Praise for

The Lizard Cage

"Connelly finds beauty and kindness and the potential for redemption in the most unexpected places. . . . There are graceful images and observations which, most likely, will remain with the reader long after he or she has put aside the book." *The Globe and Mail*

"The story unfolds perfectly and unaffectedly, with Connelly striking a remarkable balance in a tale that by turns delights, surprises and shocks." *National Post*

"Her characters are authentic, and it is a testament to her talent that she is able to get under the skin of these people, living as they are in a small Southeast-Asian country and suffering daily under the combined forces of poverty and tyranny." *Winnipeg Free Press*

"There is something beautifully—and surprisingly—tender about Karen Connelly's debut novel. . . . Connelly peels away much of the political rhetoric and gives us the human story, which is both fragile and resilient. . . . The fact that Karen Connelly is a poet . . . is very much evident here. Her prose is suffused with agonizingly sharp images. . . . It is Connelly's solid storytelling that, ultimately, is at the heart of this fine novel." *The Gazette* (Montreal)

"Connelly's writing is fluid and well-paced, and her fictive prison world, set in the actual political hellhole that is present-day Burma, is as affecting as any UN statistical report about the conditions of life in that ruined country." *Edmonton Journal*

ALSO BY KAREN CONNELLY

NONFICTION

Touch the Dragon: A Thai Journal

One Room in a Castle: Letters from Spain, France, and Greece

POETRY

The Small Words in My Body

This Brighter Prison

The Disorder of Love

The Border Surrounds Us

Grace and Poison

THE
LIZARD
CAGE

Karen Connelly

VINTAGE CANADA

Published in Canada by Vintage Canada, a division of Random House of
Canada Limited, Toronto, in 2007. Originally published in hardcover, in a
slightly different form, in Canada by Random House Canada, a division of
Random House of Canada Limited, Toronto, in 2005. Distributed by
Random House of Canada Limited, Toronto.

Vintage Canada and colophon are registered trademarks of
Random House of Canada Limited.

www.randomhouse.ca

LIBRARY AND ARCHIVES CANADA CATALOGUING IN PUBLICATION

Connelly, Karen, 1969–
The lizard cage / Karen Connelly.

ISBN 978-0-679-31328-1

I. Title.

PS8555.0546L59 2007   C813'.54   C2006-904698-0

Text design by Jennifer Ann Daddio

Printed and bound in the United States of America

2 4 6 8 9 7 5 3 1

For Ko Aung Zaw (a.k.a. Zaw Gyi) and Ko Kyaw Zwa Moe,
brothers who found each other on the other side of the border

For Ko Moe Thi Zon and Dr. Naing Aung,
brothers who lost each other there

For the child in prison

For Lucas, beloved

The possessor of this stone can fly in the air, and dive

not only under water, but underground. He cannot be

wounded as long as he has this stone on his body, that is,

in his mouth, under his hairknot, in his hands, or under

his armpits. He will be free from fatigue and disease . . .

[These] powers do not really belong to him, but only

to the stone, which by mere touch can turn lead

into silver and brass into gold . . . Thus, when

an alchemist has discovered the "stone of live metal"

he exposes himself to the danger of being

robbed of it by evil spirits or jealous rivals . . .

Evil spirits will be on the lookout for him out of

sheer malice, but the jealous rivals wish to eat his body,

because by eating it, they will come to possess

superhuman strength.

—DR. MAUNG HTIN AUNG,
FOLK ELEMENTS IN BURMESE BUDDHISM

AUTHOR'S NOTE

When the historical events described in this novel took place, the military dictatorship—which still controls Burma today—had a different name. The ruling generals called themselves the SLORC: the State Law and Order Restoration Council. In 1989, after they had arrested and killed thousands of protesting citizens nationwide, the SLORC arranged public elections. The leader of the National League for Democracy, Aung San Suu Kyi, won by a landslide. But there was no victory party; the regime refused to hand over power. Months earlier, Aung San Suu Kyi had been placed under house arrest. Six years later, in 1995, she was released for a time, but she has spent much of the past decade under increasingly brutal surveillance and house arrest.

Because of more than four decades of authoritarian rule, hundreds of thousands of refugees live in precarious conditions on the Thai-Burma border; political dissidents there and abroad continue fighting against the dictatorship from the outside, as do various ethnic armies. Burmese people remain prisoners in their own country.

In the meantime, the dictatorship illegally changed the name of that country to Myanmar and renamed itself the SPDC: the State Peace and Development Council.

THE LIZARD CAGE

The boy was twelve years old when he entered the Hsayadaw's monastery school. As the newest novice, he soon possessed the smoothest bare head; he was given dark ochre robes and taught how to wear them. With his scavenger's eye for opportunity, he saw how lucky he was. The men here gave him food, and a mat to sleep on beneath a wooden roof. He saw also that the school was a poor place, but the monks who ran it were generous with what little they had.

This didn't stop him from jealously guarding his own possessions. He even refused to be parted from his filthy blanket. The monks said it should be thrown away, but he insisted on washing the thick swath of Chinese felt himself. When it was dry, he folded it with haughty care and placed it on his sleeping mat. The old Hsayadaw—abbot of the monastery school—observed this patiently, accustomed to children who clung to the relics of their old lives.

Because the boy had never been to school, he received lessons from his very own tutor, but sometimes the Hsayadaw excused the tutoring monk and sat down to teach the child himself. This seemed like a favor to the tutor, but the truth was that the abbot enjoyed teaching the boy. He had run the monastery school for more than forty years, and this was the first time he'd ever seen an illiterate child dedicate himself so passionately to the alphabet. Learning his letters made the boy shine, and the old man liked to sit in that clean, honest light. They were both happy during these lessons, and their happiness made them laugh at almost nothing, a bird shooting through the leaves beyond the glassless window or the voice of the papaya seller in the street, calling out the sweetness of her fruit. More than half a dozen times, in the middle of the night, the Hsayadaw caught the boy with a candle burning and a notebook open in his lap, his grubby hand drawing the thirty-three consonants and fifteen vowels of the Burmese alphabet over and over, and he had to force himself to be stern when he sent the child back to bed.

The boy's name as a Buddhist novice was too long and tricky for him to write, so he insisted on learning how to spell his birth name. When he wrote it from memory for the first time, such was his jubilation that the tutoring monk whispered to the Hsayadaw, "He acts like he's discovered the formula for turning lead into gold." To which the abbot only smiled.

When he was not learning to read or trying to write, he was quiet, sometimes sullen. He was a secretive, ever-hungry boy, uninterested in playing with the other children—though he often watched them as if they were animals he was afraid to approach. The abbot endeavored not to pick favorites, but he adored this peculiar child. If only all of them were so interested in reading, and so dedicated to their Buddhist studies. It was apparent to everyone, even the more recalcitrant monks, that the boy had embraced the rituals of worship with surprising devotion. He sometimes spent hours in the temple, just sitting and watching the image of the Buddha. There hadn't been a child like that for more than a decade.

The monastery was full of boys—large boys, small boys, boys with harelips and boys with flippered limbs, boys from poor families or with no families to speak of. The Hsayadaw adopted them all. The old proverb says that ten thousand birds can perch on one good tree; the Hsayadaw was such a tree. His children found refuge in him, and he taught them to seek a greater refuge in the Buddha's Dhamma of Theravada, the teachings of the Middle Way. He did not cane his children or send them off, even if they misbehaved, because the state orphanages and reform schools were dangerous places.

The boy came to love the abbot with the same anxious tenderness he'd felt for the Songbird. This love declared itself through the laughter they shared during their lessons, through the tears the boy blinked away as he struggled with all the letters and their complex combinations. Once when he was wrestling with frustration, the Hsayadaw told him, "It's all right to cry. It's just a little water that needs to get out. We could put it in a cup if you're worried about losing it." The boy laughed, and his work became easier.

For just over three months he lived this way, making his path through hard terrain as quickly and gracefully as water. But one morning trouser-wearers appeared, two military intelligence agents who asked about him.

The Hsayadaw was calm with a lifetime of meditation, but he was afraid for his favorite son, so afraid that he broke the Fourth Precept: to abstain from telling lies. He knew it was wrong, but he lied to the military intelligence agents. He told the men that the boy was very wild, and had run away. "What did you expect, with the way the child has been raised?"

"Did he take his belongings with him?" one of the men asked.

"Belongings? He was the poorest among the poor—he had nothing but a bag of scraps and an old blanket. Of course he took them away."

The morning meal was just beginning, and the military intelligence agents insisted upon walking slowly among all the children as they sat eating on the floor. But who was to know one particular novice among sixty-seven shaven-headed, hungry little monks? The boy they were searching for was also calm, calm with a short lifetime of surviving by his rat stick and his wits. He went on eating with the other children. All of them kept their heads angled to the floor. The agents called out his name, demanding that he speak up if he was in the room. The boy didn't even blink; he would never answer to the voices of the cage again. The men came back that night and performed the same theater, but all they succeeded in doing was making a few boys burst into tears.

Two days later, petulant and angry, they returned at the hour of the morning meal. This time someone else accompanied them, a jailer who knew the boy's face. The trouser-wearers demanded that each novice lift up his head and look at this man.

Some of the boys could not hold back their tears as the big man approached them. He limped from child to child, asking questions to frighten them, to make them talk. But they had nothing to tell him. His eyes scanned the room. He barked at the other trouser-wearers to make sure they found every flea-bitten brat in the monastery compound. Then, turning to the

Hsayadaw, he asked more questions. Were some children out collecting alms? Were others washing clothes or running errands at the market? The Hsayadaw replied with great patience and a serene expression. All the young novices were present, here, in this very room. Only older boys were sent to do errands. Every child under fourteen was having breakfast. Except for the boy who had run away, days ago, the one they were looking for.

The jailer lowered his voice. "If you are lying to me, old man, you will live to regret it."

The Hsayadaw smiled his generous, open smile, all large white teeth except for the missing ones; his eyes nearly disappeared into many wrinkles. He replied, "Sir, how many men have told you the truth and lived to regret it?" He lowered his voice, so the novices wouldn't hear him. "Leave this place now, you who hunt a child like an animal. This is a monastery school. It is not your prison."

Then the Hsayadaw turned away, walked barefoot over the creaky floor, and sat down among his children. That day the abbot was so happy he had to restrain himself from dancing. He had outwitted the authorities. The day after the military men had visited the first time, the Hsayadaw had sent his favorite son to a safer place.

Wrapped in his novice robes, the boy left his first sanctuary in Rangoon and went to a small monastery in Pegu, then to a much larger one near Inle Lake and a different place after that, farther and farther north, eluding a force he equated with the men in the cage who had hurt him. Sometimes ordained monks took him in hand. Sometimes trusted novices became his guides, though they were barely older than he was, perhaps fifteen or sixteen. It was a slow, mindful, meandering escape, for it was unclear where the boy should go. He and his caretakers often walked or caught rides in the backs of open trucks.

The young monks aroused no suspicion. Even government army officers and soldiers came out to give them alms at dawn. The boy was like any other poor novice, brother to the little nuns they sometimes passed on their journey, orphan girls dressed in the dark brown or pale pink robes of their abbeys. When they arrived at a beautiful, bird-filled monastery in the hills near Mandalay, the boy thought perhaps this place was his new home, because it was very peaceful, and very far away from Rangoon.

But it wasn't far enough. The Hsayadaw sent word that the authorities were still looking for the child. They left again, traveled down into the mad bustle of the market streets of Taungyi, then Loikaw, then from village to village, through the mountains and valleys of Shan State, where the people spoke a language that recalled the sinuous chatter of birds. In a village whose name he never knew, the novice was given into the care of other, older monks, Shan men.

After leaving his dear Hsayadaw, the boy became more silent and withdrawn, but he followed the strangers with an uncharacteristic submissiveness, born of fear and the weariness of constant movement. He did not know where he was or what would become of him if he lost them too, these older brothers. The monks were kind to him, feeding him, trying to draw him out with jokes and questions in heavily accented Burmese. Among themselves they spoke Shan, known on the border as Tai Yai, one of the many tongues in that unnamed country between nations.

From the Burmese Shan hills, along the edges of Kayah State, they journeyed into Shan and Karenni territory of Thailand, down into a valley of tall thin trees and pale morning fog near the town called Mae Hong Son. Though the boy wore Buddhist robes, he arrived like so many other refugees from Burma, a dark face drawn tight around feverish black eyes. Alternately shivering and burning with malaria, he clung to his bundle of relics from the other side. They were wrapped up in his simple sling bag, which he carried on his back or in his arms wherever he went, as an older sibling carries the infant of the family.

He recuperated in the monastery at the foot of a mountain near Mae Hong Son. Once he entered monastic life again, he felt better, though the abbot of his new monastery did not smile and laugh like the Hsayadaw.

One day, a few weeks after his arrival, two Shan monks explained to the boy that he would be leaving the monastery very soon; a Burmese man wanted to adopt him. Contrary to their expectations, this news caused the boy great distress. He protested to the Thai abbot, stating his case in a heartrending mixture of Burmese, Shan, even a few words of Thai. He did not want to leave the monastery; he did not want anyone to adopt him. He wanted to be a monk. The abbot promised the boy that he could return to the monastery if he wanted, but it was his duty to meet the person who was offering him a different life. The abbot told him that while he stayed with the Burmese man, he didn't have to live as a Buddhist novice: he could give up his robes, he could eat after noon. But the boy said no. He would wear his robes, he would continue to observe a monk's diet, and he would return as soon as possible to the monastery.

The next day the Shan monks delivered him to a house built on the out-skirts of the town. A net hammock was stretched between two trees in the weedy, dusty garden. A grown man was sleeping there, his mouth hanging open like a child's. The monks and the boy stared at this man, but he did not wake. They left their slippers in the dust, walked up a few wooden steps, and stood silently at the open door. When the boy coughed, Burmese men inside the house turned from their desks and greeted them.

One of the monks whispered to the boy, "You must not cry."

The other monk added, "And don't be naughty." Following a brief chat with one of the men, they left the boy standing there barefoot. He could not bear to watch his brother monks disappear down the road, so he closed his eyes.

"Have you eaten rice yet?" one of the men asked, meaning *Are you hungry?* The boy did not open his eyes. He responded coldly, "I am keep-ing the Precepts. I don't eat after noon."

The man smiled and said, "That's a shame, because the abbot said you were free to join us for dinner. And we're going to have an excellent din-ner tonight. Aung Min has gone to the market just for you."

This made the boy open his eyes very wide. His forehead crumpled, and though his mouth opened, no sound came out.

The man thought he should explain. "Aung Min is the man who wants to adopt you. He'll be back within the hour, then we'll eat together."

The boy felt the room sway around him. He sat down cross-legged where he'd been standing. Suddenly everything made sense. Now he understood where the journey had been leading him. *Aung Min.* Instead of making him happy, the revelation made him burst into tears. The men did their best to cheer him up, but he was inconsolable. His crying quickly turned to sobbing, wet gasps and heaves occasionally punctuated with choking.

The boy's sobs were so loud they woke the sleeping revolutionary. He had children of his own, whom he had left behind in Burma. He woke thinking, I have dreamed of my son. Then he realized he was awake and a child was still crying. He swung his legs out of the hammock and took the stairs two at a time. Crouching next to the boy, he murmured in a low voice for a long time. Eventually he put his arm around him and whispered unbelievable things one after the other. "You are safe with us. We won't hurt you. Aung Min is a good man, he'll take care of you. We're happy you've come to find us. Hey—do you want a tissue to wipe your nose?"

"No. That's okay."

The boy blinked up at the man, sniffed, and slid out from under his arm. Standing, he rearranged his robes and guessed which was the bathroom door; he entered and came out with a washed face. Then he surprised them all by asking if he could have a candle, please. For his prayers, he said. They were gathered in the main room of the house; there was a little altar high on one of the walls, above a photograph of Daw Aung San Suu Kyi. Separated from the monastery for a few hours, he already missed the comforting rhythms and habits of the monks.

Kneeling before the makeshift shrine with its gold-coated plaster Buddha, holding a yellow candle in his hand, the boy uttered another humble request, for incense. The revolutionaries glanced at each other. What a strange little bird this kid was! Someone disappeared into a bedroom and returned with a dusty package of joss sticks. The boy opened it, drew out several sticks of incense, and asked for a lighter. He knelt and lit the candle and the incense and genuflected three times, forehead touching the wooden floor. The men went to the outdoor kitchen behind the house and talked in low tones about the child who was praying inside.

Aung Min arrived soon after, pulling up on a noisy motorcycle. Carrying bags from the market, he came in the back way. Yes, his men said, the boy was in the house, he was fine. Yes, he had brought his little sling bag; he rarely put it down. Aung Min peered in at the child through the half-open door but didn't want to disturb him.

The men talked over the work of the day, and cooked, and smoked cheroots. Slowly they fell silent, one by one, and began to listen as a small voice grew luminous and full in the twilight. The words of the chanted prayers came flooding back like those of an old song. Several of the men had made the same prayers, en masse, during the street protests of 1988, when they were university students. They forgot about the cheroots between their fingers. One by one the red coals went out. They stood in the darkness until the boy finished praying.

When someone turned on a light, everyone noticed the aroma of cooked rice. They stepped quietly into the house. The man who had held him earlier bent down to the boy and whispered, "We hope you will eat with us." And the boy said, "Yes, thank you, I will." The strange company, silent boy and serious men, sat down on the floor together; in the middle of their circle, various plates and bowls sat steaming, set down on old newspapers. Aung Min and the boy were introduced hesitantly, because it had been Aung Min's name that triggered the crying fit. But when the boy came face to face with the famous student leader turned revolutionary, he was polite and grave.

Aung Min watched the child hover protectively over his plate. He ate with his hands, like the men, but not a single grain of rice or bit of curry escaped his fingers. The man smiled at the boy, who glanced at him without raising his head, jaws still in motion. Aung Min realized that this was an old child locked in an old hunger. Did anyone have candy? he asked. No? What about ice cream?

Plied with sugar, the boy began to talk, first about the cold delicious cake, which he had never eaten before. How did they keep it so cold? The men smiled to see so much delight come from a sweetness they had long taken for granted.

They asked the boy about his journey. He told them. They asked him about the monastery in Rangoon. He explained about the Hsayadaw and the other children and the trouser-wearers who had tried to find him and take him away.

Aung Min leaned forward, and the boy saw that the man wanted something, badly. For the first time in that house of strangers, he felt a stab of fear.

"Little Brother," Aung Min said, "I want you to tell me about the prison."

The boy looked down at his hands. He didn't know what to say. To tell about the prison was to tell about his life, but he wasn't sure what he had to keep secret. Stammering slightly, he said, "We call it the cage."

Aung Min chose his words carefully. "I want you to tell me about your friends there."

This was easier. First the boy talked about his lizard, and the beetle in its box, and the great Tan-see Tiger, who gave him soap and a new towel before he left. Then he said Saya Chit Naing's name. "And books," he said. "My friends were books."

Aung Min's head tilted, almost imperceptibly, to the right. One of the monks at the monastery in Mae Hong Son had told him the boy was just learning to read. How could books have been his friends?

The boy started talking about a nat, a spirit who lived like an invisible monkey in a tree on the prison grounds. Several of Aung Min's men glanced at each other.

Clearly this child was many things. Inarticulate and superstitious. Malnourished. Uneducated. A variation of the boy's story had preceded his arrival, but as they sat there listening to him talk about a tree-dwelling spirit, a contagion of sighs moved around the circle. The child wasn't telling them anything they wanted to hear.

Sensing their impatience, the boy abruptly stopped talking and shrugged his shoulders. He stared hard at Aung Min as he chewed his rice. He knew exactly what the big man wanted to know about: the Songbird. Still gazing into Aung Min's eyes, he finally swallowed and said, "Teza. He also was my friend."

The men stopped picking their teeth or reading the newspaper beneath the dirty plates. Aung Min stopped smiling.

The boy pulled his sling bag into his lap. He reached into it and retrieved his meager possessions one at a time, laying them out on the floor in front of his crossed legs. Tattered postcards. A lime-green T-shirt and a turquoise sarong. A thanakha tin. His new towel. The boy touched the large matchbox with his fingertip. There were little bones inside, and a single tooth.

But Aung Min didn't care about any of that. "Little Brother, what else do you have in there?"

The boy felt the pounding rise in his chest. He put his hands on the sling bag and squeezed the cardboard edges through the fabric. It belonged to him. He glanced warily around the ring of men.

"It's mine," said the boy.

"I just want to look at it." But Aung Min had trouble keeping the hunger out of his voice, and the boy, an expert in hunger, hunched protectively over his sling bag.

"The Songbird gave it to me."

"I just want to look. I'll give it back to you."

The boy blinked, his eyes burning. Why did they always have to take everything away? He clenched his teeth. *No.* "You have to promise."

Aung Min tried to smile, but a grimace appeared on his face. Each word came out sharp and hard. "Little Brother, just let me see the notebook."

The boy glared at him, then yanked down the cloth edges of the bag to reveal the stained ledger, which he picked up and held tightly in his hands.

No one said a word; no one moved. The two of them could have been in the room alone. The boy pressed the notebook down against his legs and opened the cover. "The book is mine, so *I* will show it to you," he said. His palm splayed wide on the paper. He stared unblinking into the man's eyes.

Aung Min raised his eyebrows. Bloody kid. He stood up, waved his hand impatiently. The men on either side of the child shifted away. He sat down next to the boy, who slowly turned the first page of the notebook, the second, the third. Aung Min saw only blurred numbers, handwritten rows of accounting. He swore under his breath. The figures meant nothing to him.

Then the boy turned another page, and the words began.

The handwriting was as familiar as the voice Aung Min often listened to on a dusty cassette player.

PART ONE

THE
SONGBIRD

. 1 .

The singer is lying on the floor, a gray blanket pulled up around his chest. With slightly narrowed eyes, he stares at the ceiling. A single lizard is up there, clinging to the plaster.

What if it were the last lizard in the world? Then what would you do? Teza opens his mouth.

It's not the last lizard. Rather, it's the first. Most of them won't appear until evening, little dinner guests neatly dressed in khaki. When the halo of insects has formed around the lightbulb, the reptiles run to and fro in their jerky, mechanical way, jaws snapping. Sometimes their mouths are so stuffed with insects that they can barely shut them. Gluttons. Showoffs. Any hungry mammal would be jealous. With all that eating, you'd think they'd get fat, but unfortunately the lizards are very skinny, like most of the human inmates. Teza closes his mouth.

In response, his stomach growls, the sound as loud as his normal speaking voice. A predatory animal has taken up residence in his gut. Never mind the parasites, a small panther is mutating in there. A feral dog. Evening with its lizard bounty seems very far away.

To confirm that sad thought, the iron-beater begins to strike eleven A.M. Teza counts each blow of a hardwood pallet against an iron bar in the compound, at the base of the watchtower. *Clang, clang, clang.* The time-keeper whacks the iron as hard as possible, so that the prisoners will hear him and know their time is passing. All ten thousand of them, especially the couple thousand politicals whom the singer counts as friends and comrades, are *very* far away. The nature of the teak coffin—of any solitary cell—is that it converts everything into distance. Time, space, food, women, his family, music, anything he might need or want or love: it is all far, far away.

From solitary, the whole cage is a foreign country to him. He lives on the very edge of it, straining to hear the other voices.

T*keep! Tkeep! Tkeep!*
The lizard sings. Not like a bird, though Teza remembers from first-year biology that this common cling-to-house lizard is brother to a tiny prehistoric sparrow. Then the desert wind blew and the rain fell and the scales grew into feathers. As he stares at the lizard on the ceiling, he can imagine it: the front two legs and feet stretched out, webbing, blossoming into wings. The back feet articulated into clawed toes, which curled deftly around the thin branch of a tree. And birdsong ribboned through the steamy jungle.

But before that, who knows how many millions of years ago, there was just this somewhat alarmed chirping *tkeep tkeep tkeep* to inspire the Neanderthals. Like Junior Jailer Handsome. Here we are again, the singer thinks, smiling. Back in the Stone Age, among cavemen, in a cave. His stomach growls.

The iron-beater is still. It's past eleven o'clock now. And Sein Yun has not shown up with breakfast. Teza watches the lizard run from the light, stop, run to the wall, stop. It runs down the wall and whisks itself out the air vent high above his head.

Teza scans the brick wall around the vent. His eyes have learned the different colors of reptile and wall, lizard skin and skin of man, brick and spider. That's what he wants to see now. The spider.

It's the color of a tiny, dirty copper pot. When the bulbous back catches the light, the copper becomes iridescent, an alchemist's metal. It glints gold, then a sheen of blue-green rises toward copper again. At dusk the creature deepens to red, then fades with the invisible sun. When Teza first came to the teak coffin, the spider was almost indistinguishable against the red bricks. But now the singer can find him in seconds.

A fine web is strung high in the corner where the two walls meet, below and to the left of the air vent. The spider often rebuilds his web in a different place. When Teza wakes each day, he checks to see if his companion has chosen to abandon the darkness of the cell and build his new home outside. The singer thinks he's the sort of spider who should have green leaves around him. But the spider stays.

The Chief Warden thinks Teza cannot see out of this narrowest of windows. In a manner of speaking, he is correct. The vent is too high. Even when Teza jumps he sees nothing save another fraction of the very high outer wall and a corrugated tin overhang. But the spider sees. He crawls the outer wall, up and up. From the top, the spider witnesses the whole city, the gold stupas, the green trees, the streets, millions of men and women, the lakes Inya and Kandawgyi, Daw Aung San Suu Kyi's famous house on University Avenue, and his mother's two-story flat, surrounded by laundry and orchids. Daw Sanda loves her orchids dearly.

The spider perceives all this and more, much more: the sky with its white-backed, blue-bottomed clouds full of rain, the horizon curving like a belly. The spider sees.

And Teza watches the spider.

The fabulous copper-pot spider.

Is it male or female?

The singer has decided the spider is male: it's too depressing to imagine a woman here. He would hate to have a woman see him now.

The singer feeds his male comrade-spider secret messages, just a few words at a time, all his body can hold. Soundlessly, the spider takes in the messages and spins them out when he crawls into the world. The glimmering threads are Teza's words.

> *I love you. I think of you and send wishes of health.*
> *We have dared everything; we must win.*
> *I take strength from the knowledge that you keep fighting.*
> *I am still alive. Teza.*
> *Remember the meaning of my name.*

• • •

Forbidden to write or receive letters, he has devised dozens of ways to send a message. Every political prisoner has an elaborate fantasy of messages. Sometimes the right moment never comes, or the message gets trapped in the cell with the man who wrote it, incriminating him as only words can. But sometimes the messages escape, slip through to the other halls, where friends live. Sometimes the words pass through the first brick wall surrounding the prison, and the second one. They move secretly through the great iron gates. Hands take the place of the prisoner's legs; messages walk out into the world and speak.

The methods he has imagined are no different from his comrades'. Anxious fingers swivel scraps of paper into cigarettes and cheroots. Words are scratched onto walls and plastic bags, pinpricked onto dry leaves, stuffed into the handles of baskets, held under armpits, in mouths, wrapped in clothes, breathed nightly in prayers. The brief missives, puny as insects, as embryos, are regularly caught and crushed, torn out by the guards and warders and swept away. If the prisoners are caught sending messages, they are beaten violently; they must bleed, that is the general rule. It's also fine to knock them unconscious. Then their sentences are extended by two years, by four, by seven, by seven times two.

The singer sits down.

The spider crawls out. Like the singer's grandfather, the spider always goes outside for a morning view of the world, even if it is raining, as it is today. As it was yesterday. It will rain off and on now for months. Teza cannot see the rain, but he hears it drumming, muttering, sighing, turning over and over, out of the sky to the earth back to the sky, washing away the layer of filth created by men, which encourages them to create more.

Sometimes his dreams are very simple: rain falls into his cupped hands. In the base of that shallow well, there is a small lizard. Its tongue flicks at the clear, oversized drops, drinking the rain, which also washes Teza's palms, runs through his fingers. The lizard licks at the rainwater, perfectly calm, fearless. The singer feels the small reptilian heart beat lightly against his human skin.

• • •

The lizard dream makes him think of food, and food makes him think of Sein Yun, and that makes him mad. Where is that sneaky little bastard?

The yellow-skinned palm-reader with the long dirty nails and the jumpy manner has been Teza's server for a month and a half. He's an uncommon criminal, Sein Yun, but useful. A couple of weeks ago, the palm-reader brought in—from where, Teza will never know—some first-rate papaya, cut in cubes and served on a white plastic plate, as if a pretty lady vendor on Anawrahta Street had brought it into the cage herself. No warder or jailer would ever lower himself to the task of serving a prisoner food of any kind, or of emptying out his shit pail. Such work is reserved for criminal prisoners like Sein Yun who are trying to reduce their sentences.

Teza's previous server was Sammy, who has a new job now, as one of the iron-beaters. At least that's what Sein Yun said last week. Teza likes to imagine Sammy out there, at the base of the watchtower, the great bulk of his long dark arms beating out the hours. Sammy is an Indo-Burmese of startling proportions, over six feet tall, the whole length and breadth of him thick with muscle. But when he was a server, all his strength meant nothing to the singer, because the giant has no tongue. His awful tonguelessness was intended—and received—as an added punishment for Teza.

The only thing you want to do in solitary—besides everything else you want to do—is speak and be spoken to. Sammy could only grunt. The first time Teza addressed him, the Indian's sad mouth yawned into an empty purple cavern. The web of skin from the lower palate connected to a small, wriggling stump of flesh. The singer's first reaction on seeing that ugly amputation was not sympathy, or horror, or even distaste. Teza was so overwhelmed with self-pity that he wanted to cry.

Whatever the palm-reader's faults may be—clearly he has many—he also has a tongue, and uses it. Sein Yun is clever, happy to share his quick wit. Most important, he likes to pass on cage news. The singer already feels disproportionately grateful to him simply because he can talk.

If he would just show up with the breakfast tray, Teza would bow in gratitude. He tilts his head toward the teak door and listens. Nothing, no footsteps. Only his growling gut.

In December he will celebrate his anniversary: seven years, married to the cage. For seven years he hasn't been eating enough, but right now his hunger has passed from aching into acute. His muscles, organs, bones, have all grown teeth; he can feel his body steadily devouring itself.

His arms and shins and the backs of his knees are insanely itchy (scabies), as are his bites (bedbugs; rather, matbugs, for he hasn't slept on a bed for as long as he's been hungry), and his hair is so filthy it's beginning to smell like bad meat. All that is fine; he's used to it. Hunger is his only serious concern. He's used to being malnourished. That isn't the problem. The problem is that the food parcel, which keeps him from starving, is late by an entire week. And the last parcel, which came through three weeks ago, was a dud.

His mother sends them. But before the food reaches him, it has to pass through the holding room to be checked for contraband. Three weeks ago, warders he doesn't know, or Sein Yun, or some other lousy thief, took all but one of the dried salt fish and most of the deep-fried dried beans too.

Why did the bastard bother leaving *one* fish? What kind of slap in the face was that? The jerk was just laughing at him. Was it Junior Jailer Handsome? Handsome has only recently started to oversee the teak coffin. He and Sein Yun came together. As Sein Yun replaced Sammy, so Handsome replaced Senior Jailer Chit Naing, a man who's been a great friend to Teza. Chit Naing would never touch a prisoner's food. But Handsome is a mean bastard.

Who knows? Anyone could have stolen it. Teza is grateful to Sein Yun, but the man's always on the make. He's even friendly with Handsome. It would make good business sense: Junior Jailer absconds with the fish and Sein Yun sells them in the prisoner halls.

If the Chief Warden permits these thieves to steal Teza's food, what does he expect him to live on? Cockroaches? His political ideals? Lizards?

He strikes the wall with his open hand. Then scolds himself for hurting his palm. He touches the bricks again, gently, as if to apologize.

Above his head, closer to the teak door, a ceaseless parade of ants marches in a crooked line to where they divide into two streams. One flows into a very thin crack to the left; the other follows a right-hand route much lower down, into a bead-sized gap in the mortar. Before they reach their destination, both streams wind and loop over the neighboring bricks. This irregularity has puzzled him for years.

Why do the ants meander? Why do they not take the shortest, most direct path to the cracks in the wall?

We cannot say, They are stupid, their brains are small. Their reasons and their wisdom are beyond us. They can do what we cannot. O cell, o shit pail: how you alter the old shape of the world, the perspectives of a living man. On the floor below the bead-sized gap is a small mountain of cement dust, the ants' excavations. The ants are burrowing their way out.

Sometimes Teza hears the amber mandibles patiently crunching through the mortar between the bricks. Many legs push the bits back, back, back, passing a piece from one to the other until finally the last ant pushes it out of the wall and it falls into the pile on the floor. Of course he doesn't hear the bit of mortar fall, but he can hear the ants working, grinding away inside the prison wall. A few hours later he can see how much the pile of cement dust has grown.

After breaking a length of straw from his mat, he carefully disrupts the march and edges an ant onto the straw. The ant's antennae wave about, tasting the air. Then he pauses to clean himself.

"Yes," Teza whispers above the ant's head. "The air is dirty too. Wash yourself."

The ant obediently licks his brown hands, pulls the flexible antennae to his mouth, runs the thin feelers along his tongue.

Teza tilts the straw down. The ant crawls up. He turns the straw over. The ant crawls down. The singer paces eight by eight feet with the ant crawling up and down, up and down.

"I take the ant for a walk," he explains in English. "I am walking the ant." *Promener,* in French. But *ant?* He replaces it with *cat.*

"Je promène le très très petit chat brun."

Among his prison lessons, he has learned how to distinguish eight different kinds of ants, possibly nine, though he is not absolutely sure. He has observed the different personalities of the ants too. Some black ants, contrary to popular belief, are more aggressive than some red ones.

He wanted to speak fluent English and French. He intended also to read many books. As a boy, he touched as many books as he could in the bookstalls across from the main post office. He dreamed of owning a library to match his grandfather's library in Mandalay.

He puts an imaginary book in his hand and holds it out in front of him. Ant in one hand, invisible book in the other.

After the rainy season, the pages smell like the forest.

His grandfather's bookshelves grew high.

Hpo Hpo, why do the books smell like damp wood?

Because every book, in its former life, was a tree.

I take the ant for a walk."

The English words sound without reverberation, absorbed immediately into the walls, the heavy door. That's partly how the teak coffin got its name. Instead of having bars, the cell is sealed shut with a door made of two bolted slabs of teak. It's smaller than the other cells, and several men have died in it.

Teza inclines his head, and in Burmese he speaks with the ant about small, daily things.

An hour passes. Barefoot, he walks deeper and deeper into hunger. He'll have to stop walking at the start of the next hour, to save his energy. He won't want to stop.

Sammy the iron-beater beats out two o'clock. Curious, isn't it? Sammy used to see Teza twice daily but could tell him almost nothing. Now they can't see each other at all, but the big Indian tells him something important every hour.

Teza squats down in front of the wall and carefully returns his ant to the ant stream. A brief commotion ensues. Antennae wave. Ant hands touch ant faces as the laborers welcome their lost one back to work. Teza's fingers spread against the wall as he watches two ants break from the line and begin to unstick a flattened mosquito. The singer's blood glues the mosquito to the brick. With a mixture of clumsy determination and deftness, one worker drags the mosquito into the lower gap in the wall, where all such treasures are stored away.

Years have passed while Teza has sat or squatted or stood craning his neck, listening. To the ants. The flies. The lizards. Sometimes hungry rats trundle in through the air vent, squeaking. He knows the voices of the crows and the pigeons on the ramparts. The spider spins and respins his secret web of history. They all have a way of talking in a language beyond human.

Everything speaks. That is what he has learned here. Even ants pass messages in the labyrinth behind the bricks and mortar. Through messages they build their invisible, invincible world.

. 2 .

Six o'clock. He counts the beats carefully, hoping he is wrong.

He is not wrong. The second and last prison meal of the day is supposed to come at five o'clock. But Sein Yun didn't appear with his food tray.

The singer accepts the sad truth. Today he will not eat rice. It happens. Sometimes, if an important prison authority or general has died, or when there has been a major raid or riot in one of the big halls, or when one of the criminal prisoners attacks a warder, the meals are cut, just like that, no explanation. The news has to filter through the cage on its own, which is fine for prisoners in the big halls. If you're in solitary and your server has disappeared, there is no news at all. There is only the time passing.

He stares at the door for a while, hoping. It's his door. He cleans the years of sweat and spit and piss and crushed bugs out of its grain, twists the bolts from its flesh, tears out the locks. He returns the wood to the mill, unsaws it, heaves it back a great distance along plunging mud tracks, asks the elephants to drag it back up the steep hillsides. And then, among the profusion of thick grasses and liana and the calls of wild monkeys and birds, he sets the wood upright and it becomes a tree again, one of the trees in the last great golden teak forests on earth, the jungles of northern Burma.

He lays his hands upon the brown, pitted surface of the door. It was alive once. The mystery is how everything changes. He closes his eyes.

Do you remember the banyan tree on Mahabandoola Street, the one wrapped with ribbons and hung with puppets?

Can you conjure the smell of a lime?

Or his girlfriend's skin, the soft inner wrist before it flooded up the rest of her arm? His fingers always wanted to go farther up her sleeve.

The door remains closed. He presses his hands against the teak, then turns and leans against it, pushes his shoulder blades into the grain. He knocks the back of his head, once, against the wood, gets a sharp whiff of his black hair. He glances up at the vent. It's getting dark outside. Soon the moths will appear. Despite knowing exactly what will happen, he feels a shiver of anticipation. Attracted by the light in his cell, the moths will flap in through the air vent. The lizards will come after them.

He thumps his head against the door once more.

I t's hard to catch a lizard with your bare hands.

Sometimes they are far down the walls, already close. More often he lures them down from the ceiling with live moths, the odd fly. He once used a small praying mantis, but that was early on, before he knew better. The mantis was bright new-leaf green, a rare color in the cage, never to be used as mere bait.

The lizard hunt is a shameful compulsion. Occasionally, disgusted with himself, he has stopped it for long periods.

But it's like giving up smoking. Starting again is irresistibly attractive.

He has always needed the tiny reptiles. *Always*. How pathetic, to talk as if he'd been born here. Even when his food parcel arrives on time, he regularly supplements his diet with lizards. Despite his mother's generosity, a parcel every two weeks is not enough food, because he shares what hasn't already been stolen with Sein Yun. He's not obliged to give his server food, but it makes his life easier. In exchange, Sein Yun will bring him extras: cheroots and lighters, rags and soap. Some time ago—he can't remember if it was in his fourth or his fifth year—one of the servers, in gratitude for the extra food, used to bring Teza extraordinary and frivolous things, like real toilet paper, or a cup of warm tea. Some of the men have been as kind as the cage allows. He owes them a lot. Senior Jailer Chit Naing, for example. What would he do without him? Teza is sure that the Chief Warden himself somehow got wind of their friendship. That's why Chit Naing's duties no longer include overseeing the teak coffin.

The singer will always be grateful to the senior jailer, but when he thinks about it pragmatically, measuring out his allegiances, he knows that he owes the lizards his life. The protein has been crucial, but the best part is the hunt. The anticipation and physical prowess involved in stalking are a great relief from the boredom.

Even if you hate killing a lizard, a feeling of triumph fills you once the wriggling body goes still. Then you must eat it, because to waste the death is another crime.

F or the first couple of years of his imprisonment, Teza counted them. Three hundred and sixty-two. That may seem like a lot, but it wasn't. The early years were the worst. His body rebelled against so many kinds of deprivation. The hunger for food was only one of many hungers, but it caused him a very particular anxiety.

Three hundred and sixty-two times he sent apologies to his mother and reflected guiltily upon the First Precept, which is to refrain from harming or taking life. In his infinite compassion, the Lord Buddha would understand, but Teza suspected his mother would give him a big lecture. Daw Sanda might allow the eating of insects, but not small, four-legged creatures with red blood.

His mother has been a vegetarian for years. She is a devout Buddhist.

By the time he was an expert at catching and killing the reptiles, the numbers started bothering him, adding to his guilt. Certain records, he decided, shouldn't be kept. He talks to himself often, without embarrassment, and when he decided to stop counting the executions, he said out loud, "Some records just go missing." These words were followed by an unnatural, forceful silence. The silence spoke to him of 1988, when he and his mother lost Aung Min, his younger brother. Those eerily quiet days without Aung Min made them frantic, because they didn't know who'd been shot in the streets, or how many, or where the bodies were taken after the big trucks came through and the soldiers jumped down and dragged the students and other protesters off the sticky roads. All the bodies, even those with groaning mouths, were hauled away.

Besides the blood and the broken, hand-drawn signs, many slippers were left behind, for hours, sometimes for days, missed in the cleanup by the regime's squadron of overworked sweepers. The slippers lay scattered over the pavement, lodged in the gutters and at the base of the occasional shrine-bearing banyan tree. Shoes bereft of feet are capable of making terrible accusations. The people who scurried along the roads before the evening curfew knew ghosts were stepping into those slippers, the simple flip-flop kind with the single piece of leather or plastic that fits between the first two toes of each bony foot. During the day a few parents went out, and brothers and sisters, to search among the flip-flops, but it was hopeless, impossible to know which shoes belonged to whom. They were the kind everybody wore.

Everybody wears them still. The singer always takes his off when he paces, because it's not easy to get new slippers in the cage, and walking wears them out. He kicks them off just now, into a corner, as he always does before hunting. The flip-flop slap frightens his prey.

Anyway, eating the lizards is a necessity. Most of his warders have had no idea, and surely Senior Jailer Chit Naing never knew. That sharp devil Sein Yun probably suspects—little bones in the shit pail—but he's never said anything. Like masturbating and weeping, the singer tries to keep it private.

Years from now, the lizard hunt will be a story to tell certain friends, close ones. It will become a tale from his heroic old days in prison. He won't tell his mother, though. There are some things devoutly Buddhist mothers should never know.

Here and now, in this cage of men, the singer thinks, *Let no one see. Let no one know I do this.*

The bait is easy. He watches a moth spiral down toward the clay water pot, which he has set under the light for this purpose. Attracted to the light's reflection, various flying insects end up in the water, wings spread and shuddering on the glassy surface. He plucks a velvety, pulpy moth out of the water. Almost immediately it starts to flap and dance between his left thumb and forefinger.

Fingertips and knuckles glittering with silver dust, Teza raises the insect up as close as he can to the light, stretching his arm and standing on his toes. Within ten seconds the lizard sharply swivels its head toward the fluttering moth. Then the singer walks slowly to the wall; above him, on the ceiling, the creature follows in its darting, relentless way. From fingers to hand down through his straining arm and back, Teza's ropy muscles pull long and taut. He likes to pretend he is magic, drawing the creature down with a spell. The lizard hesitates, trying to hold on to the enormity of the hand, the figure beyond the moth, but the reptile's own predatory instinct leads it into the hand of a bigger predator. The wings whisper the irresistible *h'dah-h'dah-h'dah*, the sound of injury or entrapment, and on the lizard comes.

The singer brings his body close to the wall so his right arm—the lethal weapon—will not have to extend too much. The moth whirs like a tiny engine as Teza's elbow bends, pulling hand, insect, and lizard down. The reptile runs smoothly, then stops, returning to its jerky forward paces. The singer thinks, If I were a bird, I would pluck it off the wall this second, in my beak.

Just a little farther down now.

In the looming presence or scent or shadow of the human body, the creatures sometimes turn tail and scurry back up the bricks. Even then the singer will make a move, and he often gets them.

When his left hand is parallel to the top of his rib cage, he stops moving it and holds the moth lightly against the wall. His right hand is loose-fingered, ready. The lizard rushes for the head of the moth, unhinging its jaws and already gulping as the wings beat against the reptilian snout. The moth flaps furiously, pushing the tips of the singer's fingers. It's hard to resist the illogical impulse to release the moth, let it have a last chance at its own life. But the lizard will escape if he does this, so Teza stifles his sense of charity. Still pinching the insect as it enters the lizard's mouth, the singer takes advantage of the small, violent flurry and slaps his palm down on his prey.

It's hard to kill a lizard with your bare hands. A crude method at best.

The lizard's head and jaws and the moth between them are crushed against the brick. These are the singer's least favorite executions, because of the blood and moth innards and wing dust smeared on the palm of his hand. The lizard's legs still run, escaping uselessly into the air, while the singer picks insect from crushed reptilian jaws. Other times, he manages to catch a tail or break a couple of legs; the lizard drops neatly off the wall and lies writhing on the cement. Then Teza breaks its narrow neck as though he were twisting the cap off a bottle.

He puts the twitching lizard on the floor and moves the water pot back to its corner. Then, lizard in hand again, he squats down and pours a cup of water over the small corpse, rubbing the sides of the bloody and flattened head to get rid of the moth. He doesn't like raw insect.

It's absurd. What's the difference? Raw reptile, raw moth? May May would be completely horrified either way if she could see her good son devouring his innocent cellmates.

The singer likes to make fun, but it's true. If his mother could see him now, squatting like an old man by the water pot, avid and shining-eyed after the hunt, she would begin to cry in her silent way. If only she had howled like the melodramatic women in the Indian movies he and Aung Min grew up on. But no, they had a mother who held herself in stoic silence.

Despite these thoughts of his family, the singer is weirdly lighthearted. Squatting, he puts the dead lizard, its dull khaki skin still on, into his mouth. He doesn't bother to strip them anymore.

Yes, he is very much himself this way, teeth cutting through the meager flesh, crunching the little bones. It tastes only of what it is: lizard skin and cool blood, neither sweet nor bitter, just raw, and nothing at all like chicken, despite the evolutionary connection. He chews the lizard until he knows the bones are safe enough for his throat. At the moment of swallowing, he is without any remorse, secure in the knowledge that as long as he can do this terrible thing, he can survive the terrible things they do to him.

That night, before the lights are switched off, he eats six lizards. Or seven. Or eight. Nine? He really doesn't count anymore.

But when he's lying in the dark, a black wave of shame rolls over him. He speaks to the night in an unequivocal voice. "There is no alternative."

"And furthermore, I am not the only one."

The darkness pounds on and on, moralizing.

"Whatever happens has happened before. I am not the first. Others did this, and later, they were men again." He raises his voice, to make sure the darkness hears him. "I am still a man. My name is Teza."

. 3 .

The military intelligence agents—the MI—hated his name.

In ancient Pali, *teza* means fire, the fire of glory, of power. But that wasn't the only association that pissed off his interrogators. Teza had been the nom de guerre of the great general Bogyoke Aung San, architect of Burma's independence from the British and still revered as a leader. When the MI agents beat Teza, the young singer, it was not only his body they wanted to crush and destroy, it was that word they shared with him.

"Teza!" shouts Teza. The cockroach scurries back out of the cell, under the coffin door. It's almost breakfast time, and the morning patrol of hungry vermin is gathering at the gates.

The fire of real power and glory, Teza thinks, is the sun shining through monsoon clouds. Light drops over the high outer walls of the cage and pours through the air vent. The singer stands and steps into the warm stream. He lifts his face toward the invisible sky. From this new position, he sees that the spider has spun his web at an extraordinary angle. It gleams like the blueprint of a jewel, the spinner at the center a living ruby.

How would the spider taste?

Hungry body, abominable mind!

How long have I been hungry? How long is hunger?

"Hunger is as long as all your bones laid end to end in an empty field. Times five."

Kicking off his slippers, Teza begins to walk it out, back and forth, back and forth, between the aluminum shit pail and the clay water pot.

A s though from a great distance, Sammy the iron-beater strikes the time. Teza keeps pacing. He counts each clang with a footfall. When he turns on his heel and walks back toward the door, he stares at the stained teak and speaks to it directly. "I will be fed. You must feed me. I am truly hungry now. Feed me!" Eleven o'clock is the hour of the morning meal.

The door whispers, *Teza, you are an idiot.*

The singer nods. The door is a good-natured realist. They could leave Teza in here to starve. No one would know. The Chief Warden could report that the prisoner contracted a wasting illness. Tuberculosis, say. It's a big problem in the cage. Or dysentery, that other killer, so common and so feared.

M inutes pass. The sunlight slowly retreats. The intricate web and its ruby spider disappear. He wishes he could have a plant, some green thing in his cell. It's true that when he was first imprisoned, he believed his name was his only weapon, one that he would never relinquish. But now he would trade his name for a potted orchid.

As a boy, he knew that messages are meant to be given away, passed along, but he wondered how he was supposed to give away his own name.

The realization came slowly, through music. Like many Burmese boys, he grew up strumming a guitar, but by the time he was in high school it was clear he had more talent than most of his schoolmates. This dismayed his mother—Daw Sanda wanted him to be a doctor like his father—but delighted his friends. The girls especially loved having a musician around; Teza knew all the popular songs, including the sappy love ballads. At university he started to write and perform his own music at parties, in small concerts. He became known on the Rangoon campus as the Singer.

In 1988 he was in his last year of an English lit. degree, finishing several semesters late because of failed exams. Becoming a serious musician made him an indifferent scholar, though no one could deny that university life was good for writing lyrics and spending time with one's friends, which is why he wanted to prolong it indefinitely. The depressing specter of adulthood loomed at the gates of Rangoon University, beyond which lay a city, a whole country, perfectly empty of opportunity, especially for someone like him. Only children of high-ranking military officers or businessmen with good connections could get excited about the future.

His family was decidedly *un*connected to the regime. On the contrary, both Teza and Aung Min were guilty by association. When they were small boys, their father, Dr. Kyaw Win Thu, had been imprisoned as a communist sympathizer. Very poor, with two young sons and a husband in prison, their educated, cultured mother made a surprising but pragmatic move. She went into business for herself and opened a laundry. It was successful enough to keep them all fed and clothed and to educate the boys. As Teza grew up, however, the laundry became a source of embarrassment. He did not want to live from the proceeds of cleaning other people's clothes. He wanted to be a rock star.

But this was no solution either. In Burma, famous rock stars were just as poor as everyone else. Both the bass player and the lead singer in Teza's favorite band lived in humble rooms at the bug-infested YMCA on Mahabandoola Street. If those two jeans-and-guitar-sporting icons could stand living at the YMCA, Teza realized, he had to tolerate living comfortably from the proceeds of a laundry. Taking cleaning orders after class and helping his mother to manage the accounts, he learned to ignore what he didn't like.

Aung Min, on the other hand, lacked the Burmese apathy gene. "Little Brother," Teza said to him once, "you are not being a good Buddhist. You spend too much time thinking about the future and stewing about the past. What about the present?" He was only partly joking when he added, "Maybe you should go on a meditation retreat with May May." Their mother was a disciplined meditator. "Remember the wisdom of the breath."

Aung Min raised a skeptical eyebrow. "I would breathe better, Teza, if I were not being suffocated every bloody day."

True to his mother's wishes, Aung Min was studying medicine. He used to come home from his classes and, like his doctor father before him, talk angrily and articulately about the idiocy of the government. But he was louder and more charismatic than his father, and to May May's great consternation, he had a dirty mouth. Though he didn't swear in front of her, his voice cut right through the walls. "In Southeast Asia, only Cambodia is more fucked up, and that's simply because Pol Pot was so stupid and brutal that he killed everyone. But our old bastard Dictator Ne Win is smart and brutal enough to keep us alive! What good are dead slaves?"

May May came into the kitchen, tongue clicking, and closed the windows. Speaking out against the dictator or his regime was dangerous on the street and at home; the MI had paid informers in every neighborhood.

Listening to Aung Min's latest passionate rant, Teza carefully masked the awe he felt for his little brother.

"You remember what the country used to be called, right? *The rice bowl of Asia*. We were a huge rice producer. Now the farmers have to buy their own paddy back from the military. At [*pound!*] inflated [*pound!*] prices! [*pound!*] The farmers themselves don't have enough rice to eat. One of my professors thinks that two children in five are malnourished. In isolated areas, probably three or four in five. And most of Ne Win's cronies are so fat!" *Mataya wa-dey* was the phrase he used—*unjustly fat*. Teza burst out laughing.

"It's not funny, Teza."

"I'm laughing at the expression, that's all. Hpo Hpo used to say the same thing, remember?" He smiled, hoping to lure his brother into calmer territory by reminiscing about their dead grandfather, for whom they shared a quiet love.

Aung Min met his eye and said dryly, "You should come with me tonight."

"Uh-oh. Something tells me it's not going to be a very fun party."

"The study group is meeting."

"That's what I thought."

Teza lifted a cup of tea to his lips. *Study group* was a euphemism for the political meetings that Aung Min had been organizing on campus. Teza sometimes went to these gatherings, often to keep an eye on his little brother. If the elder student was known for his mellifluous voice and skill with a guitar, the younger was becoming famous for his big mouth.

Aside from General Ne Win's monster mouthpiece, the Burma Socialist Program Party, all political groups were illegal. Teza often chided his brother for not being careful enough; the MI had spies on campus too. The students met in each other's cluttered dorm rooms or huddled around a table at an outdoor tea shop; voices would rise to an excited pitch when they were supposed to be whispering. Even a small group of four or five people was enough to catch the MI's attention and lead to interrogation.

Aung Min spent a lot of time preparing for these meetings. He hunted down banned books for the group to read and drew up subjects for discussion, then actually managed to keep the group on topic. He made contact with members of the student protest movement from the 1970s and persuaded one of the men to give a talk. Almost fifteen years before, in a prison work camp in the north, this dissident had known their father.

T eza can still see that man speaking in his deep voice to the ring of close faces, young people hanging on his every word—words that turned out to be prophetic. He remembers everything so clearly: the pile of ragged chemistry textbooks in a corner, a tin can cut down into an ashtray, the fact that he just wanted to get the hell out of that smoky little room, away from the ominous predictions and the stifling heat. They were all sweating, wiping their faces with handkerchiefs. He was sitting close to the door—acting as a guard, ostensibly, but secretly hoping to make a break for it as quickly as possible. Yes, he'd gone to the meeting to honor the man's friendship with Hpay Hpay, his father, but after two and a half hours he'd had enough.

Yes, what about you, Teza? You wanted more than anything to leave and meet Thazin, hear her voice, touch her. If you stayed at the meeting too long, that delightful interlude would not take place, because her two roommates would return from the movies.

What were *you* doing, really, while your brother was anticipating revolution?

I was glancing at my watch. I was anticipating Thazin's mouth, her breasts.

· · ·

He is staring at the pitted teak door. The darkened grain reminds him not of blood and piss stains, but of Thazin's hair. Her voice, murmuring into the phone, used to give him an instant hard-on. This was a hilariously embarrassing problem; his longyi stood up like a tent. How wonderful, how fine, that such problems exist in the world! He is sure that some young man in Rangoon right now suffers from the same affliction, and this makes him glad.

But he felt more than lust, the body's lightning, for Thazin. He loved her, wildly, flesh and mind and heart, every gesture of her hands, the changing shape of her mouth as she spoke. This love haunts and blesses him now. Because in the end he became as caught up in the protests as Aung Min. What he believed was most personal to him, most beloved— Thazin—ceased to occupy the core of his life. She was there beside him much of the time, but the politics and the songs and that history they were all living took him over.

There was so much he did not understand. He did not know how far things would go, how bad the violence would get. Even when he was in an interrogation center being beaten black and blue, he wasn't thinking of a long prison sentence. Then they told him. Twenty years in solitary confinement. For singing *songs*? It was too absurd, even in his absurd country. How could anyone, let alone a twenty-five-year-old university student, fathom what twenty years in solitary might mean?

During the height of the demonstrations he had worked on the *Twelve Songs of Protest* every day, raw-voiced and shaking, quietly possessed, thinking, These songs are like my name.

> *Grandfather remember that other war*
> *You watched a woman with hungry children*
> *rush into her hut and fall to her knees*
> *She tore open the burlap sack*
> *of rice with her bare hands*
> *In this war Grandfather*
> *our people like that woman*
> *are tearing open history*

with their hands their mouths
Finally we will eat the truth.

Teza's songs became a manifestation of the country transforming around them, in Rangoon and its townships and dozens of cities and villages all over Burma, in the singer too, a new country was being born. The words swept through Teza's mind and flew from the mouths of the protesters, men and women and children in the streets shouting *Doh ayey, doh ayey, doh ayey.* Our business, our cause. It was the old dream, the oldest music, written again in human blood, soiled by human excrement, with shoes bereft of feet scattered all around. The chorus was a single word: *freedom.*

. 4 .

Like a dirty joke, the word *freedom* usually makes Sein Yun, the palm-reader, laugh out loud and roll his eyes suggestively. "Freedom," he likes to say, "is one more thing you can buy at market, if you have enough kyats."

Teza hears the distant sound of shuffling feet. A smile begins and fills his entire face as the feet come closer.

Despite the double-thick door, the *shuffle-slap-slap, shuffle-slap-slap* of slippers is audible to his keen ears. The singer listens for Jailer Handsome's footsteps behind the server's. Usually he waits down the hall while Sein Yun opens the door, gives Teza his food tray, and takes away his shit pail. While chatting with the palm-reader, Teza often smells Handsome's cheroot smoke.

But the familiar heavy thud of his boots doesn't come today. Odd. Teza turns his ear to the door. Definitely no boots. Just Sein Yun. In slippers that are too big for him. The shuffle is longer, more awkward than usual. Have they sent a different criminal to serve him? Has something happened to Sein Yun?

On the other side of the door, the aluminum food tray clatters down on the cement floor. The key chain rattles. Unseen fingers select the key, which slides in and turns the lock. Now the hand must throw open the outer bolt.

But the hand doesn't touch it.

Teza stares quizzically at his closed door, waiting.

No sound. The outer bolt stays clamped.

His stomach suddenly tightens. Sein Yun would have opened the door by now.

Who is there?

He controls the speed of his breathing as an old stitch of pain in his ribs pulls tight. Sweat begins to gather under his eyes, on the edge of his cheekbones.

Still the door does not open.

The man on the other side is playing a game.

The singer refuses to be undignified. He won't ask who is there. Why would they send anyone to hurt him? *He* hasn't done anything. They're the ones who aren't feeding him, who are stealing his fish. And he re- quested a haircut and a shave two weeks ago, but they've denied that too.

Twice he opens his mouth to speak but remains silent.

Just as he opens it for the third time, impatient to finish with this bad joke, the man on the other side of the door sings out, "Yooo-hooo! Is any- body in there?"

Teza jumps at the voice—Sein Yun's—then growls, "Of course I'm in here! Where the fuck else would I be? Why didn't you say anything?"

"I'm saying something now."

"Open up the bloody door, then, and bring in my breakfast. Where have you been? Why have you been standing there in silence for five minutes?"

"Had you worried, huh? Did you think I was a ghost?"

"No, I did not think you were a ghost, but now I'm sure you're an asshole."

A peal of laughter is interrupted by the clunk and whisk of metal over wood. The outer bolt slides back and Sein Yun pulls open the heavy door. Shifting the bulge in his cheek, he says, "Ko Teza, no need to get so ex- cited. I was just wrapping my betel. It's a delicate task, you know." Scoop- ing up the tray, he half leaps into the cell, which makes a clump of rice fall to the floor. Teza sighs in exasperation.

Six weeks into his association with the palm-reader, he is still taken aback when he sees the man. Sein Yun is like a creature from another star. Most of his teeth are the dark red of a betel-chewer. His lips are burgundy slashes and the lines around them leak red-black stains. Only his eyeteeth are clean. Capped in gold, they gleam like yellow fangs. A skein of grizzled hair covers his head, the shriveled scalp showing through like a rusty lemon. The little man's skin is all yellow: face, hands, neck. Even the whites of his eyes are yellow. He is a walking, talking, cursing Petri dish of hepatitis.

The wild gray hairs of his eyebrows make up for the lack of hair on his skull. But the king of hair on Sein Yun's face is one long, imposing, curly strand of black that grows out of the mole on his chin. The palm-reader often twists the wiry black curlicue thoughtfully between his fingers, just as he is doing now—stroke, stroke, and a sudden pull as he turns his head to shoot a torpedo of betel juice out the open cell door. He crouches down and drops the food tray on the floor with a clatter.

Teza begins, "Where have you been with my—"

Sein Yun's syncopated "Heh-heh-heh" interrupts him. "I have a very good excuse, trust me." He waves his hand in a downward motion, wanting Teza to crouch beside him. The singer glares.

"Ko Teza, don't be stubborn, it doesn't suit you. Come, come here. I have some news."

Teza scratches his head. Lice.

With an avid grin, the palm-reader whispers, "It's about Daw Suu Kyi."

Teza immediately drops down.

"Heh-heh. You monkey. I knew that would get your attention."

"What is it?"

"It's the reason you missed your meals yesterday." The stained lips stretch gloatingly over his teeth. "Daw Suu Kyi is free. Released from house arrest. A thousand journalists are on University Avenue right now, they've come from all over the world. It's a better tourist attraction than the Shwedagon Pagoda!" Sein Yun places his hands around an invisible box in front of his face and pumps his index finger up and down. "Click-click-click! The Nikons are out, the flashes are on. The beautiful lady is free, she's free!"

"How do you know?"

"The whole cage knows—a warder must have brought it in. Leaky warders! I accused Jailer Chit Naing, but as usual he admits nothing. The cage has gone crazy. It happened one or two days ago, I don't know exactly when. An auspicious day for Burma, a lucky day for us. Our savior is more famous now than when she won the Nobel Prize. They can finally take her picture! And she is so lovely." Gold eyeteeth flash. "But too skinny, they say. She has to start eating more bananas." The palm-reader leers, lifting his eyebrows.

Teza's mouth twists with doubt. Sein Yun might be making up the whole story.

Sensing disbelief, the palm-reader snaps, "Oh, you'll know the truth soon enough, Songbird. Your esteemed friend Chit Naing will drop by one evening when things calm down, I'm sure."

This comment sends a jolt of fear through the singer. How does the palm-reader know about Chit Naing's nocturnal visits? If he knows, he knows. It's better to say nothing. Instead he asks, "Where's Handsome? Why hasn't he come with you?"

"Ah, how sweet! You miss him, do you? Should I call him over? He's down at the far end of the hall having a smoke. You know he hates this solitary block—it puts him in a bad mood. Bad luck in here, that's what he says. All those rats down the hall. The guy is terrified of them." Sein Yun laughs and slaps Teza on the shoulder. "Isn't that funny?"

"Hilarious. What about my shower? Are you going to escort me to the shower room?"

"Please, Songbird, I don't know what you're suggesting, but whatever it is, I'm not interested."

"You are sick. Would you just tell Handsome that I want my shower?"

"Aie! Ko Teza, I'm beginning to understand why they put you in the coffin. You're a royal pain in the ass, and you don't know a good thing when it's poking you in the eye. The guy doesn't even want to come down the hallway, and if he did, he would just abuse you, because as we all know that's his karma, to be a nasty shithead. But can you leave well enough alone and just let him sit there, smoking? No, you cannot. You want to provoke him. Mr. Political, give it a rest!"

This earnest outburst is so out of character for the palm-reader that Teza has to cover his mouth with his hand to keep from laughing.

"See? See? You think it's funny! Well, you won't think it's funny when he beats the shit out of you, I promise you that. Idiot!"

"Ko Sein Yun, you're allowed to shower every day. Twice a day? I bet you have a nice wash twice a day, right? Your arms aren't covered with scabies, are they? Look at this." The singer thrusts his arms out. "You know why they bleed like that? Because I scratch them in my sleep. You know what scabies are, don't you? Tiny little bugs burrowing tunnels under my skin. Tunnels, Ko Sein Yun, tunnels! If I manage to keep away from the sores during the day, I scratch all through the night. And you get to eat, don't you? A lot, too. You have a racket in the gardens, you've told me that, fresh vegetables. I am pleased for you. But it's not like that for me. The cage is really a cage. So don't lecture me about being a good boy. If I don't complain and make demands and get in trouble, they will treat me worse than they already do."

Sein Yun fixes him with a yellow eye. "Are you done?" He spits some more betel juice. "Good. Listen again, I'll say it more slowly this time: Handsome does not want to go into the shower room because of the rats. I can't say I blame him. You're just going to have to wait, Songbird. I'll fill your water pot right to the top. You can give yourself a wash. And maybe a warder will come back later and take you."

Teza grimaces and opens his mouth to speak, but Sein Yun cuts him off. "Songbird, I'm not going to make things complicated for myself. He's a friend, okay?" Sein Yun leans over, eyes wide, and whispers, "You see, I've read his palm, and now he's mine. These guys! The toughest among them are as superstitious as old women! Even Senior Jailer Chit Naing had me read his palm! If only everyone outside were like them, all the palm-readers set up around the base of Sule Pagoda would be richer than generals. And don't be such a whiner—I've brought you something to smoke." The palm-reader stands and fishes two cheroots out of the pocket hidden inside his longyi. He proffers the cigars in his outstretched hand.

Staring at the little man's long, curved fingernails, which are caked with dirt from the kitchen gardens, Teza checks an unexpected urge to turn away. He doesn't reach for the cheroots.

"What's with you? Don't tell me you've decided to start smoking cigarettes—they're too expensive. Besides, what would you read? Do you want these cheroots or not?" This time he offers them to Teza in the formal way, with his left hand cradling the elbow of his right arm, the thick, leaf-wrapped cigars lying flat on his open palm. The singer rises and gingerly picks them up without touching the palm-reader's hand.

Sein Yun smiles directly into Teza's eyes. The force of the look is physical, as though the man has grasped his shoulder. "There's a good boy."

"Where's my food parcel?"

Sein Yun replies, slightly offended. "Little Brother, they told me nothing about it. No one tells me anything. I'm just the one who carries the crap around." To emphasize his point, he puts out his hand.

Teza turns to fetch the latrine pail. "Is there anything else about Daw Suu Kyi? Any other news? Has she been able to speak to the public?"

"Now, now, that's enough for one day. I have to get on with my work. I suspect your friend Chit Naing will be here soon enough with all the juicy details. I've heard this sort of thing interests him . . ."

Again Teza does not acknowledge the trailing bait. "Everyone, even you, is interested in what happens to her."

"True. We are all interested, but for different reasons. The men are going crazy about the whole thing. They'll gamble on anything. The bet of the day is how many weeks it will take the SLORC to assassinate her."

Teza gasps.

"Yeah, those guys in Hall Four, a savage bunch, I agree, but that's the wager. Like father, like daughter, they say, and why else would the SLORC have released her? So the generals can have her killed and pretend they had nothing to do with it, right? Then they'll announce that the house arrest was for her own good and it's a shame they ever freed her. Our heroes!" Sein Yun claps his hands, then lowers his voice dramatically. "You know, there are still rumors that Ne Win was behind her father's assassination. And if he could have the great Bogyoke Aung San and his whole cabinet shot to death right in their offices, his lovely daughter doesn't present much of a challenge."

"Ko Sein Yun! Don't say that. I don't want to hear it."

"I thought you wanted to know what was going on. That's what the men are saying."

"The generals wouldn't dare touch her. She's too well known. The entire world would despise them."

Sein Yun cocks his head to the side. "Has that ever stopped them before? It will be very interesting to see what happens next."

Teza frowns. "Ko Sein Yun, who's taking the bets?"

"Hmm?" The palm-reader is backing up, turning to the door.

"Somebody must be making money."

The slashed grin comes again, a silent part of Sein Yun's vocabulary. "Little Brother, a very good question. I have no idea. And I don't mean to offend you, but I'm sick of standing here with your shit in my hands. I'm going to empty this bucket." The cell door heaves shut.

Teza stands in front of it, shaking his head. When the leader of the National League for Democracy is released from six years of house arrest, the palm-reader responds by organizing a betting racket on the date of her possible assassination. He really is sick. And the only human being Teza speaks to on a daily basis.

Less than five minutes later the palm-reader reappears at the coffin door and hands him the emptied pail. It's surprisingly clean inside.

"What, you washed it?"

"No, I got the rats to lick it out." Sein Yun flashes his teeth. "Sometimes the tap at the latrine hole actually works. I sprayed the thing clean."

Teza stares at the pail. None of his servers has ever done this before. The unexpected kindness and weird intimacy of the act catches him off guard. He had no idea there was a tap at the latrine.

"Don't look so amazed, you'll dirty it soon enough. Take it as a token of my friendship." For once the palm-reader meets Teza's eye without making a snide comment.

Teza feels genuinely touched. "Thank you."

"Not at all. It's your shit that's getting me out of here. I'm cutting down my sentence with every pail. That's how we buy freedom in Burma." He emphasizes his statement by letting go a sonorous fart.

The singer laughs. "I am glad to be contributing in some small way to your impending freedom, Ko Sein Yun."

"Little Brother, I only wish my shit could do the same for you." He steps over the threshold of the teak coffin but turns to wink at Teza before he closes the heavy door.

"Ko Sein Yun?"

"Yes?"

"If the next food parcel is empty, I will stop eating. Let them know, would you?"

Sein Yun snaps disapprovingly, "They? They? Who is they?"

"Whoever steals the food."

"Oh, fucking politicals! If you're hungry, you stage a hunger strike. Is that intelligent behavior? Eat your fucking breakfast."

"There was only one fish in the last parcel."

"I know, I know, one fish and now you're dying. Try to remember, Songbird, you are too important for them to starve you to death. All right? The parcel is coming. In the meantime, one of these nights you should sing. You know, to celebrate Daw Suu's release. The cage would go wild. We could have a riot!"

"I could lose more teeth."

"If you ever need to pull one, let me know, I have a foolproof technique. And I can get you all the paracetamol you want for the pain. Ko Sein Yun, palm-reader extraordinaire, at your service. See you later."

He pushes the teak door closed. The bolt cracks back into place; the key turns in the lock. Sein Yun's shuffling feet retreat down the long corridor.

. 5 .

The palm-reader's smell—the ammonia of old sweat, the pungent scent of betel and lime-slaked leaves—hovers in the cell like an unwashed ghost. Teza wrinkles his nose. Then a familiar twitch sends his eyes down to the floor. He swears loudly and stamps his foot, but the cockroaches aren't afraid. They know this prisoner well. Partly because of Buddhism, partly because their guts make such a mess, Teza doesn't kill cockroaches.

He squats and glares down. They're on their way to his breakfast. The only way to keep them at bay while he's eating is to give them their own little meal. "You're worse than the damn wardens!" He collects the rice Sein Yun spilled and places it, in several discrete portions, in front of the advancing battalion.

He shifts the tray to the center of the cell, away from the roaches, quickly rinses his hands, then sits down to eat, facing the teak door. His fingers pause at the tray's edge.

Pea curry. Pea soup, really, because a curry requires spices and oil, two ingredients that are mostly absent from this gray water. Completing the menu is half a teaspoon of very low-quality fermented fish paste and a clump of broken rice.

The evening meal is slightly different: a kind of vegetable soup, also mostly water, also served with rice normally fed to pigs. Sometimes the "vegetable" is simply grass, or stalks of cauliflower. Occasionally he receives a piece of gristle in his soup. The prison kings believe this piece of gristle is meat, which shows how corrupt, well-fed men gradually lose touch with reality.

Dissatisfied with plain rice, a few of the cockroaches have begun a hesitant advance toward Teza, who claps his hands together. "Get away from me, you fascists, get away!" It depends on his mood. He also calls them socialists, capitalists, Americans, imperialists, Chinese businessmen, and bloody dictators.

With oily grace, the troop disperses, back to the rice, into the dark corners.

Still sitting before his food, the singer clasps his index finger and thumb around his wrist. It used to be that the index finger wouldn't reach his thumb. Only the middle finger could close the bracelet. But now index finger meets thumb with room to spare. The prison is erasing him.

Weighing himself this way, or looking down at the knobbed bones of his hips, or feeling the holes in his gums where teeth used to be, Teza experiences a disturbing lucidity of vision, as though he is dreaming of someone else. There he is, a man with dark eyes and famine wrists, black hair grown to his shoulders. He sits in the center of a small cell, encircled by a shifting ring of cockroaches. Taking a deep breath, he begins to eat the broken rice with his long fingers, pinching the grains into a ball, dipping it into the fish paste and the soup, lifting the food to his lips. With the third bite, his teeth close on a small stone. One of the reasons he eats slowly is to catch these dangerous bits. He once found a piece of iron the size of a fingernail in his soup.

His tongue delivers the stone out of his mouth. Like a child on a riverbank, he turns it this way and that, as though it might bear a secret mark of worth. But it's just a small gray rock. He places it on the tray's edge, for later. Nothing is useless in a coffin.

Nausea undulates through his stomach, ripples up into his throat. *Ya-deh, ya-deh, ya-ba-deh*. Never, never mind, it doesn't matter. He disciplines himself to chew, chew. No matter how bad it tastes, every meal is a small event in the abyss of prison time.

Chew, chew, chew. It's like gnawing the mat at the entrance to a noodle shop. There is food somewhere beyond it, on a higher plane.

Now comes the inevitable swallow.

He's sad to admit how good it tastes, once the first few mouthfuls have gone down. Saliva floods in. His stomach stretches inside his body, opening like the mouth of a famished child. Only after eating can he think clearly about the palm-reader's news.

What does it mean, really, that Daw Suu has been released from house arrest? He would like her freedom to mean something, to change everything, but his lips shut tightly and pull inward like an old man's. Daw Aung San Suu Kyi's hands are clean of blood and of blood money. But she's no different from her many supporters, the brave, outspoken ones, the silent ones. She is no different from her brilliant, murdered father. She is only human.

He shakes his head and gazes around his cell. His memories can be so painfully vivid. Perhaps some law of physics intersects with a law of incarceration: that is why prison chronology runs backward. The past is the most compelling evidence toward a future different from this moment: the walls, the lizards, his bucket of shit and piss, the clay water pot, its sides slicked with algae.

He touches his hair. Sein Yun is full of crap. How can he wash his hair with water from his drinking pot? Why don't they just shave his head? On a sudden impulse, he yanks out a few oily strands. As soon as the interrogators were finished with him, white began to salt the hair directly above his left eyebrow, the one split in two by a boot. Jailer Chit Naing told him there's a thick swath of white now. Teza stares at the pulled hairs in vague disbelief. No one in his family, not even his grandparents, had such pure white hair. He might as well have snow on his fingers.

He wonders if his mother's hair is graying now. After all she's been through, he wouldn't be surprised. Hpo Hpo, his maternal grandfather, had streaks of white in his always-pomaded black hair; his grandmother, who died years before her husband, dyed her hair so dark that he remembers it shining velvety purple.

They are the faces that made my face, Teza thinks. He closes his eyes and brings them to the surface of his mind one after the other. His mother. His father. His grandparents on both sides. Aung Min too. And Thazin. Daw Suu Kyi. These are the faces he keeps in his heart. His aunties and uncles, his cousins. Friends from university. Certain beloved teachers. He wonders how much the living have changed. Not as much as he has. And the dead stay as they are.

He remembers the old family photographs displayed on the wall of the sitting room, below the altar. In one of them his mother was still a girl, wearing a traditional blouse of homespun cotton, the cloth-knot button closed gracefully at the neck. She is smiling demurely, round-faced and dimpled, but from the glint in her eye and the almost ironic tilt of her head, you suspect that she wants to stick out her tongue and cross her eyes. In some of the photographs from the early years of her marriage, Daw Sanda *did* make funny faces, mugging for the camera or grinning broadly. As their lives became more difficult, her smiles grew subdued or disappeared altogether, and her arms cradled each other, as though carrying some invisible weight.

Her serious expression in the more recent pictures was similar to much older photographs of great-uncles and -aunts and grandparents. These people stared bleakly forward, pressed into time through the narrow black hole of the camera. Most of the portraits were taken shortly after World War II, and the harshness of the Japanese occupation still showed in their solemn eyes.

There were photographs of his father, Dr. Kyaw Win Thu, on the wall too, a slender man with a slightly impish grin and penetrating eyes, eyes that looked so directly at Teza that he sometimes had to turn away from their gaze. The doctor's mouth often seemed to be puckered slightly, as if he wanted to speak but was hesitating. What? What was he going to say? When Teza was a teenager, his father's photographs impressed him as much as Bogyoke Aung San's did; both men's faces showed so much purpose and intelligence. And both were inseparable from a devastating sense of loss.

Bogyoke Aung San's face was and still is everywhere. It stared out from the front wall of every classroom Teza ever entered. They had a picture of him in the family sitting room too; it was the first thing you saw when you walked into the house. He remembers Bogyoke Aung San's intelligent eyes turned toward a future they would never see. In that image the singer finds Daw Suu's more delicate narrow jaw and cheeks, the fine bone structure visible through the flesh, giving both father and daughter a severe and haunting dignity.

Now the daughter's face is iconic, revered in the same way, but it's illegal, and very dangerous, to exhibit her portrait in public. As soon as she became politically involved, images of her started to circulate. Teza once showed her photo to people in a tea shop. Country folk, in the city to join the demonstrations for a day, they crowded around his little table and asked him hushed questions about the famous lady, daughter of the great man.

She does look like him. But her popularity can't be explained solely by her link to Bogyoke Aung San. Part of her power, Teza thinks, lies in the fact that she is both Burmese and foreign. She has come from the outside world and chosen to stay in this isolated country. She is a refined Burmese woman, and a Buddhist—the latter is very important for the people. But what she carries from her life abroad is the future, which is already happening everywhere outside of Burma. She is the link between that future and Burma's past.

The last time he saw her at the house on University Avenue was in mid-November 1988.

T eza became a member of the youth wing of Daw Suu's party because he believed in the work, but he also liked being close to her. It confused him to have a crush on such an old woman. Even though she looked very young and was very beautiful, she was actually forty-three, and married, and a mother. He was very much in love with Thazin and couldn't explain his attraction to this older lady. He worked hard at keeping his feelings a secret. After the youth meetings, he sometimes played his guitar and sang songs with other musicians. Daw Suu's house was often filled with an eclectic bunch of people, not only senior politicians and activists but journalists and famous poets, well-known political comedians, actors. All of them agreed that Teza sang beautifully. Truly, his songs were written for the whole of Burma's people.

Only Teza knew that he was singing to her.

If a beautiful woman laughs in a certain way, people will fall in love with her. Certain people will hate her for it too. The generals hated Daw Suu then, for many reasons, and surely they must hate her now, which makes her release more mysterious. Why have they freed her?

Teza picks up the pebble, and holding it between his fingers like a single prayer bead, he whispers, "If Daw Suu is really free, something will shift." He holds his breath for a moment, listening as the cockroaches scratch out an incomprehensible code.

Rolling the stone between his palms, warming it, he steps to the center of the cell and closes one eye, aiming carefully at the spider's window, the air vent. He throws. And misses. The stone falls to the floor. He retrieves it, aims again. Whatever the object, a small stone or a dried pea—he's used one of his own lost teeth—the projectile must be thrown accurately and with enough force to make it through the vent.

After two attempts, the stone flies up and escapes. When he hears it hit the ground outside, he smiles, bows, dances a jig. He celebrates the lady's release with the liberation of a stone.

. 6 .

In the evening he prepares for the rest of the celebration.

Sitting cross-legged in the middle of the cell, the singer carefully places the cheroots in front of him. It's a lucky thing that Sein Yun brought him two more today. Teza doesn't like to perform the ceremony without at least ten of the long, slender cigars; the mathematical serious-ness of the number appeals to him. It's the filters he needs, not the cigars themselves. In the interest of formality and restraint, he tries not to smoke them before the ritual begins, but even if he breaks down and indulges, he carefully, religiously saves the butts. Ten cheroots take about a week or so to hoard, depending on the generosity of Sein Yun and his more irregular supplier, Jailer Chit Naing.

At university he read of the Japanese tea ceremony. From meditation, he knows the art of mindfulness. Each movement must come slowly, aware of itself but not ponderous. Sitting back on his heels, as though about to pray, he intones, "The Burmese Cheroot Ceremony" in a solemn voice.

In his second and third year, he occasionally laughed after saying this, but not a sigh of amusement escapes him now. The ritual has grown in importance with the passage of time. He performs it to mark birthdays and anniversaries. Now he will honor Daw Suu. His back to the cell door, he runs one of the cigars under his nose: woodsmoke and trees. The vision rises in his mind as clearly as one of those photographs from the family collection. His grandfather is smoking in a tea shop near the Chinese market in Mandalay.

Inside a cheroot is the smell of Burma.

After eating and meditating, the cheroot ceremony is the most important event in his life. It is a challenge to perform it well. To peel the filters apart slowly enough is an act of discipline.

The filters are made with ridged, dried straw. Holding the filters tight is a band of newspaper.

Words.

The cheroots are not all the same brand. Some are finer, some coarser. One is even expensively wrapped in plastic, and thinner than the others. That devil Sein Yun, he has good connections. Going from right to left, Teza works the circular paper label off each cigar butt.

After years of practice, he's able to peel open the cylinder of dried leaf without breaking it. He slowly draws out the filter. Then he pulls the newspaper away from the filter of rolled straw.

He pauses, holding his breath.

Nothing. No footsteps or voices outside the teak coffin.

His meticulousness is precaution as well as ritual; he is afraid of getting caught. The filter paper is smaller than a matchbook. It is actually two pieces of newsprint glued together, wrapped in a snug band and tucked into the first layer of straw. He carefully works the paper off, then separates it into its halves and lays them out before him. He tries to flatten them, but they always curl back into the shape of the filter.

Sometimes the cheroot-makers make the filters quite narrow. How upsetting! He depends on two inches of newsprint and sometimes gets only an inch or less. When a filter comes from a top or bottom margin, there are no words on it at all. While he unrolls this blank paper, his forehead wrinkles, pushing his eyebrows and nose into a scowl of accusation. He consciously smooths out his face again, as he smooths out the crinkled paper, but it's difficult to stave off the feeling of annoyance.

He attempts to make it into a joke.

Don't those damn girls know they're preparing my reading material? Don't they care?

The cheroot ceremony returns Teza to his country. Performing it, he leaves the prison. Though he's a city boy, he tramps to the villages, where the cheroot-makers work hard at their low tables. He wonders if they ever sing. At dawn the girls walk to the crumbling wooden house that serves as a factory. Fifty of them sit on the floor in a dim room. Cheroot after cheroot rolls from the girls' hands, from seven in the morning until seven at night. Through the light of late afternoon they walk home again, the lanes of red dust busy with scrawny chickens. Ox carts sway back from the fields through the tall trees. The girls fall in love with village boys and marry. They become mothers. If their babies die, they make more. They make thousands of cheroots, smoked by millions of men and grandmothers all over Burma and read by an unknown number of political prisoners held in solitary confinement.

In his mind, the cheroot-makers are beautiful, goodhearted, with pale swirls of thanakha paste smeared, powderlike, on their cheeks. If they knew they were making cheroots for him, they would find a way to put Dostoyevsky into the filter, *The Brothers Karamazov*, Tolstoy's *War and Peace*, a great tome by Pablo Neruda, and *Gone With the Wind*, a book he's wanted to read ever since he saw a photograph of Vivien Leigh in an ancient *Time* magazine. They would fill their cheroots with popular Burmese novels and bowls of curry. They would send wreaths of the sweetest jasmine to him, sticks of incense and squares of gold foil for worship. They are fine young women. Teza ceases to be angry with the blank newsprint. He thinks of girls' hands, working.

When the unwrapping is done, he lines up the tattered bits of printed paper.

He reads as slowly as possible, to make the words last.

his mother explain
but I don't trust
jealous of his love
to crying every day
escape the pressure
sure he loves me bu
not know his mother
a terrible hell.

the small America
n man killed 17 p
Including small c
n lone old woman
eapons are easy t
ate of violence d
many murders per
decaying family v
very different fr
Burma uncorrupted.

she was like a star wi
loved me in the same m
ver despite everything
without her. She was w
when she left, tears be
like rain. When I woul
without the clarity of
later understood the d
what I believed and no

child remembered
names of his former
and siblings, includ
the existence of a l
boa constrictor with
snake remained altho

boy every night, ne
nor aggression. Ko K
described flawlessly
even the kind of bla
pots and pans, showi
familiarity with all
of Mandalay Division

The singer smiles at that last one. He's sure his mother would have read the article.

May May is a great reader. She is one of those fearless women on the bus who will hold a page up to the light to read through the censorship ink. Black ink is impossible to penetrate, but if the ink is silver, you can hold it up to the light and make out the hidden words. She will even lift a blackened page up to the sky anyway, just to show her contempt. A man leaned over to her once and asked, with the urgency of fear in his voice, "What are you doing?"

In a stage whisper, she replied, "I am reading." Then she went back to trying to decipher the inked-out words.

This is his mother, a small-boned warrior. Even if she did not purchase a copy of this particular newspaper, someone in the neighborhood would have brought her the article. Someone would have seen it and thought, *Ah, Daw Sanda will be interested in this, she will tell a story.*

Daw Sanda believes in the children who remember their past lives. Their stories are printed in dozens of popular magazines across the country. She clips these tales with red-handled scissors and places them in a series of numbered folders marked REINCARNATION/REBIRTH. Stories like the one from the cheroot filter, about boys who remember the names of strangers and tame snakes and know the location of household items in houses they've never seen before, are very popular. She retells these stories with the passion of a true believer, describing in artful detail even the unpublished parts of the accounts. She explains to her neighbors that most of us forget the secrets we knew at birth. Education and parents insist that we forget.

But determined children remember. Without having been taught, they can speak strange dialects from other parts of the country. They beg to visit certain men and women who live thousands of miles away. On meeting, they recognize these strangers as their parents or friends of the past. Even friendly animals are considered to be reincarnations of recently deceased people.

Having grown up on a diet of these accounts, Teza believed in them wholeheartedly until he went to university, where he was informed that his mother was superstitious, old-fashioned. He gravitated toward those students who talked about doing away with superstitions and embracing whatever scraps of audacious modernity the world smuggled through Burma's closed borders. That included rejecting the popular stories of reincarnation. But now, with reality shrunk to the dimensions of his cell and his mind, believing has taken on a new power.

Omens, dreams, the power of the sacred places, the secret messages of the cheroots themselves: these have become crucial. Everything his mother and his grandfather told him about Buddhism, the nats, and any kind of magic has been pulled out of the well of his memory and used to slake his thirst for meaning.

That's why these tiny pieces of paper are so important. Pressing the palms of his hands together, the singer chooses another filter. The words are runes. Each piece of paper has a story, whether a sad romance from the literary section or a boring government announcement or a funeral notice. Whispering under his breath, Teza fills in the missing text.

After the story he searches for the secret, the message encoded on every bit of paper. The torn-edged missives seem anonymous, but Teza knows the world has sent them. The scraps emerge from the vastness of his country, across the rivers and fields, given by the hands of strangers. They pass through walls, gates, bars, enormous doors. They move across compounds, through cells in the halls Teza has never seen, down corridors filled with the very particular smell of imprisoned men.

<blockquote>
beyond a doubt
triumphant
prove
</blockquote>

He knows this ceremony of words and their secret messages brings illumination.

mother
trust
love
wish
escape
hell

Sometimes the messages are not secret. The meanings are miraculously evident. The scraps of paper reveal Burma's true history.

thousands killed
easy violence
decaying Burma

The tiny clippings are laid out before him. He picks his favorite one and places it in his opposite hand like a piece of jewelry.

loved
despite everything
rain
understood

Teza reads the small shred of paper again, and again. Part of the discipline of the cheroot ceremony involves sitting as though in meditation, not allowing himself to wander into memory and fantasy. He will keep this filter paper, and the one about reincarnation, instead of shredding them up with the others and dropping the pieces into his shit pail.

Until three years ago he kept all the scraps, using and reusing them, trying and sometimes succeeding in fitting bits of an article together from the same brand of cheroot. Then his cell was raided.

The warders found his little cheroot documents wrapped up in his spare shirt. He had made a kind of daily crossword game out of the bits, and the Chief Warden said they were political messages, so the warders had to beat him and threaten him with the dog cells. They used to keep dogs in them, but during a prison riot the prisoners killed and ate most of the hounds. After that, the Chief Warden decided the cages would become punishment cells. Men live in them now, exposed to the elements and trapped for months at a time with the accumulation of their own urine and feces. Teza wasn't sent to a dog cell because he would have had too much contact with other politicals. He was just given a good thrashing.

He doesn't know how that particular session ended. The beatings melt into one another because they're so similar. You have to assume a certain position—it's in the regulations. Half squat on your toes with your legs farther apart than your shoulders. Hold your hands at the back of the neck with elbows in the air. It's like stopping in the middle of a deep knee bend. Now you are ready, fully exposed: your genitals, your abdomen, your back, your face, your armpits. Your feet are bare and you are as terrified for them as you are for your balls. When the blows begin to fall, you must not move your hands from the back of your head. That is not part of the game. You must not fall over until you lose consciousness (even then they will kick you) or until they get tired, or bored, and stop.

Everything around him—the other voices, the sounds of his body being hit, the shadows and light in the room, the smells and tastes—recedes, then disappears next to the sudden intimacy of violence and the pain it creates. That pain in his body becomes the center of the world, and they keep kicking him, keep hitting him anyway. That is how they break apart the world over and over again.

It's odd, but when he thinks about the beatings, later he always thinks about making love with Thazin. It's the only other touching he's ever experienced that was as unbounded and total. But when you make love, you begin the world with another person; two small gods build the first kingdom out of the body's clay. That's why another soul, a baby, might come from it. But when a man beats you in the cage, he wants you to know that he's got the whole substance of you in his hands, your life and your death. The distance between those two points is all the agony a human body can feel.

Almost a year after the incident, Sammy, who had just become his server, nonchalantly handed him a cheroot. Teza was jubilant but afraid. "You must know I'm not allowed to have them. You'll lose your job. You'll be punished! And I'll go to a dog cell."

Sammy guffawed, in his contorted way, and waved the cheroot back. Grinning as he gave Teza a lighter, he put the V of his fingers to his lips, as though to say, "Shut up and have a smoke, man!"

So the singer began to smoke again, and returned, with heightened gratitude, to his ritual. But now every time he performs the cheroot ceremony, he throws most of the old filters away, keeping just one or two of them for a few days. He could eat the scraps of paper very quickly if he had to.

He used to throw away whole sheets of paper just because the edges were torn, or because a few unimportant words or spots of ink marred them. His old extravagance saddens him as much as the food he once left on his plate—whole pieces of chicken—because he wasn't hungry.

When he and Aung Min were small, they used to walk on the street of the bookbinders in Rangoon, near Sule Pagoda. They called it Paper Street, and discussed the possibility of working there when they grew up, just to be close to so much fabulous paper. Women carrying mountains of blank paper on their heads walked past the brothers, carefully maneuvering through the crowds and the traffic on their way to the government and shipping offices, to the printing shops. Boys walking bicycles and carts loaded with paper pushed past them with an air of adult importance that Teza envied.

It can't be any different now. The printing shops are still there. Every house on both sides of Paper Street is crammed with paper. Paper in all the colors of a Hindu temple, paper for children, for kings, rainbow-covered notebooks and looseleaf sheets of blue and green, paper with elaborate letterheads and misspelled letterheads, coarse and woody to the touch, sand-grained, or smooth as the skin of a young woman's back. Before the glut of morning traffic, the whole street smells of raw paper waiting to be filled with the stronger smell of black newsprint and love letters and rebellious missives sent from one underground cell to another.

As long as there is paper, people will write, secretly, in small rooms, in the hidden chambers of their minds, just as people whisper the words they're forbidden to speak aloud.

The generals can't stop them. Ne Win himself can't stop them. He never could. Words are like the ants. They work their way through the thickest walls, eating through bricks and feeding off the very silence intended to stifle them.

Teza reads out loud:

siblings existence remained boy flawlessly
loved despite everything rain understood

He falls asleep holding these words in his hands. By morning, the cheap ink has worn into his skin.

. 7 .

Nine days of betel-mouth's idle chatter and dirty jokes, but no chance to wash his hair. His father always used to say that bathing should be made a national pastime. He believed it was good to take two showers a day, but three were even better. In the cage, Teza gets fifteen scoops of water, more if the warder or jailer is kind. Jailer Handsome is not kind, but the last time Teza had a shower, Handsome left the room to smoke, and Teza was able to clean himself properly with forty-two lightning-speed scoops.

"First I don't get to eat and now I don't get to bathe. What would my mother say? Fuck!"

"Does your dear mother have such a filthy mouth?"

"Shut up, Ko Sein Yun, this isn't funny. I am scratching my legs and arms off. I need a proper wash. Why is Handsome being such an asshole?"

"At least he lets me put extra water in your cell."

"Splashing water all over the floor attracts more cockroaches. And I need to wash my clothes." He picks up a tightly wrapped bundle of dirty cloth and throws it down on the floor again. "This is stupid. I'm calling him."

"Oh, Songbird, I don't think that's a good idea. Really, that is a poor idea."

Teza's voice fills the cell, then breaks out of it as he pushes past Sein Yun and sticks his head out the door. "Jailer! Sir! Sir! I request permission to make a complaint!"

Silence.

The silence stretches uncomfortably, but Teza is not intimidated by silence, his most intimate cellmate. He bellows, louder still, "Sir! Sir! I request permission to make a complaint, sir!" Euphoria warms his throat. This is almost as good as singing. It doesn't matter what happens now. As soon as he opens his mouth and yells at one of them, he is free.

When Teza hears the jailer shout back, he turns gleaming eyes on Sein Yun, who whispers, "You are a bloody idiot." Slouched against the far wall, the palm-reader has shrunk his already diminutive frame further by hunching his shoulders. The boots are coming now.

Teza steps away from the door. The jailer's voice drowns out the sound of his own heavy boots. "What the fuck is going on here? Why is he yelling?" There is no time for Sein Yun to reply. Handsome walks past him into the singer's cell. He's a well-built man with a broad chest and strong forearms. Teza glances up at him. As usual, he is surprised that the jailer *is* so handsome, like a movie star, with a perfect wave of black hair combed back from his high forehead. Mothers warn their daughters against those square-jawed, full-lipped good looks, the half-raised, rakish eyebrow. Now the large, fine eyes are bright slits of anger, and Handsome's nose has wrinkled; he's smelling something unpleasant. Teza smiles very slightly. Maybe the junior jailer smells his own stinky prisoner.

Handsome's deep voice rattles off a round of rapid-fire questions. "What the fuck is so funny? Hmm? You stupid little shit, who do you think you are? You're not allowed to yell like that. Now put your head down. Put it down, I said!" He steps forward and cracks his knuckles on Teza's skull. In the presence of a jailer, prisoners are obliged to keep their heads lowered in deference, but hitting Teza like that counts as a grave offense. For a Buddhist, the head is the most sacred part of the body. Handsome pushes in, close to Teza's face, his spittle pelting the singer's cheek.

"Have you forgotten where you are? Huh? Think you're still out there, do you, spreading lies, filling people's heads with shit? Don't you know what you are, you stupid fuck? Don't you know what you are?"

Silence.

Teza's ears ring as he considers Handsome's question, seriously, and begins to answer it, seriously. "I am Ko Teza, fourth-year student of English literature at Rangoon Univ—"

The blow catches him off guard. Suddenly he is on the floor, shaking his head, opening and closing his jaws mechanically, like a puppet. But Teza's jaw isn't broken. He has fallen beside the aluminum tray that Sein Yun has just carried to him. Out of the corner of his eye he sees the movement, the flash and blur of the boot; he knows it so well. He rams his head into the crook of his elbow, grips the back of his neck with his hand to keep his eyes lodged there, blind but protected, ready for the first kick and the ones that come after. Handsome doesn't kick him, though. He kicks the food tray instead, mightily, launching watery curry and rice all over the prisoner and the cell. The aluminum bounces off Teza's elbow and clatters on the cement floor.

Silence.

But it's a conversation. It has been the same conversation since the first interrogation center, the first protest, the first song.

He waits for a kick to his stomach, or his back, but nothing comes. Carefully, slowly, he moves into the half squat, wasted rice dropping off his shirt between his bare feet. Quietly, he replies, "Sir, I request permission to make a complaint about the irregularity of my shower times. Sir."

"You stupid asshole, I'd like to break your neck right now. Permission denied, you motherfucker."

Shut up, bellows the coffin door as it slams. *Shutshutshutthefuckup.* Crack of metal bolts, rattle of keys, the jailer's voice yelling at Sein Yun, whose reply is muffled. Teza strains to hear the words they exchange, wondering why the warder doesn't hit Sein Yun too.

He stands up to survey the damage. It's always a shock to see the enormous mess made by such a small amount of food. This isn't the first time Handsome has kicked his tray. At least the jailer didn't kick *him.* He cleans, stooped over like an old man, picking up bits of cauliflower and pinching clumps of rice between his fingers, tossing all in the shit pail. This proves Sein Yun right: Teza is not as hungry as he thinks he is, because he doesn't consider eating any of the food. He wets an old undershirt and washes the floor, squeezes out the dirty water over the shit pail, washes again. It's not really clean. It never is—he has only a bar of soap to work with.

Eventually he places his sleeping mat in the center of the cell. The cleaning took him away from his anger for a while, but as soon as he sits down it floods his body and his mind. Every breath is rage. Teza wants to kill Handsome, or the Chief Warden, or one of the generals. Or all of them—he would kill them all now, if he had a gun and they were standing in the cell with him. His mouth fills with the worst curses he knows and he whispers them in a low, growling voice. He hears Handsome's words again, the shouting, feels the crack on his skull, the sudden wrenching of his jaw. When he begins meditating, he has to turn these sensations over and over until they begin to change.

The breath teaches him that. And it was his mother, years ago, who insisted on the lesson. When he was about fifteen, he started to resist going to temple with Daw Sanda. There were always things he wanted to do on the weekends, which was the only time his mother could go to the pagoda. She said, "All right, you don't have to come. But during the week, in the evenings, you have to go on your own." He was to sit down and breathe. That's all. Meditate, at least two or three times a week. Why? "Because your breath is your teacher. Your whole life, that won't change, so you must learn to pay attention to your teacher now, while you are young. When you grow up and go away from me, your breath will always be there to guide you. If you know how to follow it, you will never get lost."

He prostrates himself three times before an invisible altar and chants a low-voiced prayer. Then he sits cross-legged, hands upturned, right on top of left. Inhaling from his stomach, he follows the breath through his nose into his body. His mother used to tell him stories about the great meditators, the most learned and holy men, who can fly free through the air and walk through walls. With the inward breath they levitate. With the outward breath, they move forward. They can ignite fires with their eyes and speak directly to animals and to the spirits of the dead.

Teza is just a beginner. He cannot do any of these things.

But he can breathe. The breath rises from the center of his belly, up, up along his vertebrae into the back of his skull, then down, down, out the toes of his right leg. Beginning again, he follows the breath out his left leg.

After years of practice, sometimes moments lengthen into hours and his mind opens outward, past the smothering isolation of the cage. These are good long meditations, when he finds his own skeleton and is able to discern separate bones and muscles as the inhalations and exhalations flow through them. His breath can cool him in the hot season and warm him during the chill of the rains. His grandfather shows himself, but never his father. At peace, his grandfather has the strength to comfort him. The old man speaks very little. Often he simply appears, inclines his head, departs. Sometimes he smiles. His mother doesn't appear either, but she is always with him. She is inside him now, as he was once inside her.

As in so many other things, how right she was about meditating. As he follows his breath, he finds himself again. Despite his anger, he knows he would not kill any of the men who have hurt him. How could he, when there has been so much killing already, so many murdered and tortured?

With the in breath, he can feel the pain where he was punched. With the out breath, he can feel the pain. But each exhalation and inhalation changes its nature. His awareness moves from the ache in his jaw to his fury at Handsome. As soon as he begins to examine the fury, though, it stretches into something else, directed not so much at Handsome as at the generals who form SLORC, the State Law and Order Restoration Council. Teza exhales again and looks up.

The spider is above him, crossing his web.

Teza's mind is agitated, uneven, and he repeatedly loses the thread, but the attempt itself brings him calm. Past meditations guide him. He tries to remember all the Pali he knows from the Buddhist scriptures. Intoning the various words and phrases, he is mindful that the Buddha himself spoke Pali. It's a dead classical language, but it always feels very alive to him.

He lists the Divine Abidings: metta, karuna, mudita, upekkha. Metta is the First Divine Abiding: love and benevolence, wishing for one's good and for that of others. Karuna is the Second Divine Abiding: compassion for oneself and others. Mudita is the Third Divine Abiding: joy in the good fortune of others. Upekkha is the Fourth Divine Abiding: equanimity in the face of those things that should be let be.

"Metta, karuna, mudita, upekkha. Metta, karuna, mudita, upekkha. Metta, karuna, mudita, upekkha." He chants the words in a low voice for a long time, until the chant is part of his breath and the syllables flow together without separation. Teza realizes he is a poor Buddhist. He feels no metta for Handsome. He tries, in his meditation, but the well of the breath, rising and falling, is filled with anger and sadness.

Sadness? For himself—yes. Is there anything else there, in the chest? It would be there, the place where the ribs anchor in the breastbone. When he releases a long exhalation, he feels a sharp ache.

Sadness for the jailer? Could that be it?

There might be a small gift of sadness for that arrogant, good-looking face. During the uprisings, the students believed that their struggle for freedom was for everyone, including those who didn't understand what they were doing, even the generals and those who supported them. Therein, he knows, is the heart of the matter. Metta means to love the enemy also. In one of his Buddhist texts he once read, *The only way to end the war is to stop hating the enemy*. But he can't really do it. He tries, but he cannot. He cannot get out of the cage. None of them can get out of the cage.

He starts to whisper a prayer. "Whatever beings there are, may they be free from suffering. Whatever beings there are, may they be free from enmity. Whatever beings there are, may they be free from hurtfulness. Whatever beings there are, may they be free from ill health. Whatever beings there are, may they be able to protect their own happiness."

When Teza opens his eyes, the first thing he sees is three large cockroaches licking up traces of curry water, nibbling away at bits of rice he missed in his cleaning. He feels mudita for them, joy at their good fortune. He doesn't disturb his cellmates but lets them protect their own happiness. They eat as much as they want.

L istening to the rain of late afternoon, he decides to sing, quietly at first. "The Father's Tale," one of the *Twelve Songs*. The words resonate in the back of his throat, expanding to fill not only his body and his memory but the cell itself, as though the teak coffin has become the hollow darkness inside an instrument.

My father wrote a word
in the red dust
in the red dust
of the city of temples.
They tore the word away.

My father fed the child
by the river
by the river
of the city of temples.
They made that child beg.

My father placed the rice
at the altar
at the altar
in the city of temples.
They tore the temple down.

. 8 .

He thinks that maybe Handsome will deny him his second meal, but Sein Yun appears shortly after five o'clock with the food tray. There is a markedly large amount of rice under the thin curry.

"Where is he?"

"He sent a warder in his place. He likes to order his underlings around."

"Where's the warder?"

"Don't start yelling again, okay? You'll wreck my night. He's down at the end of the hall, reading the newspaper. Please don't make a fuss." The palm-reader points his finger at Teza like a chiding schoolmaster. "About this morning—you were retarded. I'm not going to say I told you so. You know Handsome is easily provoked."

"So am I."

"A perfect match. That's why he's your jailer."

"And why are you my server?"

"To keep you entertained." The grin cuts the serious edge off the conversation. "To wit, can I ask you a personal question?"

"No."

"Oh, come on, Little Brother, it's not *that* personal."

Teza sighs, shoveling some rice into his mouth, unable to wait. Through the food he mumbles, "Ask your question."

"What makes you cry?"

Still chewing, Teza looks carefully at Sein Yun to see if he's joking. He is not. Teza swallows and replies, "I don't cry anymore."

"What do you take me for, an idiot? You're an intellectual. Intellectuals bawl their eyes out."

"I cried at the beginning. Not now."

Sein Yun thrusts out his lower lip, a balloon of doubt. "Fine, then. What *would* make you cry?"

Teza is not insulted, only surprised by the pointedness of the question. Tears are private. He's not troubled by his lie.

"Why don't you take away my shit pail? While you're gone, I'll come up with my answer."

Hoisting the pail, the palm-reader replies, "I don't want just any answer, I want the truth! This is a psychological test."

When he returns and hands Teza the pail, the singer immediately notices that he hasn't cleaned it this time.

Sein Yun replies to his glance. "Sorry, the water wasn't running."

"Is that why I'm not allowed a proper shower? For fuck's sake, it's the rainy season. You'd think we were living in a bloody desert."

"No, just a backward country. You know what the water supply is like. So tell me, what would make you cry?"

"The sight of a clean toilet."

"Seriously, Little Brother."

"Why do you want to know? Are you helping them devise a new method of torture?"

"I'm doing a survey."

"I hope it's not for another betting racket!"

Sein Yun's yellow eyes become round. "Ko Teza! Never! I'm just a dedicated student of human nature."

The singer gives in. "I suppose eating my mother's food at home would make me cry. Especially after bathing properly with as much soap as I wanted."

"A fine answer! An honest answer, I would say. Well, that'll be me, in a year or so. Of course it won't be my mother's food, it'll be my wife's. Even if she's gone and shacked up with someone else, I'll make her cook for me, though I can't imagine it will make me cry."

"Ko Sein Yun, it's hard to imagine anything that would make you cry. Now I've answered your question, why don't you answer mine? Is there any news about Daw Aung San Suu Kyi?"

"What do you think I am, BBC Burmese Programming? All I can say is that the bets are in her favor. Fewer inmates think that the SLORC will have her knocked off. You know what that means?"

"What?"

"They don't want her to die. Even these dirty criminals adore her! They want her to liberate them from the cage so they can join the BLPA."

"The BLPA? Who are they?" It has always been a challenge to keep up with the endless acronyms and initials of Burmese politics.

The palm-reader's mouth drops open. "You don't know? Wasn't the BLPA already in operation when you were still outside? You don't mean to tell me you weren't a member of the BLPA?"

"Ko Sein Yun, what is the BLPA?"

"The Beautiful Lady's Private Army!"

"The betel is wrecking your mind as well as your teeth."

"Good thing too, or I wouldn't be talking to you, would I?"

"No news at all, then?"

"Nothing new, nothing juicy."

"Speaking of juicy things . . ."

Sein Yun holds up his yellow palm and asks indignantly, "How would I know where the food parcel is? You ask me the same question every day and I state my case: nobody tells me anything." He lowers his hand. The familiar grin begins, but slowly, changing his face by subtle degrees. "Shouldn't you be starting your hunger strike right about now, Songbird? Isn't that what you said you were going to do?"

Teza swears under his breath.

"Sorry? I missed that."

"Where is the fucking thing?"

The two men stare at each other until Sein Yun places his right hand over his heart. "You must understand—none of that has anything to do with me. The last thing I am interested in is your food, Ko Teza. Really. I have more important things to worry about. You know that the Chief Warden is pissed at the politicals because of Daw Suu Kyi's release. Maybe that's why your food parcel still hasn't come. I don't know for sure." He bobs his head from side to side and injects an Indian lilt into his loud voice. "Sahib, I will do my best to find out what the hell is going on!"

"You won't have this job for long if anyone hears you. You're not supposed to be talking to me."

"Don't worry. They've run out of people to feed you, so I'm sure I'll be visiting for a while yet. I have friends in high places."

"What do you mean? There are thousands of men here who could bring me my food and take away my crap."

Sein Yun spreads his arms. "Oh, Little Brother, you are so wrong. Not just anyone is good enough for you and your shit! Criminals who serve evil political stooges like yourself must be beholden to the prison authorities. We must be cowardly and controllable—otherwise they'd suspect us of smuggling radios to you."

"Yeah, and television sets."

"Women!" Sein Yun titters.

"News about Daw Aung San Suu Kyi."

The palm-reader doesn't miss a beat. "That's right, Songbird, and materials for building bombs to blast your way out of this shithole. Yes, the authorities took one look at me and knew I would not be such a man. I am definitely not in the movement. But I'll keep my voice down in the interests of my career. Thanks for the tip, buddy."

Teza shakes his head.

The palm-reader leans toward him with a critical eye.

"What is it?"

"You really do need a proper wash. And a shave."

"You are so kind, Ko Sein Yun."

"Just trying to be helpful. I know you don't have a mirror in here." The palm-reader slaps his leg gleefully. "Listen, you should be grateful you don't have a big beard." He delicately pulls on the wiry hair of his mole. "Shall I tell you a story?"

Teza smirks. "Of the Buddha's past lives, perhaps?"

"Ha! I knew you wouldn't be able to resist my powers." The palm-reader steps deeper into the cell and begins in an urgent whisper. "This is a verifiably true story, and someday it will appear in a book because it is a tale to warm the hearts of all people. Just a few months ago, one of the men in my hall mouthed off to one of the inspection captains, and the captain turned around and socked him in the eye, made him drop into a squat for an hour, nothing serious." He pauses for emphasis, head cocked to the side, eyes wide with the drama of it.

"But then they refused to give him a shave. The more he howled, the faster his beard grew. He was Indian, so it got to be a big scruffy thing, like a cat stuck on his face. The bedbugs almost ate his chin off. It was hot season and the poor bugger was going crazy. Anything, he said, anything, any other punishment but this! Of course that's just what they wanted to hear, so the whole hot season went by and he had this piece of fur suffocating him. Not a single inmate with a razor would touch him, out of fear of the captain. In protest, the Indian started throwing his shit through the window at the top of the cell, and one day, what happened but it landed right on the Chief Warden's head!" Sein Yun claps his hands, applauding this karmic display of justice.

"You're lying!"

"No, I'm not, that's what's really incredible! It's a true story. The Indian got the shit kicked out of him and two more years added to his sentence for gross indecency and assaulting an officer. The fuckers! But isn't it priceless? You throw a piece of shit out a window and it goes splat! Right back to an asshole!" The palm-reader flaps his arms. "Isn't that brilliant? What are the odds of it? One in ten million!"

"Come on! I don't believe that happened."

"I swear to you it did. You could ask one of the warders."

"They'd knock me in the head if such a question came out of my mouth."

"Ask Jailer Chit Naing—he would tell you."

When Teza says nothing, the palm-reader leans over and whispers, "Not to worry, Songbird. I'm just observant. I hear he is very concerned about your food parcel . . ."

"What have you heard?"

"You were getting too friendly with each other, so they sent him away to do other work."

"Away? They've sent him away?"

"Oh, don't get upset, they haven't sent him to another prison. He's still here. I saw him this morning. I think he's overseeing the first two halls now. You know, prisoners awaiting trial. He's a clever fellow. He'll find a way to visit you." The little man places a new leaf-wrapped pack of betel in his cheek. "Want some?"

"No."

"Don't worry. Your food is coming." He gives Teza a thoughtful look. "I could get you a rat. Would you eat a rat? They sell them cooked, you know."

"Where do the rats come from?" It's another one of Teza's rules, besides never eating what the cockroaches have touched. No rodents. Lizards are cleaner.

"There's a snot-nosed little rat-killer who whacks them on the head when they come out of the drains. He makes good coin selling them."

"Which drains?"

"Shower drains, as often as not. Outside the bathing rooms. I've seen him out here a few times, beside the coffin. Out by the big walls too. The cage is full of rats. I suppose he catches them wherever he can."

"Do *you* eat them?"

The palm-reader grimaces in disgust, pulling red lips back over gold incisors. "Are you out of your fucking mind? Eat a rat that's been eating who knows what?"

"Ko Sein Yun, why do you offer me food that you would not eat yourself?"

"Because you're hungrier than I am, Songbird!"

Teza exhales a defeated laugh.

"Your parcel will come soon enough. Remember, patience makes a man wise."

"And skinny!"

"But the Buddha himself was very skinny, Ko Teza, so you know you're on the right path." A sharp laugh pokes the air as the palm-reader steps out of the teak coffin. Before closing the door, he sticks his head back into the cell. "And if you're really that hungry, Songbird, just eat more of your little friends."

The door slams shut.

. 9 .

U nbelievable, really, the things you have to do to win a man's trust.
Storytelling and rat-selling and cajoling the skinny bugger
every time I visit that hole. The palm-reader wipes his hands on
his longyi. And as if I don't have enough to deal with already, I have to listen to Handsome, that arrogant bastard, laugh at me. It's a good thing he's
so useful.

Sein Yun walks a little more quickly, his oversized slippers slapping
hard. The gravel and sand have turned to mud, so he hikes his longyi up
over his knees to keep it from getting dirty. Soon the rollers will come
out—inmates who sweep the water off the compound, then push big metal
hand rollers back and forth, back and forth, to restore the surface. In the
rainy season they have to do it every day, sometimes two or three times a
day when it really pours. An absolutely useless job with no possible bene-
fits, only a sore back and blisters.

Frankly, it's better to clean up someone's shit if it's going to get you
out of the cage faster.

He walks along, past the gardens of Halls Four and Five, past the
watchtower. Near the kitchen, a guard he dislikes asks where he's going.

Keeping his head down, Sein Yun answers meekly, "To worship."

Then, in a clearer voice, knowing the guard is a bit thick, "I'm going to the shrine." The man waves him along. They might despise each other, but with the Buddha in mind they are civil.

In the circular cartography of the prison, the shrine is almost directly opposite the teak coffin. *See?* he thinks. There is a fateful symmetry in that. Passing the kitchen, Sein Yun waves at the cook, who sits just inside the door peeling potatoes with his fat hands. They exchange nods, each of them revealing a hint of a smile. It's crucial to make friends with the cook, no matter where you are. Judging from his double chins, the cook eats half of the prison food himself, gives a quarter of it to his little lover boys, and sells another big chunk of it for profit. No wonder the politicals are so scrawny.

The shrine stands between the kitchen and the hospital, not far from the main prison office and the warders' quarters. A very public place, it is a locus between the ordinary and the sublime. Fittingly, it's also where prison officials and convicts do business. All with respect for the Buddha, of course.

Sein Yun looks around with a vaguely beatific expression on his face, mirroring the Enlightened One, who sits surrounded with real and plastic flowers, ash-topped sticks of incense, scraps of colored cloth, glasses of water, offerings of shriveled fruit. Some men who have not prayed since they were small boys come here now, transformed by the cage into desperate penitents asking favors and protection. Most often they are first-timers in for second-rate offenses—minor fraud and theft, assault, disturbing the peace during drunken binges. Their short prison terms feel intolerably long because of the filth, the bugs, the shitty food, and the horny men. These soft criminals, who live in a state of infinite longing for their wives and girlfriends, become remarkably religious inside the cage.

Sein Yun finds them hilarious, swaying like the holiest of monks, counting their prayer beads. He looks over their heads, past the flaking gold face of the Buddha, and scans the first brick wall, about twelve feet high, which encloses the prison. The second brick wall looms beyond it, higher, more imposing, impossible to climb over. One of the guards in the watchtower would shoot you in the back before you were halfway up one of the lookout post ladders. Only insects and lizards can crawl over those lousy walls.

The best way to escape is by walking through the two iron doors, smiling at the buggers as you go. Never to return!

The palm-reader's whole body feels curiously itchy, as though the restlessness within him has somehow worked its way up to his skin. Despite giving his warder all kinds of vegetables for extra soap and extra bathing time, he still has infected sores from scratching at bug bites, and the pinworms drive him crazy. He wonders how many fights break out in the cage simply because hundreds of men have unbearably itchy asses.

Switching his weight from one foot to the other, he looks around, then spits. The restlessness makes him want to move. Just before money or goods pass hands, he's always agitated. He used to feel this way on the outside too, when the small plastic bags full of rubies were splayed out on the table in a contained explosion of scarlet. This is the delicious anxiety of closing a deal.

He inhales incense and sighs out nostalgia. He loved working for the colonel. Sein Yun's job was recruitment. He used to find young men to smuggle gems into Thailand. It was a real shame when one of those strapping fellows disappeared with a whole shipment. But it's best to look on the bright side. At least the colonel didn't slit his throat. In comparison, a bad beating and a prison sentence seemed like a wonderful punishment.

When the warder appears, Sein Yun approaches the Buddha and prostrates himself three times among the other mumbling inmates, then quickly rises and walks toward the hospital wall, where the man waits for him with a stony face. Sein Yun works up his most ingratiating expression—a slight, humble upturn of pursed lips, without showing his stained teeth. Oh, he knows this so well, how to make little men feel the wealth of their power. The two turn toward each other, their discretion making them obvious. The warder slips a cylindrical object into the yellow, taloned hand. Sein Yun swallows his smile.

As soon as the vial of heroin is warming safely in the pocket sewn to the inside of his longyi, the palm-reader leaves the shrine. No time for lengthy prayers today; he's a busy man. Rushing back toward the prison gardens in front of Hall Four, he starts thinking about Teza and his comrades.

He tries to be sympathetic, but frankly he dislikes the politicals' lack of practicality. All that idealism goes against his entrepreneurial spirit.

And it's not just Teza he has to worry about. He's started to run errands for a whole bevy of them, despite his general aversion. Over a dozen of them in Hall Three are planning something, brave-hearted, stupid souls. Myo Myo Than is their leader, and they are following him like sheep. The palm-reader has a plan of his own, which is why he took on the job of errand boy to these earnest fellows. If he arranges everything properly, he will get rewards all around. They're already giving him half the contents of their food parcels to pay for paper and pens.

He stops abruptly, kicks off his right slipper, and squats to pinch a brick chip out of the rubber sole. The singer comes to mind. He must squat just like this, and pick away not at a stone in the shoe but at his cheroots. Sein Yun sees the newsprint filters sometimes, when he dumps the singer's bucket. Not to mention the bones. It's hideous. Poor little Songbird, he doesn't shit enough to hide a thing!

He stands up, spits his betel juice. It's pathetic, really—all the politicals are obsessed with words. And food. Though he's walking very quickly now, a smile slowly infects his mouth. Why shouldn't he involve Teza in his little plan? Surely he would want to join his beloved comrades.

Arms swinging, Sein Yun nonchalantly brushes his hand against his hip. The vial is safe and sound in his secret pocket, ready for Tan-see Tiger, the big criminal in Hall Four. Sein Yun does a lot of this sort of thing, but carrying heroin is still nerve-racking. More inmates than ever before are junkies—thanks to the generals' hard work in the poppy business—and a lot of them know Sein Yun works for Tiger. A few would happily knife a man to get their hands on the drug.

Sein Yun coughs. Without moving his head, he glances to the left, the right. He also helps in Handsome's vegetable racket. Every week the junior jailer takes about a dozen boxes of food from each of the prison gardens and sells them to high-ranking prisoners. Before delivering Tan-see Tiger's vial, Sein Yun has to pass by one of the gardens and check on the jailer's portion of cauliflowers and tomatoes; a detail of men is harvesting today.

A fter making the rounds of the gardens—two boxes of cauliflowers and a bag of tomatoes have been set aside for Handsome—the palm-reader lifts his head to survey the sky. The clouds have gathered again. When the rain crashes down hard on the roof, it's hard to hear a man talk to you from across your cell. Not that the men usually talk. Sein Yun feels himself surrounded by bellowers, small men with big mouths. He pauses in his walk, lets his shoulders drop. The crows are flying back, cawing and arguing, settling down to roost on the high outer ramparts.

Approaching Hall Four, the biggest of the five prisoner halls, the palm-reader walks more slowly, to prepare himself. Two thousand souls live in this one massive brick building. Some of the cells contain twelve to fifteen men. He is lucky; he shares with four others, though he has the dirtiest spot, close to the latrine pail. The head prisoner and his right-hand man have bench beds to sleep on, the jerks.

Every cell has an akhan-lu-gyi, a leader, just as each big hall has a pow-erful tan-see. These hierarchies within hierarchies are the way of the world, both in the cage and out of it, but they secretly disgust Sein Yun. Take Saw Maung, the leader of his cell. He's a quiet, gray-haired man with a rough-hewn face as brutish and inexpressive as an unfinished carving. Is he taciturn because he's a deep thinker or because he's been punched in the head one too many times? Sein Yun has lived with the man for months, but he's still not sure. Saw Maung's nose is misshapen from violence. A proverbial criminal's scar cuts a pale jag across his forehead (though he got it in a car accident, not a knife fight, Sein Yun was amused to learn). The small eyes are often half closed, which leads the palm-reader to wonder if the murderer needs glasses or if he is busy plotting how to kill someone else. And who might the lucky one be?

Soon after being transferred to his cell, Sein Yun discovered that Saw Maung had won his position by killing the previous akhan-lu-gyi. After prying a brick away from the base of one of the latrines, he pounded the man to death as he slept. For this show of ruthlessness—apparently he had nothing against the man he killed—he not only won the highest position of power in the cell but gained a certain amount of notoriety in the hall. That's how it works in the cage: pound a sleeping man to death and every-one's impressed.

Sein Yun plays his part, bowing and scraping and doing Saw Maung extravagant favors. Though it was his idea to set up a betting racket on Aung San Suu Kyi, he let Saw Maung take it over. And he brings him free vegetables too. Murderers always get too much respect; that's why they rise to the top. But what does it take to kill a man? A lousy brick and a few minutes of savagery, nothing more. Then the other prisoners take you seriously or fear you. Fear is better, of course. If you make a man afraid, you've got a useful piece of him.

Far enough away not to insult the warder on guard duty, who has already met his eye, Sein Yun spits his betel juice. Yes, he needs his betel. But at least it isn't opium oil, or heroin. The junkies pass the needles around like cigarettes, the fools. Once again Sein Yun brushes his hand against his secret pocket. The little vial is still there. In a few minutes he'll hand it over to Tan-see Tiger and be done with it.

Nodding once, the warder pulls open the heavy iron door of Hall Four. The only time Sein Yun fears the cage is during these first moments of return, when his tasks for the day are done and he must go back to the hall, rows of cells on either side and around each corner, cages behind and in front, cages of dark eyes and hands and tattooed arms infected with sores. Rather than walking to the fourth row, where he lives, he takes a quick left into Tan-see Tiger's row, through the immense din.

Voices rise up around him, invading his ears, pushing against his face. The noise takes on a physical quality, a hundred times worse than any crowded market or busy street or night festival. Tiny points of sweat appear on his forehead. Supper is late again, so everyone's in a foul mood, shouting and arguing about nothing in particular.

Some men greet him as he passes, or give him a look of rivalrous disgust. Approaching Tan-see Tiger's cell, he cranes his neck, looking for the man's broad, dark face. The tan-see got his name from the big-cat tattoos that adorn his entire body—back, chest, legs, and arms—but there is something of the tiger about him too, with those languid, droopy eyes, that big head covered in a thick bristle of fur. He is a smooth-moving man, graceful and strong, given to performing elaborate exercises in the yard. He's certainly healthy and agile like a jungle cat; he can't be a junkie himself. Sein Yun has watched the muscles in his chest and back rippling, so that the cats lounging on his skin seem to stretch awake. As tan-see, Tiger is the highest-ranking prisoner in the hall as well as the head of his own cell, surrounded by a group of men who are fiercely loyal.

Sein Yun can't see him, though. He clenches his teeth. Could Tiger be out? He wills the tan-see to come right up to the bars and take away the heroin with a polite handshake. Sein Yun has instructions: he cannot give the vial to anyone but Tiger. If for some unexpected reason the tan-see isn't in his cell, Sein Yun will have to safeguard the vial all night, until he has another chance, in the morning, to visit the first row. This prospect dismays him. It's possible that Saw Maung would be more than happy to bash his head with a brick—or even the fucking latrine pail—and steal the heroin.

A thousand voices hammer their way into the very bones of his head. It's hard to think straight. His nostrils flare as he breathes the humid, human-filled air. A few more steps take him to the front grille of Tan-see Tiger's cell. The palm-reader's eyes flicker around the room, over several men's arms, white undershirts. Only the old basket-maker looks up at Sein Yun, his blind eye a swirl of bluish white.

There he is! Sein Yun is so relieved that a genuine smile opens on his sallow face. Tiger is lying on his belly on a mat, getting a massage. The little masseur—also the cage's resident rat-killer—is walking up and down the man's purple cat-filled back. The kid casts the palm-reader a suspicious glance as he leans down and taps Tiger on the shoulder, whispers something under his breath. The palm-reader bares his teeth at the masseur. Jealous brat. The tan-see turns his head, slowly, slowly, groaning with pleasure as the masseur walks up and down once more, then lightly steps off his back. Tiger rolls over on his side and smiles. He sighs. "Rough life, here in the cage."

"I can see that. You like them young."

The tan-see laughs. "No. I like hard heels and strong hands." He nods to the little masseur, who approaches the bars with his head down, his hand out. Sein Yun frowns at the tan-see, who says, "Go ahead, give it over. He doesn't bite."

It's bloody insulting, to smuggle something valuable into the hall just to hand it over to a pretty boy. Look at that: the tan-see has just rolled over on his belly again. He's not a tiger, he's a sloth. Grudgingly, Sein Yun reaches into his secret pocket and resists the impulse to toss the vial into the cell. He slips it into the rat-killer's outstretched, oiled hand. The kid steps back to Tiger and hands him the vial.

"Someone will bring you your gift tomorrow," Tiger announces in a leisurely drawl, face still turned away. Sein Yun has half a mind to demand his payment right there and then, but of course, in the interest of further work, he says nothing, just glares at the pretty boy again, who is cleaning his feet, getting ready to step up onto the tan-see's back. Sein Yun turns on his heel and retreats the way he's come, through the cave of men's voices.

To reach the fourth row, where he lives, he must carry on to the end of the first row, turn left, and pass the openings of two more rows. The long tunnels of bars make him feel as though he is looking into a trick mirror. Cage after cage is replicated, reflected through the one beside it, and all the eyes looking out are cage eyes, like his own but not so yellow, circled with the bruised purple-brown of bad sleep and bad food.

By the time he gets to his place, he has almost always regained his balance, a biting observation ready on his stained lips.

Entering, he crushes his fear, squashes it without hesitation, the same way he kills the cockroaches that come to his cell in search of food.

. 10 .

Small white cup in hand, Chit Naing stands at the door of the warders' quarters and stares out into the floodlit compound. Close to his face, moths batter the screen, trying to get to the light beyond him, two naked bulbs and one tube of fluorescence hanging over the wooden tables.

When the senior jailer finally takes a sip of his tea, he's disappointed to find how cold it is. Behind him, a dozen warders and guards waiting for their shift changes chat over card games and teapots. He angles his watch into the harsh light. No one needs a watch here, not really. An iron-beater is always there, marking their hours, their routines. Soon he will strike eight o'clock.

A swarm of annoyance follows the jailer around tonight like a fresh hatch of mosquitoes; he can't get away from it. The woman's voice singing on the dust-covered tape recorder is sentimental and twangy. He looks over his shoulder. "Whose tape is that, anyway? My ears are bleeding!" A few men laugh, but no one gets up to change the music. He sees Handsome out of the corner of his eye, watching. He is always watching, that guy. Instead of turning away, Chit Naing steps back into the room and meets his gaze. The intensity of Handsome's dislike for him is well known. They have worked the same number of years, but Chit Naing is superior in rank. The fact that his wife is from a military family has helped Chit Naing's prison career, which alternately disgusts and pleases him. In a petulant mood, he forces the junior jailer to engage in small talk, knowing Handsome is obliged to respond. "Your shift over?"

Handsome nods.

"I'm on my way out too. Do you want to leave together?"

The junior jailer replies slowly and carefully, "I'm not leaving just yet."

"See you tomorrow, then." Chit Naing steps out into the night, even more annoyed with himself. He's as petty as any of them. But it's necessary to show Handsome that he is not afraid, that he wields enough power to feign a sort of friendliness.

The Chief Warden has been using Handsome for various unsavory jobs. There's no doubt he's an active informer, telling the Chief who's doing what, where, when, how. And he's got that palm-reader working for him too. Dirt always attracts more dirt. But how could the Chief Warden have put such a violent man in charge of the singer?

Away from the cheroot smoke of the warders' quarters, Chit Naing can smell the rain and wet brick chips. When he passes under the windows of the main office, he glances up at the lit windows on the second floor. No figure passes, no figure leans out. Perhaps the Chief Warden is taking his evening bath.

Chit Naing has never liked him much, but now his dislike of the balding, bulldoggish man makes him angry. The Chief always wears trousers, even off-duty. Chit Naing has never seen him wearing a longyi or smoking a cheroot. The Thai cigarettes he smokes are becoming favorites among the young warders, who can barely afford to buy them. The Chief's son has gone to study at a school in Singapore. These details awe the younger men under his command, who mistake money for style and foreign luxuries for power. And why does he have to stay on the grounds all the time? He owns a big house in the city, but he usually prefers to stay in the suite on the second floor. It's a common perversion, the way the prison makes prisoners of men who believe they are free.

What such people hate most are those who *are* free. That's why the Chief can't stand the politicals. Asked what he thought of Daw Suu Kyi's release, he replied without hesitation that she should have been shot before she became so famous. He takes her freedom from house arrest as a personal insult, and his extreme views on the matter, loudly expounded in his office, are repeated by some of the higher-ranking warders: Why was this traitorous, foreigner-marrying bitch never locked up in a real prison? And isn't it likely that her husband, an Englishman, works for the British secret service? Eventually, through Daw Suu Kyi, Britain could come to rule Burma again.

The theory is laughable at best, paranoid at worst, but some of the warders are influenced by the Chief Warden's persuasive, know-it-all way of speaking. His charming, almost nonchalant authority makes weaker people want to believe him.

Chit Naing leaves the shadow of the office wall to cross the compound. He masks his contempt for his boss from others, but not from himself. He can't hide anything from himself anymore. Only a year ago—just before he started to oversee the teak coffin—he was sure that the substance of his life would never change.

A man has to swallow his revulsion and get the job done, even if it means living a farce. But the cage, so riddled with deceit, never lies: every broken thing in the country comes in through its iron doors and proclaims itself. Every goodhearted and idealistic thing comes in too. Since Daw Suu Kyi's release, they've rounded up a new group of politicals, her party members, some young, some as old as seventy. They've already arrived, shackled like animals. Last night Chit Naing dreamed of a student alone in a cell, his face bruised purple and bloody. He was crying, begging with a cracked voice for a cup of water. Chit Naing knew that he must not give him anything to drink. If he did, MI agents would find out about it and punish him, Chit Naing, by beating the boy to death. He started awake, heart pounding, to the cries of the baby, nestled beside his wife, who nursed their daughter back to sleep. But that was it for him; he was awake for the rest of the night. He lay in bed thinking about '88, when hundreds of students were dumped in the prison, traumatized and bloody, and, true to his dream, often severely dehydrated after days of interrogation. Chit Naing knew—everyone knew—that thousands more had died in the streets because of two unpardonable crimes: knowing they deserved a decent life and having the nerve to demand one.

He has begun to think seriously about doing something else, anything else, for a living. But the only real prospects—a transfer to a northern work camp, or those depressing offers from his in-laws—are snares, tricks to deepen the pit he already lives inside.

Just last year his wife's uncle, a senior officer at Interrogation Center Twelve, offered him another MI job. It was the third or fourth time that her well-connected family had tried to help them by improving Chit Naing's status. He politely turned down the offer, explaining that he had a duty to continue his work at the prison. When his wife found out about his meeting with her uncle, she screamed at him, "Loyalties to the *prison*? What about *me*? What about your children? There is so much more money in military work! And you insult my family once more by not accepting my uncle's offer. I don't understand you!"

He tried to explain what MI work meant. It wouldn't be like the cage, where he could protect certain inmates. (Failing that, he could protect himself by finding someone else to do the dirty work. But he never said this out loud, not to his wife, not to anyone.) An MI officer at an interrogation center, he told her, has to hurt people.

"But only people who are enemies of the state."

"How can I, as a Buddhist, torture helpless men, terrorize young women?"

She had no reply to that, but he saw from the cold, closed look on her face that she thought he was cowardly—and stupid, tossing away this opportunity when opportunities were so rare. After that argument, she refused to sleep with him.

His insomnia became a nightly rule. Four o'clock in the morning would find him beside his wife's warm body, gazing at the curve of her hip, wondering who she was. For that matter, who was he? And how could he escape going to work in the morning? Night after night he wandered around in the maze of these and a dozen other questions. During the days, only his three children gave him any pleasure. They loved simple, good things: eating, playing with their toys, watching one of the neighbor's goats escape from the yard and wander into the city street, causing a ruckus among the car drivers and rickshaw pedalers. The children clapped, they laughed. Sometimes their pureness of heart made him more frustrated with himself.

Then, as if by magic, everything changed.

Of course, it wasn't magic, was it? It was just Teza, talking. It was just a visit to a laundry.

Chit Naing smiles to himself and takes a deep breath through his nose. He loves the damp smell of the rainy season. It doesn't matter that they've cut down all the big trees in the compound. He can still smell growing things.

At the beginning of July last year, the Chief Warden assigned him to oversee the teak coffin. He'd been at it for just three days when his new prisoner surprised him by asking for a string of jasmine flowers, the kind used for offering at the pagoda. The singer's manner baffled him as much as the request itself. Teza did not cower. He didn't even respect prison protocol by keeping his head down. He stood in his cell, a bit left of center. The teak door was open. Chit Naing was on the other side of the threshold, feeling awkward because he was used to his inmates dropping to a squat or moving away from him. But after Sammy the giant had left with the latrine pail, Teza actually took several steps toward him. He looked the jailer in the eye, asked forthrightly for jasmine, then continued in a thoughtful tone, "Or even just a small branch with leaves, it doesn't matter what kind of tree. Flowers are the thing, or the smell of green leaves."

Chit Naing thought, The man is insane. Teza, the singer, was mad, and no one, typically, had bothered to inform him. Or perhaps no one knew. What else could explain this bizarre fearlessness? A request for *flowers*? He looked at his prisoner with such obvious, eyebrow-knitted confusion that the singer smiled at him, which only unbalanced Chit Naing further, because he saw that Teza was completely sane, and that with his openhearted, friendly smile, he was trying to put Chit Naing at ease. This was a complete reversal of anything the jailer had experienced in the cage. It wasn't that the singer had overstepped the boundaries between prisoner and jailer. It was that he acted as if those boundaries did not exist.

Teza kept smiling intently into his jailer's worried eyes, showing off a row of very white, very straight teeth. He'd lost a couple in the bottom row, but the gaps took nothing away from his fine-boned face, with its strong brow and narrow, high-bridged nose. Malnourishment and beatings had made Teza thin and weak, but a genuine playfulness mixed with yearning shone in his eyes. Chit Naing felt unexpectedly touched: the look on the prisoner's face reminded him of his children. Teza's smile shifted and broadened as his eyebrows rose, questioning, prompting the jailer to respond. Without thinking, Chit Naing smiled back.

Sammy rattled them from their silent communication by lumbering down the corridor, metal latrine pail dangling and clanking at the end of his long arm—and then he stared down at Chit Naing as if *he* were crazy. The jailer flushed dark red. Did Sammy think he had propositioned Teza in a sexual way? He took a handkerchief out of his breast pocket and started to polish his glasses. Sammy handed the pail back to the prisoner and grunted. Without saying a word, Chit Naing waved the server out of the teak coffin, hurriedly closed the door, and locked up.

But the next day, when Sammy left with the latrine pail again, Chit Naing pulled a string of jasmine blossoms out of his breast pocket—the sweet scent flared like white sparks against the odor of shit—and handed it to Teza. The singer thanked him and lifted the handful of jasmine to his nose.

"What will you do with the flowers?" Chit Naing asked.

The jailer's low, conspiratorial tone made Teza laugh. "What do you think? I will offer them to the Buddha."

Chit Naing glanced around the cell. "There is no altar here."

"Ha! There's no toilet either, but that doesn't stop me from doing my business, does it?" He pointed to the back wall of the cell, high up. "The altar is up there, but it's invisible. I don't need to be able to see the Buddha to meditate and pray. There's not much else to do. I never would have become so interested in Buddhism without this enforced retreat."

Chit Naing raised his eyebrows. "That's what you call twenty years in solitary confinement?"

"On my better days. The cage is a big monastery and my sentence is a very long meditation. I'm sure that's how my mother thinks of it too."

"How do you know what she thinks if she's not permitted to correspond with you?"

"Sir, she is not only my mother! She is my friend. I was fortunate to be born to her." Teza paused reflectively. "Though I don't know what she did to deserve us. She raised one son for prison, the other for war in the jungle. Now she only raises orchids, the most beautiful ones in Rangoon."

He gestured with his long-fingered hands, evoking rows of hanging orchids.

His voice rose with a childlike enthusiasm. How much the man loved and missed his mother was obvious to the jailer, but the singer wasn't sad. He seemed grateful just to have the chance to talk about her.

"She doesn't sell her orchids, though. She could by now, you know—professional growers used to come and visit her little garden. But she says she could never sell them. She says they must only be gifts. She doesn't want to make a business out of something she loves. Isn't that interesting? Of course, she already has a business, and she's a very good business-woman too. She runs a laundry."

Suddenly self-conscious, Teza pressed his lips together to stop the rush of words. Then he shyly whispered, "I'm talking too much, eh? Well, just let me finish. She is a very devout Buddhist also, and though she might not tell anyone else, I know that on *her* good days, she thinks the cage is her son's only chance for Nibbana. Out there, I could never attain enlighten-ment. I probably would be a rock star, a laundry-boy rock star, drinking every night and running with fast women. In the cage, I'm like a monk." A lilting, comical tone entered his voice. "Very celibate. Holy, even. Who knows? By this time next year I could become a Hpaya-Laung, a Bo-dhisattva. *Then* what would the Chief Warden do with me?" The singer turned his head sideways and looked at the jailer with one shining crow-like eye.

Chit Naing frowned in response. Maybe Teza *was* going nuts.

"U Chit Naing, please do not look so concerned. I don't think the Chief Warden would do anything cruel to an enlightened man."

The jailer couldn't tell if the singer was joking or putting up a brave front or just being foolish, but this curious chat intrigued him. He accom-panied Sammy to the teak coffin twice daily, which included overseeing Teza's bathing and clothes-washing breaks. He began to find excuses to lengthen those brief visits. Before eleven in the morning and five in the evening, the senior jailer felt a rush of pleasurable anticipation. In a few minutes he would see the singer.

Their conversations were often charged with an excitement out of pro-portion to what they talked about, whether it was the stifling heat or the mystery of Sammy's missing tongue—no one in the cage knew how he had suffered that loss—or the awful quality of Teza's food. Their words seemed to glimmer in the air between them, dangerous metallic threads that quickly connected both of them to books and ideas, to language itself. The jailer told Teza about the daring subject matter of the famous writer Ju's recent novel, in which a passionate young man falls in love with an older woman, but the story, as he was telling it, became a metaphor for their own deepening and forbidden association. Chit Naing talked about the magazines he had been reading, or asked Teza what he thought of this or that book. "U Chit Naing," Teza once said, "to hear someone talk about books is as good as eating my mother's curry."

Teza refused to act like a prisoner, which freed Chit Naing from acting like a jailer. For Chit Naing, the illicit friendship was dangerous, though he was sure he could trust Sammy not to betray them. After that first time, when the giant came upon them mid-grin, the server ceased to express interest in their conversations either way but stood outside in the corridor like a sentry, guarding them both.

Two months later, Teza asked him not for jasmine or a banana or another cheroot, easy things for the jailer to give. The moment Sammy had disappeared down the corridor, Teza said in a quiet voice, "U Chit Naing, my mother has not had a message from me in two years. The last person to communicate with her for me was a warder who had known my father in another prison. Will you send her a message on my behalf? You know I have nothing to pay you with but my gratitude."

Chit Naing realized he'd been waiting for something like this, because he responded as though he'd been brave his entire life. "Your gratitude is enough. What do you want me to tell her?"

That's how it began. The note was not in the singer's handwriting but in Chit Naing's: a brief missive of Teza's news, such as it was, and a message of his love. The jailer delivered it himself. He didn't want to involve anyone else, nor did he trust anyone else. Better to take the slip of paper to her on his own, under the pretext of going to the laundry to drop off some shirts.

He took a bus into the heart of the city and bought some old shirts from a noisy street vendor outside Scott Market. He caught a cab from the market and had the driver drop him off at a tea shop. Then he walked ten minutes to Daw Sanda's house and the laundry beside it. In his hand was the plastic bag of shirts. He had no intention of going to pick them up again. He placed the letter, clearly addressed to Daw Sanda, at the bottom of the bag.

A dangling bell rang when he pushed open the door. There were two women in the long narrow laundry office, but only the Indian girl sitting on a high stool behind the counter greeted him. The older woman stood at the far end of the same counter, reading a magazine.

Obviously the girl was not Teza's mother, but in his nervousness, he asked her her name as she was filling out his order sheet. She glanced up at him shyly and murmured, "Ma Sherry." He showed her the shirts one after the other without completely removing them from the bag. The letter remained undisturbed as she wrote down the number of items.

Still engrossed in her reading, the older woman lifted her head slowly, pulled her eyes away from the magazine, and smiled at Chit Naing.

He was so struck by the resemblance that he gasped, and quickly cleared his throat to cover the sound. His young prisoner was standing there in the body of a mature woman, her long thick hair pulled away from her face and gathered into a ponytail, as though she were still a girl. But she was wearing Chinese red lipstick and a traditionally tailored tamin and eingyi, pale gray-blue in color, very much the lady of business. Her smile was like Teza's smile, but smaller, and careful: a professional lady greeting her new customer. The dimples, one deep in the center of each cheek, disarmed Chit Naing. For a few seconds he stared at her, caught in the net of two thoughts: She is much more attractive than I expected. And, Does Teza have dimples or not?

Chit Naing was not wearing his uniform and felt strangely exposed without it. He looked away and coughed into his hand, as embarrassed and awkward as a country bumpkin. Pull yourself together, man, he thought, annoyed. It's a laundry, for crying out loud!

But what could he say to this elegant woman, whose intelligence marked her every feature and movement, from the candor of her gaze to the black eyebrow rising slightly above her eye to the way she closed the flimsy magazine with an air of formality? She folded her carefully manicured hands on top of it, silently asking him, *What do you want? You are a stranger here and you are acting strange*. Her fingernails were not painted, and she wore absolutely no jewelry. Not an earring, not a ring, not a strand or speck of gold or gem anywhere. So unlike his wife, he thought, who adored and coveted gold.

He glanced from the white moons of her nails to her face, the strong brow and fine nose, the seed versions of Teza's features, though her eyes were longer and paler, tortoiseshell brown. The plastic bag was still on the counter. Sherry had turned away from it to finish counting out the items of an earlier drop-off. He could leave, if he wanted. No, he *must* leave, his work was done.

But Daw Sanda seemed to read his hesitation like a preface to the note at the bottom of the bag. As he turned to the door, she said, "Look. It's begun to rain so hard. Would you like a cup of tea until it lets up?"

Chit Naing could hear Teza's voice in hers, mellifluous and strong, surprisingly direct, not a syllable hushed or withdrawn. With her offer of tea, she was telling him, *Stay here*. Chit Naing blinked at her like a schoolboy and stumbled out the words: "Tea. Yes. A cup of tea. I would like some tea."

That's how it began.

As he approaches the big gates, he gives a sharp nod to the young warder, Tint Lwin, who sits up straighter in the sentry box. Chit Naing walks more slowly, hesitating. Anyone watching—Handsome, for example, or the Chief Warden—will see that he isn't going to walk through the gates. He's not leaving the prison after all.

. 11 .

Teza smiles when the metal bolts of the window trap start clicking. Chit Naing cannot open the door on these nocturnal visits; he no longer has the key to Teza's cell. But he slides open the long metal slat to reveal his eyes, shining behind wire-rimmed glasses. The singer is always very grateful to see the bridge of his nose.

Chit Naing speaks in a deep, quiet voice but not a whisper. He has stopped whispering. "How are you?"

"Hungry. Sein Yun told me my food parcel has gone missing."

"He told you that? How the hell does he know?"

"He seems to know a lot—nothing gets by him. And the last parcel was almost empty. Do you know what's going on?"

"I'll try to find out. Be patient."

The two men look into each other's eyes. Chit Naing says nothing. How can a man who is well fed reply honestly to another man's hunger? He glances down at his watch.

Teza also looks away. The jailer is a friend who already does all he can. Changing the subject, he asks, "Is Sein Yun really a palm-reader?"

Chit Naing smiles. "Maybe that's what he writes on his résumé. He's a gem smuggler. Who made a very bad mistake. He's a special case, work-ing off time."

"As quickly as he can." Teza makes a sound like a dog gnawing at a pig's hock.

"Exactly."

"Has he read your palm?"

The jailer laughs. "Of course not."

"He told me he'd read your palm."

"He's a liar."

"Was he lying about Daw Suu Kyi's release?"

"You know about that? We will have to do something about your se-cret telephone line."

"The palm-reader knows everything. He's friendly with Handsome too, opens the cell on his own, comes in and chats, brings me cheroots."

"A regular turnkey, is he? Watch what you say. You know Handsome is always looking for an excuse to exercise his fists."

"I wish you were still the jailer around here."

"A change was coming one way or another. And since Daw Suu Kyi's release, whole blocks have been reassigned to different officers. Servers, cells, details have all been shifted. The Chief Warden is paranoid."

"She really is free, then?"

"As free as any other political. She hasn't tried to travel yet. I don't think the generals will let her leave Rangoon. But there's been attention from all over the world."

"It's a good sign, their releasing her. Don't you think?" Teza cannot prevent a bright vein of hope from breaking into his voice.

On the other side of the door, Chit Naing removes his glasses and rubs his eyes. When he puts the glasses back on again, the singer's expression of contained jubilation—the open face, the incautious smile—makes him very tired. "Ko Teza"—his voice is heavy—"it may be an encouraging sign, but it's also an act of manipulation. The generals released her to get aid money from Japan again. Her freedom is good publicity."

Teza smiles broadly. "Good publicity should never be underestimated. If the people are able to see her again, in the flesh, they will be inspired. If she finds a way to speak publicly—"

The iron-beater strikes half past eight. Chit Naing looks at his watch, then at what he can see of the singer's face. "I'm sorry, but I have to go—the night sentries are starting their rounds. All the shifts have been changed, and I don't know who will be around tonight. I don't know how often I'll be able to come."

The singer can see purple wedges under his friend's eyes. "But you *will* come, won't you?"

"I'm being warned, Ko Teza. Not directly, but warned nevertheless. It's best I don't visit for a while. I have to be careful for at least a month or two, maybe a bit more. You be careful too."

"A month? That's a long time. What . . . what about the parcels?" Teza's voice has gone slightly hoarse.

The jailer takes a small step backward. "I will do my best."

"There was only one fish in my last parcel." The singer presses his forehead against the iron rim of the trap, as if he's trying to squeeze head-first out of his cell. The large dark eyes stare directly into Chit Naing's. The jailer has never met any prisoner who looks at him this way, completely vulnerable, asking and demanding at once. His voice has become breathy, rushed, like a man speaking through fever. "I live on that dried fish, U Chit Naing, and the deep-fried beans and lentils. What if Sein Yun sells all my fish?"

Chit Naing looks away from the aperture in the coffin door, pretending to check the hall. It disgusts him to see Teza caught in the raw fear of hunger.

He looks back up at the iron-framed rectangle of Teza, his eyes shining like hot tar. "Ko Teza, I don't think Sein Yun had anything to do with the disappearance of your parcel. As for selling your fish, he has more lucrative jobs to do. He's a carrier."

"Of what?"

"Mostly drugs. Possibly selling them for someone else and taking a cut. He's an entrepreneur. Maybe into weapons too. Poke bars made from pieces of iron filed to a point. Several men have been stabbed with them in the past few months. Sein Yun isn't violent—he just helps out with the tan-see and akhan-lu-gyi of his hall. A king's servant. I don't think he's stealing your food. But I will look into it." He pauses, hoping for an encouraging response, but the singer just stands there, head against the trap. Chit Naing hears him breathing.

"Are you eating the prison food these days?"

"Since I was sick, I've been eating everything. It all tastes like shit."

"I'll pass that observation on to the Chief Warden."

"And tell my mother I'm getting fat on the stones in the soup."

Chit Naing breathes, "Shhhh!" The silver reflection of his glasses flickers down and away, like a light going out. Chit Naing once asked Teza never to use the word *mother* when the two of them are together. Teza sees him take a full step backward. They both stand still, listening, but the only sound is rain, falling lightly.

Chit Naing's eyes narrow as he steps forward. The rectangular section of his face is replaced by his fingers, sticking three cheroots through the trap. "When are you going to stop smoking?"

"Ha! When I'm allowed to read a book!"

"Some people believe smoking's bad for you."

"Some people believe reading's bad for you. And shitting in a proper toilet, and being able to see your family, and eating decent—"

"I have to go." Chit Naing raises his hand to close the trap.

Teza speaks quickly to the sliding rectangle of iron. "Thanks for the cheroots. But bring a chicken next time, would you? Or maybe a goat?"

As he turns away from the teak coffin, Chit Naing hears Teza laughing.

At the end of the short corridor, he opens the metal door, steps over the threshold, and shuts the heavy bolt. Rain falls on his head. Turning his face up slightly, he considers how tired he is of locked doors. He begins to walk back to the warders' quarters, still listening for Teza's laughter.

The migratory tendency of the prisoner's voice has been the problem from the very beginning. Though it is illegal to publish Teza's name, he remains the most celebrated singer in Burma. In secret. The Press Scrutiny Board censors even oblique references to music or art, or anything at all, if it believes the allusion is connected to Teza. Chit Naing suspects that this prohibition just makes the singer more famous. It's the same with Daw Suu Kyi: there's a nationwide ban on her name too, but rather than make people forget about her, the SLORC has turned her into a legend.

Banning her name cannot make people forget history, just as suppressing

Teza's songs has not erased them. The tapes are still made and distributed secretly. Chit Naing recently received his first copy of one as a gift from the
singer's mother, who wrapped it up like a sweet in a strip of banana leaf. After his wife and children have gone to bed or while wrestling uselessly with
his insomnia, he sometimes listens to the songs on a little tape player. Turning the volume as low as he can, he puts his ear close to the machine and holds
his entire body still to listen.

Teza does not sound young. In 1988 his voice was already an older
man's, a low baritone with rough edges. Somehow Chit Naing expected a
lighter sound, and lyrics that would be vaguely embarrassing, years after
the failed people's revolution. But the songs have become elegiac. Written
in a violent present, they bear witness to both the past and the future.
Every one of them, in some awful way, seems to foretell Teza's own imprisonment. The first time Chit Naing listened to the tape, he wept. He
wanted to pick up the tape recorder and whisper, *Leave! If you go to the border, they won't get you.* But the voice ignored him, rising and falling on the
rhythmical, unpredictable tides of a guitar, and Chit Naing listened to the
next song, and the next, with his hand clamped over his mouth.

The generals devour the holy bones and jewels
the tongues and hearts of our people
But we have turned our shoulders
to push against their crimes, their lies.
We listen to the red commandments of the dead:
When one shoulder buckles, use the other.
Stop up the dumb mouths of the guns.
Walk step by step through the room
of slit-eye and boot and bayonet
beyond, into our future's country.

He wonders if Teza's mother ever listens to the songs. He would like
to ask her but doesn't dare; he doesn't want to pry. He sees her once a
month, at a different little restaurant or tea shop in a different part of Rangoon. He has never gone back to the laundry. He has never called her on
the phone. Every meeting place is new. They make their plan to meet again
each time they see each other. At first they spoke only about Teza, then

drank some tea or ate a simple meal in silence. Now he also tells her about other politicals held incommunicado; she passes this information to the prisoners' families. Each time they meet, they have more to discuss, and so they talk, quietly revealing themselves with and without language, their eyes moving like their hands over the plates of food between them. As Chit Naing's clandestine work has become more complex, so have his meals with Daw Sanda.

Once he spooned the last delicious bit of tea-leaf salad onto her plate, the way relatives and close friends will do. They both stopped talking and looked at each other. He gave her a timid, awkward smile, the apology ready on his tongue. He waited, wanting to see what she would do. With a ball of rice on the tips of her fingers, she pinched the salad up and put it into her mouth.

They have become a man and a woman who eat together. The waiters obviously assume they are married, and neither Chit Naing nor Daw Sanda corrects or comments on this error. As he walks away from these visits, his heart almost bursts from happiness and regret. He would give anything to have made different choices.

He is making those choices now, but he is forty-six years old. Sometimes he is haunted by the thought that it's all come too late. Other times he thinks, No, what is happening now could never have happened before; I was too young and too fearful. The paradox fascinates him—as the old loyalties desiccate and the danger intensifies, he feels lighter and younger than he has in years.

But out on the street, he often looks over his shoulder. At first he refused to admit to himself why he was doing this. He pretended he was searching for someone he thought he'd glimpsed in the crowd, or trying to remember if he'd forgotten something in a shop. Gradually he has acknowledged that he's looking for a man, any man with an intent yet impudent face, a man wearing a white shirt, perhaps, and almost always sunglasses, a man who probably rides a motorcycle and is too friendly with certain taxi drivers.

He has watched these men following other people. It is easy to read the arrogance on their faces. By turns swaggering and darting through the crowd, they do not really hide what they are. There are so many MI agents now; the streets are infected with them. They have become the rats of daylight.

The moment will come when he turns his head and sees one of them behind him. Already the clicks and crackles in his telephone line make him cut his conversations short. Since Daw Suu Kyi's release, he feels eyes upon him, questions on the tip of his colleagues' tongues. Many suspect that he was the one who leaked the information of her release. When the Chief Warden took him off the teak coffin, he gave Chit Naing a long, searching look, then announced, "Forget whatever interested you so much in there. It's not worth it." Older officers and a few of the warders hesitate when they talk to him, as though he gives off a disturbing scent. They must wonder what's happening to him.

Sympathizer.

Hoping it will not exist if it is not spoken, his friends do not utter this word.

Yet how interesting they are, the many expressions of silence. He is learning the entire vocabulary of it, every pause filled with meaning.

"Ko Tint Lwin, all quiet?" Chit Naing inquires at the gate in the first prison wall.

The warder makes an admirable attempt to shake off his light sleep, like a student woken unexpectedly by a teacher's question. He's a new kid, a nice-looking boy from Pegu. He clears his throat. "Yes, sir."

As the jailer passes through the iron door, he gives the young man a knowing look and makes sure their eyes meet. "Don't sleep too deeply, friend."

"No, sir. Thank you. I mean, sorry, sir, I was just . . ."

"I know, I know. Not to worry. Anything to report?"

Young Tint Lwin opens his mouth as though to speak, thinks better of it, and just says, "No, nothing, sir."

"Is everything all right, Ko Tint Lwin?"

The new warder lowers his voice. "I just wanted to let you know that Handsome—I mean, the junior jailer—passed through about half an hour ago."

Chit Naing leans forward. "Yes?"

"And he asked about you, sir. If you'd gone home."

"What did you say?"

"I said you'd already left, sir. Because, well, because I thought you had.

I thought you'd left while another sentry was covering for me—I went to the latrine. You usually leave around eight, don't you, sir?"

"That's correct, Ko Tint Lwin." Chit Naing smiles. "Almost always. Handsome knows that."

"Yes, sir. Thank you, sir."

"Thank you, Ko Tint Lwin."

He is not surprised. It's not the first time Handsome has shown such interest in his movements. There's not much to be done, though he's grateful to the young warder. He's already reached the point where any ally, even the most unschooled, is an advantage.

The rain is coming down heavily now. By the time Chit Naing reaches the village across the highway where the bus stops, he is drenched. And glad; he craved this cool walk away from the great cage of his life. His glasses are streaked with water. All around him in the blurred green dark, the frogs in the fields and the trees chant and answer and chant again. The chorus of frogs in a roadside pond falls silent when he approaches, rises up again after he passes by. He hears their amphibious words so clearly.

The hunters are coming, the hunters are coming to catch us, the hunters will boil us alive.

. 12 .

Fish. The singer craves the salted fish his mother always sends him. Feeling himself fall into the full despair of hunger, he talks to the cell.

And listens attentively to the reply. The cell knows everything.

Is he going mad this time?

Water pot, with its fur of algae on the bottom: *speak.*

Spider. Ants. The glistening cockroaches.

Bricks.

Concrete floor.

Straw mat.

Three small, threadbare towels hang off the strap of the shoulder bag. Inside the shoulder bag is an extra prison uniform, the white cotton turned gray, and three old T-shirts he is permitted to wear. Cheroots, an empty matchbox, a lighter.

Am I going mad?

The shit pail sits across the cell from him, as far as it can be from where he meditates, eats, and exercises. The prisoner watches the shit pail. The shit pail watches him.

Food and shit. The cage controls both. A meager amount of bad food yields a meager amount of painful shit, yet there is always the stench of it, a guest who must be tolerated because he's a relative and will not leave. Though the pail is empty now, the smell remains. And the acrid stink of urine has been burning his nostrils for years.

He rips the bottom of his longyi and tears a strip off. His sleeves are already gone. He uses the material for toilet paper. Holding his little white scrap—he waves it for a frantic moment in mock surrender—he walks over to the latrine pail.

To shit or not to shit—

That is the question.

Teza read Shakespeare at university. He would love to have a few of the comedies here, with explanatory footnotes, of course.

His stomach and lower intestine twist. He sighs as he squats.

He strains for a while. Nothing comes. Too many little lizard bones.

The singer waits. Pushes until the hemorrhoids start to hurt. In this situation as in so many others, it's best not to force things. He stands up.

He hasn't shat for—what is it?—two days. His record is fifteen. But constipation is preferable to any kind of diarrhea. A battalion of intestinal parasites has conquered him already. His body is an occupied territory, a country full of worms. A serious case of amoebic dysentery is his greatest fear; he's been afraid of dysentery since he was a teenager. At seventeen, he pulled down one of his father's dusty medical textbooks and looked up the dreaded ailment. Beside the complicated English text, a few notes were carefully written in Burmese. Shocked to recognize the handwriting, Teza read his father's clinical words over and over, as if they were fragments of a letter to him tucked away in the heavy book.

He tries to be grateful for constipation. He thinks of his mother's stoic refrain, usually in reference to political change but equally useful right now: *La-may ja-may*. It will come, it will take time. You will eventually be able to crap, my dear boy.

He sits down and places his hands, palms up, one on top of the other, and closes his eyes. It's important to be grateful. And to meditate. He begins to wander through memory, searching for a place to calm himself.

He often goes to Pagan. It's a majestic, holy place, but it sends him home too. Before his father died, he took Teza and Aung Min and their mother, May May, on three vacations. Each time they visited old Pagan.

He breathes in. He breathes himself out of the coffin.

Any one of the pagodas and temples of Pagan can help him find a path to stillness. Two thousand of them stand on a wide plain above the Irrawaddy River, embedded like old jewels in the dry earth. Nine hundred years ago, the kingdom of Pagan was called Tattadesa, The Parched Land.

Walking from vaulted temple to river to pagoda again, his father becomes someone else, or more himself, a happy man who wears a straw hat and hires the most beautiful horse and buggy for sightseeing among the temples. Despite the heat, he isn't tired here the way he is in Rangoon. His short, nervous temper untangles itself and loosens into playfulness.

Teza and Aung Min follow him with walking sticks, which they use only for swatting at dragonflies and bushes and each other. Every few seconds they glance at their father, whose shoulders shift back and forth as he walks downhill, hiking his longyi up over his knees. At home they cannot get enough of him—he's so busy at the hospital, and doing the secret tutorials, and going to the clinics outside the city to listen to people's broken hearts with his stethoscope and to set their broken bones—but in Pagan they have him all to themselves, and May May too. Their eyes flit around him like birds. They would follow him anywhere, their father, and now he is leading them down to the shores of the great Irrawaddy, a river wide as a lake. Sailors unloading charcoal from wooden longboats pause in their labors to wave and smile; Teza waves back, proud to be with his father. Hpay Hpay, the boys call him—Papa.

On the very edge of the lapping gray water, Hpay Hpay prods the soft sand with his own walking stick. "Look at that," and he points with his chin to the water's edge. "There was a crocodile here last night. Maybe it was Rain Cloud himself." Inspired by the river, Hpay Hpay told them Rain Cloud the Crocodile stories last night.

"There was no crocodile!" Aung Min looks up at him, his small mouth puckered with disbelief.

"There was! You can still see the place under the water where his fat tail made a groove deep in the sand. Look! And *swish-swoosh*, he stepped into the water. See?"

Teza grins slyly at his father. The mark, already half filled with sediment, must be from a boat's keel. Rain Cloud the famous crocodile doesn't swim in the Irrawaddy but in the Rangoon River. Teza has heard the stories many times. But Aung Min is just ten years old, so of course he forgets important details. And he is easier to fool.

Now Aung Min is squinting at the imprints of men's bare feet, their toes dug, one by one, deep in the sand. With round eyes, his hands rising up and down at his sides like propellers, he declares, "There are the marks of his big claws! It's true! Rain Cloud was here last night!"

Their father leans down and whispers, "Now you see why your mother and I don't want you to come down to the river alone. Because it would be frightening to meet up with a very large crocodile. Wouldn't it?"

Even though Teza's eleven and a half, he half believes what Hpay Hpay says. He adores his father this way, making a legend true beside the water. Teza takes hold of Aung Min's bare elbow and whispers, "And Rain Cloud would want to swim us over to the other side, just the way he carried the prince over on his scaly back, remember?"

"But we wouldn't go!" shouts Aung Min, making both Teza and Hpay Hpay jump.

Their father straightens his small, lean frame. "No, you wouldn't go, because we still have a lot of pagodas to visit on this side of the river. Let's go back up to the guesthouse. May May's made lunch. She wants to have a picnic outside under the big tree. *La la la.* Come on." With a smile, he turns away from the river and begins to walk up the hill, the boys scrambling behind him.

Teza breathes in, breathes himself out of memory. He's supposed to be meditating, not wandering around in the past. Yet he would like to stay here forever with his father, his brother, his mother up the hill, all of them held safe in this realm of light and red dust and gray-yellow water, with hundreds of double-storied temple steps to ascend and mazes of brick to lose themselves in, though they never get truly lost, because the cavelike passageways always lead them out again into dry, hot sunlight.

In the Golden Age, the great King Anawrahta had an army of white elephants, a ton of ivory, many ingots of gold and silver. Anawrahta gave, with the princes and kings who followed him, hundreds of measures of bronze and iron, white copper and red copper, nine kinds of gems, to make the kingdom great for the Lord Buddha. They filled the granaries with countless baskets of paddy rice, and their gifts of salt were enough to cover the temple platforms like northern snow.

But King Kyansittha's gold has worn away from the round stupas of the pagodas. Alaungsithu and all his riches are less than dust. King Narathihapate fled from Kublai Khan's grandson Yesu Timor, the Mongol invader who ended the glory of Pagan. Only the temples still stand, the round bases of the pagodas, pounded daily by the sun, eaten away by rain and winter winds.

Teza follows his father upward. But when he reaches the top of the bank, Aung Min is no longer behind him and their father is far ahead, near one of the white temples. He looks down and sees the bare earth between his child's feet, ochre dust coating his toes and ankles. When he raises his head again, he sees Hpay Hpay walking up the steps of the many-tiered temple. A small figure under the pale, enormous sky, he follows his father.

Inside the temple, the air is cool as a grotto's. The arched windows open in three directions. To the east, there is no window but the Buddha. Teza kneels in the confluence of breezes, his toes almost cold on the flag-stone floor. He holds his hands together in reverence and bows, touching his forehead to the stone three times. Then his eyes rise above the garlands of flowers, above the flickering candles and smoking incense. He looks past the rounded knees and the plaster flaking from the still robes.

In the crumbling hands of the clay-brick Buddha, in the worn clay face, the boy catches a glimpse of his father disappearing, his features re-solving into dust.

Then only one man remains, breathing in, breathing out of his cage, swaying slightly with the pulsing tide of his own blood. He goes in deep, deeper, until his bones grow light as pumice stone. Even his stomach, bitter with acid and little bones, becomes a quiet hollow. The breathing lets him be patient before his hunger like the holy men are patient before the teachings that still elude them.

. 13 .

When Teza thinks of his father, he can sometimes smell the distinctive inky scent of carbon paper.

Even buying it was dangerous. Ne Win's regime orchestrated shortages to stem the circulation of subversive writing. His father tried to get around this by stocking up, but the military intelligence agents paid shopkeepers to report anyone who bought large amounts of carbon paper. So he gave his young student doctors money and sent them to different areas of Rangoon to buy supplies, making sure they changed their routines and varied the shops to avoid arousing suspicion. If questioned, they always said the paper was for their tutorials.

And so it was. For almost a decade Hpay Hpay managed to run secret tutorials without detection, supplying thousands of people in Rangoon and Mandalay with an underground news source. He executed this clandestine operation at the kitchen table, with the smell of curry and garlic wafting through the air.

Teza remembers how the carbon paper on tutorial evenings slowly won out over the tantalizing kitchen smells. His father read slowly and succinctly from various pieces of newsprint and hand-copied missives. Teza sat at the back of the kitchen on a small stool, listening to the quiet, persistent stream of Hpay Hpay's voice without understanding what it meant. Young men and women, faithful interns from Rangoon General, sat on either side of the kitchen table, bent over the inky sheets, writing hard.

Sweat beaded on skin, slid down necks and noses while words filled page after page. Sweat dampened shirt collars and the waists of longyis. Windows were closed to make sure no one in the side street heard the doctor reading; the kitchen became a sauna. The interns treated Teza's father with great deference and affection. If he murmured past the last of the cicadas into the cricket-song of night, the young doctors followed his quiet voice with black-smudged hands. The carbon paper rustled and sighed, sending a strong scent of ink to the small boys who sat poised on the periphery of the writing circle, anxious to be inside it, where their father was. They were both jealous of the young men and women, who knew how to read and write. Teza had just learned to read, and Aung Min, a year behind him, was still memorizing the alphabet.

Though the interns changed every two or three years, their work remained the same: they pressed urgent words through several sheets of paper, then left the pages with May May, who organized the notes. She and the doctor passed them out to friends and colleagues, who in turn passed them on to others, until an elaborate network of people had read and absorbed the worn hand-copied writings.

The boys knew the work was a secret. Their parents told them many times that they were never to talk about the tutorials with anyone but the fledgling doctors. No one was allowed to hear what they were doing. Then, one particularly hot April night, Hpay Hpay suddenly stopped reading. Teza waited for him to take a drink of water. He did not. The interns shook out their cramped hands and began to wipe handkerchiefs over their faces. The doctor turned around. Everyone waited. He seemed to be examining the closed windows. Looking over his shoulder with a mischievous grin, he asked, "It's too hot, isn't it?" His voice was unexpectedly loud. "We're going to suffocate in here. Just what Ne Win wants."

He slowly unlatched and opened the windows. The young men and women looked at each other. Daw Sanda put three fingers over her mouth as her husband pushed the wooden shutters open. A current of cool air immediately poured into the room, bathing everyone's faces and necks. Teza's father turned around calmly. Before picking up his papers and continuing, he leaned over, his palms spread wide on the stained wood of the table. "Let them hear," he said. "We are all cowards at heart, but we must try not to be afraid. If we are always afraid, they will always win." He read for the rest of the tutorial in the cool air of evening.

They copied widely, everything from banned news items and political satires to translations of Che Guevara and Lu Xun and directives from the Communist Party of Burma. The CPB sent out information about political and guerrilla action as well as strike organization. The doctor wasn't a card-carrying communist, but he was ready to consider any alternative to Ne Win's dictatorship.

Shortly after Teza's fourteenth birthday, he lay restless in bed, trying not to wake his little brother, who breathed steadily beside him. That night his father had given him wonderful news: he would be allowed to have his own sheet of carbon paper and try his hand at writing with the interns. Perhaps his copy wouldn't be usable, his father warned him, but he would be permitted to try.

Finally the ink would be his, smudged on his fingertips and shirt cuffs; he would join Hpay Hpay in his heroic, clandestine work. Sleep was out of the question. He lay wide awake in bed, pleased with his insomnia. Downstairs, right beneath him, his parents murmured in the sitting room. Teza wished he could join their serious conversation.

Lifting up the shadow of the mosquito net to feel a breath of chilly December air on his face, he thought about the grand and daring act he would soon perform. The secrecy surrounding the tutorials was something he savored, a treat his friends at school were not allowed to eat. With one hand touching Aung Min's back and the other flung extravagantly and bravely outside the mosquito net, he began to drift off, imagining how impressed the young doctors would be when he sat down with them next week, the newest and youngest recruit.

The knock yanked him out of shallow sleep. Why would his mother knock at the bedroom door? He rose up on his elbow, dream-addled, half smiling in his confusion. The knock came again. This time he understood someone was knocking at the front door. Not the hurried rapping of a man with a sick child or with a wife in early labor, it was strangely polite. Who else would be calling so late?

Teza held his breath. Aung Min was still asleep beside him. When his mother rushed into the bedroom, whispering, "Wake up, wake up! Come and say goodbye to your father," Teza was already swinging his skinny legs to the floor.

"Aung Min!" He shook his little brother's relaxed body until it tensed awake. "Aung Min! Get up now. Hpay Hpay's going away."

There were three men standing in the room. As soon as Teza saw that one of them was wearing trousers, he knew his father was in danger. Dr. Kyaw Win Thu did not like to be demonstrative in front of strangers, but he dropped to a crouch and enfolded both his children in his arms, so tightly that Teza lost his breath. When he released them, he continued to hold each boy tightly by the hand. He spoke quietly and quickly.

"You must be very, very good boys while I am away. May May needs your help. I will be home as soon as I can. Don't forget me." He smiled at them, but neither was fooled. Their eyes began to shine with tears.

The doctor squeezed his wife's hands while looking into her dry eyes. She was not going to let military intelligence agents see her cry. Later the doctor was to wonder what more he could have done or said in the act of farewell. He had spent so many years loving her, it did not seem possible to convey this emotion in a brief, exposed gesture. He thought of his favorite endearment for her, "my moonlight"—a reference to the ancient Pali meaning of her name—but he could not say it in front of military agents. So he simply held his wife's hands for a moment longer.

Somewhere behind and below them, Aung Min asked, "Where is Hpay Hpay going? Why is he going?"

The authorities sent the doctor to a work camp in the north. The expense and the two days of travel involved in reaching the prison camp from Rangoon prevented Daw Sanda from visiting him very often. Taking the children with her on the buses and trains and, for the last leg of the journey, the ox cart—for a thirty-minute visit with their father—was exhausting. Twice they reached the camp and were refused permission to enter. Sometimes she had to bribe the guards to let her and the boys in. As months stretched into years, she sold most of their furniture. The wedding silks went too, then her jewelery, then her mother's and most of her grandmother's jewelry. Each possession paid for the next trip upcountry, and for her husband's food. He was the first to wait for parcels from her.

Three years after he was sentenced, the doctor woke one morning during the rainy season with a fever. He had been feeling tired, almost sick, sore in his muscles for a day or two, but he had attributed it to his new work detail in the nearby stone quarry. When the fever started, his first thought was malaria. The rains brought mosquitoes; some of the men in the camp could barely stay upright. He already had the more common vivax strain in his body, so he hoped to sweat out the attack on a little supply of paracetamol and quinine. He waited for the chills that follow malarial fever. They did not come. In the middle of the second night of high fever, violent cramping in his gut twisted the length of his body from one side to another, a whip of pain snapping inside him.

Dr. Kyaw Win Thu realized it wasn't malaria at all.

The vomiting and diarrhea came before morning, with such violence that two friends held him over one latrine pail as he heaved into another. Such is the work of amoebic dysentery. During their invasion and colonization of the intestine, the parasites produce a poison into the mucous membrane of the gut. The weaker the body, through malnutrition or fatigue, the more severe the illness. The raw lining of those long, many-folded coils and loops refuses its normal task of absorption and begins to secrete fluid instead. The doctor tried to drink water but immediately threw it up. He knew he was dehydrating from the inside out. He also knew that if he didn't get antibiotics, the parasites would burrow into the intestinal wall, causing peritonitis, or they would enter his bloodstream and infect other organs, most likely his liver.

The prison camp dispensary had only aspirin and alcohol. With money, he could have bribed the prison doctor, begged him to buy the proper medicine outside. Or he could have paid the akhan-lu-gyi. Unlike Teza, he wasn't confined in solitary; he lived with other men, criminals and politicals. The akhan-lu-gyi often received favors from the warders in exchange for protection money extorted from weaker prisoners.

The doctor knew precisely how to cure himself. More precisely, he knew that he could not. After a series of convulsions, he lay on his mat in a tight fetal fist. The whip snapping through his guts had transformed into a knife. The blade slashed this way, that way, deep in the center of his body. The pain was so intense that he only longed for it to be over.

In his lucid moments, he kept thinking how simple the world was, how unbelievable. He didn't need magic powers or a miracle to save his life. He just needed money, enough to bribe the akhan-lu-gyi or the tan-see. One of their people could fetch the medicine or at least send a message outside. Daw Sanda would have left the children with her cousin and started immediately on the journey.

Later, she thought it out: she could have sold the last of her grandmother's gold to buy his medicine. He needed so little, really: a course of antibiotics and an IV of Ringer's solution. He needed clean water. Clean water and medicine meant his life. All he had to do was survive for seven more years. Then he would return, to Teza, to Aung Min, who was beginning to look very much like him, and to Sanda, his moonlight.

For a long time afterward she made the calculation repeatedly, as though it were an alchemical formula for pleasing a powerful nat, one of those animist spirits that preside over the shadows of Burmese Buddhism. On a piece of paper torn from one of her sons' exercise books, she scribbled down every possible variable, her forehead propped on her other hand. Always more or less the same calculation, it equaled nothing—two gold wedding bangles and the thin gold wedding chain were enough for the antibiotics and for the long journey. A bridge washed away in the rain, the trains slowed, the road a swell of mud: even with these obstacles, if she had known, she would have gone forth. If she had received a message, she might have reached him in time.

"There has been a small epidemic," the prison doctor explained in his letter.

"Small? How do you define a *small* epidemic?" she cried, stricken, furious.

When this letter reached their house in Rangoon, when May May sat at the table in the kitchen with the piece of paper shaking in her hand, her beloved husband, their father, had already been dead for sixteen days. They were never able to discover where he'd been buried.

. 14 .

Nine strikes against the iron. A moment after the last beat sounds, the lights go out. Darkness, like a guard he cannot see, pushes him into an empty well.

Suddenly he becomes conscious of the way his mouth draws in, the lips bunching slightly like an old man's, like the old man his father never became.

When Hpay Hpay died, Teza stopped playing the guitar; he was just seventeen. His grief for his father demanded suffering, and hardship, and loss.

But Teza's mother—in spite of her worries about a musician's life—didn't want sadness to guide her son. "Teza, your father bought you that guitar because he knew you were gifted." Teza could play. Not just a few chords, not just a bit of street strumming in the evenings, but complex patterns, fingerpicking and blues triads. He could play any tune at all, anything. He used to echo the radio, just a few beats behind, or play complementary wandering riffs in the same key. Whatever he heard he could play, and he sang like a bird with honey on its tongue. "Teza, a gift is a responsibility. Go. Go upstairs. The guitar's in your room, isn't it?"

By the time he was in university, he was playing for himself again, quickly gaining recognition as the Singer, a handsome young man. In love.

Teza touches his lips. He closes his eyes. Sound looms before him like a sail.

Thazin. He's not sure if he can remember her voice or not. Her life has continued without him. After his first year in prison, he understood she could not wait. He had to release her, and he did, in his own mind, as he was never permitted to communicate with her directly. In the third year, the news came to him, passed from one mouth to the next, that Ma Thazin, the famous singer's love, had married someone else.

Still he tries to find her.

At Rangoon University, the boys saunter by Convocation Hall under shade trees like enormous green umbrellas. The girls refold their blue, yellow, orchid-purple tamins, their sarongs of fine patterns, fine cloth. Ugliness does not rule the world and Teza is twenty-two and will be handsome and talented for the rest of his life, which is forever. Why not? The girls remind him of butterflies breathing. When their sarongs loosen from walking, they pause, stretch the extra fabric out to the side, fold it across their bellies, and tuck it in tightly again. Some continue walking as they do this; some stop briefly on the path. The motion is the loveliest he knows, a gesture both discreet and laden with promise. All the girls do it, because every girl wears a tamin. Every curve of belly and slope of thigh is momentarily accentuated. When a girl walks through a pool of light coming down through the branches, her colors become as vibrant as wet oil paint.

Gitah-shay, the boys whisper of the girls walking by the tea shops. "Guitar shape" is the highest compliment he and his friends can give a girl.

As the finest guitar player, he is a favorite for serenades, when dusk stretches indigo into evening. The trees with their shadows sway above them like dark green water. The scent of jasmine and night flowers fills the air; the boys, hoping the smell is perfume, drift toward the girls' dormitories. They smoke cheroots without coughing; they attempt to swagger. On finding the windows of those they most admire, Teza tunes his guitar. Cheroot ash falls on the frets.

Aung Min blows the ash away and whispers, "I'm starved. She better give us food."

Teza pauses in his tuning, stares at him. "Little Brother, you have no anadeh." No shame, no proper sense of decorum.

Teza begins to play. The boys sing their hearts out. Girls lean from the windows like flowers. When they like what they hear, they throw down snacks, packages of pickled tea leaves and deep-fried lentils, peanuts, Chinese sesame bars, deep-fried Indian pastries.

Ma Thazin throws down a book.

Aung Min leaps forward, snatches it off the ground, and brandishes it above his head, crying, "Sister, we don't need literature, we need something for our bellies."

As the girl stretches boldly out the window, a chorus of high-pitched laughter rises behind her voice. "That's not for you, you little brat. Give it to your brother!"

The book is a photocopied, cardboard-bound version of Bob Dylan's songs, in English. With chords and music.

Teza falls in love. He meets her at her favorite tea shop, on Inya Lake. They walk along the paths through the People's Park, devising dozens of elaborate ways to rub shoulders, touch elbows, skim the backs of each other's swinging hands. They go to movies, daringly alone sometimes, but more often with a group of her friends from the Faculty of Medicine. The idea of marrying a lady doctor thrills him. His father would have liked her. Even May May approves of this pretty but earnest young woman. Three times Teza pretends he is sick and three times Thazin becomes wonderfully serious, asking him to stick his tongue out, open his shirt so she can place her important stethoscope there on his pounding heart. "Breathe deeply," she instructs, but how much more deeply can he breathe? Three times she scolds him: "You'd better not be faking it, Teza, or I'll stop speaking to you."

But she speaks to him again and again.

He sees her rewrapping her scarlet tamin, doing up the cream-colored blouse, her small fingers deft with the gold buttons. He mourns those buttons, and the shadow of a bra beneath her blouse. Once, after they had made love all afternoon, she jumped up and rushed to get ready to go. The sight of her bare feet on the wooden floor made him hungry and hard again. When he reached for her, she laughed and hit his hand. "Absolutely not! *You* are insatiable and *I* always miss this class!" He fell back on the bed and let her leave. He regrets that now.

Everything would be different if he could reach up one more time and pull the mother-of-pearl comb from that black waterfall of hair. Or watch her fine, strong feet walk toward him.

He takes his hands from his eyes and lays them on his chest. He loved her.

He knows she loved him also. That is why he remembers.

His hands slide down over his ribs. The blades rise out of him, xylophone keys placed side by side. The sensitive place beneath his left nipple, the bruised feeling, is another beating. The cracked rib didn't knit properly. Interrogation Center Fourteen.

The jutting leap from his ribs to his lower belly would sicken her. He is glad she cannot see him now, with hipbones protruding like hooks.

His hands slip under the unknotted longyi. He scratches. He picks one, two, three bedbugs from his pubic hair. This act brings enough pleasure to release a flood of lust and the memory of lust. His yearning will be satisfied in seconds.

Certain moments rest in his body from the time before. The places she marked him are far below his skin, but he searches for them. Not scars, there were no scars with her, only the deep, worn groove where the shyness and fear of two virgins yielded to love in the body. His desire sings to hers, coaxing it forward, and her desire comes toward him. He unbuttons her blouse, pulls away the soft material of the bra; her nipples harden under his lips. Shy, she covers her breasts with her hair, hiding his face also. He floats above her, afraid to rest his weight on her, knowing he will have to use his weight, he will have to push. The nexus of tenderness and force confuses him. He did not expect to be so afraid of hurting her. Echoing his own thoughts, she whispers, "I'm afraid. You'll hurt me."

Maung-go lo-ba-deh. Chit-pa-deh.

Despite their fear, these are words of love.

The spasm charging through his body makes no sound.

Wasted pearl fills his hand, spills down his wrist.

He rolls over on his side, jawbone chafing straw mat. The ants between the bricks have gone still, as though the wall itself has clenched tight and crushed them all.

. 15 .

The sky becomes ocean. Rain comes in waves, rises and falls; tide after tide of water beats the roofs and walls of the prison, drips into some cells, spares others, transforms the compound into an expanse of brick-chip mud and puddles. Teza sleeps through the pounding nightly lullaby, the iron-beater counting the hours of darkness.

He sleeps while the drainage stream behind the big halls and latrine holes swells like a river. In the tangle of weeds and garbage there, a snail battalion continues its endless labor of eating green. Rain crashes down even as the night turns, by imperceptible degrees, toward dawn. Teza sleeps through the mighty chorus of frogs, through the shouts of warders in the compound, through the spider plucking his web.

He dreams.

A child again, he sits with his grandfather on the front stoop in Mandalay. The old man is tight-lipped, unsmiling, looking down at something in his hand. The boy pulls his grandfather's arm low enough to see what's there, cupped in the palm. Then he jerks back in horror.

Bones. Tiny bones, white and fine as ivory toothpicks.

The boy rises, guilty. He wants to run away, to escape, but the old man grabs his arm and asks in a stricken voice, "What have you done, Teza? Why did you kill it? Every lizard is a small naked man."

The old man is still his grandfather, but the child begins to cry when he looks down at the birdlike claw that grips his bare arm.

T eza opens his eyes in wild fear of the dream. Yet there is no solace in what he sees. He wonders how many times a man can be broken by dreaming, then broken again by waking. Still lying on his mat, bone-chilled, the sound of rain all around, he searches the wall for the spider, but the spider is gone.

Exhausted, he rouses his limbs with great effort. To stand up is work. Conjuring is work, remembering, remaking himself as he was in the world before the cage, the disappeared world: a person among people.

T eza turns his head toward the teak door. He holds his breath to listen to the footsteps. It cannot be eleven, tray time. Surely he has not slept so long as that. He tries to hear through the crash of rain. It's not Sein Yun, not the drag of flip-flops. Boots are coming down the corridor, solid, steady. Purposeful.

When the door opens, Teza is waiting with his head down.

"Come on, then. Shower day has come at last, because you stink so bad I can smell you down the hall. Get your stuff—hurry up."

Teza silently pulls his shirt over his lowered head, steps out of his longyi. He picks up his slice of soap, his tin cup, clean clothes. He removes his slippers and stands there in threadbare shorts. Handsome moves away from the door, shouts, "Forward!" and spits down the hallway. Teza begins to walk. When he reaches the phlegm on the floor, he swerves around it. Handsome grunts, then punches Teza between the shoulder blades. The warder barks, "Back up. I said back up!"

The singer moves his feet back, step by step, through the spit on the floor.

"Now walk in a straight line."

He advances through it again.

● ● ●

The walk to the shower room at the end of the corridor comprises the entire geography of Teza's world. The room is a large brick-walled cell without a door or window. On the back wall and in the center of the room are two concrete troughs. A dripping faucet sticks out over the back trough, which is full of water. Since the building houses only Teza, the other trough sits empty. At the threshold of the room, Handsome barks, "Go ahead," meaning *Go scare the rats down the drain.*

When Teza steps into the cool, dark room, he claps his hands. There is no general scurry. Cage rats are like cage cockroaches, fearless and perfectly accustomed to competing with humans for space and food. He steps deeper into the room, the cement floor cold on his feet. There is only one light, in the corner by the entrance, and it takes a moment for his eyes to adjust. Under the empty trough, a few feet away from the drain, he spots a shifting huddle of gray.

As he walks toward the gray shape, it melts into three, four, five separate darknesses, like a ghost disintegrating and seeping out over the floor. "Out, out! Get out."

Handsome's voice suddenly booms, "Make sure you get rid of all of them, Songbird, or you won't get your shower."

The rats seem to float toward the drain, leisurely, taking their time. Teza stamps with his feet and hisses. "Yes, sir. They're gone now, sir. The rats are gone."

Handsome enters the room and scans the floor, looking left and right. "Okay. Begin."

Teza is already standing almost naked at the edge of the trough, tin cup in hand. The jailer stands behind him and off to the side to avoid being splashed. The jailer's silence, his refusal to enter into even the most mundane exchange of language, makes Teza afraid of him.

"Throw!"

Teza dips the cup into the trough, then quickly tosses the water under his arm. He has to move as fast as possible, lathering up the slice of soap, scrubbing—

"Throw!"

He rinses off with the next toss of water, combs the soap out of his hair with his fingers—

"Throw!"

Angular elbows and knees pump up and down, both to keep warm and to make sure he cleans as much of his body as he can with the small amount of water available to him. He counts the throws, keeping track of how much more water he can afford to use on any particular part of his body. It has become a refined athletic skill to step speedily out of his underwear between the commands and wash his genitals in three or four scoops of water. A bath is fifteen scoops; sixteen or seventeen if the jailer loses count.

"Last throw!"

Teza's naked toes grip the wet cement. Eleven. He's only counted to eleven. He still has to wash his legs, where the sores are the worst. He needs to wash his legs. Eleven cups of water is not enough. Handsome lost count.

Teza takes a deep breath, breathing a word with the exhalation. "Sir?"

"What is it?"

"Sir, I believe I have four more scoops of water."

"I don't care what you believe, your bathing time is over. Dress."

Teza's tongue moves back and forth behind his teeth. He should just be quiet. Putting his hand out for his clean longyi, he thinks, *Teza, just be quiet.*

But the scabies on his legs are itching. In the absence of medicine, only bathing helps them and prevents the open sores from becoming infected. Why shouldn't he ask for his share of water?

"Sir, if I could just wash my legs quickly, I would be very grateful."

"You skinny little motherfucker." Handsome steps forward and cracks Teza on the back of the head with his knuckles, "if you don't get dressed right now, you'll go back to your cell naked with my boot up your ass, so shut the fuck up and put on your longyi!"

It infuriates Teza that tears rise into his eyes involuntarily when he experiences pain. Tears should be saved for more important things than physical pain. Ears ringing from the crack on the head, he blinks the tears back into his eyes.

Water drips from the faucet into the trough.

He stares at the tin cup in his hand. He is very cold now. The jailer stares at the back of his prisoner's head, at his shoulders, which have begun to tremble visibly.

Quick as a market thief, Teza scoops water and tosses it onto his legs, then lifts the right one and begins to lather the soap over his shin. He doesn't dare to bend down with the jailer right there behind him. He is sure his disobedience will incite violence against his naked privates, so he is doubly shocked when Handsome grabs him by the back of the head, his big hand closing on both hair and thin muscle.

Teza hadn't thought about the water at all. Suddenly his head is going down and the water shoots up into his nostrils, displacing the cry in his mouth. Handsome's bellowing is muffled and the singer is already coughing upside down, sucking in steely cold liquid.

When the jailer yanks Teza's head up into the air, he feels the entanglement deep in his throat, water flooding all the passages even as it pours from his mouth, his nose.

"Want to bathe, do you? Let me help you get clean, you dirty fuck!"

His head is cocked back for an instant in the air, then he is choking harder, more water surging into his throat and nostrils. His limbs kick of their own accord as his head bucks against Handsome's grip. His shoulders go under while his arms flail upward, his hands grasping the jailer's hands, but it's like trying to pull apart pieces of iron. *I will drown in a bathing trough.* He tries to control the muscles of his throat, to keep from choking more, but he can't.

Teza begins purposely to splash as much water as he can out of the trough, hoping to get the jailer very wet before he dies.

Handsome yanks him out. Water pours from his mouth. His face and neck are flushed; his whole head is pounding, pulsing with blood. Just as he feels a tiny sliver of air open his throat, Handsome pushes him under again. Now he tries his best not to move, but it's hard to do this, to let life sink away. The grip tightens in his hair, around the muscles in his neck. How long is the jailer going to hold him down? Against every instinct— he wants only to rise fighting into the air—Teza gives up.

Handsome lets the singer drop to the floor, then grabs the edge of the water trough for purchase and begins to kick, expressing his fury in articulate jabs. Teza curls into himself, protecting his genitals with his knees, his face with his hands. He is still choking. Behind his hands, his mouth opens and closes, opens and closes, a fish in the wrong world. Water drenches him, the cement floor, the jailer's trousers. The boots that kick him are wet now, propelling his body one way, snapping him back the other.

It is astonishing, to have throat and mouth and tongue but no way to cry out.

H e doesn't know how long it takes to get back to his cell. Handsome swears at him each time he falls down, kicks him again. Seven minutes, half an hour? Pain has no respect for time; it makes up its own beginnings and endings.

"There! You stupid prick, happy now? You've had enough water, haven't you?" Handsome blocks the open door of the cell. Teza stands before him, head down, drenched, praying only to be allowed to go back inside, to be locked away, safe from the jailer. "Answer! Have you had enough?" Handsome knuckle-hits him on the top of the head.

It's hard to get the words out. "Yes, sir."

The jailer steps aside and pushes him through the door. "If you want more, just let me know, you stupid fuck. If you're lucky, maybe Sein Yun will fetch your clothes later on. Until then, enjoy the cool weather."

Shivering in his wet shorts, Teza stands before the door until it slams shut. Then he limps to his mat and lies down, testing each vertebra, shifting his left hip, not putting any weight on his right elbow. He carefully pulls the gray blanket over himself. Prone on the floor, he begins to touch his head with his hands, as though he were a doctor and the head belonged to a misshapen newborn. Tears start in his eyes as he feels the delicacy of his own skull, how he can't protect it. He cannot protect his own body. His fingers spider over his head, through his wet hair, trying to locate the source of the pounding. It feels as though an artery has burst somewhere at the front of his brain, just above his left eye, though surely if that were the case, he would be dead by now.

He is surprised to discover that nothing but his nose is bleeding. He's cold, because he is soaked, but shivering is good, because it will keep him awake. He pinches the top of his nose to stop the flow of blood.

Above all, it's important to put the beating out of his mind, to return to the relative safety and familiarity of the cell, the four walls, the benign water pot, the lines of ants traveling the walls. Now the teak coffin is his protecter, his only home. The worst thing of all is to be beaten in one's own cell, because then it too becomes a vicious place full of weapons. He stares with curious gratitude at the latrine pail.

There is nothing to be done with the memory of the violence, as there was nothing to be done with the violence itself, except to endure it without becoming it, which is his most important work in the cage, his way in, his way out. It is strange that sometimes, when the beating is very bad, his anger is not so intense. He feels none of the fury he felt the other day when Handsome kicked his tray, for example. A different feeling surfaces in him now, which he does not fully understand. He feels tenderness toward his own vulnerable, hungry body. Poor thing! It's as though he's found a wounded animal on the roadside and wants to take care of it. The feeling of metta—compassion—is so great that there is no room to feel anger at the one who hurt the animal. He would not do to Handsome what Handsome has done to him. He knows this. And that knowledge is also a kind of tenderness.

He cradles his skull in his hands and closes his eyes. When he opens them, he sees more lizards than usual on the ceiling, stalking insects around the light. He whispers to the creatures above him, "Ha, you've all come back to the cell for a visit, have you? You must know that Hpo Hpo told me to stop eating you." What did his grandfather say? *Every lizard is a small naked man.* How easy escape would be if every small naked man were a lizard! Teza would just walk away through the air vent, bidding farewell to the spider on his way out.

He's pleased to see that the spider is back and busy spinning a new web some distance away from the air vent, in the corner where the walls join the ceiling.

Comrade Spider, little eight-legged friend, show me how you live.

By making strong nets out of almost nothing.

I aspire to such a vocation myself. But it's not as easy, comrade, as you make it look.

. 16 .

He is grateful to find that the punishment ended with the beating. Handsome hasn't cut off his meals or his drinking water, because Sein Yun shows up as usual with his breakfast tray. What a blessing!

The palm-reader curses the junior jailer for being such a bully. On his way back with the latrine pail, he shuffles down to the shower room, rinses Teza's clothes, and brings them back to the teak coffin. "You have to admit, Little Brother, I warned you, didn't I? And, as you can imagine, he's now in a pissy mood." He lowers his voice and takes a small step into the cell. "But here's some good news." A high, anxious note pulls taut like a wire in his whisper. "I think you might have a bit of food coming tomorrow."

Teza tries to rise from his mat, but his ribs are so sore he winces and drops to the floor again. Sein Yun waves his hand. "Ya-ba-deh! Never mind, I don't have anything else to tell you and I've got to go. That bastard's getting impatient at the end of the hall, I can just feel it."

Teza passes the entire day trying to decipher Sein Yun's words. Is the palm-reader himself arranging some extra food for him? Or is another political sending Teza something? Could Sein Yun have meant the htaung win za? Is the food parcel finally here?

When the palm-reader comes with dinner, Teza is standing at the teak door, anxious to get more information. He's frightened by Handsome's sudden bark; the jailer stands, hidden, to one side of the door. "Hurry up in there, palm-reader, I haven't got all fucking night!" Teza is puzzled. Why didn't he hear Handsome's boots coming down the corridor?

Sein Yun thrusts the tray into Teza's outstretched hands, then backs out of the cell and closes the door. Still confused, Teza puts down his dinner and tries to hear what the palm-reader and jailer are whispering on the other side of the thick door. Their low voices are drowned out by the shuffle-slap of slippers and the familiar clomp of Handsome's boots. Teza wonders briefly if there's something wrong with his hearing.

He stares down at his tray—the same broken, dirty rice, the same watery curry.

The next morning the singer begins to wait, consciously, patiently. Then he waits in growing annoyance. The pain from the beating diminishes as the growling, gripping cramp in his stomach intensifies. The stomachache gives him a headache.

Swearing, he stands up, too quickly, and loses his balance; he grabs the wall to steady himself. The headache reasserts itself with a sudden ferocity, so he sits down and rests his back against the wall. Slowly the awful drumbeat in his skull recedes.

When the iron-beater finally begins to strike out eleven, Teza is so relieved he could cry. Five minutes later he hears the palm-reader's slapping footsteps. To his dismay, he also hears the sound of Handsome's boots. Strange. Did he just miss them yesterday?

The jailer swears above the rattle of his keys, whisks the bolt back with a harshness that Sein Yun never displays. Teza bows his head in submission. Handsome opens the door and spits into the cell. The phlegm smacks the floor close to him, but Teza doesn't glance at it. He doesn't move a muscle. The jailer grunts, steps back into the corridor, and shouts at Sein Yun, "What the fuck are you waiting for? Just give it to him!"

The palm-reader shuffles into the cell and stands before Teza, grinning like an idiot. In his arms is a large htaung win za; the food tray is balanced on top. Teza blinks. Food. He opens his mouth but restrains his desire to

let out a whoop of joy. The parcel is big, bigger than usual. He looks past
Sein Yun's shoulder, through the cell door. Handsome glares; Teza drops
his eyes.

The palm-reader is subdued in the presence of the jailer, but only in
volume, not in character. He takes another step into the cell and the space
fills with his throaty chuckle and his smell. "It weighs a ton, too. She must
have thought you were setting up shop inside, Little Brother. There'll be
enough food here for you and all your friends."

Teza glances at Handsome again, who has turned his head away and
appears to be staring grimly toward the shower room. Sein Yun jabbers on,
his voice jumpy, pitched too high. "I hope you share some of this wealth.
I can already smell the salted fish. I'll make it worth your while, of course.
You wouldn't expect any less from me, would you?" He tilts his head this
way and that, too quickly, nervousness making him a caricature of himself.

Teza hurriedly takes the tray off the top of the box, sets it down, then
lifts the food parcel out of Sein Yun's arms. He whispers, "How did so
much get through? And in a cardboard box?" Usually parcels come
wrapped up in plastic bags.

Sein Yun raises a finger to his lips but says loudly, "I'll take the biggest
fish in exchange for thirty tablets of paracetamol. You suffer with toothache, right? How can you enjoy eating if you're in pain? Give me your
pail, no chatting."

When Sein Yun leaves to empty the pail, the jailer steps to the threshold of the cell and growls, "Your food is poisoned," then slams the door.
Shaking his head in bafflement, Teza looks down at the parcel in his arms.
Sein Yun was right; he can smell the fish! His mouth begins to water even
as he tries to hear what Handsome is saying on the other side of the door,
but the men move off down the corridor and their voices disappear.

Five minutes later Sein Yun, still out of breath and jumpy, pulls open
the heavy door and hands Teza his pail. He winks and jerks his head backward, indicating that Jailer Handsome is waiting to lock up, his impatience
audible in the clatter of the key ring against his leg. He whispers, "Remember not to eat too quickly, Little Brother!"

When the door heaves shut again, the air is still filled with the palm-
reader's nervousness. Teza waits for the footsteps to fade out, then squats
down in front of the parcel. Having been searched, it is already open, but

he carefully and slowly folds back the flaps of cardboard. It is a gift from his mother.

There are plastic bags filled with peanuts, deep-fried beans, sesame seeds, the pickled tea leaves he particularly adores. He takes the packages out, carefully sets them on his mat, surprised to see she has bought a new brand of la-phet, tea leaves they've never eaten at home. It doesn't matter. He is so pleased, so surprised to receive this food. He takes deep breaths, trying not to rush.

The cheroots have come through all of a piece, thirty of them in a sealed pack: he'll be able to perform the cheroot ceremony for three weeks without relying on the palm-reader. And he'll smoke a little more freely.

When he takes out the bundle of fish, tears of relief fill his eyes. This is what he has been waiting for, the dark brown and gray half-coils of these water creatures, their bodies preserved with salt. They are life to him. Strangely, they're wrapped in oil-stained paper instead of the cloth she usually sends. His mind lights briefly on Handsome's threat, but he knows the food is not poisoned. And if it were, he would eat it anyway. Only his sense of formality stops him from tearing into one of the fish, bones sticking out of his mouth like opaque pins. There are an unprecedented twelve of them.

A gathering sense of foreboding competes with his pleasure in this bounty. Twelve fish. Usually there are eight. Once there were ten. Why did they allow such a large parcel through?

Four blocks of thanakha slide into view. Rubbed in a little water in his hand, the fragrant bars of ground bark become a paste he applies to his sores. His mother claims that thanakha is the reason that Burmese women have such lovely skin. While he was growing up, she smeared it on him for reasons as varied as heat rash to boils to insect bites. He peels the plastic wrap off one of the bars and smells it: the faint scent returns him to a childhood morning, when he left the house in a sulk because she forced him to go to school with thanakha swirled on his cheeks. Like a child, or a girl! He stopped at a tap in a friend's compound and indignantly washed the offensive cream off his face, only to get scolded by his friend's mother, who knew exactly what he was doing.

There are four large packages of deep-fried beans mixed with spices. There is a new towel, and two new pairs of underwear. Most worrisome of all, there are two bars of soap. He has never received two bars of soap. Someone always steals the soap.

Teza's nervousness mounts as he takes out each longed-for item, holds it. Daw Sanda, May May, his mother: he cannot feel her touch here. Though everything is in place, something is missing. Some of the food may have been sent by her, but someone else put together the parcel, which explains the uncustomary cardboard box, the unexpected quantities.

The abundance feels like a bribe. But that is ridiculous. What can he possibly be bribed for?

Out loud, he whispers, "Keep going."

He flips up the cardboard flaps at the bottom of the box. A half-cry rises from his mouth.

Paper.

White, coarse-grained, and folded at the bottom of the box. He tilts the empty parcel. A white ballpoint pen rolls out from underneath a cardboard flap. The paper is blank, and the pen looks new.

The singer swears under his breath.

Now he understands Sein Yun's jumpiness.

Minutes pass. He stares at the various items of food and toiletries placed carefully on his sleeping mat. Then he looks at the paper, three sheets. A white pen. They are like bombs meant for children, enticing him, drawing him forward, designed to explode in his hands. He does not touch them. He sits in the cell tilting the box back and forth. His headache comes back. The pen rolls under the cardboard flap, disappears. Rolls back out. He cannot escape it.

He tucks the paper and the pen back under the flap at the bottom of the box, out of sight, and turns to the food. What he craved so badly has suddenly become a distraction.

Still, as soon as he pulls a chunk of flesh off one fish and puts it into his mouth, his body remembers that food is the center of the world. The rice on the tray is particularly sandy today, but no matter, he has fish to eat and he eats it, feels the salty flesh bypass his stomach completely and go straight into the long wasted muscles of his thighs and arms. *Thank you, thank you.* He carefully picks at the needling bones. It's almost a medical procedure, the precise, methodical stripping away of the meat.

The cardboard box sits beside him like a disturbing companion, but he ignores it, surrendering instead to the deep hunger of his body. He eats and eats, slowly, carefully, making himself stop and breathe, stop and breathe, knowing he must not go too fast or have too much at this first sitting. Forgetful, he chews and swallows, licks his lips, eats too much. To keep himself from eating more, he stands and paces for a few minutes.

All afternoon he has left the pen and paper in the box, pretending they are not there. When the iron-beater strikes five o'clock, Teza begins to stare at the door, willing Sein Yun to appear. Sometimes when a parcel is delivered, the next prison meal is mysteriously forfeited. Teza waits, but Sein Yun does not come to explain to him what is going on, where the pen and paper came from. By six he understands that the palm-reader will not be making an appearance.

In his agitation, he eats another whole fish. And a package of la-phet. Then peanuts. He chews each peanut carefully.

Soon he must put all the food back in the box and start moving it around, trying to keep it from the ants, who have already abandoned their excavations in the wall to come and have dinner with him.

Polite creatures. He crushes a peanut and puts it on the floor to distract them from the larger store of food. This will work for a while.

He removes the pen and paper from the box and tucks them into his little bundle of clothing. He will not touch them again until he knows how they got into the parcel. And where the parcel itself came from.

His curiosity rises with the evening mosquitoes. Does the pen actually write? He retrieves the ballpoint and sets the nib to the muscled flesh of his palm, just under his thumb, like a surgeon aligning a scalpel. The entire surface of his palm sweats. His hands, he notes unhappily, are shaking. Imagine holding a gun! He surely would blow his foot off. He thinks of Aung Min on the border, an armed revolutionary.

"Aung Min," he whispers, "I can barely hold a pen."

He begins. Nothing. The point skids along his damp skin. He wipes his hand on his longyi and tries to write again. He swears. Of course the pen writes. Blue ink. He knew it would write. As soon as the ink makes its mark—he loops the line—he rubs it away with the thumb of his other hand. How amazing that these mundane objects, the tools of clerks and civil servants, should alter his narrow world so completely. He has not held a pen since he signed a confession after being tortured.

Through the air vent comes the guttural sound of a guard clearing his throat. Caught unawares, Teza drops the pen. The plastic clatter causes him an anxiety as acute as physical pain. His first impulse is to run. Run to where? Eight feet away, to the opposite wall? He knows the guard could not have heard the pen drop, but sweat floods his skin. He stands as still as he can, the white pen on the concrete floor somewhere below him, his head turned up to the air vent, where the spider rests in the center of his web. There is nothing wrong with his hearing.

He listens with his whole body.

No one is there, neither outside in the rain nor on the other side of the coffin door, but he remains motionless, straining to hear. Handsome could be sneaking up on him, ready to heave the door open and catch him.

With paper, pen. Contraband items.

No one is there.

The guard has long since passed on his rounds.

Suddenly the lights go out. Nine o'clock. Blackness falls like a blanket with a silver hole: through the air vent he can see the illumination of the floodlights high above the coffin. But the cell is in complete darkness. Teza lowers himself to his knees and begins to search for the pen. Under the watchtower, the iron-beater begins to strike out the time.

"Fucking Sein Yun."

His own words surprise him. He has not realized until now, with his hands carefully sweeping the floor, stretching out farther, farther, coming in again, that he is angry. In fact he is furious, which helps to keep his growing sense of panic at bay. He is sure Sein Yun is responsible for this. Certainly he has made it possible. While his hands pass over the layer of grit on the cold cement—the bloody thing did not fall so far! or did he kick it when the lights went down?—it becomes very clear to him that the three sheets of paper and this lost-in-the-dark pen will only make his life more difficult. He does not want them. The last beating, the drowning, is still too fresh.

If he is discovered with pen and paper, Handsome will thrash him, to death perhaps. If he survives the beating, they'll just extend his sentence. There doesn't even need to be anything written on the paper; they would sentence him by intention alone. Two, four, seven more years? Seven. Probably seven. Or ten.

There. There it is. His fingers close around the pen. *Tsshik-tsheek.* He clicks the point in and out, then crawls over to his sleeping mat. In the dark, his fingers burrow into his little bundle of clothing, where the three sheets of paper are wrapped in a clean undershirt. He slides the pen in beside the paper. Where else to hide them? There is no broken cement on the cell floor, no broken or breakable brick in the wall to create a hiding place. The ants' chambers are not thick enough for the pen. His latrine pail? Obviously not. The water pot?

Hiding places are useless anyway. In a raid, the warders miss nothing. They check the bricks to make sure they are sound. They tap the floor and dig up raw earth. If they look for something they will find it, even if it isn't there.

. 17 .

When Sein Yun comes with his breakfast, Teza does not stir from the back of the cell. The palm-reader almost skips toward him, eyes shining, and leans down to the singer's ear. "You have the paper?"

He whispers, "Yes."

Sein Yun smells of sweat and betel and cooking oil. Many of the criminals in the big halls are allowed to cook for themselves. "And the pen?"

"Yes." Teza's voice is thick with suspicion. He wonders if Sein Yun also hears the fear. Both of them glance repeatedly at the open teak door. Handsome is at the end of the hallway.

"Your friends will be pleased. They are writing messages to Daw Suu Kyi, in celebration of her release."

Teza does not reply.

The palm-reader drops to a squat. "The politicals in Hall Three want you to write something about prison conditions. They want you to write it to Daw Suu Kyi with the plan that a whole collection of letters will be sent out to the UN."

Teza quells his surprise that Sein Yun can say "UN" without a hoot of laughter and some rude comment about Westerners. No, Sein Yun's yellow face is grave. Teza asks, "Which politicals?"

"Myo Myo Than and his group in Hall Three."

Teza glances at the door. "When did you find out about this?"

"Right after Daw Suu Kyi was released. They wanted my help. Of course I said no, are you crazy? I'm a hardworking criminal, not a political gofer. But they kept at it, and I must admit they came up with some danger pay. I've earned it a hundred times over, listening to all that shit about solidarity and the movement and prison conditions—as if I don't know about prison conditions! I agreed to bring you pen and paper as long as it came in a food parcel. Forgive me, but I didn't want to carry anything on my body. Heroin and vegetables are one thing, Songbird, but paper and pen is another kettle of fish, you know what I mean? I have no idea what happened to your last parcel, but a friend of yours kept this one hanging around for a week in the holding room, until it was safe enough to repack it."

"What friend?" Teza stares hard at the palm-reader.

"You know, your powerful friend."

He can only be talking about Jailer Chit Naing, but why doesn't he just say so? Teza rubs his eyes, hiding his confusion. Something is wrong. Why didn't Chit Naing tell him directly that something was going on? Because he didn't want to incriminate himself?

As though reading his mind, Sein Yun whispers, "Let me tell you, it has been a nerve-racking time. A lot of people are risking their necks. More people than you might imagine."

"Which people?"

"The fewer names you know, the better, in case someone fucks up. Just remember that you have friends. Another criminal prisoner has agreed to take the messages out. A criminal! So don't think we're good for nothing. He leaves in four days, and the releasing officer has been doing business with him for years, so he won't be checked when he leaves." Sein Yun clasps his hands together and stands up, then squats down again just as quickly. His gold teeth gleam among the stained ones as he bends closer. "So can I tell them you'll join them?"

Teza doesn't know what to say. Sein Yun's yellow eyes shine with urgency. He breathes the words: "Why do you hesitate?"

"Because I am surprised."

"Are you afraid?"

Teza cannot reply.

Sein Yun impatiently shifts his pack of betel from one cheek to the other. "There's not much time. Myo Myo Than is waiting. We have to get the messages together."

The *we* enters Teza like a needle. *We* is the movement, the people. *We* is what he longs to feel viscerally, but cannot. He is alone. Though he is a political prisoner, he does not feel like a politician.

Myo Myo Than was Aung Min's good friend, a fellow strike leader and organizer. He was arrested just before Teza. For one week they shared a holding cell at Interrogation Center Twelve. Teza spent night after night listening to the strike leader screaming in the room across the hall. Myo Myo Than, in turn, spent his mornings listening to Teza. The destruction forged a tender bond between them. Myo Myo Than was the only political prisoner Teza shared a cell with as he became one himself.

"I need time to think."

"Songbird"—the voice is quiet, almost coaxing—"time is exactly what we don't have."

As Sein Yun backs away, he executes a serious bow. Then he picks up Teza's shit pail, makes a rude joke, and leaves the cell.

When he returns with the pail, he is petulant.

"When do you need the letter?" Teza glances at the open door.

Sein Yun carefully examines the singer's nervous countenance before answering, "Tomorrow."

"Tomorrow! How can I do it so quickly? I need to think—this is a serious decision. How can I just sit down now, after years of not writing, and do this?"

"I would have thought that nothing would prepare you better than years of not writing." Sein Yun smiles. "Listen, it's good that you only have until tomorrow. The less time this stuff is in your cell, the better."

The open expression of bafflement on Teza's face closes again into suspicion. "Why are you doing this, Ko Sein Yun? I thought you didn't believe in politics."

"I don't. But I thought, Why not do these poor bastards a favor? It's the big dream, isn't it, for you guys, sending out a message."

Teza is conscious that whatever he says will sound like an excuse. "Precisely. It is a dream. The reality is more complicated. I can't do this without thinking about the repercussions. If I am caught, if my sentence is extended, my mother will suffer as much as I will. Perhaps more." While this is true, Teza is keenly aware of his own possible suffering. Thirteen years left of a twenty-year sentence, plus seven more. Or ten. No chance, then, of an amnesty, an early release. It's hard enough for him to say *thirteen years* to himself; it sickens him to think of yet more time stolen from his life.

Sein Yun stares at him, disappointment plain on his face. "I hope you'll know what you're doing by dinner. Five o'clock. Tonight I'm supposed to tell them how the delivery went." He squints for a moment at Teza, his head cocked to one side. "You know, among your friends, there was no question that you'd join them. Perhaps you've become so much the prisoner you've forgotten the power of your name."

He spins around and takes a few mincing steps out the coffin door. A good palm-reader knows when to shut up.

T eza sits with his back pressed against the back wall of the cell. He closes his eyes and does not move. It is a hopeful paralysis. If he sits this way long enough, will he be exempt from making any decision?

To think how he craved this parcel.

Opening his eyes, he tries to keep them from straying to the bundle of clothes where the paper and pen are hidden. He tries to imagine who got the paper and pen, who put them in the box. If it's not Jailer Chit Naing, then a warder or a guard must be in on this. There could be no other way. The thought of someone with power in the cage knowing about the plan makes him feel so vulnerable that he stares for long unbroken minutes at the teak door, straining to hear the sound of them coming.

He knows there is a web outside his cell, one he cannot see and can barely fathom, because he's always lived in solitary. There are deals that people would not make in normal times. An elaborate scaffolding of secrets and lies holds up a reality no one would choose if given a choice. Who would choose to build a prison, to be part of the prison world and then thrive inside it? But the prison is manmade, and the regime is manmade;

they all made choices that brought them to this place. And when have times in Burma been normal? When has there ever been a time to make the right choice without risking one's livelihood, or one's life?

The beginning of the letter should come easily to him. He has written so much in his mind. Why does he hesitate now, when he has the paper and the ink to write the words down? What would his mother say about this hesitation? Would his father be ashamed of him?

He cannot answer his own questions.

He stares for many minutes at the brick wall, his mind circling the paper, the pen, the letter, the beautiful woman in an old house on University Avenue. Daw Suu. The woman with flowers in her hair who faced down an army. During her election campaign tour, there was a time when soldiers kneeled before her entourage and raised their guns. Teza was already in prison then, but the story made such an impression on people that a warder *and* a server told him about it. Warning her student companions to stay back, she walked toward the soldiers, calmly, stepping toward the guns like a woman stepping into fire. The battalion commander lost his nerve and ordered the men to lower their weapons.

The iron-beater strikes noon. Five hours to pass before Sein Yun comes again.

This day will be longer than other long days, and dedicated to the Paper and the Pen. He won't touch them. He'll leave them tucked away among his fraying clothes. His hands cross over his chest to rub warmth into his goosefleshed shoulders. *Tsshik-tsheek*. He still hears the satisfying sound of the inky ballpoint clicking out, clicking in.

But he won't agitate himself further by touching them. Empty hands, clear mind.

. 18 .

The iron-beater strikes one. Sixty minutes, sixty seconds to a minute, three thousand six hundred seconds in the step between twelve and one. Yet that solitary strike is one of the easiest hours of the day to miss.

Sitting, turned away from the teak door, the singer hunches over like an old man. The thin sheaf of unfolded paper rests in his left hand. In his right, he holds the pen. The longing overtook him without warning, intense, almost erotic. Now he's undone by the sweetness of blank paper. The pen has such a particular weight. He clicks the nib out and sniffs the ink, then looks down at the pale rectangle of paper; it's like the light contained by a door frame. He could go through it and be outside, speaking to the world.

The paper is not really white, it's rough second- or third-grade stuff, the color of very fine ash. There are minute constellations of flaws, blurred gray galaxies. He leans over to kiss the first sheet very lightly. His nose touches the paper, catches the earthen scent of it, damp because the cell is damp. This reminds him of his grandfather's books. He thinks of his father, the tutorials.

He knows his mother would want him to write a letter. His father? It's hard to know what he would say from across the border of his death. Myo Myo Than is writing a letter; other politicals are writing letters.

Teza returns the paper and pen to their hiding place and begins to walk back and forth, considering his options. If the letter doesn't make it out of the prison, he may very well be pacing for seven or ten extra years.

What will be left of him? Not very many teeth. Such vanity, to think first of his damn teeth! But the decline of the body can be made into a joke, if one is still capable of joking. He's afraid to think of what will happen to his mind. He already struggles to maintain a connection to the movement outside the cage, then beyond, outside the country, where his brother and thousands of other Burmese exiles live. The Thai border is not so far away.

His grandfather used to take him to a monastery in the Sagaing Hills. From his child's memory of those vine-twisted slopes, he conjures an idea of jungle and envisions a bedraggled column of men tramping through the rain on paths transformed into mud and, farther on, into muddy water. Most of them have open sores on their feet and are wearing rubber flip-flops. His brother must be somewhere among them. That's what Aung Min wanted, didn't he? To fight the regime.

He was shocked when Daw Sanda supported Aung Min's decision to go. Now he wonders what would have happened if they had left together. Obviously, the past seven years would have been very different. But Teza was determined to stay in Burma, and he did his best to persuade Aung Min not to leave. By that time his younger brother was a Che Guevara in the making. He sometimes wore a peculiar flat black cap, which drove Teza crazy—it seemed so pretentious, so un-Burmese. Tears jump, ridiculously, to his eyes. That stupid black hat. Che Guevara became Che Aung Min, though it was not socialism or communism that interested him. It didn't matter that the Western world was already making fun of democracy's many failures and hypocrisies. The Burmese didn't have that luxury. Flat black cap or not, Aung Min had already decided he was joining the armed revolutionaries, and he couldn't understand why Teza wanted to stay behind.

He left at the end of October 1988, with a flood of other student dissidents. Doctors left too, and journalists, teachers, workers of various kinds, longtime political activists who'd been released from prison or hounded by military intelligence agents.

A couple of weeks later Daw Sanda sought out other parents whose sons and daughters had departed for the border. Some of the students had phoned home in tears, or spoken in the cold, resolute voices of children who had become adults in the space of weeks. Many did not call at all, for fear of incriminating their families. Phones were tapped; private letters were opened as a matter of course. Aung Min, out of fear for his mother and brother, never called home.

Yet by routes circuitous and secret, Daw Sanda ascertained that her younger son was alive and a new member of the student militia that was being trained for combat by the Karen National Liberation Army. Teza tried not to be too impressed by the thought of his brother running around with a machine gun slung across his back, or his chest, or wherever one slings a machine gun while running; he had no idea. He asked, "They're armed?"

Daw Sanda scratched her neck.

Teza waited. His mother said nothing. "They are armed, aren't they?"

"Not exactly."

"What do you mean, not exactly?"

"Apparently there are not enough weapons for them. So they are training with . . . with sticks."

"With *sticks*? And when they attack the SLORC troops, will they throw the sticks or charge and hit the soldiers over the head?"

May May gave him a black look. He knew he should feel guilty for making the joke, but he didn't. "And their food. What are they eating?"

His mother's fine-boned face lost its regal contours; she began to cry. Ashamed of himself, Teza shifted closer and put his arm around her shoulders.

She cleared her throat. "The man I spoke to said that the last shipment of rice from a humanitarian group failed to reach them, and the Karen Army didn't have enough rice for them all." The Karen Army. Teza knew so little about the people of the borders, their struggles. He wondered how student politicals from central Burma would communicate with the Karen guerrillas of the jungle. He wanted to ask May May whether they even spoke the same language, but he bit his tongue.

Rallying herself, she said, "Besides, it's still raining. Both sides are in retreat. They're not in danger of being attacked."

They were truly mother and son in that moment, wife and child of a doctor, thinking simultaneously of rainy season diseases—malaria, wound and eye infections, typhoid, cholera. Dysentery. If the students-turned-soldiers didn't have rice, they surely wouldn't have quinine, or antibiotics, or proper wound dressings.

But Daw Sanda had learned to manage the unmanageable, the unbearable, the patently ridiculous, and the insane. Her next words sounded almost triumphant. "So they've been out in the jungle learning to snare animals for food. The Karen soldiers are also teaching them how to build huts out of bamboo. And the rice will come soon enough. It's just a matter of time. La-may ja-may," she said, that dependable Burmese refrain against ruin. *It will come, it will take time.* Daw Sanda had been saying that ever since Teza could remember. Composed again, though somber, very much the cool, beautiful moonlight of her name, she wiped her eyes as if some dust had had the audacity to blow into them.

W hen the iron-beater strikes three o'clock, Teza stops walking and stares into the stolid face of the teak door. Memory has summoned the brave ones of his life so he can ask them what he should do. He ponders what he knows, what he does not know. Two whole hours until Sein Yun comes with his tray. It's crucial to make the time go down bit by bit, like a fishbone lodged in the gullet. He begins to pace again.

. 19 .

You haven't written anything yet, have you?"

Sitting on the floor at the back of the cell, Teza shakes his head.

The five o'clock food tray clatters down. "I can't believe I've stuck my neck out like this for nothing. I'm not being paid enough!"

Teza whispers, "You said tomorrow. It will be ready when you bring the morning meal."

Already turning to the door, Sein Yun stops and stares hard at the singer. "They are counting on you, Ko Teza." Something very much like pleading—or is it fear?—raises the pitch of his voice.

"I said, it will be done tomorrow." Teza stands up, steps toward his food tray. "Give my regards to Ko Myo Myo Than."

"Of course I will."

A mosquito buzzes near his chin, lands on his chest. The singer remains motionless, watching the insect draw a long draft of blood. Who can tell what a single word, the right one, might do? He considers an entire letter. How far will it travel, whom will it find, what will it carry or leave behind in its wake? Whatever he writes will mean *You have not si-lenced me. Despite all your power, you are not all-powerful*. Men have often reduced his voice to gasps and weeping. They have crushed the power to speak from his body, from many bodies. But words written down outlive the vulnerability of the flesh. His songs still fly through the air like swallows. Recorded words can be passed along. In one form or another, they *will* be passed along. Movement is their essential nature.

Teza unwraps his contraband items, clears a place on the smoothest part of the cement floor. He picks up the white pen, pushes out the nib, scribbles again on his hand. Leaning over the paper, one knee folded in, the other leg stretched out, he begins his letter to Daw Aung San Suu Kyi with a pounding heart and a sweating brow. It *is* like writing a love letter.

He bites his lower lip as he begins, and cannot hold the pen without clenching it. How strange to see the words appearing, to feel the familiarity of writing come back into his hand like a surge of blood. He wipes his sweaty palms on his longyi. Twice he stands up and walks around, whispering the words to himself, not wanting to make a mistake on the paper. Just a few minutes before nine o'clock, when the lights in his cell go out, the letter is complete. Then the paper and the words and his anxious eyes are plunged into darkness.

The parcel is in the center of the cell. Something is wrong.

He crosses the teak coffin in agitation.

Ants have got into the box. Within the sharp anxiety of the dream, he knows they're in there, eating his food. He has to hurry. They are dangerous ants, soldiers. They will eat everything and he will go hungry again. But he can't get the parcel open. Someone has glued down the cardboard flaps. What kind of glue is this? He struggles, tearing at the top of the parcel with his long fingers.

Finally the cardboard slats give way. He peers into the box to see what's happened to his food, but only ants are there, hundreds of big ants, a busy swarm crawling out of the box up onto his hands. He shakes them away, but they keep coming because he won't let go of the parcel. Something is still inside, hidden.

He tilts it to the side. What slides out from beneath the bottom flap? Not the white pen—something else, raw pink, flecked with ants. It's a lizard, the skin already eaten off. Now the ants begin to devour the flesh on the skull. The two black eyes are still untouched, still alive. They peer up at his face.

He stares at the skinned body, the writhing mass of ants. Their heads swivel this way and that as their mandibles close on the flesh. The understanding comes as a slow wave of horror. He opens his mouth to cry out, to call someone, but no sound comes. It's not a lizard at all, though the shape is the same, the tail is there, the four short limbs. But it's not a lizard. It's a very small human fetus.

He wakes in the dark, sluiced in sweat, shaking. He whispers, "Just a bad dream, Teza." His voice sounds hollow.

The iron-beater strikes four.

He curls up like a child and rocks himself to sleep.

With lights-on at six, he wakes and checks his parcel. Indeed, the ants have discovered it—not the big ones of his dream, but the smaller breed he knows so well from their innumerable treks on the coffin walls. He picks the creatures away one by one, then lifts the parcel and walks back and forth with it in his arms.

He paces for twenty minutes or so, to make the ants abandon the hunt for a while. Then he puts the parcel down again and rereads his letter, trying to commit what he has written to memory. There are several smudges of ink, which he regrets. Two drops of sweat blur a few words.

He spends the morning in scattered meditation. A few minutes after the iron-beater strikes eleven o'clock, his stomach begins to churn. A rising anxiety causes him to sit for a long moment listening to the empty corridor.

As soon as the palm-reader opens up, Teza whispers, "It's ready."

Sein Yun hands him his food, puts a finger to his lips, whispers, "I can't take it yet. Give me your empty tray. I have to go."

"But the letter is finished."

"Handsome just asked some questions. Shh!" They freeze, listening. "He's coming down the corridor. I shouldn't have anything on me right now. I'll take it tonight." He holds his hand up before he leaves, like a traffic cop. Stop. Wait. And indeed, Teza stands there unmoving, quiet.

There is no sound in the corridor after Sein Yun's slippers slap away. Teza hears the outer door of the building close too. Server and jailer are gone. The light overhead suddenly flickers, flares, flickers again, rippling over the objects in the cell. The singer unwraps the letter once again, holds the paper in his hand. There's no need to reread it. He has it memorized.

His bare feet thump lightly across the cell. The sound reminds him of a heartbeat. Or a moth caught between his fingers. The letter sits in front of him. Evidence, he thinks. He puts it away again and paces, listening to the sounds in the corridor. In the space of an hour, he hears seven rats and as many mice pass. He can tell the difference between them by the speed of movement, the weight of small, clawed footfalls. Outside, beneath his air vent, a work detail goes by, criminal prisoners laughing and swearing; a guard coughs and spits. Occasionally there is the grumble of far-off thunder.

An hour passes. He eats another fish and drops the bones into his latrine pail. Then he paces with the food in his arms again, to confound the ants. He listens to his stomach. He waits this way all day, until the time when he begins to expect the sound of Sein Yun's footsteps. He wonders about the warders who will be on duty. Will Handsome appear again? Many things must fit into place in order for the letters to get out safely. What if a particular guard's shift changes unexpectedly? What if there is a random search that no one predicted?

He stops pacing, drops his head to the side like a puzzled dog.

Out loud, he whispers, "What is it?"

He doesn't know. He goes still, trying to hear with his body. Only his eyes move back and forth, from the air vent and the spider's web to the door, from one corner to another, crossing, going forward, sweeping back. Sudden wind howls through the tunnel between two buildings. A cry reaches him, as though across an enormous field, from another part of the prison. He listens for another cry but hears nothing.

Now and then the thunder booms in low tones, like explosions in a rock quarry. A vision flashes into his mind from last night's dream: living black eyes gaze up at him from inside the ant-filled box.

Teza crosses to his pile of clothes, takes the letter out, unfolds it. The fine hairs on his arms and neck stand on end.

He folds the letter over, once. Holding his breath, holding the edges of the folded papers, he slowly and carefully rips them in half. At first it is easy. The thin layers of paper offer no resistance, though the sound of tearing is like the world leaving him behind. He keeps at it, putting the torn halves back together between his thumbs and index fingers, tearing them again in half, in quarters, eighths, until the muscles in his hands and forearms cramp with effort. He tears the letter into fragments just slightly larger than the cheroot filters.

The smallest pieces escape, slip and flutter from between his fingers or lift off the neat piles he has set down in front of him. He carefully gathers them up. Salt sting in his eyes now, he blinks, blinks, squints. *What would make you cry?* He shakes his head slowly, back and forth, not knowing why he is doing this. But it does not feel like cowardice. He is not a coward.

The iron-beater begins to beat out five o'clock.

The scraps of paper go soft on his tongue, absorbing saliva easily. When he chews them, they become hard nuggets and hurt his teeth, so he tries to keep them small enough just to swallow them down.

ry harsh but I have becom
ounger I had to force myself
ison provides discipline beyo
mind myself of the sacrifice
your father. So history is m
complish true change is not
willing to give that up.

is belief continues to be
solace in the tenets of Bu
e all wish to tell you how
courage and metta for al

re deserving of dignity, b
strong in our commitmen
our struggle to make our coun
  deserve. The long night of Bur
  said, "All they have are guns."
also have the people's fear. Thi
strange but I am no longer afra
have dared so much, we must w

Ladling a cup of water, he keeps balling the words up on his tongue, swallowing them down. He wonders if he will be disappointing his comrades, but feels sure he is not. He feels no guilt as the letter slowly disappears back into his body. Near the far right edge of his web, comrade spider sits patiently, waiting for his dinner. Teza stops chewing as he stretches his neck to look up at the spider, the air vent. He smells the coming rain. All the warm muscles and tendons in his neck and upper shoulders are taut. The singer feels the pounding in his throat before he hears it with his ears. It's not the sound of thunder or heaving rain but the footsteps of men in the corridor.

Half the paper is already in his mouth as he pours the cup of water over the rest of the scraps in his hands, jumps back to the water pot, sloshes more water up to his mouth, swallows, gags, swallows. Coughing now, trying to cough quietly, fearing he will start choking and not be able to swallow, he pushes the rest of the wet paper into his mouth and holds his breath as he chews, willing the reflexive muscles in his throat to be calm. He has to chew to get the paper down more quickly, and he flinches at the stabbing pain deep in the roots of his bad teeth, but it doesn't matter. He moves rapidly in the small space, gracefully, as though he is a dancer and has practiced it many times, the leap back to his blanket where the pen is wrapped up.

As he uncovers the pen and crosses the coffin, he is listening hard, counting. There are at least three men. Or four. Not Sein Yun, no flip-flops. They are all wearing boots. Voices now.

The men are halfway down the corridor. The keys jangle and the long chain that holds the key ring rattles and clanks. Is it Jailer Handsome? Teza cannot tell, but he knows the meaning of the sounds. He has experienced this before, the jailer and the others coming, that chain.

The pen in his right hand is poised to the right of his right temple, pointing upward like a dart. He takes aim at the air vent, but he has never played this game with anything bigger than the bits of gravel and the uncooked peas.

The sweat gathered on his forehead trickles in rivulets onto his eyelids, into his eyes. He feels sweat on the fingers holding the pen.

They are near the door now. The singer holds his tongue between his teeth as he takes aim again.

The pen shoots from his fingers, flying upward, but too high. It falls down, narrowly missing the web. He snatches it up again and throws while he is still moving backward.

How long is a second? A minute? Ten extra years? The pen seems to float; he thinks it will go through, his shoulders have already relaxed in relief. But it hits the bottom edge of the air vent and drops into the spider's web, tearing through the silk strands and falling to the floor. The small plastic clatter causes a cramp to twist his stomach.

What would make you cry?

The heavy bolt cracks back hard, that smack of metal against metal, not unlike the smack of bamboo against human bone.

Teza! Teza!

It's his brother's voice, not his father's, not his mother's. Aung Min always had the better aim with a slingshot.

Stand still. Don't back up any more. And please, stop moving. This is your last chance; they will crash through the door in four, at the most six seconds. Close your left eye and aim a little higher. You've always aimed too low. Stop shaking. Now!

Teza exhales a small cry as he lets the pen go. His is not the spear-throw of a warrior. It is a full surrender to the realm of absurdity where he lives in the teak coffin and men break into it, where his teeth fall out and the spider's web tears away and his brother whispers to him from a country he's never seen.

The key turns in the lock a moment after the pen flies from Teza's sweating hand.

. 20 .

The small cell fills with an invasion as uncontainable as floodwater. The men crash in, brown-clothed limbs to every bare corner. Three warders and the junior jailer surround him. Each one wears boots, though he recognizes only Handsome. Teza stands, head down. There is no way to contain the flood; no matter what he says, no matter how he replies to the questions, it will not stop. The story is already written, the scene set in this cramped theater. The ending is always the same. As the voices break the air in the cell, Teza prepares himself.

We have a report of contraband now a search yes sir no sir no it's not the case Lying will not be tolerated you singing pig I do not know sir there is nothing here Your comrades from Hall Three we know them they're in the dog cells already we have reports they told us your name How do you like that your own friends betrayed you I don't know what you're talking about Where are the contraband items where are they Sir there is nothing here I swear to you sir.

Teza feels the thunder in his teeth, but the storm is inside. Four men search for something they cannot find. The prisoner is their center and they cut around him, kick apart the old sleeping mat, tear through his clothes, swearing all the while, making ugly jokes about the latrine pail. Handsome sticks his finger into the seam of the singer's single collared shirt and rips the collar off. Nothing is curled up and hidden there. A ball of clothing hits the wall, falls into the water pot. One warder, his face still soft, curved with youth, lifts up and dumps out the food parcel. Handsome begins to tear open each of the remaining seven fish. He glances repeatedly at Teza, who, head down, watches the show through the fringe of hair hanging in his eyes. The smell of salty, dried fish fills each man's nose. Inside the fish there are only delicate bones. Handsome drops the ruined pieces one by one on the floor.

"You can't hide anything from us, Songbird."

"That's because I don't *have* anything to hide from you, sir."

"What did you say?"

"I said I don't have anything to hide from you, sir."

The jailer approaches. "Lift your head. Lift your ugly head!" With only one word in his mind, Teza raises his chin. *Breathe, breathe, breathe.* On the exhalation, eyes closed, the hammer of knuckles lifts and falls, striking his cheekbone. The skin does not split, but the singer knows humans are different from animals. There doesn't have to be the smell of blood to incite bloodlust. With the first act of physical violence, the close air of the cell immediately changes, assuming a higher charge of danger. The men move more quickly. Fingers probe the corners, flat-palmed hands run over the bricks, search for the dug-out fissures, hiding places. Behind Teza's back, one of the men kicks over the water pot. Water sloshes against the wall and the singer imagines his stomach being kicked. From the corner of his eye he sees another officer upend the latrine pail over the mutilated fish. The officer spills gingerly, slowly, careful of his trousers. The smell of shit and urine mixes with that of fish.

While the warders perform the search, Handsome cleans his hands on one of Teza's shirts. He watches his men and keeps his eye on the prisoner; he scans the cell, its floor, the walls, the ceiling-without-lizards, Teza's hands hanging at his sides. Walls again, brick by brick. Back wall. Air vent.

Teza feels Handsome looking at the air vent, measuring the distance and the height with his eye. The staccato of rain is a many-layered sound the singer would like to crawl into, disappear inside.

Handsome begins to laugh, long on the exhalation, hiccuping on the inhalation. The smile on his face is that of discovery, the pleasure of sudden comprehension. The warders stop their work to look at the jailer.

They're not in on the joke yet. Teza keeps staring at his feet; he understands only too well.

"That's good, Songbird. Why didn't I think of it right away? I'm surprised at myself." Handsome approaches Teza, nodding, but addresses one of the warders. "Come with me. We're going on a treasure hunt."

Two minutes later Teza and the two warders inside the coffin hear Handsome and his helper outside in the rain. The warders stare at the air vent. Teza stares at his feet, filled with regret for their nakedness. They're like twin children he cannot save. Handsome's voice splices into the drumming rain. The other man's voice is not loud enough to hear.

"You forgot the fucking umbrella."

". . . through this puddle."

"No, it wouldn't . . . far. Here. Here." The squelch and slide of the boots is lost to the listeners inside the coffin. "Is that . . . ? No, there, in the mud!"

"Stupid bastard . . ." and then some more words the men inside the cell cannot make out. Teza's gut turns over inside him like a jellyfish. He should have told them at the beginning. They have license to beat him more savagely now, for lying.

The boots return, at a faster clip, almost running. Teza glances at the warder closest to him. Their eyes meet for an instant. He is the young one. The simple beauty of his youth is jarring, dissonant. He doesn't yell at Teza for lifting his head but immediately looks away, to the still-open door of the coffin.

There is no pause at the threshold. Handsome is suddenly back in the coffin, his fists bunched under Teza's chin, gripping the threadbare cotton shirt. "Where is it? Where did it go?"

Teza begins to cough violently. He puts on the show as well as he can, stealing a few seconds to decide whether the question is a trick, to make him lie again, to implicate him further. Handsome found the pen, didn't he? Didn't he? How could he *not* have found it? Teza closes his eyes to reply. "I . . . I don't know what you're talking about, sir." The hammer again, in his face, against his nose, which begins to bleed before the jailer has lowered his arm.

"Don't lie to me, you little fucker. Don't you lie to me! Remember, we can kill you. We can kill you just like that." A glistening lock of pomaded hair spills onto Handsome's forehead as he yanks the wooden truncheon from his belt, brandishes it threateningly. He hits the wall beside him, leaving a pink mark where the brick skin chips off. The jailer spins away from the singer, looks wildly around the cell, and screams, "Tear these open," to the young warder. He rams the truncheon back into his belt, then kicks the packets of peanuts and deep-fried beans to the young man's feet. The two other warders, halting their fruitless search to watch, form an audience.

The singer realizes the young man is being trained. Perhaps he has never done a search before. Teza recognizes the mouth clenched against its own inarticulate protest. He speaks quietly, not to Handsome but to the young warder. "If the bags are sealed, how can anything be hidden in them?"

Handsome shouts, "What the fuck did you say?"

Ignoring the junior jailer, Teza holds the young officer's frozen gaze. "I said, how can anything be hidden in the packets? They are machine-sealed. Why do you have to tear them open?"

Handsome gives the order. "Hit him."

Rain drums the roof.

"Ko Tint Lwin, hit the prisoner! I command you to hit him! Now!" Handsome turns away from Teza to face the younger man. "Tint Lwin, fucking hit him! Hit him!" In a single motion, Handsome grabs the truncheon from his belt, takes a step backward, and strikes the wall again.

"Ko Tint Lwin, you don't have to hit me. You could refuse him. You are not a dog, and he is not your master. You are free to make your own—"

"You stupid cunt!" The blow from the truncheon knocks Teza against the back wall of the coffin. His knees buckle, but his fingers grip the bricks behind him. He does not fall.

"But sir, you know I'm right. Even you don't have to do this, you are a Buddhist, it is the First Precept, we must not harm another living—"

"You fucking political prick, you are not a living being, you are just a mouthpiece for that colonialist bitch, shut the fuck up or we will kick your guts out your mouth!"

Terror has been loosened now, the tether slipped from its leg, and frantic wings beat around the cell. Handsome screams at the two other officers, who add their fists to the blows of his truncheon.

After a few well-placed hits on Teza's head and back, the jailer stands away and yells, "Ko Tint Lwin, get in there! Now! Or you will be court-martialed, you will be sent up north as a sympathizer!"

Teza is on the floor now, his eyes hidden. The young man begins to kick him. Tint Lwin, twenty-two, feels the tears coming and keeps them from his eyes by kicking. He will never again eat dried fish of any kind. The slightest whiff of it will tighten his throat to retching and remind him of this terror that is not Teza's. The singer has already retreated deep into his writhing body, though somehow he throws his voice up like a rope, and each of them, Buddhists all, hears his words, twisting as his back twists: "You will remember. You will remember breaking the First Precept. What merit can you make for this?" Now the terror in the cell belongs to the four men, whose transgressions have been witnessed by their victim and given back to them whole. When the question comes again—"What merit, what merit for your crimes?"—Handsome kicks harder.

Teza cannot tell which direction the blows will come from. He twists away from one boot and another cracks against his ribs. He does not try to shield his body, only his head, his face, his mouth. A nail of pain shoots behind his eyes, pounded deep into his ear with one stroke. Everything rings, rings, as though the iron-beater were close by, counting out the hours. Three minutes swell into four, five. Teza whimpers, groans.

"Stand up! STAND UP!" Handsome's voice. The men back away from the body at their feet, whose breath scratches the floor like an insect.

"Stand up."

In Teza's ears, Handsome's yelling reverberates as an insulated, high-pitched ringing. When he moves his head to try to turn off the ringing, a pain stabs so deep in his ear that he wonders if someone has kicked him again. He manages to push himself up onto his hands and knees, but he knows he won't be able to stand. There are other pains in other places—a jaw mauls his lower back, the teeth driven deep into the muscles at the base of his spine. His legs have begun to swell already. His longyi has come undone and fallen down his legs. He rests more of his weight on his knees, to free one of his hands. Very slowly, he pulls the bloodied white sarong back over his buttocks and legs. When his weight settles into his feet, he realizes that something has happened to his toes. He pushes himself up onto his knees and drags one leg forward, bends it as though to launch himself into a standing position. But the pain is literally breathtaking. He cannot flatten his foot; several toes are broken. A dark liquid drips on the floor.

"I can't."

"Stand up!" Handsome kicks him in the stomach and he collapses again.

The jailer waves his hand. Tint Lwin and the second officer pick the prisoner up. This is another reason that the young man will never again be able to eat dried fish; its scent blends with the animal smell of Teza's blood, which flows from his nose, his left ear, and the gash above it. He sees up close Teza's raw face, already several shades darker with contusions, the cheeks puffed out and soft like bruised mandarins.

Handsome growls, "Where are the contraband items?"

"There's nothing here." Teza works to keep the slur out of his voice. His toes—they've done something to his toes; he will fall, he is so dizzy. He leans back on his heels and reaches for the wall behind him. "You searched . . ."

"Where are the pen and paper? Where are they?"

"Sir?" Teza's voice is clearer now. Handsome and the three other officers wait expectantly. The singer continues. "Do you ever say our Buddhist prayers? *Sabbe satta abyapajjha hontu.* Whatever beings there are, may they be free from hurtfulness."

"You motherfucking asshole, what do you think you are, a holy man? Is that why you think you're here, you cunt?" Handsome slaps the prisoner across the face, then wipes his soiled hand on his leg.

Teza sways like a tree about to go down, but he does not go down.

Handsome steps close to him and roars spittle into his face. "Where is the paper? Where is the fucking pen? Where are they! If you stuck them up your ass, we'll find them!"

"*Sabbe satta avera hontu.*" Teza continues to recite the Pali prayer. Whatever beings there are, may they be free from enmity.

Handsome slaps him again.

Teza lets his head hang down. Watching two different streams of his blood drip onto the floor, he thinks of another line in the prayer. *Sabbe satta anigha hontu.* Whatever beings there are, may they be free from ill health.

Handsome nods with his chin toward the youngest warder. "Check his asshole. Maybe the pen's up there."

Tint Lwin looks from Teza's head to the junior jailer to the floor.

"Are you fucking deaf? Check his ass. Stick your finger up there." To Teza, Handsome barks, "Drop your longyi!"

The singer doesn't move. Though leaning against the wall, his legs shake from the effort of standing. His head is so heavy. But slowly he lifts it and opens his eyes.

Handsome's face has purpled; the veins in his neck and forehead bulge out. Tint Lwin is frozen, staring at Teza. The singer is covered in blood and swaying. The warders exchange nervous glances; the Chief Warden told them to exercise restraint.

Handsome notices their hesitation and gets angrier. "Didn't you hear what I said? Or are you deaf too? I'm surrounded by fucking deaf-mutes." He takes a step closer to Teza, who keeps his head up, his eyes on the jailer's eyes. But Handsome does not really see him. He screams, "Drop your longyi, you little bitch! Then turn around and bend over! Now!"

Teza astounds them all. He utters three small words. "Ma lok boo." *I will not.*

"How dare you! I'll find that letter! I'll find that fucking pen! Is it up your ass? Here, I'll help you turn around, you stupid fuck!"

The warders watch the sudden arc of Handsome's arm, rising, cutting through the air. Tint Lwin thinks *skull* and holds in his own cry as Handsome's truncheon whacks the singer's face. Teza's jawbone cracks loudly, like wood split with a machete. Catapulted sideways by the force of the blow, the singer is thrown hard against the wall, his head leading the trajectory of his body. He slides to the floor, his mouth falling open, full of blood. His mind hauls off, deep through the great banyan trees, into the dark.

. 21 .

Handsome is filled with a palpable desire to break the palm-reader's fingers one by one. How difficult could it have been to give a desperate political prisoner a few sheets of paper and a pen? It was the simplest of arrangements. The contraband would go to the prisoner in his food parcel, he would write a letter to Suu Kyi, just like the politicals in Hall Three, and then the whole filthy lot of them would get a sentence extension for breaking prison regulations. It was to be the Chief Warden's personal way of celebrating Suu Kyi's release from house arrest. Sein Yun, for his work, would get to leave the cage in eight months instead of two years. Handsome would get his recommendation to the MI. What the hell happened? Stupid palm-reader. Handsome is wondering how to explain the fuck-up to the Chief when one of the warders pipes up, "Do you think he'll croak?"

"Who?"

"The singer."

"Of course not, you ass. He's lucky I just knocked him out. That'll keep him from singing for a while."

"The Chief will be pissed if he croaks."

"What are you talking about? Nobody ever died of a whack to the face. It's good for him—he's a fucking troublemaker."

Brick gravel crunches under four sets of boots. The officers pass the watchtower now; the central prison office, where Handsome has to report, is just beyond it. As if orchestrated, the four men look up at the lit windows of the Chief's office. Handsome wonders if he has time to stop at the warders' quarters and drink some tea.

The warder won't shut up. "There were no orders to beat him like that."

"Were you in charge of the search?" Handsome grabs the warder by the elbow. "You haven't been promoted while I wasn't looking, have you? No? Still just a low-ranking warder, right? So shut up!" Handsome smirks. "I know what the Chief said. *Exercise restraint.* But you should see me when I'm unrestrained. What are you going on about, anyway? We were engaged in a cell inspection; the inmate was being uncooperative. You sound like Tint Lwin, for fuck's sake, first day out on a real job and weak in the knees."

To Tint Lwin he growls, "I'm reporting what happened in there to the Chief Warden. It'll go in your file."

Keeping his head down, Tint Lwin replies, "Yes, sir."

At the warders' quarters, Handsome glances at his watch. "I have to go and make my report."

"Should one of us come with you?" The big-mouth warder again. Tint Lwin slips behind the other men, trying to melt into the wet air.

"That's all right, I'll take care of the old fart. Go eat something. Miss Tint Lwin, where is that fucking umbrella?"

He would like to throttle the kid with the umbrella. He knows why he gets the new ones—he can be trusted to put some mettle in them—but it's an aggravating job. After two minutes of cleaning up at the sink behind the warders' quarters, he walks over to the central prison office. The Chief's apartment occupies more than half the second floor. Handsome stares grimly at the wooden building as he approaches. A staircase leads up to the Chief's door. The jailer spits at the bottom of the stairs, places his foot on the first step, pauses, looks around for witnesses, puts his foot back down. It's not that late; the Chief can wait. A cheroot will calm his nerves. He still craves a cup of tea.

All this *crap* over a pen and a couple sheets of paper.

How to explain the situation? Where are the fucking pen and paper? He stubs out the half-smoked cheroot. The rain's finally stopped. The twin demons of self-loathing and envy hover around him on his ascent. They knock at the Chief Warden's door when he knocks, which is why his fist on the wood makes such a murderous sound.

When the Chief himself opens up the door, Handsome is disconcerted. He regrets pounding so hard; usually there's a lackey. But the jailer has forgotten the time—it's late; the servant must have left already, or gone for dinner. The Chief asks him, "Have you eaten rice yet?" the polite greeting. "Yes, sir, thank you, sir" comes the polite answer from the famished man. They exchange empty smiles as the heavy-jowled, balding Chief Warden steps back and lets Jailer Nyunt Wai Oo in. Handsome's prison name disappears here.

The hallway opens into a spare room: wooden walls, simple but elegant also, the polished teak benches like sofas, covered with leather cushions the color of dried beef. A red-and-gold-trimmed Burmese harp is the centerpiece on the low table. It could be anywhere, a nice house, a fancy hotel lobby even, but there are files here too, a couple of pens, a sheaf of loose, closely printed papers, letters written in ink and turned facedown, and it's not anywhere, it's the Chief's sitting room and private office, his living quarters. Rumor has it that he doesn't go home to his place in Rangoon because his pretty young wife is screwing one of the SLORC generals' cousins. Everything, from the parquet floor to the ornate shrine on the wall with its colored electric lights, to the framed pictures of lily ponds, is nicer than in Handsome's house. That's what decades of taking bribes will do for a man.

They're still standing when the Chief lobs the grenade. "So things didn't go well with the singer."

How the fuck does he know already? Somebody must have been watching the cell during the raid. The place is full of spies. "That's correct, sir. There was no contraband in the cell."

The Chief smiles coolly. Handsome thinks, *I am fucked*. After motioning him to sit down on the opposite bench, the Chief sits down too and taps a cigarette out of a soft package. Marlboros from Thailand. Rich bastard. Then he leans forward and tamps the tobacco down by knocking the filter end on the table, just like any man does with a cheroot; it's not so different.

"Cigarette?"

"No, thank you, sir."

"Yes, you like our good old cheroots, don't you?"

Fucking superior asshole with his stupid foreign cigarettes. "I just had a smoke, thank you, sir."

"So what happened, Officer Nyunt Wai Oo?" His cigarette lighter is a gold rectangle.

"I haven't had a chance to speak to inmate Sein Yun yet, who was our aide in the work, but there was nothing in the cell, sir. I mean, nothing illegal. Some cheroots, but nothing else."

"You did a thorough search?"

"Yes, sir. We searched the area outside too, in case the inmate managed to dispose of the items in question. As you know, there is a small air vent in his cell." He hates talking like this—*dispose of the items in question*—but the Chief approves of proper speech. He's a major, and a military intelligence officer, and one of his many responsibilities is recommending prison employees for MI positions. When those employees talk like stupid peasants, the Chief tells them they will never get a job with military *intelligence*. This tired joke doubles as his favorite insult. Handsome has heard it several times and laughed politely, even mocked himself, or apologized. He courts the man's favor because he must, and he is not above dignified groveling. The military recruits prison officers who show promise, gifted men like Handsome, but the only way his talents will become known is through the Chief, who sits in front of him smoking expensive cigarettes. He's already said that in due time he will put Handsome's name forward for MI work. *Junior Jailer Nyunt Wai Oo, son of Maung Maung Gyi*. Handsome has seen the paper, but when will the Chief send it up? If he had a family connection to the upper echelon of the army, things would be much easier; he might already be out of the cage. As it is, he is very much here, hungry and tired, drained from the adrenaline rush that fueled him less than an hour ago.

"We can't prosecute Teza without evidence."

"I realize that, sir. When I spoke to Sein Yun yesterday, he said he had delivered the pen and the paper to the prisoner, just as he had delivered the same to the politicals in Hall Three. The raids there were successful, sir. As you know, there are fourteen politicals in the dog cells now."

"Yes, I know that, but we discussed the importance of inmate Teza, for the sake of . . . How to put it?" He waves his cigarette, searching for the word. "Publicity. His brother is a student leader on the border. And Teza's become an Amnesty International poster boy this year. It would be a good way of replying to all those bothersome letters and postcards—show them that we abide by rule of law in Burma, even in our prisons. If the prisoners break prison law, they face the legal consequences." The smile warms almost to beneficence as the Chief reaches down and straightens some of the papers on the table. "You know, Officer Nyunt Wai Oo, that I retire in two years. I was hoping to leave inmate Teza with an extra seven to ten before I go." The heavy cheeks and jaw quickly absorb the cordial smile. "The cell raid was very important. Obviously that didn't prevent you from botching it. If you didn't find any contraband, we'll have to drop Teza from the list of defendants. The whole point of these raids was to prosecute legally. Talk to Sein Yun. Find out why he didn't do his job."

"If you permit me, sir, I believe he did do his job. But somehow the inmate changed his mind about giving over the letter, and he disposed of it before we got to him. Someone must have helped him. Perhaps Jailer Chit Naing."

"Please, Officer Nyunt Wai Oo, keep your petty rivalries out of this office. Chit Naing has his faults, serious ones, but he's not an idiot. He's being watched and he knows it. Besides, I've already checked—he hasn't been to see the singer for more than a week. Something else happened, and I would like to know what. This was *such* a simple job, Officer Nyunt Wai Oo. You will never get a job with military *intelligence* if you can't find your ass with your hands."

"Yes, sir." His voice is genuinely apologetic, even repentant, though in his mind he has conjured up a vision of the Chief's young wife. She's on her back, and some young pig with a full head of hair is stuffing her. The thought gives him strength.

The Chief uncrosses his legs and leans over for his package of cigarettes, the gold lighter. "Now, tell me, what did inmate Teza have to say about all this?"

"He maintained that there was nothing in the cell."

"You encouraged him to tell the truth?"

"We did, sir." Handsome emphasizes *we*, trying to share the responsibility. He clears his throat.

"And he didn't change his story?"

"No, sir."

"That's odd. He's never been much of a liar, our earnest songbird. Did you consider that he could have been telling you the truth?"

"But Sein Yun said he delivered the paper and pen. In the morning, Teza told him the letter was ready. Sein Yun refused to take it, saying he would come back at five o'clock. He carried out his orders, sir."

"I see." He sounds so reasonable. But Handsome knows what's coming. The Chief Warden's nostrils flare as he speaks, "Then where the fuck is the letter and the pen he wrote it with? Just how much did you encourage him?"

There is simply no mercy in this world. "Well, sir, we beat him."

"I know you beat him. How did you *leave* him? In what condition?"

Handsome clenches his teeth. It's so infuriating that some little gofer ran up here right away to tell the Chief about the beating, some sneaky junior warder, picking up extra money or a big pat on the back for being a spy. "He was very uncooperative, sir. He was insulting." The Chief chews the inside of his cheek and waits for the answer. Handsome's neck suddenly feels sunburned; his face is hot. "I think we may have broken his jaw."

The Chief butts out a half-smoked cigarette—a terrible sign. "Who broke his jaw?"

"Sir, I said I think it *may* be broken. I'm not a doctor, so I don't know if it really is broken or not."

"Officer Nyunt Wai Oo, I respect you. At least, I try to respect you, but you don't make it easy. I'll rephrase my question so you understand. Who do you *think* may have broken the inmate's jaw?"

"I think I did, sir."

The Chief clears his throat before speaking. "Officer Nyunt Wai Oo, I gave you instructions, a *command*, to exercise restraint. I suppose you know what happens when a man has a broken jaw."

Handsome numbly examines the boatlike shape of the Burmese harp.

"When a man has a broken jaw, you fucking idiot, he cannot eat. All we need now is another bad cold to turn into bronchitis to turn into pneumonia. Remember? That's what happened with your last important political. It was AIDS on the death certificate, but the old man didn't have AIDS, did he? He died of simple pneumonia. That was a mistake we could absorb, but the singer is more important. He has to last years, as an example from '88, a living, breathing, imprisoned example to new students." The Chief Warden considers his own lecture for a moment, pleased that his own son and daughter are so well behaved. His lovely girl attends the elite school attached to the Institute of Education; his boy is studying in Singapore. It's useless to send them to regular Burmese schools, because the universities close down every time there's trouble. Then the students complain that the government is impoverishing the country intellectually by closing down the universities, but what choice do the generals have, when the campuses are infested with anarchists and subversives? This train of thought returns him to the task at hand. "Was he at least conscious when you locked up?"

"No, sir." Handsome is staring at the harp strings. They are just cotton thread; they are not real. The harp cannot make any music.

The silence lasts a long time. Finally the Chief exhales a long breath through pursed lips. "You contravened a direct order." He stands up, crosses over to Handsome's side of the table. The jailer is keenly aware of the other man's height, his gold belt buckle, his head turned away to the wall as he speaks, sharply, clearly, as though to a servant, orders obviously composed before Handsome even walked into his office. "The doctor will see him the moment he gets in tomorrow. Tonight we're doing a cell transfer. Inmate Teza will go to the white house. It will be done tonight, after lights-out. There are five new politicals in there now, NLD members. Take them to a holding cell until the teak coffin has been cleared. Open up the cell beside the coffin too, because four more men are expected tomorrow. Chit Naing will handle the singer. He's already received his orders. You are not to have contact with inmate Teza again. He is no longer your responsibility."

This is much worse than Handsome anticipated. He is scared to speak; his words tumble out in a small, gruff voice. "But sir, Chit Naing already has had close contact with the singer, we know he is sympathetic—"

The Chief interrupts. "I told you not worry about that, Officer Nyunt Wai Oo. Someone else is already keeping an eye on him. That's another duty of which you are relieved. At least I know that Chit Naing won't break any more of the prisoner's bones. Or sell his food." The Chief crosses to the office door before Handsome can defend himself against the last accusation. "It's late. That's more than enough for now. You're capable of letting yourself out, no? I'm sure that's not beyond you."

"Yes, sir." Stupid prick. He puts his hands on his knees and wears his humblest expression, his lips completely soft, his eyes downcast as he speaks. "Before I go, sir, may I just ask one question?"

The Chief Warden looks at him coldly.

Handsome meets this dead expression with the submissive hope of the inferior, the beggar. His entreaty shines in his eyes. "Will you permit me to make a search for the pen, sir?" Just getting the words out emboldens him. "I am sure it was in Teza's cell. And I am sure the inmate also wrote a letter. Paper is easily destroyed, but the pens were all marked, and I would like to try to repair some of the damage I've done by finding the one Teza used."

"A search for one pen in a prison of more than ten thousand inmates? We don't have the manpower to send warders on impossible searches, Officer Nyunt Wai Oo."

"Of course not, sir. But as I said, the pen is marked. It's traceable. And I suspect it will end up back in one of the political sections, or in another solitary cell. That's where I'll start. I'll work on it myself, overtime. You know what the politicals are like when it comes to writing. They're always trying to get their hands on pens. I also want to question the warders who were on duty. Someone will know something." He allows himself the slightest smile. "Someone always does."

The Chief Warden pulls his hand down over his mouth and ends by rubbing his chin. Handsome knows from this gesture that he's going to give his permission. How could he not? He too wants his monument, wants to be remembered for his work. "The letter-writers will be kept in the dog cells until they go to trial six weeks from now. You can have three weeks, no more. If there's anything to find, you'll find it, and I will be pleased to add Teza's name to the case. But no false evidence. This is going to be a legal trial. Personally, I have my doubts that Teza ever had the contraband items to begin with. Someone made a serious mistake." The Chief looks at Handsome's face. "You know why the palm-reader is here. Perhaps his bad luck is following him."

"Yes, sir, I have to acknowledge that as a possibility." It's a blessing that there's someone else to take a portion of the blame. But Handsome was the one who chose Sein Yun to do the work; he was the perfect, un-scrupulous accomplice. "Will he still receive his sentence reduction, con-sidering the work he did, successfully, with the inmates in Hall Three?"

"That depends on what you turn up. I'll have to think about it. Nor-mally gem smugglers who lose their boss's gems also lose their balls, so all things considered, sentence reduction or not, he hasn't had a bad deal." The Chief gives him a bland look. "All right. Report back to me in a week's time."

"Yes, sir."

"And Officer Nyunt Wai Oo?"

"Yes, sir?"

"Be discreet with the search. Control yourself. No skull-cracking, all right? No fuck-ups. We've had enough of that for a while." The Chief nods. Handsome stands and lets himself out of the office.

Walking back down the hallway, the jailer imagines pissing in the um-brella stand by the door. Humiliation provokes in him a palpable desire to make things dirty. *We've had enough of that for a while.* That stupid fake harp; it would crack over his knee like kindling. The Chief is an asshole. Handsome's always known it, but the man's never been so blatantly insult-ing before. And he's giving Teza back to Chit Naing. It's unthinkable. They're all assholes. Sein Yun is an asshole *and* an idiot. The world is crawling with people who are no better than vermin; the weakest and the strongest of them, they are everywhere, like cockroaches. *Obviously that didn't prevent you from botching it.* Handsome opens the door, shuts it with restraint, and descends the stairs quickly, letting the wood take the full pounding weight of his body.

When he's more than halfway down, the rain-slick tread lets him go. He slides and stumbles, then slips down the remaining steps, grabbing awk-wardly at the handrail. A loud yelp escapes him before he gets to the bot-tom, his leg twisted, most of his weight bearing down on the unprotected joint of the knee. Naked-faced in pain, he glances around. Too late. A guard on watch at the end of the building lopes over. "You all right, sir?"

"The fucking wood is slippery."

"Is that ankle sprained?"

"I'm fine. What are you gawking at? Go back to your post. You have a job to do, don't you? Go do it!" As the man turns away, Handsome curses under his breath, "Fuckers, all of them." He takes a careful step. The ankle is tender, but some deep tendon or ligament wraps flame around his left knee, shoots fire up the back of his leg. He walks on, refusing to limp. Even with the floodlights, it's dark, it's impossible, but he doesn't care, his eyes sweep across the brick chips, the mud, the puddles. Paper, pen, the words. Where have they gone?

. 22 .

Sir, why ask *me*?" Sein Yun puts his hand to his chest, fingers point-ing inward like a classical dancer's. "I did my job, just as I did my job with the politicals in Hall Three." In the shadow under the eaves, he glances up, almost coquettishly, at Handsome. His betel-red mouth squeezes into the shape of a shriveled heart. Then it opens. "I won-der who made a mistake?"

The little joke does not have the desired effect. The jailer grabs the palm-reader's sweater with both hands and uses it to swing him around, pushing the small, wiry body against the wall. Sein Yun's head whacks the bricks. "Sir, I've already told you the truth. Teza had the papers, he had the pen. He said he wrote the letter."

"He said he wrote the letter, did he?" Under the compound floodlights, the jailer's fine white teeth shine mauve. He holds those teeth shut to keep from talking too loudly, and the result is a demonic hiss. "Did you see the letter?"

"I . . ." The palm-reader rushes back in memory, trying to separate the papers, the hands, the cells of the past week. "I . . . don't . . . remember. I don't think I did. But maybe I did. I'm not sure."

"Remember, you little shitbag, remember! Either you saw it or you didn't. I'm not in the mood for this crap. I want to know what happened to the pen and the paper, and you're going to help me find out. Did you see the letter or didn't you?"

"No. But I'm sure he wrote it. I told you he seemed afraid to at first, but I coaxed him, talked about his friend Myo Myo Than and the others. I am sure that when I was there this morning, the letter was in his cell. He was scared when I wouldn't take it away with me. I told you that, remember?" Handsome drops the palm-reader's sweater and takes half a step backward. Sein Yun cautiously levers himself off the wall.

"Then where is it? We interrogated him. He said there was no contraband in the cell, he never had any paper or pen."

"He was lying. Or someone took them away before you got there. Who visited him during the day?"

"No one. One of my men stood guard until we got there at quarter to five. We came as fast as we could, after we did the raids in Hall Three."

"Maybe someone bribed your guard. Chit Naing . . ." The name floats in the air.

"No. Chit Naing isn't one for bribes, and the guard would never double-cross me." The jailer stares at Sein Yun's face.

"Nor would I, Jailer Nyunt Wai Oo. You know that. We've done all sorts of work together, haven't we, and I've never let you down." He returns Handsome's glare with a submissive expression. Careful not to provoke a new attack, he pulls the neck of his rumpled sweater away from his throat and coughs politely, his hand over his mouth. He has a burning desire to ask what this unfortunate disaster means for himself, but he knows it's best to allow Handsome to continue his bellowing.

"I don't even have access to the singer anymore," he yells, then immediately lowers his voice. "He's being transferred to another cell. I'm going to start a systematic search for the pen, but the Chief is right, how can you find one pen among ten thousand men? It has to be the white pen, the real one, not a fake or a plant. The trial will be legal. How about that? If there's no evidence against the singer, he won't go to court with the rest of them." He messes up his slick hair with a nervous hand, then begins to rifle through his pockets for a cheroot.

"Here, take this." Sein Yun hands him one, a good brand, still wrapped. The palm-reader can't help being amused by all this talk of the court case's legality.

"You know what this means for you, don't you, palm-reader?"

Sein Yun lifts his eyebrows slightly, trying to maintain a neutral expression.

"The Chief might not cut your sentence at all. Two more years in the cage instead of a tidy eight months."

Sein Yun is momentarily at a loss for words. "Hmm" is the sound behind his betel-stained lips as his mind scurries forward. *Eight months* is a little shoulder bag, easily slung about, just the right size for a few interesting souvenirs. *Two years,* on the other hand, weighs him down with many heavy packs and boxes of bad luck. He's taking pills for his yellow skin, but who knows what kind of pills they really are? The prison doctor is a quack or a thief or both. Six or eight months, yes, he can wait to get to a good doctor in Rangoon. Two years and he'll turn into a yellow sack of bones.

"Hmm." Sein Yun makes the sound again. His eyes are brighter. He pulls the long black hair on his chin. Though it's past lockup, he suddenly feels awake, the adrenaline mainlined right into his tongue. "Then we have to find out where the pen went, don't we? Even if the letter was destroyed, the pen has to be around somewhere. It couldn't just disappear. It's too valuable. We'll find it. I marked them all, you know that, three little cuts with a razor blade at the top, three cuts at the bottom. It can't be that difficult."

"It's going to be like searching for a needle in a haystack."

"Ah, you don't know what a palm-reader's hands can do. I've found many needles in many haystacks. You will see."

"You're full of shit. If you hadn't fucked up in the first place, I wouldn't be in this position. You bet your bony ass you'll help me with this search. We'll talk more later. I need to eat something and get the fuck out of here." Handsome's eyes stick to Sein Yun. "Go back to the hall on your own."

The palm-reader bows slightly, whispers, "Yes, sir," and steps out of the shadows.

Catching a glimpse of Sein Yun's gold eyeteeth, the jailer turns his head sharply to see if the little bugger is mocking him. But the palm-reader is already hurrying away, holding his longyi over his knees as his slippers slap the muddy ground.

. 23 .

They're on a narrow path through the trees, walking at a brisk pace. He is young again, twelve, thirteen. The child is with him, holding his hand, sometimes running a few steps to keep up. When Teza looks down, he smiles, though it hurts him, and his whole body feels a surge of love for his brother, Aung Min. Then he hears a voice calling from behind them on the path, a sad, old voice. Who is it?

His grandfather. He looks over his shoulder without stopping, but he cannot see the old man.

Teza, Teza, where are you going?

He doesn't have to call out. He just answers in his head—Hpo Hpo will hear: We're going home. The Old Man Lord of the Banyan Tree will help us find our way through the mountains.

But you said you were going home. Beyond the mountains there is only the border.

Yes, into the forest.

But my dear boy, you come from the city. Why are you going away?

We need to find the tree, Hpo Hpo, the banyan tree with the shrine. He turns to the little boy, who walks and half runs at his side, trying to keep up. Remember, Aung Min, we saw it that day when we went to Sule

Pagoda—remember? Glancing upward, the small boy smiles a solemn smile. The two of them walk more quickly, away from their grandfather's voice.

But my dear boy, Sule is in the heart of Rangoon. Don't you remember that, Teza? Teza? Can you hear me? Teza?

He *can* hear; but his decision is made. His brother's thin arm swings with his own, a small, warm hand in his hand. They will find the tree, and its nat, its keeper, the Lord of the Banyan Tree. And then they will go home.

Chit Naing is squatting beside the singer. The aluminum cup in his hand has so far proved useless. Unconscious men, even dehydrated ones, do not drink water. "Ko Teza, can you hear me? Ko Teza!" He looks at the bloody mouth that cannot drink and the horrible new angle of Teza's swollen jaw, the chin hanging loose.

A high-ranking warder has accompanied him to the cell, to help with the transfer. He stands silently beside the open door, staring down at the senior jailer and his prisoner. Sensing how carefully the man is watching him, Chit Naing tries to harden his face. The warder makes him nervous. After another fruitless attempt at reviving Teza, Chit Naing snaps, "I can't wake him. I don't know what's wrong. Go get the medic and make sure he brings morphine."

When the warder is gone, Chit Naing stands up and swears at the stench and the mess of the cell, the chunks of fish, the torn sleeping mat, longyis and shirts wet with shit and piss. He picks through the detritus until he finds a mostly clean undershirt and pours some water on it, then, squatting again, hesitates over Teza's face. He glances at the open door. Not because he cares who might be there, but because he doesn't want to look too closely at the bloody pulp near his hands.

He lowers the wet rag to Teza's left cheek, swollen but not bleeding, and slowly wipes some of the dirt away. Teza's left eye is blackened and shut, and his left ear and the cut above it are still bleeding. Chit Naing looks at the door again, anxiously this time. Where is the medic? He doesn't know what to do. If the ear is damaged inside, will he do more harm by pressing it, to stanch the blood? He is also afraid of touching the lower part of Teza's face. He places the rag against the cut above the ear, gingerly at first, then with more pressure. Very quickly the blood marks an outline on the white cotton, right around his fingers, rose deepening to crimson, dark red blossoming out under his hand until the cotton is as heavy and warm as a filet of raw meat.

"Teza. Teza!" He speaks the name loudly now, asking him to return. "Teza, Nyi Lay, wake up. Wake up, Little Brother." He presses the blood-ied cotton harder against the wound. The singer groans. His legs move slightly, walking in the air. "Teza, wake up!"

The singer's eyes don't open, but a blur of words emerges from his broken mouth. The pain of trying to speak is the rope that pulls him for-ward. Chit Naing keeps pressing the gash on his head. "Pyan-ma-la-boo." Is that what he's saying? *I'm not coming back.*

Chit Naing's fingers are slick with blood. "Little Brother, come back. You have to wake up now. Wake up, Nyi Lay." The jailer can hear the need in his own voice. "Open your eyes."

The left eye is swollen shut, but the right one opens so suddenly that Chit Naing pulls away in surprise and has to put his free hand on the floor to steady himself. He leans back over the singer, whose eye is still wide open, blinking, blinking, blinking. He's in shock; he doesn't know where he is. "You're still here, Teza. I am Chit Naing, Jailer Chit Naing. Remember?"

Sound heaves out of the singer, contorted like his jaw. The enraged cry, made of a single word, reverberates in the cell, lifting the singer's head and shoulders off the floor. The jailer can't understand. He only knows that he's pulled the singer back and Teza is furious. He starts to kick as he howls misshapen words. Suddenly the medic is there, on the other side of Teza's convulsing body. Without a word to Chit Naing, he plunges a nee-dle into the prisoner's thigh. The appearance of another man and the vis-ceral jab of pain, rather than the drug, subdue Teza. He stops thrashing immediately, but the eye, shining black and white, will not close for sev-eral minutes.

"There," says the medic, "that'll calm him down." He drops the nee-dle on the dirty floor.

"Was it morphine?"

"No, another sedative. But he'll be out for a few hours."

Chit Naing puts his hand on Teza's shoulder. It is the only gesture of comfort he dares to make. *The needle, the needle.* "Was it clean?"

"What?"

"The needle. Was it new?" His voice is too loud, unsteady. Again he becomes conscious of the warder's watchful presence at the door.

The medic tosses out a bitter laugh. "Where do you think we are, Rangoon General? I don't know—we try to sterilize the needles. Sure it was clean." He pushes his chin at Chit Naing. "You should be worried about yourself. Look at your hands—they're covered in his blood. Do you know if *he* is clean?" The medic flicks his hair off his forehead and hops over Teza. Wearing latex gloves, he probes the gash and the inflammation around it. "It's a superficial wound. He wouldn't bleed to death from that. The skull's not cracked. There are lots of blood vessels in the scalp, that's why it bleeds so much. I don't know about the ear. Punctured eardrum? The worst thing is the jaw. I can't touch that." He tilts his head sideways and down, following the contortions of bone. "It looks pretty fucked. The only one who might be able to fix that is a good surgeon." He whispers to the unconscious man, "Good luck, buddy." Then he looks up at Chit Naing again. "A truncheon, right? Who did it?"

"Handsome."

"Ah, right. We're used to cleaning up his work."

The medic scuttles the length of Teza's body, still in a squat, checking his rib cage, abdomen, pelvis, legs. When he gets to the feet, he lets out a little whistle. "I wonder how they broke so many of his toes. You can't set toes. They have to heal on their own. As far as I can tell, he doesn't have any internal injuries." With a condescending grin, he asks, "Jailer Chit Naing, sir, wouldn't you like to go wash *your* hands now? We don't know if he's sick or not. He's incredibly thin, though; that's usually a sign of it."

"That's because he's starving, not because he has AIDS." Chit Naing clenches his jaw to keep from yelling. His eyes flick from Teza's gaping mouth to the medic's bored face. "Did you bring any morphine with you?"

"Of course not. There isn't any. To get morphine, we need the Chief Warden's permission."

"You have his permission."

The medic shoots a skeptical glance at the jailer. "He'll sleep now anyway. He won't wake up until late tomorrow morning."

"If at all."

"With that jaw, he'll wish he hadn't woken up. But he will. He's not going to die from this beating—he'll live, the poor fucker. After the doctor checks him tomorrow, I'll come by and shave his head. His hair is filthy. When we're through with him, he'll be as good as a brand-new political prisoner." Chuckling at his own joke, he jumps up to retrieve his bag from the warder. "I'll wash him up a bit and dress his wounds."

Chit Naing stands up much more slowly. "I'm going to wash my hands."

"Could one of you please bring me back some water?" The medic looks around. "What a bloody mess. But here, this will do." He hands the jailer Teza's clay water pot.

It's a menial task; Chit Naing should let the warder do it. As though prompted, the other man has already stepped forward, but the jailer shakes his head. "Ya-ba-deh. It's not a problem. I'm going to the shower room anyway." He smiles perfunctorily. "You stay here and make sure our medical man doesn't accidentally kill the inmate, all right? The Chief is already in quite a state over his condition."

As he walks down the corridor, Chit Naing puts his hand out, touching the brick wall to steady himself. There is no use in hating Handsome, less use still in fearing him, but Chit Naing feels his stomach curdle with these two poisons. He gazes at the cement-block walls, the single bulb with its requisite contingent of moths. The air smells of cold water and rat shit, decay. Chit Naing knows that even his concern for Teza is tainted. The singer gives him a sense of something he desperately needs: atonement for his presence here.

He quickly turns on the tap and rubs his hands under the hard, splashing stream. What is he going to tell Daw Sanda? How can he tell her the truth and save her from it at the same time? The stink in the shower room is like the smell of his own shame.

PART TWO

FREE
EL SALVADOR

. 24 .

He opens and closes his eyes. Next blink, he opens only the right one; the left hurts too much. An unfamiliar breeze pours in, spilling like water over his face, his arms, puckered with sores. Something has happened to his head. He feels cool air on his skull. Shaved. All his dirty hair is finally gone.

He thinks, *Fuck, the things you have to go through to get a haircut in this place.* He lifts his hand to touch his head and opens his eye to look at his hand. Beyond his hand he sees a blue wall.

No, it's not a wall. Sky.

This creates a sudden vertigo in him.

Blue through the metal bars, above a dirty white wall, a real wall, plastered and stained. Out of habit, he turns his head to look for the spider in the corner. He gasps in pain and the gasp makes it hurt more. His mouth is full of scalding water. No, not water, pieces of glass. Tears jump to his eyes. He breathes, in, out, slowly, studiously, taking stock of his body. His toes. The legs. The lower back. His breath is articulate enough to tell him about the bruising, the swelling, the dislodged toe bones. With the telling he remembers Handsome, the three warders, beating him. The young one with the beautiful face: he was named. What was his name? This is a detail he won't be able to find for several days. Where is the pen? This is not a detail, it is a mystery. But it's not important now; *breathe, breathe*. He is a sac full of thudding pain, burning pain, sharp pain, so many different voices trapped in his body, calling out, falling or rising in intensity depending on where he sends his breath. His left ear. His left eye. Just like years ago, in the interrogation center. At least this time he can see out of the slit. His whole head is a throbbing sphere. There is glass in the jaw, shattered. No, not glass: fragments of wood stuck deep in his mouth, also the lower left side—his entire face feels broken. Not wood. Bone.

He breathes. The breath goes where it must, like the flow of groundwater. Rain. It rained while they were searching. Yesterday? Two or three days ago? He remembers the doctor coming in, leaving, coming back. And U Chit Naing was here. Arguing with the doctor? At a great distance, past the deep heart of all the pains, something else is pinching, crawling, pinching. It's from the outside, new, almost reassuring; his skin is alive enough to feel the bites. Where did all these bedbugs come from?

Bedbugs are a prisoner's sons and daughters. Monk's children.

The pinching becomes more insistent as it works its way through to his waking mind. They have climbed the mountain of his body, migrated to the warmest places, his armpits, his groin. Bedbugs. Why are there so many of them? He crushes a few between his nails; dozens more replace them. His blood feeds them, so many hungry mouths.

But he has lost the spider. The pen fell down and tore through the web. More carefully, he shifts the heavy anchor of his head again: *sky*. The realization gathers like a wave and crests over, the exhausted synapses connecting at last. I am not in the teak coffin anymore. I have graduated to a cell with sky. That's why there are so many bugs. Before me, two or three prisoners must have been kept here.

His face is close to the metal door, which has a swing-trap at the bottom and long bars above, all the way to the top, so he can look *out*. The white wall facing the cell is like a blockade, so that he cannot see into or be seen from the rest of the compound. But the air is fresh. At night he will be colder, but it doesn't matter; the monsoon won't last forever. *Sky*. The color is like food. As though in agreement, his stomach begins to growl. Eating the blue with his eyes, he retreats from his ruined flesh and goes down into memory.

Blue and blue and blue and blue, fathoms deep, a band of it high above the cage. Sunlight during the rains is a gift for everyone. The children are playing at the curbs; boys are covered in mud on the steaming school fields, kicking the ball back and forth, yelling. *Did you know*, his grandfather says, *that even during the day there are stars shining in the sky? The sun is a big star, closer than the other ones.* Encouraged by his grandson's surprised face, he continues in a hushed voice, leaning forward, imparting the secret: *Teza, the origin of all life is starlight.*

There is no past tense. Breathing in his slice of sky, Hpo Hpo is there with him, inside that color suffused with starlight. Who knows how old he was when the old man gave him that little gem, but here it is, in an invisible pocket all this time, filling the sky over the cage. He suddenly remembers the moon. He has not seen the moon for years. Sanda, the moon. His mother's name.

He mustn't cry. Not one tear. It would be a waste of salt. He may need them—salt and tears—later. To cry would sap his strength. Or, more accurately, compound his weakness. He will not even feel now; he will lie very still and think of football.

He remembers the mud drying in ragged stripes on their backs, down their brown legs. Aung Min, unsurprisingly, is the better football player, faster, trickier. Grass and tangled weeds border a green field that slopes here and there into soggy puddles. Give it a piece of food—*blue*—and the spirit jumps with longing, sends him running to buy cubes of ripe papaya on Anawrahta Street. He wants the orange splendor and perfume-scent of the fruit stacked on the cart, he wants the worn wood and painted green aluminum of the cart itself, set against a powder-blue wall. Now he has something bright and sweet in his mouth, easy to swallow. From there he enters the chaotic animal brilliance of a market and glories in the fabulous, overwhelming profusion of *things*. He rushes to the rows of fabric—Daw Sanda will be there, shopping for a new tamin—and gazes at the bolts standing in their places against bigger bolts, so there is no wall in this universe, no brick wall, no concrete wall, no wooden wall, no bars at all, only varying widths of rolled-up color. Black and ochre loops, the brightness of yellow birds, violet butterflies, smooth, solid expanses of cherry and pink and aquamarine from the women's dazzling patterns. The men have deep green and rust checks, deep-ocean blues, burned reds, burgundy, washed purple.

I will not return to songwriting. I will sell football uniforms to school-boys. I will grow papayas. And sell longyis. My hands will unwind rain-bow after rainbow of brightly dyed cotton.

Still staring at the blue sky, envisioning his career opportunities, Teza hears slippers approaching. This sound, like a switch turned on, returns him to the throbbing in his jaw, his eye, his ear. A breath later, he knows the gait is not Sein Yun's, that bastard. He does not move his head. Be-tween the bars, he sees striding toward him an orange rubber flip-flop and a burgundy velvet one, the latter of the sort usually worn by women. Above the slippers rise two bony ankles, two scarred shins, two moon-faced knees eclipsed by a turquoise longyi, also a woman's, judging by its color and sheen. The length is pulled up between its wearer's legs, tucked in at the small of his back, transforming the longyi into a pair of pantaloon shorts. Above this garment, a lime-green T-shirt makes a proclamation in faded English. Despite the pain, Teza's eyebrows knit together as he reads the bold black letters: *FREE EL SALVADOR*. If he could smile, he would. The T-shirt must have come from a plastic bag filled with white people's old clothes. Packed in charitable good faith on the other side of the Pacific, the shirt was sold for profit on the unpredictable streets of Asia. How very far *FREE EL SALVADOR* has come.

The impossibly colorful garments are in front of him now. The slap-ping slippers assure the singer that he is not seeing a ghost or suffering hal-lucinations. The colored flip-flops stop a few paces behind the swinging trap in the bottom of the door. As Free El Salvador squats, food tray in hand, Teza's eyes rise to his face.

Is *this* my new server? The singer blinks several times, looking past the shirt, focusing on the blue sky, then returning to the new face. No, he is not dreaming.

The server is a boy.

His face is close enough for Teza to see a dirt mark on his cheek. To see his eyelashes. And he is not just any boy.

This is the first step his mind makes: Aung Min. Teza is simultaneously amazed and disbelieving. The boy looks like Aung Min twenty years ago. When he and his brother were small, people often confused them as twins. Only Teza's height revealed him as the elder. If the boy resembles Aung Min, he also looks like Teza.

His jaw in splinters, the singer cannot speak. He looks both ways, up and down the dirty white wall, but no one—no one else, no one *big*— is there.

Teza's eyes roam the boy's face. The boy, for his part, doesn't look at Teza. Like an animal about to be captured, he holds still while Teza looks at him. So much time has passed since the singer has seen a child; perhaps any boy would remind him of his own childhood. But there is a true similarity in the narrow, high bridge of the nose, the large eyes and generous forehead. He has a rather square face, just as Teza and his brother had; a face with a solid jaw is unusual among children beloved for their fat cheeks. Teza thinks of the tea-shop children, the orphans and poor boys sent from the country to wash dishes and run trays in the city's sidewalk shops. Free El Salvador is nothing like them. His face, marked in places with faint scars, betrays none of their bewildered sadness, not a trace of their scrappy joy. He looks stoic and tough, wizened despite the broad cheekbones and chin. He has the large bony knees of chronic malnutrition, a feature the singer recognizes from his own body.

Teza slowly turns on his side, carefully lifts onto his elbow, which makes him wince. The boy starts to push the food tray through the trap at the bottom of the door. Teza leans over and pushes it back. The boy turns his head away, catching Teza, for a split second, with an almost angry narrowing of the eyes. Now the singer is not so sure. From this angle, the child's face is feral, the chin pointed, not square. The boy is a mongoose.

Teza waves his hand and tries to say, "I don't want to eat," a sentence he cannot finish because of the sudden ripping of flesh inside his mouth, as though the bone fragments are newly exploded shrapnel. The words are a cry as Teza's hand jumps forward, pushing the tray back out of the cell. The boy looks down at the food: curry soup, rice boiled to mush for the invalid. Watching Teza for a sign, he raises an imaginary dollop of rice to his mouth. Teza waves his hand, managing one word, "Sa!" *Eat.* Slowly, carefully, the prisoner lies down again and closes his eyes.

Squatting in front of the tray, the boy glances left and right, picks up the metal spoon, and slurps and swallows as fast as he can. Even if the prisoner changes his mind, he will not be able to complain, because his face is so broken he won't be able to tell anyone. There was no mistaking *Sa!* The boy's nervousness does battle with his appetite down to the last mouthful, but he eats everything. Then he carefully holds open the trap and slides the empty tray through.

Teza's eyes are closed, but he is not sleeping. He lifts up his hand: *Goodbye.* The boy turns and disappears behind the white wall like a marionette whisked from the stage.

. 25 .

After a few days, the kitchen staff, who are also prisoners, begin to eat a mouthful of peas or a scoop of boiled rice from the prisoner's tray. Through cage telepathy, they know Teza is not eating, so why should the little rat-killer get all the spoils? The boy picks up the tray at the kitchen, walks past the shrine and hospital at a clip, then slows down as he approaches the solitary cell. He doesn't want anyone to see his excitement. Once he gets inside the wall that encircles the white house, he sets the tray down on the bare wet earth, hunkers over it like a dog, and eats all but the last four or five curried peas, fishing them out of the soup with dirty fingers, scooping the watery rice into his mouth as he goes. If there is a piece of potato, he eats that too. His body is going mad with growth, but cannot grow. The rats do not help.

At night, when he tries to sleep, he feels a demon gnawing the bones inside his legs. The demon growls, *Longer*, and grinds its teeth into the bladed shinbones, the femurs, the way you might gnaw a piece of leather to stretch it. But the boy doesn't want to grow. Let me be small, he thinks, lying in his shed outside the warders' quarters. There is not enough food for big people here. Let me be small. Please. Let me be smaller.

Let me be a cockroach. He smiles. They are so quick, so *shiny*.

No. Let me be a bedbug.

He crushes one of them—there are many living in his rag bed—and looks at the blood on his fingers before he wipes it on the corrugated metal wall of his shed. If I were a bedbug, I could live off the prisoners. I would never be hungry.

The boy has treasures, which are not to be mocked. Certain people in the cage don't understand his wealth—one of the corporals regularly teases him about his beetle—but the taunts don't bother him. He is used to the ignorance of convicts and warders alike.

Sometimes his wealth is obvious. In comparison to the prisoner, for example, who has nothing but his dirty white prison garb and a blanket and a few clothes, the boy knows he is rich.

In addition to his bedding, which consists of a Chinese felt blanket and a few old longyis given to him by departing prisoners, the boy proudly cherishes the following items:

the turquoise longyi
the lime-green T-shirt
the once-white-but-now-gray T-shirt
the green school longyi
the navy-blue-and-black-striped sling bag
the box with the beetle in it (the beetle is black with red markings on
    its back, and very much alive, after two months of solitary
    confinement, on a diet of lizard shit)
Nyi Lay the little lizard
a man's tooth, upper left incisor, kept inside an empty thanakha tin
nine books of various sizes and colors, traded to him by various
    prisoners, usually for rats or drug deliveries
the big pair of underwear
many candle stubs and two lighters
half a tin can: a small shovel
the other half of the tin can: a candleholder
a stone-sharpened nail, for killing rats
the postcard of a golden-spired building, which he recognizes—not
    from memory, but from Jailer Chit Naing's explanations—as the
    Shwedagon Pagoda in the heart of Rangoon

the postcard of a Buddha from Pagan

the photograph, on cheap newsprint, of Bogyoke Aung San, the
  great general. It is stuck to the corrugated wall of the shed with
  rice-paste glue.

the photocopied photograph of Bogyoke Aung San's daughter, Daw
  Aung San Suu Kyi. Her mouth is open, talking and smiling at
  once. She does not look at the paper in her hand but out, directly
  into the boy's face. He keeps her tucked away in a book.

the lovely but rapidly disintegrating iridescent purple butterfly he
  found by the stream that runs at the edge of the prison grounds.
  It is one of the most beautiful things he has ever seen, but the
  ants keep finding it. Every time he changes its hiding place
  another flake of wing or segment of leg drops off.

Lastly, most extraordinarily, the boy owns a ballpoint pen. This is a recent acquisition. Its presence in his life is both miracle and disaster. The
pen is still so new and so wonderful, such a lucky find, that he ignores the
disaster part of the equation.

The boy is known for hunting. He stalks plastic bags, bones, good
rocks, anything useful and all things edible. One of his many jobs is rat-
killing, smashing the squeakers with his stick. He's learned to gut them
and sell them too, because prisoners who don't get food from home need
to eat rats.

When there's a storm, he's sad, because rain drips through the roof
of his shack, but he's also happy, because he knows exactly where the
rats will go.

Inside. Like giant, gray-haired cockroaches, they scuttle up the drains
into the shower rooms. They prefer the smaller buildings, where there
aren't so many people. And if it rains for a long time and a building
floods—like Hall Two, which is built in the lowest part of the compound—the rats come scurrying right back out again. But the other day,
as the storm stirred up, the boy rushed for the closest shower room drain-
pipe; he knew the rats would be scurrying in. Before he reached the shrine,
rain was already running down his face. He was racing the rats, but he
knew they had the advantage. They're the only ones in the cage who
are permitted to run. Everyone else has to walk; it's in the regulations. The

boy walked as fast as he could, almost skipping, hoping he wasn't going to be too late.

When he got to the teak coffin shower room, he stood stock-still over the open drain, his trusty stick raised in the air. His eyes scurried like the rats themselves, from wall to wall to wall, but he didn't see a single one. Rain drenched his clothes. He swore under his breath. No rats.

Just a warder walking by, who laughed at him. Shit! He was too late. The squeakers had already gone into the pipe. The men who wanted rat for dinner were going to be pissed. Still holding his stick in the air, the rat-killer started to calculate how many kyats he would lose, how much Outside food.

Blinking water out of his eyes, he growled, "Fucking rain, fucking rats," and let the end of his stick thump against the ground. He started back toward his shack and the warders' quarters, holding his skinny body close to the wall, under the narrow eaves, but the wind was so strong that sheets of rain snapped against his arms and legs. Angry to be wet and rat-less both, he put his head down and hurried forward.

That's when a small, blade-shaped thing hit the brick-chip gravel directly in front of him. A white dart. He was moving so quickly he stepped over it before his brain registered *treasure*. He carried on a few more steps, then stopped and energetically scratched his shin, as if he had a bad mosquito bite there, which he didn't. He just wanted to look around before he returned to the treasure. He peered backward, past his arm. He glanced ahead. Close to the main prison office, three warders were herding a large work detail toward the big halls; warders and inmates alike rushed to get indoors. On the far side of the watchtower, he could see warders standing guard at the doors of the big halls, but the rain and the storm's early darkness blurred them. The floodlights wouldn't come on for another hour.

The rain he cursed became a screen to hide behind. Staring at the brick chips, water puddling around his bare feet, he shuffled back four paces. Five. Standing below the air vent and above his prize, he heard the ominous drumming of boots.

Handsome's voice cracked like lightning into the cell.

Outside, the smallest hand in the cage reached down and picked up the glowing white pen.

Then, against the rules, he ran.

• • •

He takes out his prize and examines the fingerprinted length of it. When he presses the button at the top, the nib comes out at the bottom, with a quiet *tsshik-tsheek*. He draws a circle on his dirty hand. The appearance of the blue ink is like magic. He was brave enough to take the pen, so it belongs to him. He would like to keep it forever, but it's worth too much. Right now it's still too dangerous to show around, but when things calm down, he'll exchange it. The politicals will trade anything for a pen with ink.

Dried fish, meat. To feed the demon gnawing the bones in his legs.

. 26 .

The boy can't forget and tries not to remember his own story. Not-forgetting not-remembering is the best way to live in the cage. Any prisoner and most of the warders will tell you that.

His father, who was a low-ranking warder, never said such a thing, but then he wasn't much of a talker. His mother talked, and she could sing too, before the time of whispering began. But that was so long ago. And who remembers the voice of a dead woman? What he remembers-forgets is the illness that killed her.

Money meant three things only: rice, rice water, medicine. She ate all the medicine and nothing came back but blood, strings of it out of her mouth, baby snakes, such a dark, clotted red they might as well have been black. She died so long ago that he doesn't think of her anymore. Living in a world inhabited entirely by men, he forgets what a woman is, what a mother does. A very small boy, he came to the prison to help his father. He ran errands for the other warders to earn his keep. He watched his father begin to die in the same way his mother had, coughing up snakes.

They lived outside the prison grounds, across the big road, past the palm and mango grove, in a village where some houses were built of wood, but most were made of thatch and scraps of metal, random boards, even creatively mounted lengths of old linoleum. If the wind blew the wrong way, the smell of pigs and latrines filled the air. Walking back and forth every day, the boy stayed close to his father, rarely holding his hand but often touching his leg or his hip to make sure he was still there. Already his skeleton had started to ache, protesting the rice and rice water and meager vegetables, crying out in its silent bony way *not enough not enough*.

At night he sometimes heard men fighting in the streets after long sessions of drinking. They fought with knives, broken bottles. The prison was safer, a kingdom of guards with giant dogs, where the bad men were locked up and could war only among themselves. The boy stayed close to his father, watching him, making sure he wouldn't get away. When the sickness made him cough at night, the boy brought the medicine quickly. He gave him the pills, ran and brought him a cup of water without spilling. He cared for his father with a fierce tenderness but also with a clear motive of self-preservation. He was afraid of being taken away to an orphanage or becoming a road-builder. That's what you might have to do, his father told him, when I die. Carry stones or cement at one of the building sites in the city. That's where you'll have to go.

The boy fell asleep on the floor beside his father and woke every time he coughed.

But it wasn't the cough, the black snakes that got him. It was very early in the morning, still dark out. They were crossing the big road before the prison. Farther along, it opens out into a smaller road that leads up to the big gates. The truck wasn't going to the cage, though; it was barreling along on its way to Rangoon. The driver had been driving all night, on his home run from Mandalay. His eyes were full of crazy medicine, pills to keep him awake.

That's how Jailer Chit Naing explained it later.

The boy should have been killed too, because he was so close to his father, two fingers tucked into the waist of the thin man's longyi. The truck came over the rise roaring, a beast without eyes. The headlights were broken. The boy thought the truck swerved—not to miss them but to hit them, for they'd almost reached the dirt and weeds beyond the pavement. They were two steps away. He felt his father's hand hit him in the back harder than he'd ever been hit in his life—one heavy blow—and the ground shoved dirt into his mouth and pounded the air from his chest. The boy coughed as though he had the sickness; he couldn't breathe. Tears stung his eyes as he fought for air. Then he just lay on the ground for a little while, resting, pushing small pieces of dirt out of his mouth with his tongue. He felt dirt clinging to his lips and chin.

The stillness of the morning had returned, but the sun was up now, exhaling red light and heat. In the distance, he saw women walking from their village path onto the road, just as he and his father had done, except they were going in the opposite direction. He watched their straw hats until they disappeared into the rising sun. For a long time he stared at the places their bodies had occupied. Then he lay again on his side. Once, he lifted his head and looked along the side of the road, thinking his father would have fallen close by. Not until his eyes reached the middle of the lane did he find what he was looking for. He could see his father's bare feet stretching out toward him. Like hands, he thought. His eyes flitted here and there over the asphalt, searching. He felt a pang of sorrow; where were his father's slippers? They were almost new. Hpay Hpay would be very angry to lose them. He saw his father's legs too, also bare, his longyi torn and yanked up around his waist. But his body was twisted in such a strange way that the boy could not see his bloody head.

When no one came—the place was a fair distance from the prison— the boy stood up and walked to the prison gates. He discovered that one of his teeth had pierced his lip when his father pushed him; he put his hand to his mouth, then looked at the blood. He did this again and again. He told the gate guards what had happened. Two men went out with a truck and took his father's body away. The boy never knew where. No one washed the blood off the road. Afraid to go home, the boy stayed at the prison that night. He didn't want to cross the road because of the ghost of his father. Where had they taken the body? The boy didn't know, and he was afraid to ask. But he knew that an unburied body had no choice but to become a ghost, a wandering spirit. The boy felt guilty about this. But how could he have buried his father by himself? He didn't own a shovel.

He walked as far as the blood. The flies had been busy all day, licking it up. It would be gone in no time. There was a thick black mat of them making a fierce noise. Two days after the accident, he saw a bit of white sticking up out of the coagulated smears. Brushing away the flies, he squatted down. It was one of his father's teeth. Shocked that he could recognize it, he wished he'd looked carefully at his father's body. From the forgotten-remembered image of his mother, the boy knew his father's image would fade too, merge into the faces of the other men, the faces from the cage. The flies covered the tips of his fingers while he picked out the tooth. Then they sank into the small hole where the tooth had been. The flies were green as peacock feathers. Some were blue-backed. Some were brown. Many were black. He was afraid of the wasps. All together, the noise they made was like an engine, like the roar of the truck that had killed his father. He wiped the blood-rust on a leaf, put the tooth in a small box, put the small box in his sling bag, and ran back to the prison.

Only once did the boy walk across the road, through the field, and into the shantytown. He went for his other clothes and his father's clothes. Little else was important enough to take. He took his mother's tins of thanakha without knowing exactly why, for he'd already lost the childhood habit of smearing the fragrant paste on his skin. The landlord was waiting. As the boy walked down the road, the landlord came up behind him and asked for the rent. The boy explained that he had no money. The landlord said, "I'll call the police and they'll come and take you to jail."

The boy replied, seriously, "But that's where I'm going."

The landlord slapped the boy's head and grabbed his shoulder.

When the boy explained he was working at the prison now and promised to bring the rent in small amounts, the landlord released his shoulder, poked the soft place in the joint with his forefinger, and warned the boy not to lie. The boy was astounded by the uncanny way grownups could read his mind. His lie to the landlord was his first real lie. He swore he was not lying, which was his second. He understood, at seven years old, that this was a skill he had to work hard to perfect. He never went back to the house made of bamboo and leaf thatch. The cage became his world.

At first he lived in a little open storage shed near the shrine. It was a favorite place for warders to take naps and read the newspaper, and they didn't mind him bedding down in there at night. But the shrine and the storage shed sat between the hospital and the kitchen, and both Chit Naing and Tan-see Tiger warned him away from the big cook. It was the jailer's idea for the boy to make a little place outside the warders' quarters. There are more men here, coming and going, and the cook never uses the warders' latrine, because the warders hate his guts. The low-ranking warders hardly make enough money to feed their families, while the cook runs a food racket and gets fatter and richer every year. The boy made himself a shed from scraps of wood and strips of corrugated metal. The shed is low, like a doghouse, but it's his home. His treasures are safe.

The boy works hard. For cage work, he gets paid in rice and in cheroots, which he smokes like the small, fierce man he tries to be. As a rat-killer, he is popular with the inmates who do not have families to send them food. The rats are city rats, not paddy rats. Very tough, they have the taste and smell of garbage in them, like pigeons. He sells them to the prisoners, five kyats per rat, depending on how poor the prisoner is, occasionally ten kyats if the rat is big and the guy's got money. When he eats rat himself, he gets a terrible stomachache. He dislikes rat meat so much that he will trade one rodent, or two, or three, for any fair amount of Outside food, but to hold his bargaining power he keeps his desperation a secret from the prisoners.

When the men have visitors from Outside, they usually get some money. Outside is where money is made. The boy imagines that the paper kyats come from a place bigger than Hall Five, a cage full of paper and scissors. Spotting a pair of black-handled scissors in an office he was cleaning, he asked one of the other floor-scrubbers what they were. He then dared to open and close the long jaws. The cleaner took a piece of paper from the wastebasket and began to snip away. The boy watched in silent wonder as a crooked, five-pointed star fell out of the paper.

He would love to have a pair of scissors, but he's never seen them anywhere but in that office. He has seen razor blades inserted into pieces of wood, and the junkies' syringes and the metal bars whose ends are sharpened into points for stabbing—these poke bars are the best murder weapons, he knows, especially if you get the heart, the lung, or the intestine. With a few pokes in the stomach, it's hard to stanch the blood.

But with a pair of scissors, he could cut shapes out of the paper in his books. He would cut his hair instead of getting it shaved. He would cut Bogyoke Aung San's face out of a blue five-kyat bill and glue it to the wall beside his other picture of the famous general. The tan-see of Hall Four, the ruling convict of all the convicts in the entire hall, has given the boy many lessons about the Bogyoke. The big man even has a picture of the general hanging on the wall in his cell. Bogyoke was a hero, a great *soldier*. At the word *soldier*, Tan-see Tiger raises his arms and his voice. None of the soldiers today are as great as the *great* Bogyoke. And the generals, the *generals* of today are just a bunch of crooked *pricks,* nothing like the Bogyoke. He defeated all the terrible *British* and all the cruel *Japanese* who had overrun *the whole country,* which, the boy supposes, is Rangoon, Mandalay, and the immense field in between.

Sometimes the boy dreams of going to visit Rangoon. Chit Naing has told him it's less than an hour away by car, more on the bus. But the boy would never go in a car or a bus or anything else with an engine. He would walk.

And when he got there, he would see everything: the Shwedagon Pagoda, the Sule, Chinatown, the Chinese temples. These places, he knows, are made of pure gold, with real mirrors (not pieces of shiny metal) and walls full of rubies and emeralds and sapphires. Mahabandoola Street. Scott Market. Inya Lake: the prisoners have told him it is beautiful and big and shines in the sun; there's more water in the lake than he has ever seen in his life. But by foot, those places are a thousand lives away. And everything about the city feels dangerous. Next year, he thinks. I will save up some money and go. He doesn't like the road with its roaring trucks and buses. He remembers the men in his neighborhood getting on a bus with a horde of people crammed inside, going off to Rangoon to work. So many *people* out there, so many *streets*. Sometimes standing at the big cage gates makes him anxious; everything about those looming metal gates means unfathomable, dangerous departure. The man who killed his father might live in Rangoon. All those buses and trucks and cars and people, they could so easily crush a boy. Chit Naing chides him, "Nonsense! You have to go to Shwedagon Pagoda, you're Burmese. Are you just going to live out here forever and never go into the city? You have to go to a pagoda, a temple. Have you ever been to a temple?"

The boy stares at the ground. His father was a Zairbadi, a Burmese Muslim. He has dark-morning memories of his father kneeling and praying. He watches the Muslim prisoners bowing down during the day and murmuring their mysterious words to Allah. The Buddhists pray too, at the shrine before the Buddha. When Chit Naing told him that the Buddha is not the same as Allah, the boy felt the insult like a nasty pinch. *Of course* the two are not the same—what does Chit Naing take him for, a retard? Chit Naing is a kind, wise man, but sometimes he, like so many other old people, underestimates the boy's intelligence. Allah is invisible and powerful and big as the wind—that's why the Muslims bow down and whisper so much—while the Buddha is solid as clean gold, still and calm like his statue at the shrine. The boy knows these two holy forces, but no one has ever taught him how to pray. His mother was a Buddhist, and she kept a small altar in the house, but she was too weak for the pagodas.

"Well?" repeats Chit Naing. "Have you ever been to a temple?"

The boy shakes his head. The senior jailer knows many things, but how can he know the fear of getting crushed by the city? He is too big.

"Someday you will go to the pagoda, and you will like it very much. It's a peaceful place."

Yes, someday, thinks the boy, peaceful. But not now, not yet. He has too much work to do. He himself is liquid, part of the prison currency now, slipping through the corridors with messages, on missions. The boy speaks so rarely that some convicts presume he is a deaf-mute. This reluctance to talk makes him popular among the prison authorities, who sometimes choose him to do jobs on their behalf. He once overheard a senior warder say, "The little rat-killer was born with the ability to keep his mouth shut. Some of our men should take lessons from him," which pleased the boy immensely. He doesn't know what he was born with, but he quickly learned the importance of safeguarding a secret. It doesn't matter whether it belongs to a warder or a jailer or a prisoner; they're all the same. So the doctor sometimes uses him for black-market drug runs to the sick and needle runs to the junkies. Another senior warder once used him as a server to a very hairy Indian, who was on rationed meals for offending the Chief Warden. And now he has new work, serving the Songbird, which is the criminals' name for the singer. It's a job of some notoriety, a position that demands respect. The boy pretends he doesn't know this; stupidity makes his life easier.

Thus he goes about his business with great care while looking unconcerned. He moves through the cage knowing exactly how it works and who rules whom, while his thin arms swing lightly, swiftly, showing the world that he is just a child rushing along under the eaves to keep out of the rain. Without a word he delivers drugs, weapons, alcohol, little slips of paper tucked in the folded waist of his longyi. He works often, and with great loyalty, for the tan-see of Hall Four, the one who gives him history lessons about the great general. Besides running errands for him, the boy gives Tiger a massage twice, sometimes three times a week. It's *just* a massage—he walks on the big man's tattooed legs, kneads his tattooed back— Tiger doesn't like screwing boys, big or little. More than once he has said, "You just let me know, Nyi Lay, if one of these faggots tries to fuck around with you, and old Tiger will bite off his dirty head," and then he lets go a mighty, theatrical roar, grabs the laughing boy, and lifts him up over his tattooed shoulder.

The boy has his share of pleasure. In the hot season there are occasional water fights with Tiger's cronies, and now, during the rains, he enjoys long, meandering walks along the stream that runs under the cage walls and out into the world. Sometimes he listens in on jokes he can't understand, and he laughs with the men, who laugh at him for laughing. He spends some of his time with the Thai prisoners, a few of whom have become his friends, for lack of a better word. The Burmese inmates make fun of the Thais, getting back at them for wars of long ago and saying things like "Who is the economic miracle of Asia now, big guy?" The boy doesn't care about all that. He's more interested in the weird, ever-present fact of their language. If the men are in a decent mood, their chatter is like listening to birds tell stories. Before he started visiting the Thai cells, he took it for granted that everyone in the world spoke Burmese. The Thais taught him otherwise, and he hungrily learns words from their singing speech. In turn he provides them with important Burmese phrases that few others are willing to share. And because the Thai teak and drug smugglers are shocked to see a child roaming around in the cage, they always scrape together something for him to eat.

This place of brick buildings and high walls is his school and his playground and his home. He does not think of it as strange. He remembers-forgets playing with other children in the village, a long, long time ago—when he was very small. In their kindly misguided way, the Thais are right, and the boy agrees: the prison is no place for little children. Fortunately, he is not a little child. The screams in the middle of the night, the sounds of torture, the growls and stifled cries of fighting, of men raping, being raped, the stench of human shit in the dog cells, the clear evidence of men going mad or becoming cruel, the sight of men sobbing, of men dying: he is old enough to know about these things.

He trades his labor and extra cheroots for food, for treasure, for the gray, fingerprinted books he adores. Once he found a praying mantis. He fed it flies and little leafhoppers. The green mantis escaped him, though. It flew away. Now he has his beetle in a box. If the beetle leaves, he will always have the lizard, because the lizard is free but *chooses* to stay with him. The lizard walks up and down the walls, waits above the candle flame for his dinner. Sometimes the lizard chirps a little song. Like so many of the men here, who call the boy Nyi Lay, Little Brother, the boy has taken to calling the tiny reptile by the same name. One of his greatest pleasures is feeding his little brother flies and moths.

Far from the Outside, an hour-long bus ride away from Rangoon, forgetting-remembering as much as he can, the boy grows into his own life, sharp and choiceless as a thorn. He is twelve years old.

. 27 .

Because only old or unlucky men have limps, Handsome makes his sore knee carry its full weight. He walks *one two three four, one two three four*, as in police officer training, years before he came to work in the prison. He turned eighteen just before his stepfather got him a job at the local police station in their township. His future was clear early on, because the job was perfect for him: order, precision, strength, obedience. *One two three four*. He's on his way to the warders' quarters, at lunchtime; it's good to eat with the men, it builds camaraderie, a shared sense of purpose. He walks tall and winces only once, when he turns around suddenly to see who's behind him. Just that brat, the rat-killer; little bugger, he's always sneaking around. The boy keeps his head down and rushes like a small dog into his doghouse.

Handsome swears under his breath and pivots again, careful to take the weight on his good leg. The knee will get better on its own. *One two three four*. When he was a kid at the police station, it was just paperwork at first, running around for the sergeants and filling out forms and picking up supplies, but he was so good at getting the job done that they put him on guard duty the second year, and then sent him through officer training. *One two three four*, military march, it's not so different from being a military man.

That's really what he should have done, gone into the army, like anyone with a brain; that was and still is the best way to rise. But his mother wouldn't let him go; the job at the police station was already there, waiting for him. Never mind, it's not too late. All he needs is a good recommendation from the Chief Warden, and that'll be that—he'll have a new job and a different life.

That's one crucial measure of Chit Naing's lack of loyalty. The MI have wanted him for years, but he won't go. At least that's the rumor, but it has the smell of plain truth about it. Jerk. It would be such a relief to find some proof that he's not merely a sympathizer but a traitor, helping those political pricks directly. If Handsome had more money, he would put someone on him, get a man to follow him night and day, find out what's he up to. The Chief says he's taking care of it, but so what if someone's watching him in the cage, it's outside that really counts, it's outside where he'll fuck up, thinking he's safe.

Handsome pulls open the door and the men lift their heads, fearfully or obediently, or with that dull look in their eyes that means they are tired, tired of this room with its metal chairs and wooden benches and the wall calendars of the pretty singers wearing traditional dress and smiling with glossy lips, tired of the rain too, and the shit food from the kitchen every day. The warders eat what the prisoners eat.

The men turn back to their plates and begin to chew hurriedly, afraid that Handsome will call them to order before they've finished—it's happened before—and they'll have to begin the stupid search without lunch. A moment ago Handsome was hungry, ready to sit and eat and talk, but it's never like that. Whenever he walks in here, he feels the coldness, the turning away. He knows they're just afraid of him, or jealous of his status, though he tries to be the same as they are. He *is* the same, isn't he? He is also a man. But there is an invisible wall between them.

He is ready to forgo lunch and start bellowing instructions when lowly Warder Tint Lwin, umbrella-carrier, saves the meal. He is brave enough to say, "Here, sir, please sit with us, there's a lot of food left at our table." The jailer casts a disgusted glance at the men and sits down to the communal plates of food, cheap rice and cheap fish paste. At least they are served the best vegetables, properly cleaned. There is dried fish too. "Here, go ahead," says Tint Lwin, pushing the plate with the fish toward the jailer. "Please eat it."

Twenty minutes later the meal is done and fresh tea rings are sinking into the deeply stained wood of the tables. The warders who are not in on the search have already left for their hall duties, and the others are fighting the urge to close their eyes and lie down for a nap. Each of them will fit the work in around their regular duties and also work overtime for two hours without pay in the evenings. All of them are paying off debts or favors or punishments of some kind. Pretty Tint Lwin is here to prevent an insubordination charge—for not following orders during Teza's cell search—from being added to his file. Two men owe Handsome money. Another was nabbed months ago for stealing from the infirmary, and rather than disciplining him, Handsome let him keep the medicine, saying, "You will pay me for this later, you asshole." So it goes.

Handsome stands at the table, obliging everyone to look up to him as he reads the names from a sheet of paper. "Ko Tint Lwin, you will work with Ko Ohn Kyaw." He reads out the rest of the list. "U Soe Thein, your partner is Ko Win Win Gyi. The first three pairs will work in Hall Three. The second three in Hall Five. The last three go to Hall Four."

Much older than Handsome, Soe Thein is not too intimidated to speak. "But there are no politicals there."

"No, but criminals know how to write too. This is a general search for all writing materials, pens, pencils, paper, books, everything."

"We're collecting all that stuff? From the criminals too?" His voice is quiet, but the disbelief is audible to everyone.

"Yes."

"Even from the tan-see and the akhan-lu-gyi?" Hall and cell leaders are allowed unusual leniency in certain things. It's not uncommon for them to have pens, paper, books. Some of them have short tempers too, and poke bars, and razor blades.

"Yes, we're doing a full search, and any contraband items are going to be confiscated."

"But aren't we looking for a particular letter, and a pen? A white pen?"

"It is not just a letter and a pen. They are important pieces of evidence, though the letter has probably been destroyed."

"Forgive me, sir, but if we're looking for those two items, then why are we doing a full-scale raid? Why get the men all riled up about losing their love letters and their pencils for word games?" The other men laugh at their colleague's lighthearted tone.

Handsome cuts in. "If you think this work is a joke, I ask you to visit the Chief Warden and explain to him why you are so amused. We will collect *all* writing materials in Halls Three, Four, and Five. If we don't find what we're looking for there, we will also search the sentencing halls, the workshops, the kitchen, and the hospital and infirmary. Report back to me at the end of every day."

When the junior jailer begins to spout vitriol about political prisoners and their wily ways, Soe Thein breaks in. "Sir, I'm sorry to interrupt you, but one o'clock was just struck and we have other duties to attend to before we begin the search."

Handsome glares at him. Soe Thein holds his gaze for a few seconds, then looks down. There is a communal sigh of relief when Handsome says, "I hope all of you are as keen to get to work as U Soe Thein. Just one last thing. If anyone finds the evidence we're looking for, it's better not to talk about it, even to your partner. Report to me immediately with the item in question and leave the inmate who had it to me. I will do the interrogating."

After the jailer dismisses them, they file out in twos. As they pass through the doors, their voices return in the form of light conversation about the weather; they wait until they are past the central guardhouse to begin complaining about the ridiculousness of the search.

"We'll never find it."

"Of course not, any fool could see that."

Soe Thein speaks for the first time since they left the warders' quarters. "We just have to do this job as best we can. If you're not going to follow orders to the letter, then keep quiet about it so that the rest of us won't get shit if he finds out. And keep in mind that if we find this magical white pen, it might be the thing to make Junior Jailer Handsome disappear."

"What do you mean?"

Tint Lwin interjects, "He's doing this for a promotion."

"No, that's wrong. He doesn't want a promotion. He wants to leave the cage."

"How's he going to do that?"

Soe Thein lowers his voice. "He wants a recommendation from the Chief for the military. He wants to become an MI. In interrogation."

Like a pair of shackles clamped on a convict's ankles, these words silence the men and make them look down. An MI? A torturer.

"So be careful," Soe Thein warns, glancing around the small cluster of men. He adds, "But if you do manage to confiscate a bra and maybe some fancy underwear, I'll buy them off you and take them home to the wife." There are hoots of laughter before the men walk off in pairs to begin the search.

. 28 .

Sitting at the table, drinking one last cup of tea, Handsome swears when he hears the distant laughter. Pricks. The bloody warders can laugh at him as much as they want, providing they do the job. He takes out a cheroot, thinks better of it, puts it back in his shirt pocket. In a few minutes he has another meeting with that yellow rat. Besides making his regular rounds with open ears, the palm-reader says he's employing ancient techniques of divination, trying to find the pen with fortune-telling and a swinging amulet. Sein Yun can burn incense and pull magical herbs from his asshole for all the jailer cares, as long as he keeps plying people for information. Handsome gets up to leave, pulling shut the double doors behind him. Thirty paces away, he hears the faint squeal of one of those doors opening again. He looks back automatically, checking to see who's on break, but whoever it was has already slipped into the small building. This piques the jailer's curiosity. It's rare for any warder to move so quickly unless he's under orders.

He turns on his heel, leaning forgetfully into his bad knee. Exhaling a curse, he strides back to the warders' quarters and pushes open one of the doors. The boy, scraping leftover rice into a plastic bag, looks up, openmouthed. The enameled rice bowl slips from his hands and drops with a hollow clatter onto the table. "Kala-lay, what the fuck are you doing in here? Get out, you little thief. Get out! Leave the plastic bag."

Kala-lay. Sometimes the men say it offhandedly, even with affection, *little Indian*, but in Handsome's mouth it's a slight. The boy is frozen, wondering how he can slide past Handsome without getting a whack to the side of the head. Very slowly, he places the plastic bag of rice and vegetables on the table. He makes his voice small. "I'm very sorry, sir. I missed breakfast this morning, and I'm hungry, and I knew that everyone had finished lunch, sir. I'm very sorry, sir." He has taken a few paces forward, his fingers running lightly along the edge of the table. "I didn't think of it as stealing, sir."

"You didn't think of it as stealing, eh? Think again, you little brat. If you want the leftovers, you have to ask for them, not just walk in here and take whatever you want. Understand?"

The boy does not say, *I understand, sir, I have asked permission from Jailer Chit Naing, who always lets me have the leftovers.* Instead he moves with small, shuffling steps toward the door, head down, bent over in obeisance and asking-for-pity. It's working. Handsome, though still grumbling, has softened. He pulls open the door and the boy passes through it into the daylight of the compound, his neck tensed slightly, ready to receive the blow. Another moment passes; it doesn't come. He feels Handsome walking behind him, and now he's in front of his shack, which he tries to pass by nonchalantly. Standing between the shack and the jailer makes him nervous, because the treasure is in there, wrapped up and buried in a pink plastic bag, and they're looking for it now. He heard the whole thing, the big talk in the warders' quarters.

Unfortunately the jailer doesn't just swear at him again and let him off the hook. He stops right in front of the small lopsided shack. Unable to stand it, the boy looks down and closes his eyes very tightly. As if Handsome can see through corrugated metal walls and rag blankets and earth and plastic, he angrily demands, "What the fuck is this?"

To steady himself against the blast of Handsome's voice, the boy puts his hand out and grips the ragged metal edge of the low roof. Thinking that Handsome *knows*, the boy forces himself to open his eyes. And almost pees himself with relief. Of course the junior jailer can't see through the walls and under the ground. The boy solemnly answers the question at hand. "It's a stick, sir." Head still down, his voice comes lizard-quick.

"I know it's a fucking stick. What do you use it for?" The long stick is leaning against the boy's house. Handsome picks it up and swings it back and forth, fast, so it sings as it cuts through the air.

The boy stares at the jailer's boots.

"Are you really fucking deaf, then? I asked what you use this stick for."

"To kill rats, sir."

Indeed, there is a scab and splatter of dried blood at the bottom, and many gray hairs stuck in a tiny split in the wood. "How do you kill them?" Handsome's voice has shrunk.

Why is the jailer asking him these questions? Handsome has seen him hunting out back, near the stream, carrying that very stick. "I hit them on the head, or the back, or the neck, to break it." If they don't die, I stab them with my nail in the back of the neck, but the boy doesn't mention the nail because he knows that, like the convicts, he's not supposed to have anything made of metal.

"That would be a shitty way to go, wouldn't it?"

The boy is surprised. The jailer's voice is quiet and thoughtful. "Yes, sir. But at least it's fast, sir. They die really fast." The boy allows himself the speediest glance at the jailer's face, which looks very peculiar.

"I fucking hate rats. Hate 'em." Handsome talks from far away, though he's still here. He asks slowly and seriously, "Do you know why?"

Is it a trick? Will the jailer hit him now, when he least expects it? The man still has the stick in his hand. The boy tenses his neck up again to whisper "Why, sir?" though he doesn't really want to know why the jailer hates rats.

But Handsome wants to tell. "Because once, when I was about your age, I stole some money from my stepfather, just like you were stealing food."

The boy thinks, It's not the same at all. There is never leftover money.

"He was so pissed off at me that he locked me in a rice storeroom for the night, and guess what came out and crawled all over me when it got really dark?"

The boy, head still down, whispers, "Rats, sir."

This time the child's voice wakes the man up, and his voice rears up big, very loud. "Yes, rats! It was a good punishment. It was the last time I ever stole anything. So if we catch you stealing things, money or food or anything else, we'll do the same to you, kala-lay, do you hear me?" He shouts as he leans down, "Do you hear me?"

The boy whispers, "Yes, sir," but thinks, I'm not afraid of the little squeakers. He stands there waiting, knowing it will come, and it comes, a smack to the side of the head, not with the stick, very fortunately, but with the jailer's empty hand. The boy holds his ground; he doesn't let the blow knock him off his feet and he doesn't let the tears squeeze out of his eyes. Blinkblinkblink, he swallows them.

"Now get back to work, kala-lay, no more fucking around. And no more stealing."

"Yes, sir, thank you, sir." He bows a little, as though his throbbing temple were a gift. He sighs. *Never mind, don't cry.* The leftover rice will be thrown away. He reminds himself to check the garbage bins later that afternoon. He moves away from his shack as quickly as possible and walks purposefully in the direction of the kitchen. But when he gets there, he passes by, turns the corner, and heads toward the stream. Partly fed by kitchen runoff, it's a place of culinary possibilities: cauliflower stalks, old potatoes, bones. He rubs the lump on his aching head. When he kicks at a bit of brick chip, something moves.

A rat. Clambering gracelessly over a bunch of discarded tires, the medium-sized rodent carries some unidentifiable orange thing in its mouth. Mandarin peel, or mango? Or a scrap of cloth? The squeaker raises one paw from the old rubber and looks over its gray shoulder at the boy. This reminds him of a prisoner in Hall Five who requested a rat this morning.

But he doesn't have his stick. He left it behind because the jailer was still holding on to it. As the rat steps off the hill of tires and disappears into the tall grass, the boy realizes that he's glad. No stick, no whack. What a relief. Sometimes he gets sick and tired of being the rat-killer.

. 29 .

The singer meditates and sleeps. Morphine encourages both these activities. He sleeps because he cannot cry, and he cannot cry properly because he cannot open his mouth. Whenever he moves his mouth in any way, the pain takes his head and breaks it open, from jaw up into skull, a round bone under a sledgehammer. The tears amass inside him like pus.

His meditation practice is full of halts and stumbles. Sometimes he cannot be calm. Anger flamethrows through his chest and throat for hours before burning into ash and black shadows, the stuff of mourning. Unable to pace because of his broken toes, he doesn't know what to do with himself. He can't eat, he can't smoke, he can't walk. He has killed all the bedbugs in the cell. On these bad days, his rage and despair seem to be without release. They build to the point where he takes a great jungle machete in his hand, crashes through the brick wall, and emerges, slashing the air until he gets to Handsome's throat.

The worst is true. Despite his pacifism and dedication to human rights and dignity and democracy, he is a murderer, because he wants to kill them—Sein Yun, who must have betrayed him, and Handsome, that sadistic prick. His killer's hand stretches out. The Chief Warden dies. Every asshole warder he's ever had is imprisoned for three lifetimes. All the MI interrogators and torturers are executed or imprisoned for five lifetimes. The colonels and the generals are summarily executed, especially Ne Win, that superstitious old tyrant. The crooked businessmen who support the SLORC go to flooded prisons in Bangladesh, and the university administrators who abandoned the students when they were striking all go to one of the lower Buddhist hells. The soldiers who killed peaceful, unarmed people with bayonets and rifles are murdered in their turn. The Lon Htein riot police who drowned the first student protesters in Inya Lake are drowned. The soldiers who let the students suffocate to death in a police van are smothered. Every hairy, pasty-faced white businessman who uses the desperate labor of the Burmese people spends fifteen years bent over a sewing machine in a windowless, firetrap factory. In his pure, raging heart, Teza makes the old saying come true: *No one goes unpunished for his crimes*.

He has no idea how many people he kills and imprisons. Hundreds. Thousands. Sometimes these long, systematic acts of revenge arise during his meditation, and he abandons his breath and charges forward like a soldier, shooting wildly into the dark wall of trees where the invisible, ever-present enemy is waiting.

When these orgies of violence end, he wants to howl like a wounded dog, but taking up vengeful murder has not enabled him to open his broken mouth. He remains unable to weep. Spent, deeply sad, and chastised by the futility of his emotions, he returns to the humble work of meditation and inhales. Exhales. Inhales.

Teza wouldn't execute the prison doctor. He would just pulverize his face and then force him to spend an agonized convalescence with a quack like himself. The doctor is a nervous, cheerfully dishonest man with bad acne. Of Chinese extraction, he has round cheeks, a bulbous nose, and watery eyes. On each of his visits he takes Teza's hands in his own, poking and prodding the fingernails. "I check for blood flow and mineral absorption, is that all right?" It's a genuine question, as if the prisoner might refuse him. Then he slides his fingers over the still bruised and swollen skin of Teza's jaw and cheek, clucking his tongue, occasionally shaking his head. Upon finishing the examination, he lies with a smile. "Everything is fine. Don't worry. The fracture is clean, not much fragmentation of the bone, it's healing well. The only problem is eating. You have to eat. Every day, without fail. They send you extra boiled rice and fish, no?"

Teza nods.

"You eating it?"

He nods again. The doctor is not the only one who can lie.

"And no talking, even when you've had morphine. If there's too much motion at the fracture site, the bones won't knit. It could get infected, because there's lots of tearing in your left gum—that's how the bacteria in your mouth can get into the wound. And you know the mouth is a dirty, dangerous place, don't you?" The doctor laughs. Teza laces his fingers together tightly and looks past the doctor's head, through the barred door to the sky, which is mercifully blue and full of scudding white clouds.

Two weeks have passed since the beating. The doctor tells him, "The pain will lessen considerably within a month." Teza should be able to talk, after a fashion, in the same amount of time, depending on how well he heals. Before the grizzled old warder steps up to secure the locks, the doctor always smiles. This last false grin is the worst thing about the entire checkup.

Chit Naing visits him too. He is overseeing Teza again, so he comes by three or four times a week. But Chit Naing's visits are not what they once were; the old ease is gone. The jailer's anxiety infects Teza like a virus, aggravated by his pain and his inability to speak. He wants the old Chit Naing back, the serious, helpful jailer who could also crack good jokes. Eating little food, Teza craves the restorative nourishment of humor. Free El Salvador doesn't talk, the old warder doesn't talk, so Teza wants words from Chit Naing. His own speechlessness infuriates him. He can push out monosyllables if he's had a shot of morphine, but that's not enough to ask Chit Naing, "Have they found the pen? Are you bribing the doctor for the morphine? Did my mother give you the money? Have you seen her? Does she know what's happened?" Teza can't imagine where else the money to buy the drug could be coming from, because it's hardly prison policy to give pain-easing opiates to politicals. He wonders too how much longer the shots will continue.

One warm, beautifully sunny morning, Chit Naing stands at the barred door of the cell and repeats things Teza has already heard. His eyes light upon and leave Teza's face quickly, repeatedly. The singer knows that

Chit Naing can barely stand to look at him. His words are awkward, his voice full of cracked notes. "The doctor says the jaw is not so badly broken." Teza stares at the jailer's mouth and tries not to let fury get the better of him. *Anger is a bad fire.* "He says that setting the jaw would be like breaking it all over again. All the muscles would spasm. You would be in more pain. Agony." *As if pain can be measured. As if any of them can imagine it. My face will always be crooked.* "The doctor says that to do a proper job, to calm all those muscles, they would have to put you under general anaesthetic. And you know that's impossible here." *They will not take me to a real doctor outside, in a real hospital.* "And they might have to wire your jaw shut. You would lose too much weight." *Already I eat so little.* "The pain, the doctor says, will eventually subside."

Teza looks at the bones of his knees. Having recently finished his meditation, he's still sitting in half-lotus position in the middle of the cell. When Chit Naing begins rattling his keys, shuffling through the noises of departure, Teza turns back to him and holds an imaginary cheroot to his mouth.

"But how can you smoke?"

Teza shakes his head and twirls his index fingers around each other in a tiny treadmill motion. Smoking is impossible, no matter how much he would like to. He just wants to unwrap the cheroot filters. *Reading material.*

"Ah, of course. I didn't even think . . . I forgot . . . I'll see what I can do," Chit Naing quickly replies. He salvaged as much as he could from the teak coffin: soap, thanakha, Teza's clothes and blanket. There were also two plastic bags of la-phet, pickled tea leaves, still sealed. Teza regrets that he did not eat everything faster, the tea leaves and roasted sesame seeds and peanuts. It's depressing to remember the dried fish, so stupidly destroyed.

"The boy will be coming soon, with your breakfast."

Teza nods.

"Try to eat, all right?"

He nods again. Chit Naing has the courage to hold his gaze for a long breath, but he always leaves the cell without really speaking.

The singer has his generous moments, when he would like to tell the jailer, *U Chit Naing, it's not your fault. I know you're trying to help and I thank you.* But when his shattered jaw has woken him in the night and ravaged him, exhausted him with pain, it pleases him that the jailer feels awkward and ashamed. Someone should. Teza has that, at least, the power of the victim. But he knows it's a tainted weapon, all righteousness one moment and the next his own long list of executions.

He has never wanted to be the broken one. He hasn't allowed himself to be. Even crushed physically, as he was after the interrogations, as he is now, he has always sought the power beyond the body. He grew up bathed and fed and watered with the teachings of Buddhism, learning and relearning that the mental self and the physical body are only small, mutable parts of the world, ever changing and illusory, shifting like clouds. The soul, that spark of flame, continually moves toward rebirth and enlightenment, the great unbinding, where finally there is no separation. That's why the great monks do not fear death. They know their deaths come to them just as their bodies did, not as ending but as movement, the next step. It's the one thing everyone has in common.

So when the man with power stands on the other side of the iron bars, asking to be forgiven no matter what his mouth is saying, Teza on his better days tries to reply, head nodding, hands tracing thought in the air. His eyes shine with the labor of communicating a message he barely understands himself. The daily, decades-old, entrenched battle of their country ends between them, not because Teza offers forgiveness—he is not capable of that—but simply because he sees that Chit Naing is also trapped. They are both caught and struggling.

It is the First Noble Truth: *Life is suffering.* Buddha spoke these words the moment after his enlightenment. *By seeing, accepting, and comprehending the truth of suffering, eyes arose, insight arose, wisdom arose, and the light arose. Such teachings have never been heard of before.*

When his meditation goes well, Teza remembers those lines from the Buddha's First Sermon. Other times, pain sears everything from his body and memory. What light can arise from this violation? He tries to focus his meditations on letting the pain do its work without clinging to it, without identifying it as himself. This is very hard to do, especially in solitary.

. 30 .

Three weeks after the beating, Chit Naing carries a new food parcel to the white house, opens the cell, and gives the htaung win za over into the singer's long-fingered hands. A painful, gargled cry escapes Teza as he stares down at the parcel, two plastic bags wrapped around and around with sticky brown tape. It's so obviously from his mother, and full of food he cannot eat. The senior jailer had the parcel cleared the day it came in, before anyone had the chance to put his dirty hands all over it and steal whatever he wanted.

Chit Naing leaves the cell very quickly, excusing himself with talk of other duties. Teza barely notices his departure. The htaung win za is more important; his mother is inside it. Once again Teza examines the items of a food parcel.

There are five fish. Two bars of soap. Several small packages of tea leaves and sesame. Curry-dusted deep-fried beans. Peanuts. Ha! He cannot imagine eating a single peanut.

No, he cannot eat, but her presence is a different kind of sustenance. Before he undoes the careful wrapping, his double-jointed fingers move over the items one by one. She likes to fold things up in small pieces of cloth, often just scraps of old material left at the laundry, but among these pieces is a small treasure, the clearest message: a threadbare white handkerchief, its edges still embroidered, very simply, with sand-colored thread. Folded inside are two cream blocks of thanakha. The very old handkerchief is a testament to the decidedly English influence his paternal grandmother experienced while growing up. It was she, who died when Teza was still a boy, who had embroidered his father's handkerchiefs.

Outside the cage, the parcel means very little. It would be only what it is: plastic bags filled with food and toiletries, perhaps the possession of a traveler or a student going upcountry on the train. But in the cage, nothing that comes from home is inanimate.

Laying the items out on the floor, he thinks, *What I've lost comes back to me now. Not the way it was before, not the way I want, but transformed. I cannot understand it. How to comprehend the threadbare square of linen in my hand that sings to me about my father? I can only hold it, lightly, and if I could speak, I would say, Yes, I accept this gift, the love that brought it here. I hear the song in this silent thing.*

An hour later, at eleven, his server arrives. The strange boy. He's wearing the green *FREE EL SALVADOR* T-shirt again, with the turquoise longyi pulled up between his legs like shorts. His other outfit is an old white undershirt and a green school longyi. Where in the cage did he find a student's school-issue sarong? This is a minor but compelling mystery, one more reason that Teza wishes he could talk—not that the boy would answer his questions. In his green T-shirt and shimmering sarong, he comes as a bearer of color and food, not words.

Whenever Teza sees a flash, sudden as heat lighting, in those keen eyes, he expects the kid to speak. Every day he sees that spark, unveiled, and every day the small, thin body twists away from him, away from the cell. Teza wonders if it's because of his battered face, the chin warped toward the broken jaw. The black eye and other bruises are healing very slowly. Is the boy frightened of him? Has it come to that?

Two or three times a week, either Chit Naing or the old warder comes, opens the grille, and lets the boy take out the latrine pail. But whether or not an adult accompanies him, Teza is always impressed by the child's politeness. It's a matter of form, of course—the singer knows the kid eats some of the food before he appears, but he never eats it all. And when he arrives at the cell, he is a creaturely little gentleman, lifting his fingers to his mouth quickly, repeatedly, his black eyes wide with the silent query *Do you want to eat?* If Teza gives a short wave toward his body, fingers pointing down, Free El Salvador squats and pushes the tray through the aperture. If Teza shakes his head or waves his hand away, the boy drops down as he did the first day and eats everything save a few spoonfuls of the soupy rice. If they've given him boiled fish—that's what really sick ones get—the boy leaves that too. He fears the prisoner will get hungry later and regret losing his whole meal. Knowing that the free food depends on Teza's continued generosity, the boy doesn't want to offend him by appearing greedy.

While Free El Salvador deftly slurps down the boiled rice, the singer examines his face. The inflamed scratches on his cheeks and arms are from mosquito bites he has worried to bleeding—Teza has a few of those himself—and the boy has the rashes of scabies too. But where did the scar on his cheek come from? And the other gash, on his forehead?

Why is he working in the prison? Teza hasn't tried to ask Chit Naing—there are always other things to worry about when the jailer visits. Teza stares hard at the boy, as if the intensity of his gaze might open the child's guarded face. Free El Salvador's aloof expression rarely changes, not even when he's eating, head down, concentrating. Teza is no longer sure if the child resembles Aung Min at all. Maybe all boys have the innocence of brothers until you see the scars on their faces.

Chit Naing has told him the boy can talk, but for Teza, this new server is worse than the tongueless Sammy, who at least had a varied vocabulary of grunts and sighs. The boy is silent in both speech and body. The grating sound of the tray, pushed into and out of the cell, is the child's only voice. And though he makes a small, grateful inclination of his head after he eats, he also shows that he's not beholden to Teza. Occasionally, when the singer waves the food to him, he doesn't want it. He pushes the full tray into the cell and quickly leaves. Teza understands this as Free El Salvador's claim to independence.

Teza tries to draw him out. Some days he points to the sky or smokes an invisible cheroot, but the boy gives him neither a childish monologue about the weather nor a single smoke. Planning a new solicitation, Teza pushes yesterday's dented tray out of the cell. Picking it up, the boy glances at the singer, who jerks his thumb back toward the latrine pail with comical exaggeration, then rises into a half-squat and graphically mimes his need for toilet paper. Free El Salvador tosses him a lopsided grin, which might just as well mean *You are a fucking nutcase.* Then his face goes cool again. Teza sees that unreadable mouth and knows the boy won't come back with a few squares of toilet paper.

He's looking past Teza now, deeper into the cell, where he's glimpsed something on the floor. Plastic bags, small squares of laundered cloth. A little oblong block of thanakha. Things from Outside! Now the boy lifts his head slightly and actually sniffs. Teza sees him searching it out. Through the latrine pail and the damp and the prisoner's sweat, the boy catches the old-seaweed odor of dried fish.

Free El Salvador glances up fearfully, as if caught in a new act of theft. That spark in the boy's eyes has become a flare lighting his face. Without a word, the child speaks, and Teza recognizes the familiar cry: *Give me something to eat!*

But when the boy looks from the food to the singer, his expression is not one of supplication. No, he glares at the man. Teza blinks. He can't talk yet, can't move his mouth to make the words *Wait, I* will *give you something,* though he takes a step back, ready to turn and get a fish. But the boy is already standing, an angry sneer on his face. Teza gurgles sound out of his throat, trying to call him back, but Free El Salvador has turned, he's marching away. His jutting shoulder blades, the nicked velvet of his skull, and his rapid stride all proclaim that he is a boy who does not look back.

And he does not.

. 31 .

The boy hurries across the compound, fists clenched at his sides. Even that old broken-face gets food from Outside. So what? The boy doesn't care. He knows how to find his own food. He doesn't like the way the singer needles him with desperate eyes, trying to find things out. Whatever the boy's secrets are, he will keep them to himself.

He thinks of the pen. It's his now, not the singer's. Anyway, Handsome would have confiscated the pen from the Songbird. The boy's glad he buried it in his shack. No one can take away his treasure.

Wearied by this unexpected storm of emotion, the boy would like to crawl into his shack right this minute and pull his rag blankets up over his head.

But he has things to do.

First of all, he's going to fetch his own damn fish. When he returns the used tray to the kitchen, he also picks up his payment. This is a fine new job, because it gets him a fried fish every day. A small one, but not stinky and dried; this fish is cooked in oil.

Unfortunately, he must ask Eggplant the cook for his payment. Eggplant is the only fat man the boy has ever seen, a giant, oil-sweating pervert in the kitchen of the world. The boy has learned to stay away from him. He does nasty things to the young convicts who get sent up for kitchen duty. Sometimes these new inmates seem barely older than the boy, and they are much less savvy about the cage. They stumble out the back door with a beaten look on their faces even though they're not bruised.

The boy wipes his mouth and lifts his chin, trying to get a better view of his enemy. Though he hates Eggplant, this food-filled kingdom attracts him. Sometimes there are smells of fried chicken. Sometimes big bones still laced with meat sit on the chopping counters that line the entire west wall of the long building. The boy looks over the wet concrete floors, past hundreds of pots and pans, piles of vegetables, big sacks of beans and lentils. Beside the last row of gas burners, near the back doors, the cook is stretched out on a small mountain of bagged rice. His eyes are closed, but he's not sleeping. One fat hand covers his mouth as the opposite hand picks away at his teeth.

Just inside the entrance, the dishwashers squat among piles of battered trays, talking and joking among themselves. They pay no attention as the child silently adds Teza's tray to the others and then takes off his slippers, darts over to the chopping counters, and stealthily makes his way toward his fish. If the chance arises, he will steal something to eat. Beyond the cook, against the back wall of the building, two important pots contain the chief warden's food, rich curries with tender lips of fat still hanging off the meat. The boy thinks about them every time he visits the kitchen, but he'll have to wait for months before he can touch them again.

During March and April, when heat puts Eggplant to sleep like a drugged pig, the boy sneaks in after the morning trays have been collected. The cook lies on one of the cool wooden counters, a trail of saliva on the lower half of his cheek as though a snail has just emerged from his mouth. When the boy hears his guttural, sloppy snoring, he steals into the back part of the kitchen and tiptoes past the cook. By the time he reaches the big frying pans, his heart is thumping and his mouth is salivating uncontrollably. Careful not to knock any of the aluminum pots off the burners or hit a stirring spoon to the floor, he slowly lifts the large pans to his lips and drinks the leftover curry oil. There is no other taste like that of spiced, stolen oil.

He sighs. It's late August now. The sleep-inducing heat of March is still very far away.

Eggplant rolls over on his side. A crease parts in the man's oily skin, a single eye slivers open. "Come here, Little Brother, I've got something nice for you to put in that mouth of yours."

"I'm here for my fish, sir."

With surprising ease, the big man sits up and swings his legs off the sacks. "Yeah, yeah, I know what you're here for, you little brat." The cook throws his toothpick on the floor. "Are you sure you just want fish? Huh? Have you eaten rice yet? How about some nice curry? I'm sure you'd like it." He rumbles a low laugh, his hand moving back to the knot of his longyi. The boy knows better than to make any trades with Eggplant.

"I'm here for my fish, sir."

They stare at each other. The cook snorts and goes into the back kitchen, a large, covered area outside the main building, where prisoners, under Eggplant's direction, take care of the rice-boiling and soup-making for thousands of men and fry the fish for those who can pay for it.

The cook turns to one of the big scalloped frying pans, grabs the boy's payment by the tail, and quickly turns around, tossing the fish onto the slick concrete, where it flips and slides as though coming back to life. "Oh, no! The oil made it slip from my hand! But don't you worry, the floor's so clean back here you can eat off it."

The boy does not make a move to retrieve his payment from the filthy cement, but calmly stands and stares at Eggplant.

"What the fuck are you looking at? Pick that thing up and get out of here, you little Indian bastard!"

But the fat man leaves first, shaking his fat fist, calling out angrily to the dishwashers. When Eggplant has gone back inside, the boy bends down and collects his payment.

Just outside the back kitchen, he rinses off the fish at the water tap and eats it whole, bone-ladder and all. After drinking from the tap, he watches the water rush down a twisting gutter and feed into a shallow stream. On the narrow strip of land between the buildings and the high prison walls, several streams of refuse from the kitchen join other ones from the hospital. During the monsoons, this dirty confluence transforms a meandering thread of water into a real current.

The boy scans the gray-bellied clouds. It won't start raining for a while. There's time to follow the stream down to the prison walls. He steps into the water. When the stream becomes shin-deep, the gravel under his feet gives way to velvety silt. He stops to wiggle his toes and dig them deeper into the cool mud. Plastic bags bump against his calves, and thick messes of dirty cotton, oily rainbows, old leaf-wraps from betel nut, clumps of gristle, chicken feathers, the occasional chicken foot from the kitchen or a tumbling knuckle of bone. The stream is his classroom: he studies the precious refuse it carries, the creatures who drink from it and the spirits who gather between the water and the prison walls.

The current disappears under the first wall and the second wall. A warder told the boy that crocodiles and poisonous snakes live in the ravine between them, and the boy is sure that when the snakes and crocodiles go to bed, all the ghosts wake up. They are the restless spirits of everyone who has ever died in or near the prison, whether they went in a poke-bar fight or with a knife or after a beating or with dysentery or hepatitis or malaria or any other plague, including madness and sorrow and speeding trucks.

Outside the cage, the water filters into a great cesspool where mosquitoes breed by the millions. When they smell the blood of the prisoners, they rise up and fly over the snakes and the crocodiles and even the ghosts. Mosquitoes enter the cage of their own free will and torment everyone who lives there.

The boy absentmindedly scratches one of his mosquito bites as he walks with the current, enjoying the mud-suck at his toes. When he spots a half-rotten potato bobbing along the litter-strewn bank, he grabs it, wipes it on his longyi, and drops it into his sling bag. A few paces farther on, he finds a smooth green stone, and picks it up. Treasure.

He watches the banks, squints into the monsoon crop of grass and weeds. Soon one of the guards will scythe the plants down again—long grass can be used as a place to hide weapons—but for now he enjoys the green profusion with its show of purple morning glories. After checking for scorpions, he steps into a patch of grass and wipes the mud from his feet and legs, all the while humming low so no one can hear him. Sometimes in his little shack he sings a few lines over and over, a scrap of song he doesn't know how he knows. Singing makes him small again. It changes his face and gives him gooseflesh, just like when Nyi Lay, his pet lizard, comes out for a visit and eats a moth from the boy's fingers. His eyes shine then with the luster and lust of a real child, as they do now, because he's spotted the prize, a few steps away. The green lizard with a blue neck has come out of his hiding place.

This lizard is nothing like his pet; he will never live in a shack. He needs the long grasses and the rocks and stones. He's wild, like a snake. And magic, because he can change color.

The boy loves to watch the lizard slowly transform from deep green to the color of dusty aluminum. If you didn't know he was there, you would just go tramping stupidly along. The guards and the warders would never see the lizard unless he ran away from them. But the boy sees. First the blue neck fades, then the blue around his legs, then the whole bright length drains away, slowly and quickly both. The lizard can't know how it's happening, but it happens. Now he walks with lordly steps to a clump of greenery nearer the stream. He delicately stretches his head up to a blade of grass and licks at a drop of water until it's gone. Then his head clicks downward on a little hinge, and he drinks another drop. His tongue is pale red. The boy watches until his mosquito bites get the better of him. After giving the lizard a polite nod, the boy rises and backs away, scratching.

The air smells of warming earth and green stuff and flowers. Two old generators, gutted of all usable bits, sit at odd angles against the first brick wall, sunk in several inches of water; they are surrounded by a few desiccated car batteries and some discarded latrine pails. Morning glories have taken over one generator, and vines grow through the rust holes in the pails. The boy steps close to the burgeoning purple flowers and carefully gathers a collection. They wilt almost immediately, but that doesn't matter. Flowers in one hand, new stone in the other, he turns and scans the back of the kitchen and the hospital. A guard stands outside the hospital, smoking. The boy waves. The man raises his hand for a moment, then bends his head away to relight his cheroot. The boy hopes he won't watch.

Behind the hospital, close to the first of the prison walls, there stands a small tree, rooted valiantly in a bare mound of earth. The boy doesn't know the proper name of a single plant on earth, but he calls this one *holy*. Some of the warders have tied red and pink and orange ribbons around the narrow, sand-colored trunk. It's not impressive, nothing like the groves of mangoes and palms across the highway, but it's the only tree left in the

cage. The guards who believe in the spirits of trees come and leave flowers at its base or tucked between the smooth bark and the colored ribbons.

When the boy reaches the nat tree, he lowers his head, puts the stone
under his arm, and self-consciously folds his hands together for a moment.
One breath. Two breaths. Then he jumps forward and quickly tucks the
flowers into one of the ribbons. He doesn't bow down or say words,
though he thinks of his father and his mother. He could ask for protection,
but it doesn't seem right that he should ask for anything, because he's just
a boy offering wilted flowers. Should he leave the stone as an offering? But
that would be the only one, among the dried-up chains of jasmine and
branches of foliage. Some of the warders, along with prisoners who work
in the hospital, come and place tiny glasses of water and clumps of rice in
the altar box, which is painted red and sits in the crook of the tree's lowest limbs. The boy never touches this food. It's for the nat.

He squats down with his father's graceful furtiveness, but he doesn't
kneel and bow before the tree as some of the men do. If they saw a boy
whose father was Muslim bowing like a Buddhist, would they forbid him
to come here? Squatting, he stares at the colorful ribbons while fishing a
lighter and a half-smoked cheroot from his sling bag. The cheroot is
strong, stronger near the stub. Swooning, the boy puts his hand on the
ground to steady himself. He waves the smoke away from his eyes like
Chit Naing, who often tells the boy he must not smoke. After another
heady drag, he lets the coal go out, then tucks the remainder of the cigar
behind his ear.

A faint breeze stirs the leaves above him, and behind, closer to the water, something sighs through the grass. The boy smiles at the sound, and
holds his breath to listen. A lizard is licking water off the long green
blades.

. 32 .

Inside the white house, the singer stares up at his narrow slice of bright sky, darkening cloud. He wonders if somewhere in the world grows a fruit whose flesh is the same intense blue. Heaven fruit, it's called. From Africa. Or from the deepest jungle of Brazil. And what would it taste like?

Not that he wants to put anything solid in his mouth. The thought of chewing horrifies him. Managing his rice gruel in the morning is still excruciatingly painful. He has started to keep the Eight Precepts, which means he eats only his morning meal. This is a great relief for his jaw. There's an old saying that it's easy to keep the Precepts when the belly is full, but maybe it's easier when the belly is empty. In solitary confinement. With a broken jaw. Ha-ha. He lists the Eight Precepts to himself, like a child memorizing a lesson.

To abstain from harming or killing sentient beings
To abstain from stealing
To abstain from wrong conduct in sexual desires
To abstain from telling lies
To abstain from alcohol and intoxicating substances

To abstain from eating food after midday
To abstain from singing, dancing, and indulging in sensual pleasures
To abstain from high or luxurious beds

A good Buddhist must try to keep the first five. People in meditation retreat keep all eight. Monks have an even longer list. Teza wishes he could say them aloud, but he doesn't want to move his mouth. For the past few days his palate and his gums have been bleeding so much that he's swallowed a great deal of his own blood. The doctor says he should spit it out or let it drain into his cup, but moving the spitting-out muscles is so agonizing that Teza just lets the blood slide down his throat.

As though on cue, he hears someone cheerfully greet the gray-haired warder, who has arrived to open the cell. The doctor in his dirty white coat steps around the wall, holding his black bag in front of him like a badge. Or maybe a blind man's cane. "Né gaun la?" he asks, peering between the bars. Your health is good?

The fucking twit! How can the singer reply?

He can't. He just stands as the warder opens the grille. The doctor trundles in, glancing around nervously. Teza doesn't understand why the man should be so anxious; he's not the one who's being treated, is he? And *treatment* is a misnomer. He does little more than listen to his patient's heart (the clammy stethoscope sticks, as though dirty, to the singer's bone-rack chest) and look at his deeply ridged fingernails ("Mineral absorption very good!") and lecture him about moving his jaw. This is the only honest and useful counsel he gives. "You might be able to talk a bit now. But no talking!" Though he stands so close that Teza can see the festering state of the acne on his nose, the doctor still needs to shout. The singer closes his eyes and takes a deep breath. Loud sounds cut right through him these days.

The doctor yells, "No talking out loud! We have to stabilize the fracture. Your jaw is still very swollen." When he touches the distended, discolored chin, Teza can't feel a thing. "I'm worried about an infection. Today you get *two* needles." His voice drops to a dramatic whisper—"Your morphine"—because the first needle is contraband. "And it's a full dosage, more than you usually get." Then the volume goes up again. "And some antibiotic, very good quality, from China. The Chief Warden himself makes sure you get this. The Chief Warden!" His voice deepens with awe, as though he's talking about some powerful nat. One after the other, the needles go into Teza's thigh, where the veins are bigger. The ache blossoms right there, then fans out, *whoosh*. He immediately recognizes the deep flood of morphine, then feels himself falling into it.

Go, go, he thinks, watching the doctor's mouth move. The loud voice still booms off the walls, but within minutes it no longer hurts Teza the way it did before. Wherever the morphine is coming from—his mother or Chit Naing's private dealings or that most powerful nat, the Chief Warden—the singer is very glad to have it. Once he feels the drug sliding in and through and all around, coating him from the inside out, he can pronounce that he doesn't need it. He can manage the pain on his own.

Twenty minutes, half an hour later—whenever, perhaps a century after the fucking doctor has gone—there it is, here it comes, the pain. It's like this sometimes, a series of unexpected spasms. Or contractions. He is giving birth to . . . What?

The fracture throbs up and down like a bloody grasshopper. Trapped grasshopper. How will it get out? The doctor must be wrong—clean break, ha! *I am stoned.* Isn't this a good time to be honest? There's a mess inside, a grasshopper with razor legs jumping, flying inside his flesh.

But the pain is foreign, apart from him. It's like watching a horror movie happening inside his own body, but instead of being frightened, he just stares at it, fascinated. What grasshopper? If he indulges in metaphor this way, is he breaking one of the Eight Precepts? Only if poetry counts as a sensual pleasure. Does it? He is *very* stoned. Is being stoned on morphine breaking one of the Eight Precepts?

Relax, Teza. He lies down on his mat. Just breathe. He pulls his gray blanket up over his body. There is no bloody grasshopper in your mouth.

It is very similar to meditation—you can still feel the pain, but it doesn't really hurt. Or it hurts, very much, but you are far, far away from it, listening to some other music.

There's a sudden flicker at the wall's edge. Free El Salvador, his grubby little hands!

But it's not the boy. It's a lizard, scurrying up the wall. Hunting.

Watching the reptile, the singer feels various emotions expand and fill his chest like clouds that change with the wind, curiosity shifting to sadness billowing into grief. But not only grief, something else. He sees and hears pieces of the strange dreams he's had these past few weeks. His grandfather's disembodied voice calls out through tall trees. Ants devour a fetus. Lizard claws curl around his arm. The visions of a man, he thinks, who wants to leave his cage.

His eye flits up again, following the lizard on the outer wall as it rushes forward, eats a black speck of insect. An unexpected gratitude washes through him. He's happy to see the creature but have absolutely no interest in eating it. The days of that awful hunt are over. They will not come again.

What will come in their stead? With this question shimmering in his mind, he closes his eyes and immediately drops into a deep, blue-dream sleep. He's floating in the sky. No, it's water. Yet he's not wet.

And I'm not really sleeping! he thinks craftily, like a child who has succeeded in fooling his parents. I'm just dreaming. No, it's not a dream. I am remembering. But the memory has the measurements of a dream, the same lucidity and length and weight. He is sneaking into their neighbor's compound. And Aung Min is just ahead of him, crouched like a warrior.

My eyes are closed, yet I see everything. He knows he's in the cage, but the memory-dream pulls him down inexorably. Teza's the rear guard this time. Aung Min's the scout. His own little brother. He recognizes his longyi, the shape of his body, and feels a sharp jab of pain in his jaw. He mustn't shout out loud. Only inside the dream. The memory, where he can say anything he wants. He could even sing.

Aung Min!

Aung Min turns and grins, then waves him forward. He creeps along, eyes on the wall. Teza glances back to the low gates of the long, narrow yard. They don't want the wrong person to catch them at it. Though they're allowed to enter U Toe Khaing's compound, what they're doing could get them into trouble. Old Uncle Toe Khaing wouldn't care. If he were sitting outside his little flat right now (as he likes to do, in that saggy canvas chair), he might not even notice, because he's always reading a dog-eared magazine, his thick glasses perched at the very end of his wide, flat nose. Sometimes you can't tell if he's snoozing until the magazine falls out of his hand. Teza's not worried about him. But if May May finds out . . .

They are both avid slingshot warriors. Aung Min holds his hand behind him—*Wait!* They both go still, eyeing their prey on the plastered brick wall. Slowly the younger brother cradles a rock in the thick rubber band of the sling, stretches it back, and sends the missile flying through the air. A small gray-green house lizard gets it right in the head—there's the bull's-eye of blood on the whitewash—and drops into the grass below. Aung Min always hits more than Teza. But both of them are delighted enough to let out bloodthirsty shouts of triumph as they rush to the wall and squat over their kill. The creature's still convulsing in the weeds, flipping around like a burned leech. The head is all red and misshapen, but look—he's trying to run away and keeps falling over instead, legs kicking the air. To see a lizard fall over and wriggle like that is very odd—they're usually so quick, so agile. The sight of it makes the boys feel strange, embarrassed for the pathetic thing. Looking for distraction, Teza takes aim at a bird, shoots, misses so badly that his prey doesn't even fly away. It just squawks, as though irritated, and hops to a different branch. Aung Min laughs. "You've never hit a bird in your life!"

Then they both hear the sound and freeze. A she-tiger. Other mothers nag or scream in high-pitched voices. But when their May May is angry, she mutters so quietly under her breath that it sounds exactly like a growl. Teza whispers, "Oh, shit." The brothers turn around together. There she is, slowly walking in their direction. By the time Daw Sanda is standing before them, her arms crossed over her chest, she is silent. Aung Min squirms beside Teza, who stands very still. Daw Sanda pierces her sons with eyes like black-tipped darts.

"May May—" Teza begins, his voice cracking.

"Go home. Now."

Back in their own flat, they have to sit in tall wooden chairs in the front room, where the black-and-white photos hang on the wall. Teza looks at the altar above the pictures. He can smell the incense lingering in the air. Because the boys are sitting, May May glares down at them from a great height. "You know that when you kill anything, you break the First Precept—*I refrain from killing*."

Guilty sons. They cannot look at her, their good mother, who ostensibly goes without meat to purify herself but in fact gives her share to the boys.

"And can you imagine how afraid you would be if some giant, boy-hating nat came and started aiming stones at your little heads?"

Squirming, Aung Min interjects, "But we were just playing—"

"Playing? That's how you play? By taking the lives of other creatures?" They shrink in their chairs.

"Imagine if some angry nat was playing with you that way, throwing stones at your head, making you run this way and that in the street, without a place to hide, like the lizards on U Toe Khaing's newly plastered wall? Not even a single crack to make an escape! You're so much bigger than they are!"

Aung Min has killed more lizards, so he cries more. Tears drown his eyes and spill down his face. Teza is less remorseful but more ashamed. As the elder son, he should know better.

"No, no," she announces, imperious. "No crying. Go to Sule Hpaya before it gets dark. And get up with me in the morning to give alms to the monks. Making merit is better than crying."

It's not the first time she has sent them alone to the pagoda. This puzzles Teza. Normal mothers do not send their children alone to temples and pagodas. But Daw Sanda is not normal. She is very tough. She wants her sons to become responsible for the religion.

They stand immediately, eyeing the door. "I will give you enough to buy flowers and incense. Nothing else! And keep in mind, this is your allowance money." Teza pockets the change. Once outside, they walk quickly through the late-afternoon heat. In an attempt to remain solemn, they discuss the possibility of a giant nat pounding down Mahabandoola Street like Godzilla, pelting them to smithereens with stones.

"Do you really think it could happen?"

"No, Nyi Lay, she told us that because she doesn't want us to kill lizards."

"But maybe it could happen."

"There are no giant nats."

"How do you know?"

"Nats are always the same size as people. Or smaller. Maybe sometimes just a little bigger. She was only making it up to scare us. And you're scared."

"No, I'm not."

"Yeah, you are."

"No, I'm only thinking of where I would hide. He wouldn't get me. I would hide. I would run away." At this word, Aung Min's feet tumble into running, but it's far, four blocks. Teza catches him by the shoulder and declares, with the unquestionable authority of an older brother, "If we run, we'll drop dead in the sun before we even get there."

The buses of Mahabandoola Street roar past, men hanging off the window struts, dozens of people squashed inside. The roads around Sule Pagoda are filled with women and men going home from work or coming out to Anawrahta Street to sell their wares for the evening. Holding hands, the brothers cross the busy thoroughfare of roaring cars and buses. They maneuver around bicycle rickshaws and men pushing noodle and fruit carts. The moment they enter the pagoda, they move more slowly. They walk past the fortune-tellers and sellers of prayer beads. Ascending the stairs makes solemnity rise into their faces. Even though the flower-seller smiles, they buy their yellow and white bunches in silence, serious about the money passing hands.

Teza reflects upon the lizards. Aung Min suspects there *are* giant nats, despite his brother's doubts. They go up into the pagoda, where other people are sitting, praying, and chatting quietly. Buses honk on the streets below, a few girls laugh on the stairs, but the two boys step forward in silence, crouching down to offer flowers and light the candles and incense. There he is, the Buddha, looking calm as usual, good-humored. Teza knows he was a real man, from India. If he was a man, then he was a boy once too. He was a prince—so he must have gone hunting himself, before he gave up his rich kingdom and became a holy seeker. Long before Prince Gautama rid himself of desire and defilement and attained enlightenment, he probably had a slingshot. A trace of smile curves the golden mouth. Teza stares up at the smooth face and suddenly, unaccountably, feels very sad. He swallows, angles his head down. Already kneeling, he joins his hands palm to palm before his face and bows, hands opening to let his forehead touch the tiles. His little brother follows him, three times, almost in unison. After genuflecting, they sit motionless in the aspect of prayer.

Leaving the pagoda, they step slowly down the stairs, silent, their boyish faces calm and still. They ignore the palm-readers and souvenir peddlers. They don't have enough money to buy sparrows and release them for merit, but they stop, as they always do, and chirp into the small bamboo cages. Then they reenter the city. For a few minutes they will be immune to the noise and rushing energy of the streets. They walk without speaking through Paper Street and the street of moneychangers, where old Indian men sit at small tables, arguing over chipped white cups of sweet tea.

Going to a temple or a pagoda always makes them feel serious and lighter at the same time. A little later happiness will come and knock sound out of them, like strong wind against bells. Teza announces, "We won't do it again." Distracted by the smell of frying noodles from a roadside shop, Aung Min replies, "Maybe not." Teza gives him a push. "I bet she won't let us keep our slingshots," Aung Min adds with a sigh. They walk more quickly, their breath pulling them through smells of curry and bus exhaust and snapping oil. The leaves of the trees in the slant of twilight glow like green liquid jewels. When Teza suggests, "It's not so hot anymore," the brothers, understanding each other, begin to run.

They move in pace, not racing, sometimes they skip and giggle like girls, they are boys, after all, elastic and strong, they can do whatever they want, their elbows and knees are endless pistons. They leap over the broken teeth of cement and exposed sewers, laughing for no reason but to claim the joy of their voices even as they release it, send it flying into the air of this township, in their own city, Yangon, a name that means *the enemy is gone*. The brothers hoot and jump and run without flagging, five blocks home and beyond, their breath lifting them like birds through the brilliant dusk.

May May is watering her orchids. The expression on her face is the same one she wears for giving alms, praying, and thinking about their father. Some of the more common purple flowers rise spindly out of clay pots, their faces openmouthed, as if they're surprised to blossom on such flimsy stalks. But her favorites are attached with twine to wooden posts, cradled in burlap sacks and growing more as they would in the jungle, on trees. Green netting covers them, keeps them safe from the sun. It's early evening, the sky like faded mauve and salmon silk, the air around them that same silk fallen from the sky.

Teza wants to know her secret. "May May, how did you find out what we were doing? Did U Toe Khaing tell you?"

"No, he did not. I just knew that you and Aung Min were up to no good. It was a shiver at the back of my neck."

"May May, *really*, how did you know?"

"I already told you. Something came into my head and I needed to find out what you were up to. Stop gawking at me like that. I don't need to see you, or Aung Min, to know what you're doing. You're my sons. And you two are brothers. Never forget that. Wherever we are in the world, we will always be connected by something very strong, even if it's invisible. A thousand little threads. Or ropes! I don't know exactly what they're made of. Your grandfather's fishing line, perhaps, which was very strong indeed!" She laughs. "Now go play with Aung Min. And remember what I said. The slingshots are for target practice and mangoes only!"

Where is my slingshot now?

Less than a year later, Aung Min loses his trusty weapon, leaves it behind on a secret mission to Pazundaung Creek (they get into trouble for that too, because once again May May finds them out). The two brothers become a one-slingshot hunting party, but they never kill lizards again. The next year, in favor of other games, Teza no longer wants to shoot bottle caps off the fence or hunt for mangoes. In their little upstairs bedroom, alone, he wraps the thick rubber band around the hand-worn wooden crook.

I kept changing its hiding place so Aung Min wouldn't find it. I didn't want him to outshoot me with my own slingshot.

The two grown brothers eat in strained silence. Their mother keeps adding another spoonful of food to Aung Min's plate. Teza looks askance at him gobbling down the curry. He himself has little appetite.

"Aung Min, I think it's a mistake."

"Sorry?"

"Your leaving. It's a mistake."

"We've already talked about this. It's not as though I have a choice. I'll be arrested if I don't leave. You're at risk too, you know. You think you're not, but—"

Teza interrupts, "Why don't you go into hiding for a while? To Mandalay or Sagaing, into one of the monasteries until the situation quiets down? The monks have hidden other students."

"The situation is not quieting down."

Desperation spikes Teza's voice, making him sound much younger than he is. "Think of what Hpay Hpay used to say."

"Oh, Teza, not this again. It's not the same thing—we live in a different time."

"I think his words are still true. *When you pick up a gun, you become a dictator.* That's what our father used to say."

Aung Min pushes away his empty plate with such force that it spins to the other side of the table. As Teza reaches to catch it from falling, his brother shouts, "Stop *our father* this and *our father* that. He's dead. They killed him! It didn't matter to them what he believed. How many more people have to die before the regime changes?"

"That's exactly what I'm asking you."

"Then this argument is over, because our question is the same."

"But our answers are completely different."

"That's democracy in practice. Get used to it!" Aung Min can't restrain a grim yet triumphant smile.

Daw Sanda presses her lips together and fights to keep her tongue still. Each of her sons must decide what he has to do on his own. She looks sadly across the table at Teza. He can see from her expression that she too thinks he should leave. This only hurts him more.

She touches Aung Min's arm and whispers, "It's past nine." He will catch a night bus upcountry, where he's meeting a small group of friends. Together they will cross the border into Thailand near Mae Sot.

"Teza, I have to go. You will not come with me?"

"I'm staying in Burma. My own country. This is where I belong." He believes what he says. He isn't staying because he's a coward. He doesn't want to leave home, his mother, his beautiful Thazin, but that's love, not cowardice. He and Thazin will get married next year, or the year after. If she would come with him, then he might consider leaving, but her parents won't let her go. They think the border is too dangerous. And she is too good, too respectful, to run away.

Teza stares at his hands as Aung Min turns, lifts his legs over the long kitchen bench, and stands up. *He is still my only little brother. Nyi Lay. But we will never be able to protect each other again.*

When Teza walks into the sitting room, Aung Min is already at the door, a small knapsack on his back. The very last of the family gold—a bangle, two necklace chains—is sewn into the lining of his blue jacket. "Just wait, don't go yet." Teza sprints up the stairs and returns with a small gift wrapped in old brown paper.

Aung Min accepts the package and gives it a squeeze. "What's this?"

"Open it when you get to the jungle. I'm sure you'll need it out there, dodging bullets." Teza laughs, though his throat feels tight and his jaw is clenched. Again he is the one being left behind. It's already happened once, with his father. And this time it's worse, because Aung Min is choosing to leave him. He can't help but feel betrayed. When his brother embraces him, Aung Min whispers, *I love you,* but Teza doesn't respond. The words in his mind can't pass through the knot in his throat.

Then his brother, his almost twin, walks out the door, through the little wooden gate. Daw Sanda remains in the flat, but Teza steps into the garden compound. He closes his eyes and listens to Aung Min's footsteps fading down the road. When a few talkative teenagers pass by, it's hard to distinguish Aung Min's flip-flops from theirs, *slap-slap slap-slap.* Their laughter is so dissonant, so *awful,* that Teza has to open his eyes. He looks around himself and blinks. Everything has changed. Suspended on their posts, the pale-faced orchids glow in the dark like hanged children.

With a flick of gray-green tail, the lizard has disappeared over the top of the outer wall. Sitting now, rising out of the morphine deep, Teza stares at the iron bars without seeing them. He thinks of the shelf in his childhood bedroom, where he used to keep an old biscuit tin full of mementos. Old Burmese coins, long out of circulation. A photograph of his father as a serious, slender teenager. His grandfather's nibless fountain pen. The shimmering blue-green eye of a peacock's tailfeather. A rolled, unused piece of carbon paper.

The tin is probably still sitting on that shelf in his and Aung Min's room. Teza knows it was still there on November 29, 1988, because he was staring at it when the MI knocked on the door at eleven-thirty at night. The only treasure missing from its contents was the parting gift he'd given to Aung Min one month before: his old slingshot, its *Y* of wood still smooth and dark with the sweat and dirt of a boy's hand.

The officers took Teza just as they had taken his father. After he was escorted from the house—he saw this as clearly as he felt the rough sack close over his head, the boot on his neck when they pushed him down onto the floor of the car—Daw Sanda went into the kitchen and sat down at the table. It was true, what she had told him; Teza didn't need to be there to know exactly what she was doing. For the first time in her life, Daw Sanda wept in rage and sorrow loudly, openly, for there was no longer anyone left in the house to hear her.

. 33 .

The morphine lets him sleep through most of the afternoon, but he's relieved to wake up when the iron-beater strikes four o'clock. Free El Salvador will appear soon with his dinner, and Teza doesn't want another misunderstanding like the one they had this morning. He unfolds the largest piece of cloth his mother sent him in her last parcel. Then he sticks his arms through the bars and lays the worn cotton on the floor. Carefully, he places various offerings there, then pulls his arms back in and surveys the picnic. Who knows? In exchange, maybe the kid will say a word or two. Then, to insulate himself from disappointment, he thinks, But it's fine if he says nothing at all.

Like a suitor critical of his own gift, he puts his hands back out into the corridor and rearranges things. Craving agitates his fingers, makes his gut clench painfully. *Hunger, hunger.* It's a second heartbeat. He looks down at the bounty on the other side of the bars. *Don't cling to what you cannot have.* He pinches an ant off the display and drops it behind him.

When Free El Salvador swings around the outer wall and nears the singer's cell, he sees the flat body of a dried, salted fish laid out on white cloth. It stops him in his tracks. Beside the fish, a package of green-black tea leaves, a pouch of sesame seeds, three more of peanuts and deep-fried beans and garlic. The boy frowns. The Songbird sits cross-legged, hands on his knees like a statue. His eyes are closed. The boy wonders if the prisoner is going crazy. He glances back to the food.

He takes a step forward, suspiciously. You never get something for nothing.

Teza still hasn't opened his eyes. The boy cranes his head forward. Is the singer *dead*? Can you die sitting up?

No. He sees Teza's skinny chest rise and fall. He's meditating, like a monk. There have been monks in the cage before, in trouble, just like the politicals, and they do a lot of this sitting-breathing. The boy wishes the singer would open his eyes. If Teza gave him a certain kind of glance, the boy's question (*For me?*) would be answered. Maybe the fish and the la-phet are for someone else. Maybe for a nat? Or Jailer Chit Naing, his friend.

He takes a step closer.

Not only the fish but Teza's silence reels him in.

A few paces from the singer, he squats. Shoulders hunched, eyes flicking back and forth, he begins to eat the rice soup. He pauses to listen for the sound of boots. Slurping down the last spoonful, he peers up at Teza's face.

The jolt of it makes him jump backward—the singer is staring right at him with big gleaming eyes. The startle upsets him like a bad practical joke. Teza whispers quickly, the same word he said to the boy on the first day, "Sa!" Eat.

With bony fingers pointing down, wagging inward, he waves Free El Salvador closer to the fish, the la-phet, the peanuts. He whispers the word again. "Sa! It's for you. I can't eat it." Even after he soaks it in water, the salted fish is too hard. Teza still cannot chew at all, cannot grind his teeth together. When he closes his mouth with any pressure, the pain makes him nauseous.

Free El Salvador is confused. And frightened, though he doesn't know why. The man is giving him good food; there's nothing to fear. The skinny prisoner, jaw askew, is harmless. Even if he *were* dangerous, he's locked in a cage.

But that's not where the danger lies. It's the way the man surprises him, catches him off guard, not with violence or harsh words but with kindness. The boy cautiously pulls his sling bag around, off his back, opens it like an envelope. Teza watches as he picks up each little pouch of la-phet and squares it away in the bottom of the cloth bag. He moves slowly, thought-fully, as if he understands that he will enter the history of the man's life by eating his food.

On the other side of the wall, the rest of the cage unfolds, the large compound with its various buildings laid out in the shape of a warped ox-cart wheel, but Teza places the beginning of the world there, almost reach-able, through the iron bars, five steps away, in the boy's eyes, inside the boy, who thanks him for the gifts in a wary voice. Teza pushes the used tray through the trap, aluminum scraping concrete like primitive words between them. Free El Salvador picks it up and leaves, walks around the dirty white wall, out into the rest of the world.

Teza closes his eyes again. Before he's settled back into his meditation, he thinks how mysterious, how ordinary the breath is, this thin line of air cast between spirit and death, always here. Until it's gone.

He shakes the thought away and breathes

in

     out

in

     out

in

. 34 .

Lying in his rag bed, the boy stares at the plastic bag suspended above him. On the rare occasions when he has extra food, he hangs it from the roof beam to keep the bugs away. Soon he'll kick down the piece of corrugated metal that serves as a door, but for now false night fills his shack with stars of light shining in through small holes in the walls.

The twist of fish and fishbone over him looks strange in the dark, like another creature. He closes one eye, sees fish. He closes the other eye, sees monster swimming through plastic sack. He opens both eyes and grins, deeply pleased. The pleasant stink of his dinner fills the close space.

Treasure above, treasure below. Wrapped in another plastic bag and buried half a foot deep, under the small of his small back, lies the ballpoint pen, *tsshik-tsheek*. Jailer Handsome and his ragtag team of warders are still trying to find it. Giggling to himself, the boy snuggles deeper into his bed of old longyis and Chinese felt blanket. He searches out the spot of felt that's still furred and holds it against his cheek. With the door shut, he can nuzzle his head in the blanket like a child.

He inhales the monsoon, the smell of cloth never dry. The mildew comforts him, reminds him of sleep, the privacy of this small house, built a little longer than his body and high enough for him to sit up, crab-walk inside. He worries about growing. If he gets big, the shack will get too small. They probably won't let him build another one. Shhh, never mind. He closes his eyes. In the big matchbox, his carrion beetle claws against the thin cardboard. Scratch, scratch. Shhh, don't tell a soul!

In a population of ten thousand criminals, a couple thousand politicals, hundreds of warders and guards, no one else knows where the pen is—only the beetle and the little lizard and the boy who feeds them. While Handsome searches every nook and cranny of the cage, swinging threats around like a rat stick, the boy sleeps on top of the ballpoint pen. In the evening, as he leafs through a paperback by candlelight, the pen pulsates beneath him like a glowworm.

Last night, hours after Handsome left the cage, the boy pushed his rag bed to one side and dug his treasure out. He shook the clay dirt away from the plastic bag and held the pen, poised it in his fingers like the men do, as if eating with a single chopstick. He opened one of his tattered paperbacks and willed himself to make a mark somewhere on the printed pages. But he was afraid. If Jailer Handsome somehow got hold of the book and saw ink scratches in the margins, he would be suspicious. What would the jailer do if he *found* the pen? Beat the boy to a pulp? Or throw him in a dog cell with the other politicals?

Sometimes pragmatism slaps the boy in the head like an angry warder: *You have to get rid of the fucking thing. It's too dangerous to keep.* He could dispose of his prize this very morning, when he empties the latrine pails for a cell in Hall One, where prisoners wait to be sentenced.

As he held the pen in his fingers, he imagined letting it go, dropping it into the stink and pouring each load of crap right on top, flies rising around his hands in a noisy black net. He gripped the pen tight in his hand and clicked the nib in and out. *Tsshik-tsheek tsshik-tsheek*, it said, a sound so fine, so mysterious—like the whisper of many words hidden in the ink—that he knew he could not do it. Drowning the pen in shit would make him a . . . He searches for the word. A criminal!

The squeaky door of the warders' quarters announces the departure of several men. The boy abruptly sticks his head out of his rag-bed and rises on one elbow to listen. Several men walk by the shack, but they say nothing of interest. The boy listens carefully all the time, trying to catch news and gossip about the pen search. Mostly the warders complain about Handsome, but sometimes they talk about how angry the criminals are, because of the raids.

This morning the warders are just teasing each other and laughing and coughing. The principal cougher loosens a bunch of muck from his throat and spits loudly at the side wall of the little shack. The boy grimaces, but he doesn't take it personally. In the cage, everybody spits a lot. Tan-see Tiger calls it the universal language. The routine of throat-cleansing starts with lights-on. The hawking, gagging, and propelling of phlegm into corners, between bars, into garden vegetables doesn't stop until the first meal of the day.

The boy grins at his fish. He's already planned his day's menu. For dinner, fish with rice. For lunch, some of the Songbird's la-phet, with rice. And very soon he will have his special breakfast, which he eats once a month (twice if he's lucky).

He pushes down the propped-up door with his feet and sticks his head outside. Out of the thin morning light, the colors have pulled themselves together: reddish gravel, gray walls, wet brick walls and wooden buildings, another round of khaki-brown legs passing him. He glances at the door of the warders' quarters. Cups of tea, milky sweet or bitter green, have been left behind on the tables. He used to sneak in to drain the tasty dregs, but he hasn't done that since Handsome caught him stealing leftovers.

Never mind. He has the pen and Handsome doesn't. He also has a fine breakfast coming. He skips to the sink behind the warders' quarters and splashes water on his face. Then he hurries off to Tan-see Tiger's cell.

Halfway down the long row, three cells away from Tiger, the boy stops. Though he's never heard the man yell, the tan-see's voice gets very sharp when he's angry, like he's stabbing the one he's talking to. The boy doesn't like to be close to that sound, in case he accidentally gets in the way, but if he remains standing in the corridor, the other prisoners will start to tease him or ask for favors. He begins to walk again, slowly, head down. Five steps later, he pauses and carefully, needlessly, reknots his longyi.

He's close enough to make out Tiger's words and hear him pacing back and forth, back and forth. "I don't care if he's going to read your palm for the rest of your life, you stupid twit. The guy's an asshole, and if you want to get chummy with him, you're out of this cell. Got that? If he wants to work for me, he has to come down here and bring me the stuff himself, not hand it to one of my men in the gardens. Never *ever* accept anything on my behalf unless I tell you to. And don't even talk to that asshole. Can't you see what he is? He works for Handsome. That's reason enough to stay away from him. Understood?"

"Understood, Tan-see. I made a mistake." The boy knows this voice too, slippery and slick, a worm. It's skinny Hla Myat, the youngest inmate in Tiger's cell, who has a nervous habit of running his dark, long-nailed fingers through his greasy hair. He's a big talker too, which irritates the older men, especially Tiger, who regularly tells him to shut up. In turn, Hla Myat often teases the boy when he comes to give the tan-see a massage or fetch money for breakfast. But today Hla Myat won't be nasty, because he's in trouble.

"A *mistake*? A mistake like that could cost you your life. Why do you think I use Sein Yun anyway? Because he's trustworthy? Because he reminds me of my grandpa? No, you jerk. I use him because the deliveries have become so dangerous that he's likely to get knifed one of these days. That's how bad the business in this place is getting. Since all that bullshit with the search, I *hope* he gets his throat cut, because he's in on the whole thing. Helping that prick Handsome. They took all my letters! Fuck!"

"Nyi Lay, would you stop skulking around out there? You're making me nervous. Come here and I'll give you the breakfast money."

The boy's eyes open wide in surprise—how did Tiger know he was there?—but he marshals himself and steps forward. When Tiger grins at him with his big white teeth, he is relieved enough to snatch a glance inside the cell. There's Hla Myat, and beyond him, sitting in the corner, is the old basket-weaver, rolling strings out of plastic bag strips. The other men are out on work details. When Hla Myat sneers at the boy, he quickly looks back at Tiger, who sticks his fingers into the breast pocket of his nice blue shirt and takes out some money. He also pulls out a short gray pencil and, riled again, shakes it at Hla Myat. "This is all they left me with. And I had to bribe one of the warders to let me keep the damn thing. It's outrageous. How am I supposed to write my letters with a pencil? Those bastards!"

Tiger nods the boy closer. "Don't worry, kid, I'm just in a shitty mood.

A good breakfast will make me feel better." He puts his big paw through the bars and presses the bills into the boy's palm. "Three bowls. One for you, one for Uncle in the corner there, and one for me. There's enough here for you to get an egg for yourself, okay?" Tiger must be very mad at Hla Myat, to exclude him from food.

Nyi Lay whispers, "Thank you," and slips away.

He passes through the cage gates, holding the kyats close to his body. Just outside the prison, a grumpy man in his sixties runs a noodle stand. Warders eat here sometimes, for a treat, and newly released prisoners, and people who've come to visit someone inside. But often the little wooden tables and stools sit empty, as they do now. The worn bills leave the boy's dirty hand and return as a bowl of mohinga with one fine whole egg. When he's finished, he'll go back to Tiger's cell with two plastic bags full of the same noodles.

Whenever he eats here, he sees the big road to Rangoon. If he's feeling brave or bored or pissed off, he eyes that road and makes plans. Next year, he thinks. Next year, he will go to the city. But most of the time—this morning, for example—he turns his stool in the other direction, toward the fields, leans over his bowl, and carefully shovels the magic food into his mouth.

The white noodles are made by women. Breakfast food. *Mohinga, mohinga.* Sometimes he whispers this comforting word to himself before he falls asleep. He forgets-remembers that his mother used to sell mohinga under the twin banyan trees at the edge of the village, but he doesn't think of her anymore, just that taste, salty-sweet soup drowning soft rice noodles. The food takes him back to a feeling he cannot name.

When there's nothing but the egg left in the bowl, he lifts his head and looks out to the monsoon fields, green on burning green, colors undiminished by scattered villages and roadside tea shops, daubed here and there with figures tending bean plants, vegetables, rice. With great attention he watches the land, patched with fallow tan and mud but mostly spread out green, a color to stretch the eyes, pull the vision forward, farther, as if there were no end to how far he might see if he could just sit here all day, outside the cage walls. In a few of the paddies the rice shoots are still like slender young grass, while in others they have become an emerald flood. The water they grow from reflects gray or blue or white cumulus, the whole glimmering sky stitched or thickly woven with rice.

The fields make him happy in a way the road to Rangoon never does. He smiles at the green expanse before him, then glances down and remembers. The egg.

It's time to go. He has to deliver Tiger's noodles. Then do his awful latrine detail for that crowded cell in the sentencing hall. By the time he's washed up after that job, he'll have to deliver Songbird's breakfast. He pulls a plastic bag from his sling bag and quickly wraps the excellent, broth-soaked egg.

. 35 .

Until Handsome broke his jaw, Teza never realized how much he spoke aloud: long minutes in monologue, or in discussion with the ants and the cockroaches and the copper-pot spider. One of the worst things is not being able to talk to himself and hear his own voice. This affliction is different from the physical pain, but there are moments when it's almost as difficult to bear.

He knows he is sane, despite the physical agony that leaves his mind raw and shaky. He is sane, but he misses the spider dearly, the web spun and respun according to the creature's secret need. He misses the perfection of that architecture in the midst of so much ugliness, and he misses the constant presence—even though the spider went outside, he always came back. Teza feels real concern. When the pen fell, did it hurt the spider? He knows how delicate and breakable they are, a spider's jointed legs.

The singer rubs the smell of old urine away from his nose and gingerly touches his swollen eye. He pulls his knees up to his chest and stares down the sharp slope of shinbones. He has five broken toes, two on the left foot, three on the right. Though he has no clear memory of it, he suspects that one of the warders, or Handsome—probably Handsome—must have jumped up and down on his feet. The toe bones are the broken pieces that have healed most easily. With tolerable pain, he is able to hobble. Talking is still very bad. And not talking is also very bad. Eating is the worst. His entire jaw is tight, raw-feeling, but the left mandible is the site of the fracture. No mirror, of course, but he leans over the water pot and sees the wavering reflection. His whole chin has shifted to the left, sunken into the shortened, half-shattered bone. His chin is the only place on his lower face that doesn't hurt now—because it's perfectly numb. The doctor says the nerve in that area has been severed.

The buzz and echo in his left ear come back at least a few times a day. Sometimes he thinks he's gone deaf in that ear. Other times he still hears as well as he did before. Or does he? What worries him most is that he doesn't know for sure. The left eye is bruised and still swollen but has stopped running pus. He washes it several times every day.

Taking stock this way is a necessary task, like returning to a city after the invading army has left, but it leaves him feeling like the most exhausted man on the planet. Chit Naing has told him that all the men who wrote letters to Daw Aung San Suu Kyi are in the dog cells. There hasn't been a trial yet, but that doesn't matter. Each man possessed "illegal" materials, which means they'll all get an extra seven to ten years.

I was wrong to trust Sein Yun. We were all wrong to trust him.

But you cannot remain human if you never trust another person.

That is the crux of it. I am exhausted because I remain human.

Sammy strikes the time, but the singer isn't counting anymore. Whatever time it is, he is old. He covers his crooked face with his hands. His long fingers pass over his cheekbones, his head. He smells the dirt on his hands and gets up to wash them at his water pot, using soap. He knows the sadness will leave him. It will change into something else. This is the truth of annica: all things are impermanent. He moves carefully to his mat, clears away a dirty undershirt, and wraps himself in his blanket. Forming a mental image of the Buddha, he turns toward the outer wall, the bars, and genuflects three times. He still bows gracefully, as he will until the day of his death, his head touching the cement through the triangular opening formed by his thumbs and index fingers.

Kneeling, his hands held before his chest, his eyes closed, he silently recites the Pali prayer:

Sabbe satta aham sukhita hontu.
Sabbe satta nidukkha hontu.
Sabbe satta avera hontu.
Sabbe satta abyapajjha hontu.
Sabbe satta anigha hontu.
Sabbe satta sukhi attanam pariharantu.

Whatever beings there are, may they be happy.
Whatever beings there are, may they be free from suffering.
Whatever beings there are, may they be free from enmity.
Whatever beings there are, may they be free from hurtfulness.
Whatever beings there are, may they be free from ill health.
Whatever beings there are, may they be able to protect their own
    happiness.

He bows again three times and begins to breathe.

Though his eyes are closed, something interrupts him. Free El Salvador stands beside the outer wall, his body hidden behind it, his head visible, hovering over the food tray. Teza completely forgot that it was time for breakfast. The boy shifts his weight from one foot to the other, somehow asking if he's welcome.

Teza cannot smile, but his eyes soften as he waves the boy closer. How long has Free El Salvador been watching him? With the fluidity of a mongoose, the boy comes forward, crouches. Teza notices that his expression is different. Why does he look more like a child today than he did yesterday?

Chin dipped against his chest, eyes lowered, Free El Salvador carefully pushes the tray into the cell. It's shyness. The boy has become shy! Teza is delighted to recognize this emotion in the hard nugget of a face. Quietly, still looking away, the boy utters that single, beautiful word they share.

Sa.

Eat.

Teza whispers his thanks. "Tzey zu bay, Nyi Lay."

The words, garbled because he cannot open his mouth, are clear as fire, and hang like fire in the air between them, burning with many meanings: nyi lay. Little Brother. A prison child. The lizard he keeps in his shack. Aung Min, living in a border country that Teza can only imagine.

Nyi Lay. Jailer Chit Naing calls both child and singer by this casually affectionate name.

Teza is still kneeling, the blanket gathered about him, while the boy squats with his hand on the tray and pushes it into the cell. His head almost touches the bars.

The boy whispers, "Sa! You're too skinny."

Teza points to his jaw and makes a falling ax of his hand. "It's not easy to eat."

Free El Salvador points to the tray. "Sa. Sa!" He sticks his arm in through the trap and pushes the tray closer to the singer, but Teza still doesn't look at it. He's too excited; the boy is finally speaking to him.

Free El Salvador says, "Pass me your dirty tray." Now the singer will see. There is the familiar sound of aluminum rasping cement. Then a faint intake of breath. The boy snatches up the used tray.

The singer squints with his good eye, confused, then disbelieving. There it is, poorly concealed with a few spoonfuls of wet rice, something he has not seen for years. An egg.

When he looks up, his hands rise too, fingers spread, asking for an explanation, but Free El Salvador is gone.

H e pulls the tray toward him. Yes. It's a hard-boiled egg, the white turned brown with fish sauce and oil.

Teza picks up the slippery egg with his long fingers and inhales deeply. *Noodles.* On the other side of the egg, he finds mohinga. Mohinga! He smells the Forty-Second Street Tea Shop, behind the old jute factory. You have to be there before eight-thirty in the morning if you want to be sure to get a bowl. It's a famous place. The crowds on their way to work or school stop for breakfast, then drink sweet tea or bitter tea or instant coffee, deliciously thick with condensed milk.

He breaks the egg with the edge of the metal spoon. It's backward augury, for he cannot read the future in the yellow center, only the past. Early mornings with Thazin bent close over the corner of a low wooden table, his knees touching her knees, the bowls of mohinga empty and the sweet tea finished and the pots of bitter green tea beginning, that lovely, endless stuff, provided compliments of the shop, allowing them to stay longer, too long, drinking not only tea but each other's company, away from their friends and families, enjoying each other as much as they do when they borrow a dorm room or find a secluded spot in a park. Mohinga and the whole tea-shop ritual often made them late for their first classes.

He breaks the egg again, in quarters, then mashes it up without mixing it into the boiled rice, not wanting to dilute the taste. With the blanket pulled up around his shoulders, Teza eats his first egg since the days before his arrest in 1988. He eats slowly, his tongue pushing the crumbled yolk against the roof of his mouth until it becomes a wet paste. He winces, stops, keeps going.

The salty, sulfury taste is both utterly unexpected and deeply known. Home, the noodle and tea shops, the young woman he loved. Eating mohinga with Aung Min before they go to play football. And from far, far back, his father, who takes him to visit the Shwedagon in the new light of dawn. He is four or five years old. Aung Min is too small to come. Teza is a boy gloriously alone with Hpay Hpay, who buys jasmine and orchids from one of the flower-sellers on the grand stairway that leads to the gold stupa. He puts his son down to take the flowers, chatting and laughing with the old lady who sells them. She touches Teza's cheek with one hand as she hands him a string of jasmine. Father and son climb a few more steps, stop again to buy incense and candles. Another small conversation ensues with the vendor, about the coolness of the morning, the coming heat of the day. Near the top of the staircase built into the angle of the hill, Hpay Hpay lifts Teza and carries him up the last of the steps into the round, glittering courtyards of the great pagoda. All around them, invisible and visible among the many shrines, monks are murmuring and chanting the prayers of dawn. Both father and son offer flowers. Hpay Hpay lights the incense and candles, then makes his own prayers with Teza sitting cross-legged beside him. After a while they bow again to the Buddha—Hpay Hpay places Teza's hands in front of his head—then they stand and walk the night-cooled stones around the large circumference of the stupa. The small boy is patient and quiet, happy with his father in this circular labyrinth of many Buddhas and brightly painted statues. He knows what awaits them, after they descend the long staircase under the arched and painted ceiling, after they return to the wakening clamor of the streets around the pagoda. There's a mohinga stall nearby. Each of them has a bowl. The little boy gets an egg in his noodles. To help you grow big and strong, Hpay Hpay tells him.

I am eating an egg. He revises it.

I am eating my whole life.

Rain begins to fall, all at once in steady rhythm, a wet broom sweeping out the sky. Fresh air billows into the cell. The rain has a mantra: egg, egg, egg, egg.

With a fleck of yellow yolk stuck on his lower lip, Teza makes up a stupid joke.

What comes first, the chicken or the egg?

The political prisoner, of course.

He swallows as slowly as it's possible to swallow without choking. He revises it.

What comes first, the chicken or the egg?

The boy. Free El Salvador, who brought the political prisoner an egg from a bowl of mohinga.

Before Sammy beats out five o'clock, Teza places another dried fish outside his cell, laid carefully on a piece of cloth from the parcel, surrounded by four small pouches of peanuts, tea leaves, and sesame seeds.

When the boy arrives, his eyes fall immediately to the offering on the ground. Obviously surprised, he glances at Teza, who manages to say, "Thank you. For the egg this morning."

Shyness comes to Free El Salvador again. He approaches the cell. "Was it good?"

"Very good," Teza replies, a smile in his voice. "I haven't eaten an egg for a long time. It made me think of my father."

At the word *father*, the boy lifts his head. His mouth is not quite closed, not quite open. The dark lips are full, as innocent as they are sensuous. Beautiful, really. The old anger whipcracks through Teza, asking one question: *Why is this child living in a prison?*

The singer takes a deep breath. The boy's still looking at him, newly direct, almost complicitous. And wanting. Wanting what? To be loved, of course, like any child. Teza points to the food outside the cell. "It's for you."

"De gé la?" Really?

He breathes out a laugh. "Really, Nyi Lay. Who else?"

The boy scratches his cheek. It wrings Teza's heart, to watch him struggle against his own longing. "Be quick. The warder might come." The child drops to a squat and deftly wraps the fish in the little white cloth, secrets the pouches of la-phet away in his sling bag. He thanks the singer almost formally. "Ako." He pauses. "Tzey zu amiagee tin-ba-deh." Teza nods, touched by simple words. The boy is still too shy to say Teza's name, but *ako* is a beginning. Older Brother.

A few mornings later Nyi Lay brings the singer a fried fish. After deboning it, Teza makes a paste of the soft white flesh to mix in with his boiled rice. The boy watches him drink the soupy mixture, occasionally whispering, "Sa, sa," like the parent of a fussy child. In turn Teza leaves him more food—another fish and some deep-fried beans—from the parcel. The next day the boy brings him a very ripe banana.

Two days later he leaves Teza a small twig of diamond-shaped leaves and the singer gives him another dried fish and one of the little bricks of thanakha.

The next day, squatting in front of the cell, Nyi Lay sticks his skinny arm through the bars and opens his hand. Lying in his dirty palm is a pale green stone. He whispers, "It might be jade," and looks up at Teza. Like a diver, the boy takes a big, audible breath before plunging in. "Maybe it's a jade *amulet*. Tan-see Tiger has a jade Buddha that he wears around his neck. On a gold chain. He pays the warders so they don't take it away from him. And he says that the Buddha image *protects* him." He flushes, embarrassed to be talking so much, but he can't stop. "And he has some other amulets too, all for protection. One's a *bullet* that was taken out of his chest. For protection against other bullets! And you can still see his scar!" Out of air, Nyi Lay falls silent.

Teza raises a questioning eyebrow. "If the stone is for protection, don't you want to keep it?"

There is a long pause. The two of them gaze down at the glinting little rock.

If it *is* an amulet, then he should keep it for himself. The Songbird's right. Because of Handsome and the pen, he needs all the help he can get. Yet he doesn't close his fingers and pull his arm back through the iron grille. The green, gray-fissured stone lies on his open palm. He *wants* to give it away.

With long, thin fingers, Teza picks up the stone and turns it this way and that, into the light of the corridor. "If you need this talisman back, just ask. I'll hold on to it for you." The boy stands. Teza says, "Wait, don't go yet. There is one more dried fish from my parcel. Do you want to take it today or tomorrow?"

As the boy watches Teza wrapping it up, an explanation opens in his mind easily, lightly, like a door made of thatch. If the Songbird keeps the amulet, the boy can keep the pen. The trade keeps both of them safe.

. 36 .

From the white house, he walks along with Teza's empty tray, the pleasant weight of more good dinners stowed in his sling bag, bumping against his thigh. He pauses to check the fish and reknot his longyi.

Amulet for pen for protection. What can he do to make sure the exchange works?

He will make an offering. That's why the men pray, and leave flowers and food for the nat of the last tree in the cage. They believe the nat will help them.

Between the hospital and the kitchen stands the Buddhist shrine. Though he needs to return the singer's tray for wash-up, he finds himself stopping at that special in-between place. If he makes an offering to the nat, then maybe now is the time to make one to the Buddha, who sits calmly above the fresh and wilted flowers, the fresh and dried branches of green. Incense smoke curls up and disappears above his knees of peeling gold. A warder has placed a glass of water and a plate of oranges beside him. It must have been a warder, or an officer, because the convicts gobble up fresh fruit right away, peels included. Untempted, the Buddha sits placidly beside this plate of juicy oranges, tapered fingers grasping nothing. The long gold arms slope smoothly into his draped lap, like those of a dancer who has decided to sit down forever.

The boy stands behind the half-dozen worshippers, prisoners sitting cross-legged with eyes closed, lips forming inaudible words. Two of them count prayer beads; the boy hears the tiny *click-click-click* as the beads pass under fingertips. He won't get down on his knees and bow three times. Not yet, not with so many prisoners around. He knows it's three times because he's watched the men so often, and the Songbird too. He just stands there, staring at the golden face.

Then he sees it.

A thousand times he has watched the gold mouth, wondering if it ever speaks. But he has never seen the holy man smiling as he is now. The Buddha has changed. Almost imperceptibly, the full lips curve upward, as though he knows the boy's secret—*amulet for pen for protection*—and promises, with his closed, smiling mouth, that he will tell no one.

The boy meets the Buddha's gaze and makes the same face back. Putting the tray under his arm, he raises his hands in prayer position, makes three little nods with his head—as close to bowing as he dares—and closes his eyes.

"Why don't you kneel down like the rest of us?"

This unexpected voice, close and hot against his ear, makes him jump. The aluminum tray falls noisily to the ground. A worshipper turns, scowling. Sein Yun smiles an apology and raises a diplomatic yellow hand. The boy has already retrieved the tray and taken several steps backward.

Sein Yun gets down on his knees. Now he is like a midget. Instead of genuflecting before the Buddha, he casts a wry sideways glance at the boy, who knows he should leave. Maybe it's the Buddha himself whispering, *Go, don't stay here*. But the boy doesn't move. He's never been so close to Sein Yun's face. He examines the yellow skin, the curly-haired mole on his chin, the betel mouth with wrinkles radiating from lips stained red and brown. When the palm-reader waves to the boy, Nyi Lay stares at his fingernails, exceptionally long and rounded like hooks.

Sein Yun's smile reveals his dark teeth. "Don't just stare, Nyi Lay."

"Sorry, Uncle." His apology is without meaning.

"Oh, I don't mean at *me*—stare at me as much as you want. I mean at the shrine. La-ba. Come and join me. We will worship together."

The invitation takes the boy by surprise. He has always wanted exactly this, one of the men to teach him, to help him, but no one has ever offered, until now. Why does it have to be the nasty palm-reader?

Sein Yun's smile is nothing like the Buddha's. His wrinkled face squeezes up like an old mango. His lips rise; the two gold eyeteeth glint. Sein Yun jerks his chin downward, meaning *Kneel beside me*.

The boy has a good excuse. "My father never went to the temple."

The palm-reader stops smiling. His face becomes less squeezed and more sad, but the boy doesn't believe that moony look. "Your father has been dead many years."

Nyi Lay glances down at the cement between his feet. What does the palm-reader know about it?

As though reading his mind, Sein Yun says, "I knew him."

The boy's throat squeezes like a vise around two words. "My father?"

"Yes. He played cards with us. He was a good card player when it wasn't for money. When it was for money, the poor fellow always lost. But he used to win cheroots by the dozen. Remember when we played at the little tea shop in your village? You'll remember if you try—you kept asking to go home. You were very, very small then. Maybe you've forgotten. Or do you remember?"

The boy drops his head. He forgets-remembers many things about his father, whose image has blurred in the midst of so many men. Cage faces—even the warders'—share a certain tightness, as though the bones are too large for the skin that contains them. It's like a mask the prison gives to every man who passes through the gates. The boy sees it on Sein Yun's face too.

He forgets-remembers so much. Now a clear memory from the other world rises up and takes hold of him. He is a small child again, walking past a late-night noodle shop, his fingers tucked into his father's longyi as they rush through the rectangle of bare electric light that falls from the small building. The boy hears voices first, then turns and sees the happy ruckus, men at the tables, the laughter and shouts that mean toddy rum and cards. The father feels his child turn, sees the hungry look, the longing. The child wishes, inarticulately, deeply, that his father could be there, among those laughing men in the unshaded light. He has almost never heard his father laugh. But the man misunderstands. Yanking the boy forward, he growls, "If you ever start that nonsense, I swear I'll lock you up. Never play cards. There's enough gambling in this life as it is." The child has no idea what gambling is and only the merest comprehension of *cards,* but he doesn't try to explain. He only replies, "Yes, sir," like a tiny soldier. The two of them keep going, walking quickly along the dark road.

The boy looks into Sein Yun's face. Liar, he thinks. Stupid liar. My father never played cards. He smiles at the palm-reader. "What was my father's name?"

Sein Yun's mouth gapes open. Then closes into a dark red *O* surrounded by deep betel wrinkles. "I . . ." He taps his head. "You know, I've forgotten! I must be getting old."

Nyi Lay would like to spit, but he does not—he is at the shrine. So he just removes his eyes from the palm-reader, like an adult looking away from something unpleasant, rotting food or a dead animal. He shifts his gaze back to the Buddha, hoping that the secret smile is still there. It is.

The palm-reader is like a man trying another key in the lock. "Nyi Lay, you can worship here, even if you don't know the words. The Buddha will not mind. He is very generous. Besides, your mother was a Buddhist."

Anyone who knows cage business would know his mother was a Buddhist.

The palm-reader smiles, more ingratiating now. "Come, why don't you kneel down and pray with me?"

"I have to deliver the tray. Then I have other jobs."

"Ah, yes, you're doing the singer now. I was his server before you, you know. It's important work. Well done."

The boy doesn't want the man to compare them, to make them the same just because he has taken over Sein Yun's job. The skin on his back contracts, shivers, the way it does before he throws up. He is surprised at himself, confused by this tumult within him that suddenly wants to get out. Before he knows what's happening, the words begin to escape, though they are not rushed or fearful. They do not act like escapees. "His mouth is all broken. I take him his food, but he cannot eat. Because of you."

"My dear boy, what do you mean? What are you talking about?" Sein Yun's smile disappears as he becomes wide-eyed with incomprehension.

The boy's voice sounds clear in his own ears. "You know. You were the singer's server before me." It's a voice barely used, like a new bell but sharper, different in function, closer to a very small silver blade. He stares into Sein Yun's eyes. "You ratted on him, remember? And the politicals in the dog cells. They are there because of you."

Caught off-guard, the palm-reader is at a loss for words. In that silent gap, the boy turns and walks away, his orange flip-flop and his burgundy velvet flip-flop slapping against his heels.

. 37 .

Sein Yun doesn't stay at the shrine for long. He never does, unless he has business to conduct with someone. The little rat-killer was not business, he was just a thought, a probing. Little sack of bones. Shit with eyes. And a tongue.

It's not so strange that the kid knows something about Sein Yun's part in last month's raid. It's no longer a secret, because the pen search didn't exactly go as planned. Where did the damn thing go? During the past month he's read palms for free and chatted up the guys left, right, and center, feeling through metaphorical pockets like a whore. There's nothing to find.

The warders did the main convict halls, they did the sentencing hall. They tore up the gardens and combed the compound three times. They even stirred up the latrine holes—what a stink that must have been. The palm-reader's done his part too. He got the cook to harangue his work details and helped him search the kitchen. He sucked up to the medics and prisoner-helpers in the infirmary and the hospital, but there's nothing to find, anywhere. Or a lot of things all over the place—pens, pencils, razor blades, notes, love letters, newspapers, an American five-dollar bill (a sheer miracle, kept for good luck, and pocketed immediately by Handsome), a working transistor radio, batteries new and old, magazines, makeup and pantyhose and sexy nighties (the faggots have nicer clothes than his wife), even a broken telescope, but no white pen, razor-nicked at the bottom, razor-nicked at the top. Scuffles broke out among the convicts in Halls One and Four. Some jerk in Hall Five, angry about the raid, attacked one of the warders and the whole place went crazy, had to be locked down for two days. Four cons were sent to the hole for a week, with nothing to eat for forty-eight hours.

That stupid little brat. Sein Yun realizes he is too polite—he should have smacked that kid a good one. As if the palm-reader doesn't have enough shit on his plate. Handsome's pissed at him, and Tiger's making noises about finding someone else to do his heroin runs, all because he lost his pens and a few sheets of scented paper. Unbelievable. Sein Yun walks away from the shrine. Without knowing it, he's developed a curious tic, one he shares with Handsome. He scans the brick-chip ground as he walks.

Where did it go? The singer could have eaten the damn paper, but who could eat a pen? Impossible. You can't eat a pen. It would make you choke.

Really, it verges on obscene, that brat making his accusation, as if the palm-reader has broken some sort of code. Little twat. There's nothing more annoying than a voice full of its own innocence.

He doesn't feel guilty. No. Absolutely not. He didn't *touch* the singer, didn't lay a *finger* on him. The thought never entered his mind. He doesn't like violence; he is a civilized man. And Teza's not a bad guy, for a political. Sein Yun tried to be good to him. Remember the cheroots? And that time he took him papaya? Pure altruism! Merit-making!

Besides, this is a *prison*. If you were charitable every day, you'd be eaten alive. People do what they have to do.

He had no idea that Handsome would fly off the handle like that, none at all. Let's face it, the guy's dangerous; everybody knows that. He wants to be an *MI*. The warders say he had orders not to do any work on Songbird and he's in shit now for breaking the guy's face. But that's what happens in the cage.

Little brat rat-killer. It's none of his business. Sein Yun had nothing to do with that savage beating, it wasn't his fault. It's not like he was standing outside the teak coffin, cheering them on.

Sein Yun stops walking.

He is a restless, sick-yellow man, stricken most of the time with a frightful inability to keep still. But he has gone very still.

The pen.

He's found it. Right there, staring him in the face. It's wearing mismatched flip-flops, in a monsoon storm, waiting for rats near the shower-room drain.

. 38 .

Free El Salvador brings a new gift with the five o'clock tray. He
pushes three cheroots into Teza's cell, along with a lighter. Then
he sits back on his haunches to watch what the Songbird will do
with the offering. All prisoners are pigs for cheroots. The singer who cannot sing sits down, holds a cigar to his crooked mouth, mimes lighting it.
His eyes squint shut with pain as he speaks. "I still can't smoke. Hard to
suck, you know?" He exhales a stuttering laugh and nudges the lighter
back out through the trap. It's like playing a very odd game of checkers.
The boy looks at the little red rectangle, then back at Teza, who says,
"Watch."

He breaks the filter off the first cheroot and removes the green wrapping of dried leaf. There they are: small words on a thin band of newsprint.
He finds the place where the newsprint is glued, picks at it until it opens. He
unwraps the words, letting the inner filter of straw leaf fall away. Holding
two small pieces of paper in his palm, he leans forward, close to the bars,
closer; his hand reaches through. Cautious but curious, Nyi Lay stretches
his arm out. Teza drops his paper offering into the grimy open hand.

The broken mouth doesn't make any difference; the singer's eyes smile
and smile. He whispers, "Zaga-lone-dwei."

Words. The boy looks down at the two curled pieces of newsprint covered in the circles and dots that make words.

Then, as though it were a secret, Teza whispers, "Bathazaga."

Language.

A light comes into the boy's eyes. Bathazaga. This is a word he knows but he thinks only of its first half, *batha*. That's a different word altogether separate but part of the other one too. One word lives inside another, he thinks, surprised. *Batha* is a word for every day, like breathing or drinking water. It means to bring the Songbird gifts, or to visit the nat's tree and make an offering of flowers, a little clump of rice placed on a leaf. Batha.

Batha is religion. Bathazaga is language. What does it mean when one word holds the other? He doesn't know how to think about it, yet something is there, like the lizard in the grass who can change color. Batha is the Muslim men praying in daylight and darkness, their voices an echo of his dead father's voice. Batha. Zaga-lone-dwei. Bathazaga.

He can't understand how one word gets inside another, and why, and what it means. He turns the newsprint over in his fingers, roughly. One of the pieces tears, and he squeezes both scraps in his small fist. Why is the singer making him think about farther-away things, words he can't understand? Many thoughts rush into his head. He thinks of the tattered paperbacks in his shack, his hoarded treasures. He thinks of the white pen. The singer's pen. He thinks of writing.

Here is a silence filled with many voices. Though neither child nor man speaks, they are talking—their thoughts drift into the air and ribbon together like smoke, twisting, dissolving. Teza thinks, When he's frustrated, how much he resembles Aung Min! The boy opens his hand again, glares at the crumpled scraps of newsprint, then lifts his eyes. Suddenly they flick away from Teza, toward the sound of footsteps crunching gravel.

Their reactions are identical, resembling those of lovers caught in a guilty embrace. The boy springs to his feet. Teza rises and steps backward unsteadily, tucking the cheroots into the waist of his longyi. He and the boy lower their heads.

Both of them expect to see the old warder who sometimes comes to open up Teza's cell so Nyi Lay can take away the latrine pail. Their guilty surprise turns into something else again when Chit Naing rounds the corner of the white house. His official mask breaks open when he smiles, first at the boy and then at Teza. "What are you two up to? A football game? Playing cards?" The boy's guarded expression cracks enough to reveal a smirk. The jailer peers into the cell.

"Has Nyi Lay given you a file to escape with?" Chit Naing laughs, then notices the boy's indignant expression. He smiles and touches the bony shoulder. "I'm only joking, Nyi Lay. I know you're doing a very good job, as usual. Here, why don't I open up and you can do our inmate the favor of emptying his pail? I'm sure he would be very grateful. Correct, Ko Teza?"

The singer replies, "Yes, that's a good idea." This is the first time since the beating that he's seen Chit Naing in such an easy mood. The ring of heavy keys clanks against the iron bars as the jailer unlocks the grille and lets the boy through. Nyi Lay hoists the pail and rushes out.

Chit Naing knows he's walked into something. It's like stepping backward through a spiderweb in a dark room. He feels it pulling, stretching behind the boy, who has already disappeared behind the outer wall. When he turns and looks more carefully at Teza—his hands folded in front of his body, his slightly hunched back—the jailer is sure of it. Some private act has taken place between them.

The thought of a sexual transaction crosses his mind, but he dismisses it. Teza is not a homosexual. Even if he was, the boy never makes himself available.

"Was I right? Has he really given you a file to escape with?"

"No, no. *I* gave *him* a file to escape with." Teza winces. Too much talking. He breathes out the next stinging words, "Why is he here?"

"I suggested to the Chief Warden that he would be an excellent server. I know he's not much of a talker, which the Chief appreciates. He's also very obedient." And, as the Chief was only too happy to point out, completely uneducated, therefore without politics.

Teza shakes his head. Chit Naing has misunderstood his question. "Why is he *here*, in the cage?"

"Well, he . . . ah, lives here. His father was a warder who died several years ago. There was nowhere else for him to go." That was another reason why the Chief let the boy have the job. He lives in the cage, knows nothing but the cage, so he could never be bribed to take messages out or bring contraband in.

"Why not an orphanage? Prison is too hard. He's only a boy. Why isn't he living in a monastery school?"

"He doesn't want to leave the prison. I talk to him about it sometimes. He's never even been to Rangoon, if you can imagine that. He's afraid of the city."

Teza steps closer to the open door. "But he's only a boy."

It dawns on the jailer that this is it, this sympathy is the illicit interaction. Teza's feeling sorry for the kid! Chit Naing smiles slightly and asks, "How are you? You sound better. Far too thin, but better. I see the swelling is down."

"Yes, I can open it now." Teza blinks his black eye.

"The doctor will come by before he leaves today to give you a shot of morphine. And you're still getting your double ration of rice, aren't you?"

Teza nods, though he doesn't add that it has been many days now since he's eaten the evening meal. He knows Chit Naing will be angry with him if he finds out about the fasting.

"I have good news for you." This must be why the jailer is so relaxed, even making jokes. The haze of guilt and reticence that has surrounded him for weeks seems to have lifted. "The Chief Warden is tired of this search for the pen. He gave Handsome a bit of an extension, to keep looking, but he and his men can't find anything." Chit Naing looks carefully at Teza, whose face doesn't change. "It's been almost a month since the raids started. They still have no evidence to incriminate you. The papers for the list of the defendants and the charges against them have been drawn up. Your name is not there. You know what that means, don't you? You won't go to trial. They can't extend your sentence." The jailer tries to gauge Teza's reaction to the good news. Chit Naing doesn't tell how he removed the court files last night and replaced them this morning with trembling hands. While they were in his possession, he copied them at a safe shop and dropped the copy off at a small hut in an open-sewer satellite town outside the city. Today or tomorrow, the papers will be picked up by an old man, an agent who carries information to the revolutionary and dissident groups on the border.

Chit Naing likes to imagine that Teza's brother will read the files before they are compiled and published. All tribunal records within the prison system are highly restricted documents. The jailer wonders if any copies of prison court proceedings have ever left the country. He's already planning to smuggle out the trial documents themselves, when the hearings are over. The thought of doing that fills him with an excitement indistinguishable from happiness. That is how the singer perceives it too. *Chit Naing is happy*. Though the jailer is deeply relieved that Teza is not among those charged, primarily he's sailing on the adrenaline of his own subterfuge.

Waiting for something from Teza—some celebratory gesture, however subtle, or an indication of relief—Chit Naing pushes his glasses up his nose and leans through the slightly open door. Teza only nods, as though distracted, and looks past him. Chit Naing wonders if Teza's injuries have rendered him apathetic. The jailer carefully examines the dark green and purple skin around the eye, the broken jaw hanging loose, various bruises and swelling still visible on his face and neck. Between the injuries and the shaven head, Teza has changed so much that it's hard to remember what he looked like before, and *before* was only a month ago.

It was the beating that pushed Chit Naing deeper into measured recklessness. That's why he was able to steal the list of defendants and pretrial papers. Though he comes to the prison every day, he's not working for the generals anymore. He wants a response from the singer, not of gratefulness but of recognition.

"If there is a general amnesty for politicals in the next couple of years—"

Teza finishes the sentence, "They will not let me go."

"But they've let others go, men who served only eight or ten years."

"Thirteen years more. Because of the songs." Still out there, flying around like birds.

"At least they won't add an extra seven or ten."

Teza only says, "Think of Myo Myo Than, the others."

"You can be sure they are happy for you."

That word again—how odd it sounds. Teza closes his eyes as the flame shoots up inside his jaw, into his skull. He wrenches his head to the right, to get away from that searing, but he cannot. The morphine will be a blessing tonight. Eyes closed, he says, "The boy. I would be happy to help the boy."

Chit Naing is nonplussed. "What boy? The rat-killer?"

Both prisoner and jailer turn at the sound of the metal bucket clanking against a knobby knee. Free El Salvador looks up and grins widely, carelessly, out of character, because these two men are kind to him, in their different ways.

The small dark face sparks and for an instant gleams, returning the child to an innocent country he's never lived in. Teza hasn't seen the boy smile like that before, and it has already disappeared, subdued into a goofy, self-conscious smirk. Free El Salvador slips to the edge of the cell, handing the singer who cannot sing his bucket, which was not full. Lips pressed together, he waits for the jailer to tell him he can go, which the jailer does.

The boy glances at Teza, then he's gone.

But that moment of clean light in his face was enough. Teza knows now. He knows what he intends to do.

. 39 .

That night, while Teza is thinking about the boy, the boy is thinking about words.

The corner of the shack where he lays his head, as far as possible from the door, is the driest place. His collection of nine paperbacks is stacked in two piles between the wall and his face, each pile on a brick. He keeps the books off the ground because water often seeps in. Curling like a cat, he turns his back to the books, head on his arm, knees near his belly. The candle flame flares high in a sudden draft, then drops again.

Nyi Lay the little lizard clings to the low roof above the candle. For a long while the boy lies there watching him eat small moths and mosquitoes, happy that the lizard can get his dinner so easily. There are always enough insects for him.

One moth, swooping in erratic circles around the candle, finally crosses the flame and *ssssttt* singes its wings. It falls free and clear of the wax, unlike several others, which are stuck to the candle, embalmed or burning up a mothy stink. The boy picks up the fluttering moth and, propping himself on an elbow, holds out the offering to Nyi Lay.

Now he can smile without embarrassment, without even thinking of it, as Nyi Lay approaches his fingers, dives at the moth, and grabs it in his small jaws. *Shake-of-head-swipe-of-lizard-hand*, and the scrap of burned moth silk is gone, eaten up, just like that, swallowed into Nyi Lay's stomach. The boy can still feel the slightest touch of lizard nose on two of his fingers. He would like to hold Nyi Lay, to have him ride around on his shoulder like a monkey—one of the prisoners had a monkey once, but then another prisoner had his food parcel stolen, so he was hungry, and he killed the monkey and roasted and ate it, and there was a big fight and a lockdown. But Nyi Lay doesn't want to ride on anyone's shoulder. He doesn't want to be picked up at all. When the boy tried, the lizard ran away. So it's better just to watch him and feed him and listen to him chirp-chirp his few words.

The boy lies on his back, knees to the roof. From this position he can see the books. They did not disappear while he was feeding Nyi Lay. They are still here. Sighing, he looks at the variously worn and naked spines, the dried yellow glue. Why do I keep them? Why do I keep It? He can feel It beneath him, under the rag blankets, buried in the earth, wrapped up in the plastic bag. It pokes at his ribs like a bone-white finger, asking him the same question with wretched insistence: *Why do you keep me? Why do you keep me?*

Through the drumming rain, he hears his beetle pawing in its box. *Kratch-kratch kratch-kratch.* The beetle has grown to twice the size it was when the boy first picked it up near the watchtower. He reaches over and opens the big matchbox. It pushes against his fingers and makes a brief inspection of his palm before climbing over a knuckle. The boy strokes the red triangles on its back as it marches purposefully up his arm, fearless, over his lime-green shirtsleeve and onto his shoulder, onto his bare neck, without trying to get away. He's relieved that the creature never stretches out a hidden pair of wings. A flying beetle would want to fly off into the world.

He pulls up his shirt and prods the armored insect down, letting it walk over his bare brown chest. The claws catch, small hooks in the boy's flesh, but they only tickle. They never hurt, unless he plucks the beetle up too quickly; then the claws dig in, trying to hang on.

Visiting with the beetle is not as much fun as it used to be. When both of them were younger, he used to play with the creature for hours, making little tracks in his rag bed and devising small adventures—the beetle pushes a pebble, the beetle hangs on to a finger upside down—but at the moment it's pure distraction, to keep him from thinking about the books. He looks at them again and forgets the beetle as it crawls onto his longyi. Only when it reaches the inside of his bare knee does he sit up, giggling. He carefully detaches the little soldier from his skin and drops it back into the box, then pushes the cardboard drawer closed.

Kratch-kratch-kratch. "Hey, you. Sleep! I'll feed you tomorrow." It's a carrion beetle, patient muncher of dead stuff and lizard turds, nothing to recommend it but the red markings on its armor.

The candle gutters and snaps, rippling shadows over the rippled walls. *Kratch-kratch.* The boy looks around, finds a few of Nyi Lay's turds stuck to the wall, picks them off, and puts them in the box. Now the beetle will be quiet.

Finally his hand darts out and grabs the book on top of the smaller pile. Books! The picture on the cover is a faded landscape of trees and sky. In the foreground, two tiny figures face each other on a curved bridge. Something about the picture makes him sad. He tries to see who the two people are, but their faces are indistinct. Inside the cover are lines, circles, and dots on cheap gray paper.

Words words words words words words words words words words words, zaga-lone-dwei, like the very ones he speaks, bathazaga, but language written down, in dots and circles and pieces, by a hand that knows what it's doing or one of the clattering machines in the main prison office. People can write words with their fingernails on plastic bags, and with pencils and pens too, ballpoint pens. Chit Naing once tried to explain writing. Every word is made of letters, and every letter is one of these curved spots. Understand?

The boy didn't understand, but not wanting to disappoint the jailer, he whispered, "Yes."

Edging closer to the candle, he flips the well-thumbed pages. He stops at a random page and searches through the long printed lines. He wants to find the beginning, the way he found the beginning of his shack at the place where he dug a hole and sunk a wooden post into the earth and buried it again, to hold up a slab of corrugated metal. Isn't there a word like that, the beginning word that holds up a whole book? The boy grips the flimsy cover with both hands, tensing the muscles of his forearms and shoulders.

But it's not like lifting a slab of that corrugated metal or hauling bricks on his head—the thing can't be done with the strength in his back and arms and legs. These books! They infuriate him even as he asks the inmates who are leaving to let him have any leftover printed treasures. He watches warders and prisoners alike read comics, magazines, bits of newspaper. After money, food, and weapons, printed words are the most valuable things in the cage. Occasionally the men laugh as they read. Other times, with a piece of paper from the prison office in their hands, their faces drain still and pale.

With eyes steady on a gray page, the boy carefully copies the facial expressions of the men. Nothing comes of it but the sting of tears, which makes him bite his lip until the sting goes away. He cannot do it. He cannot find the beginning word. The tight lines of script do not open up. How is it possible that he can speak and know his language but fail to know this other thing, which is part of it, so close to it?

The same time Chit Naing explained writing, he also explained reading. The Burmese alphabet, he said, has thirty-three consonants, fifteen vowels. Consonants? Vowels? thought the boy, frowning. The alphabet? All of them are letters, these little lines and circles. The jailer's hand swept over the sheaf of printed papers on the table, beside the teapot and dirty cups. The boy nodded dumbly, though what he really wanted to do was bang his head against the wall. Who could learn all the letters, and remember them, and put them together to make language?

All that's left for the boy is to pretend, just like he does at the nat tree every day now, without fail. He says a prayer to the nat and makes an offering, pretending he knows how it works, he knows what to do. If he pretends well enough, his prayers will be real, his offerings accepted.

His hard little hands hold a book—but never, ever upside down. Once he held a book upside down while reading and the warders made such fun of him that he retreated into his house in rage and didn't go out to piss for hours. Now, by carefully examining the cover of the book and the first pages, he knows if the letters are right side up. On the threshold between his shack and the prison compound, the boy's eyes maneuver over the page slowly, laboriously, like two ants carrying a piece of food many times their own size.

The candle gutters again on another draft of air, but the boy ignores it.

He has a very important job to do now: reading. Letters make words and words tell stories. Books are full of silent stories. Chit Naing explained that to him too. It was the one thing he really understood, because the cage is full of storytellers, men talking all the time, telling their lives large and small about the time before the prison so they remember that world and the people Outside. That's why prisoners and warders alike are hungry for books, these very ones, this wobbly altar of musty paperbacks. Without making a sound, they are full of the world.

The boy holds the book and believes it: *I am reading I am reading*. In the flaring, shifting light, the damp pages tell the story of the good nat and its tree beside the stream, where the big lizard lives who is green but also gray; and of the singer who cannot sing but prays; and of the boy who holds the book and reads what's not yet written while the rain falls and the small lizard talks and the candle burns and burns, its flame reaching out, like each of them, like every one of us, for the invisible air.

. 40 .

The boy is not the only child in the cage. He's just the only one who looks like a child. The rest of them are hiding, inside the bodies of men.

One of these men sits at his desk in the small office he shares with one of the prison accountants, who, fortunately, is off pencil-pushing in another building at the moment. He is relieved to be alone. Under his right hand is a ballpoint pen, which he spins around on the wooden desk.

He's thinking about the power of the unexpected, decisive gesture. He is a tall man, barrel-chested, with large hands, the hands of a builder's son. That's how his mother referred to his father. The builder. For reasons the grown son knows nothing about, his mother left his father and took up with someone else, a policeman who was not overly fond of his stepchild. He was suspicious, jealous of the child from the beginning. When his new wife didn't get pregnant, the policeman grew resentful, then angry. Without offspring of his own to weigh the balance, he began to feel unfairly burdened by another man's child.

One night after he'd been drinking, the policeman began to fight with his wife, goading her with a nasty joke, an insult, another harsh joke. This was normal enough. For a while she jousted back, her voice wheedled sharp with bitterness. Eventually she left the small room where they ate to-gether, seeking an escape in the outdoor cooking area behind the house. It was the one place where her husband usually left her alone. This time, though, he followed, standing above her as she squatted and began to wash up the bowls and plates. He kept at it, accusing, poking.

When he finally found the sharpest weapon to stick in and twist—shouting that she was like a dead-end street because she couldn't bear his children—the insult broke her open, not to tears or an equal insult, but to rage. She replied, quite unexpectedly and not without a certain grace, by throwing a pan of cooking oil at him. It wasn't that hot, but it hurt enough to infuriate him, and it ruined his uniform. He responded by grabbing her hair and dragging her a few steps to the kitchen water vat, one of the old clay ones. He pushed her down, hard, into the water. When he yanked her up, her face was purple and twisted with choking and coughing. He pushed her down again. Then again. Each time he pulled her out, her face was darker, more unrecognizable. But her six-year-old son recognized her. He came running out of the house to save her. When his stepfather screamed at him, he shrank away and began to cry. After a few more minutes of watching, his fear caught in his throat so that he couldn't breathe properly.

Finally the policeman let her fall to the ground. Choking, water bub-bling from her nose and her mouth, she slowly found her breath again. When her husband was certain she was all right, he beat her. The boy watched his mother being drowned, then beaten, not with the cooking pan, which was too unwieldy, but with the policeman's baton, which was always close at hand. The child knew the beating was his fault. He crawled under a low table and made himself very small. That is how his mother found him, when she was able to haul herself off the ground where her husband had dropped her. The man had fled the house, still cursing, but her child was there, in shock, shaking violently, milk teeth clacking together.

The boy is a grown man in an office now, spinning a pen on his desk. His memories of that evening are small arrows lodged deep inside him, remembered-forgotten, slivered through his brain and his body. The mo-ment he recalls vividly is the beginning: his mother's unexpected reply, the amber oil flying through the air, his stepfather's face frozen in mid-yell, comical in its utter surprise. It's a relief to laugh about his stepfather thirty years later, to consign him to ridiculousness, just another powerless township copper lording it over his wife. The man's terror as a child, and his anger, and his useless love—it saved no one, his love—are locked in a deeper mind, the mind of his body, heart and head and limbs, the strong legs that carry him to work every day.

Since his accident on the stairs, Handsome's knee bothers him constantly, but even in pain his body is as faithful as that old story about a terrified child. Determined to tell itself, that story has become the work he does, the man he is.

It's upsetting to think that this business over the pen might lose him his recommendation to work as an MI, but the Chief Warden is furious with him. He says the pen search has been a farce, causing more problems than it's solved. In Hall Five, one of the convicts attacked a warder, and half the block joined in the cheering. Luckily it was Warder Soe Thein in charge and not anyone else. A few more minutes and there would have been a riot instead of just a lockdown.

But no matter what happens, he'll manage. He can do this work. He could do whatever is involved in being a military intelligence agent, any grueling job, he's sure of that. He runs on a fuel that will not run out. If he had to name its source, a child's anger and fear would not cross his mind, though he still thinks of cooking oil flung hot through the air. He thinks of the beautiful shock of the violent, righteous act, how it has the power to stun and silence.

There is a slight tap at the door, which is already open, but the fellow hesitates at the threshold. "Come in!" Handsome calls out, and looks up to see the accountant. The young fellow is carrying a tray in his hands, two cups of sweet tea on it, along with a small pot of le-phe-yeh, the bitter brew. Handsome greets him, softens because of the two cups.

He holds the tray out, very politely, he's a nice guy, in his midtwenties, Chinese, clean-cut but not geeky like most of the pencil-pushers.

"Thank you," Handsome says, taking the proffered cup. The accountant sits down at the desk opposite Handsome and takes out one of the smaller ledgers. He licks the nub of a freshly sharpened pencil and begins copying a list of figures he's brought over from the administration offices. Handsome stops playing with the pen and picks it up instead. He's supposed to be writing a report on the results of the search.

What a waste of time. He raises the cup of hot liquid to his lips. A bad smell drifts in, from the open window perhaps; the latrines are not so far away. The sweet tea, light brown in color, is already in his mouth when he realizes that the smell is so sudden because it's right there, on his lips, that stink is in his mouth. There's fury and disgust in his volcanic cough; he's spitting out the smell and taste of shit, spraying it over his desk, the paper and pen. When his knee jerks up against the bottom of the desk, he gasps in pain, coughs harder. The accountant looks up.

Handsome yells, "What's in this tea? What did you put in the tea?"

The remainder of the liquid flies from his cup and splashes from the accountant's stunned face onto his desk, soaking ledger and papers. An unsteady "Ak-haa-hrrgggaa!" escapes him, rising two octaves at the end, part pain because the liquid is hot, part fear because Handsome is coming toward him.

"There's shit in the tea!"

Fear overcomes the young man's confusion. He begins to plead, "Sir, it's just tea, I got it from the warders' quarters. What's wrong?" He stands behind the shield of his desk, measuring escape routes. There are only two. Window or door?

Handsome screams, "There's shit in my tea! Which of you bastards did this?"

The window is the only way. The accountant knows he'll never make it to the door; Handsome is blocking the way. Behind his desk, he carefully steps out of his flip-flops; it's always better to run in bare feet. He makes a desperate appeal, "Jailer Nyunt Wai Oo, sir, if there was anything in the tea, sir, I didn't put it, I didn't put it, it wasn't me."

Handsome picks up the pot of bitter tea and fiddles with the aluminum top, but in his haste he can't remove it. "Fucking bastard Chink!" he yells, hurling the pot as hard as he can at the accountant's head.

The young man ducks just in time; the teapot crashes against the wall behind him, splashing hot tea on his back. Like a martial artist in a kung-fu film, he takes a running leap for the open window. He bangs his shins hard on the frame and dives roughly into a roll on the ground, shoulder first. The flaying pain of the dislocation rips an indiscriminate, high-pitched scream out of him: "Eeeeeeeeeeeeh, aaaiiieeeeh!" Upon seeing Handsome's face at the window, he becomes more articulate. "Help! Help me! I'm being attacked!"

He struggles to his feet and takes a few quick steps, hanging on to his shoulder to keep it from flopping around; then he starts to run, crying, toward the administration office, where other civilized men, clerks like himself, will protect him from the madman.

Bitter water and dark green leaves drip in abstract arcs down the wall, over the desk, dousing the open ledger again, which was already wet from the cup of sweet tea. When Handsome picks up the ledger, tea pours off its surface, smudging the figures. How could such a small vessel hold so much liquid? He clears his throat. This sound, in the empty room, is strangely menacing. If he were to speak now, he doesn't know what he would say. Would he recognize his own voice?

It's better to be quiet. Better to be still for a moment.

Holding the drenched ledger, he crosses back to his own desk and carefully picks up the white teacup. From a distance, he sniffs. Strong tea, condensed milk. He sniffs again, more closely. He can't smell anything else, anything offensive. He lifts his head and inhales.

The whole office is scented with sweet, milky tea.

. 41 .

I'm not being nosy. The junior jailer was supposed to come find me yesterday at the shrine or in the gardens, but he never showed up. That's the only reason I'm asking." In nervous excitement, Sein Yun works the dirt out from under his nails. He speaks as politely as possible with the warder on duty outside of Hall Four, but it's hard to contain himself. "So. Where is he?"

The warder responds with a smile.

"Come on. I'm sure to find out soon enough."

The man turns his head in the other direction.

The palm-reader grumbles and sticks his hand down his longyi, into the hidden pocket. "You guys would strip the skin off a mangy dog, you're so greedy." He fishes out a cheroot and hands it over.

The warder pouts. Sein Yun reaches back down and drops another cheroot into the still-outstretched hand. "So?"

"He had trouble with the junior accountant yesterday. It was a bad day. He had to deal with the Chief."

"What kind of trouble?"

"He'll tell you himself if he wants to."

"Two cheroots for that? Why don't you tell me what the fuck is going on?"

"I said, he'll tell you himself. Out of pure generosity, I will let you know that a bunch of underground dissident agents from the border were brought in this morning. From an MI center. They're in the poun-san khan right now. That's where Handsome is, venting his frustration."

"That's hardly news. Where else would he be? Listen, will you tell him I need to see him? It's about the search."

The warder guffaws. "He won't be interested. The search is over and done with. That's the word from the Chief."

"Just let him know I have something to tell him, okay? It's important. Surely he won't be with the politicals all night—he has to eat like the rest of us. If you see him at dinner, tell him I'll be in the gardens till lockup. After that he'll have to send for me or come to the hall himself."

Curiosity piqued, the warder whispers, "Did you find the fucking thing? Do you have it?"

Sein Yun grins. "Just tell him I need to talk to him, would you? I have some news that will make him happy."

Teza's mouth is full of a steady, bloody throbbing. But he doesn't care how much it hurts to talk. The moment Free El Salvador appears, the singer asks, "Where is your mother?"

It's like a brick dropped on the tray in the boy's hands. He lurches forward, knocked off balance by the power of a word. Not *motherfucker*, which he hears often enough and is sometimes called.

May May!

Can a word be color? Light falls in yellow bands on the bamboo floor. The flowers are yellow and fuchsia; they open across the lime-bright cotton of a tamin, wrapping her hips, stretching across her thighs as she sits down on her knees. She leans over the palette of stone and the broken mirror. She sprinkles water on the stone, then grinds the soft wood against it, around and around, until the gray palette turns ivory with the wet fragrant paste of thanakha. Stretching out her first two fingers, she touches the palette, spreads the cream on her face, touches the palette again, spreads the cream on his face, around and around, the scent growing on their skin like a white flower after the first rains. With a small blue comb, she draws a swirl of lines in the circles.

May May!

Who remembers the voice of a dead woman?

Zaw Gyi, chit day, chit day, muh-may-neh naw. I love you, little one, don't forget.

Something stings the boy's eyes; he rubs them. Holding the tray with one hand, he steps forward so quickly that the boiled rice jumps out when he shoves the food into the cell. He seems about to stand up and bolt, which makes Teza regret speaking so bluntly.

But then a mighty exhalation deflates him. His tight-muscled frame loosens; his weight shifts back onto his heels.

Teza crouches down slowly, not wanting to scare him away. They each see a face framed by iron bars. The boy meets the gaze of the man and the man finds the eyes of the child. Free El Salvador is so still the singer can see him sway forward, sway back, small bent tree in a breeze. He's felt this breeze himself, while sitting in meditation, his body pulsing almost imperceptibly with his heartbeat. But he's never seen it in another person.

His voice reaches through the bars like a hand. "Do you know where she is?"

Free El Salvador opens his mouth, but nothing emerges. The answer is somewhere in him. The whole story is in him, but where is the beginning word? His gaze drops to the cement.

"It's a good thing, if you know. Do you know?"

"She's dead." The voice is small and cool. *She* is an unfamiliar sound. *She* of colors and long hair wound up and fastened with a plain old comb, a coughing woman who hid bloody handkerchiefs under her mat. She was a woman who sang, making mohinga noodles, and hummed, washing out the aluminum bowls.

"And your father?"

"Also dead."

"Can you leave the prison?"

"Why?"

"Can you go away from the prison?"

"Where?"

"Outside. To the city."

The boy turns his head, blinks at the wall. He doesn't feel very well; maybe he's getting sick. He will say only a few more words before leaving. "My job is here."

"But this is a prison. A big, ugly cage, Nyi Lay. None of us want to live here. It's not a good place to live. And you're the luckiest one among all of us. Do you know that?"

The boy replies by baring his teeth like an angry gibbon. This is how he feels about his tremendous luck.

Teza tries not to laugh, because of the pain, but sharp puffs of laughing-breath blow out his nose. "But you *are* lucky. You are. Of course you know why."

What is the singer talking about? Has he gone crazy? Maybe he is just stupid. "Why am I lucky?"

Teza puts his hand around one of the bars. "Because you are different from everyone here, warders and prisoners alike. You are free to go, Little Brother. You can leave the cage."

With Sein Yun gone, the warder pockets his two new cheroots and immediately makes his way to the poun-san khan cells. Halfway across the compound, he hears Handsome shouting commands at the new politicals. A couple days in these instruction cells get fresh prisoners ready for the pecking order. Usually high-ranking criminals are dispatched to "teach" the new arrivals how to behave in front of warders and prison officials, but Handsome keeps new politicals for himself.

The warder sends a guard in, with the news of an important message for the junior jailer. Waiting, he lights up one of his new cheroots and listens to a stuttering cry of pain, then a low sob. Handsome is too dedicated to his work.

When the jailer finally appears, he's red in the face from physical exertion and his eyes are buggy. The truncheon is still in his hand. Noting these details for a future storytelling session among his workmates, the warder proceeds cautiously. "Sir, I am very sorry to interrupt you, but I have a message from the inmate Sein Yun."

"What is it then? Can't you see I'm working?"

"Yes, sir, I'm sorry. But Sein Yun wants to see you as soon as possible. He has some important news about the search, sir." The warder lowers his voice conspiratorially. "He says it will make you happy."

"Oh, really? The prick. Where is he?"

"In the gardens, sir. I wanted to let you know right away, sir."

When the man's gone, Handsome pulls a handkerchief out of his pocket and wipes the sweat from his face. His concentration has been broken. The attending warder can finish the session tonight, but the jailer will be back tomorrow to give those bastards another lesson. There's one guy in there he wouldn't mind having a long talk with, alone. He didn't come off the border but out of some satellite town near Rangoon. The report from the interrogation center says his little hut was being used as a safe house for activists and underground rebel agents from Thailand. They worked on him at the center—electric telephone, riding the motorcycle, kneeling on glass—but he isn't broken at all, he isn't afraid. Why didn't the MI guys beat that self-righteous expression right off his face? If Handsome were an MI agent, he wouldn't let such a dangerous prisoner go until he was crying under his boot. One inmate like that in the poun-san khan and the whole atmosphere of the place changes, because the other new arrivals think they have a big hero. It's the brave ones who have to be shown up and knocked down. Like the fucking singer. Handsome regrets all the trouble that Teza's caused him, but he doesn't regret breaking his flapping jaw in two.

These thoughts tick through his mind as he unrolls his shirtsleeves and heads across the compound to the gardens in front of the big prisoner halls. He sees the palm-reader in the distance, carrying a large bucket to the edge of the mud. Handsome doesn't think for a moment that Sein Yun has found the pen. The little yellow fiend is just grasping at straws now, because he suspects that his own sentence reduction has been lost in the wake of this mess. Well, he doesn't have to suspect anymore. Last night the Chief made it clear that Sein Yun would not be getting a cut to his sentence. He also told Handsome that he wouldn't be offered a position with the MI anytime soon. There's "internal restructuring," he said, which means no more jobs for nonmilitaries. After the fiasco with the accountant, no fucking wonder. The only good news is that the Chief told him he wouldn't record that "unfortunate incident" on his work record.

What was he going to do, mark it down with a big black *X*? All Handsome did was toss some stinking tea at the guy, and the cunt had to jump out the window and wreck his shoulder! Handsome stuck to the story that there was something offensive, even poisonous, in the tea, but the Chief Warden didn't care. "I am not interested in your excuses, Officer Nyunt Wai Oo."

Fuck you! It wasn't an excuse, it was a *reason*. Though he knew he'd made a mistake as soon as he smelled the cup afterward. Why did he fly off the handle like that? He's not really going crazy, he's just pissed off. The hellish day turned into a hellish night, because he went home and had an argument with his wife. As if he's responsible for the rising price of chicken!

He stops walking abruptly and uses the pause to light a cheroot. It's his knee. If he's not going to limp, he has to rest for a couple of minutes every now and then. Sein Yun's caught sight of him; Handsome can tell by the way the palm-reader has stuck his nose out like a hungry rat. The jailer leans down and digs his thumb into the cramped muscles of his lower thigh. His whole leg aches. His knee is obviously connected to his brain, because when he thinks too much, it starts to burn. Yesterday, after the accountant jumped out the window, just before the warders on guard duty came into the office, the swollen joint buckled under his weight, and he would have fallen down if he hadn't caught the edge of his desk. His wife says he should go to the doctor, but god only knows how much that will cost. She says, Go to the prison doctor, it's free, but he wouldn't let that quack touch him with a ten-foot pole.

The palm-reader talks to the guard now, gesturing in Handsome's direction, getting permission. Good. It's better if he comes over here anyway, away from the other men; no need for all of them to hear whatever he has to say. Sein Yun scurries around the outer edge of the garden. Along with the scent of shit-rich mud, the jailer smells Sein Yun's excitement. He's almost leaping over the brick chips, hitching his longyi tighter around his waist as if it's a warrior's belt. Fuck, he's an ugly guy, grinning like a dark-lipped ghoul. Handsome pulls out his handkerchief again and wipes the last layer of work sweat from his upper lip and forehead. Then, stepping carefully into the torn brace of his knee, he walks toward the palm-reader.

. 42 .

F ree El Salvador." Between broken jaw and accent, the sound is
fee-a-sabado.

The boy gives him a quizzical look. "What does that mean?"

"Those are the words on your shirt." Teza points to the holey T-shirt,
which the boy awkwardly pulls away from his body, trying to get a better
look. Those straight and sticklike letters, with hardly a circle and not a single dot among them, look very unfamiliar.

"It's a name. El Salvador. Not in Burmese but in English. And Span-
ish. It's the name of another country, a small country far away, where . . ."
Where what? Teza knows very little about El Salvador, except that it was
something like Burma. The people wanted to run their own government,
but the military wouldn't let them, and so many innocent people were
killed and imprisoned and disappeared. He read about it once in an old
copy of *Time*. "The word at the beginning is *free*. Lut-latyeh. Because El
Salvador was a prison country, like Burma, and her people wanted to be
free. Because you wear that shirt, sometimes I think of that word as your
name. Sabado, for short." The obvious question strikes Teza. "What is
your real name? What is the name your family gave to you?"

The boy rubs his nose to avoid the question. He has to go soon; he's already been here too long, as usual. He looks up again. The singer's still staring at him. He's seen eyes like that before, in the skulls of addicts and inmates transferred from the northern work camps, the ones who haven't eaten enough for months. Those men are frightening too, like Teza.

But how can he be afraid of the Songbird? He squares his shoulders and looks at the thin, battered man. Why does Teza want to know his name, anyway?

Tan-see Tiger knows it, and Chit Naing, but the boy asked them please not to use it. He prefers his prison names—nyi lay, rat-killer, brat, the boy, kala-lay, any of the nicknames the men use for him. They are easier. They mean what the men want them to mean and nothing more. His real name is like his father's tooth and his mother's thanakha tin. He wants to keep it hidden. Safe.

How small the boy looks now, like a very young child, six or seven years old. Watching him wrestle with the question, Teza worries that he might do some shocking, normal-child thing, like burst into tears. "Never mind—Sabado's as good a name as any, no? Sabado, don't you want to go to school?"

The boy raises his eyebrows. "School?" How could he go to school? He's not even sure what school looks like. It's the same with women. This morning some of the convicts in Hall Two were talking about women, describing their bits. The men said that women don't have cocks at all, but holes. Holes! Right between their legs. When the boy staunchly refused to believe this, the convicts laughed so hard they almost fell down. He looks inquisitively at Teza and lowers his voice. "Do women have cocks or holes?"

"What?"

"Do women have holes or cocks?" He doesn't know why, but he's sure the singer will tell him the truth.

Teza's the one rubbing his nose now, thoughtfully, buying time. That the boy extracted this question from the word *school* proves he is a trapped and thwarted teenager. The singer carefully answers the question. "Holes." Sometimes the truth sounds so crude. He tries to fix it. "Special holes."

"Special?"

"Like your cock is special. All those hidden things we've got, you have to take care of them. You protect them, they're . . . special places. A woman takes care of her special place."

"Her hole."

That word again, so raw. Teza's not prepared for this. "Yes, that's right."

"Why *don't* women have cocks?"

Teza breathes a sigh of relief. He knows how to get out of this. "Because the woman is different from the man. She has the babies. They come out of the hole."

"That's why the woman is the mother!" This is the one thing the boy knows about women.

Teza nods again. "And the man is the father." With luck, that will be the end of it. What if he asks about where babies come from? But he need not worry, because the boy suddenly sits down, heavily, on his side of the bars.

His voice is weighted with defeat. "I can't go to school."

"Why not?"

In a whisper, he admits it. "Because I don't know how to read." Each word is a scrap of sandpaper on his tongue.

Teza reaches his hand through the bars and touches the boy's shoulder. "Don't worry. That's what school is for. I know a place where you can learn to read. And the people there will look after you."

The boy tilts his head to the side and asks suspiciously, "What kind of a place?"

"It's a monastery school. Run by an old man who was a friend of my father's."

"You have a father?"

"Everyone has a father. My father is dead, but . . . well, I still have him. And the Hsayadaw is like a father to all the children in his school."

The boy gives the singer a doubtful look.

"Nyi Lay," Teza leans toward him and whispers, "he would teach you how to read. I know he would. Do you know what reading is like?"

Though the boy has many thoughts on this topic, he shrugs his shoulders. He doesn't like to talk about leaving the cage. He's too hungry.

"It's like flying. Reading a book can take you anywhere in the world."

"Ko Teza?" This is the first time the boy has used his name.

"Yes?"

"I have to leave now or I'm going to get in trouble. But can I eat your rice soup before I go?"

"Of course. Go ahead."

He watches the boy eat, his pace increasing as the gruel disappears. The spoon scrapes against the tray, a desperate crescendo. It is the sound, Teza thinks, of pure determination. The boy picks up the dirty tray and the two of them stand together.

"Tzey-zu-tin-ba-deh," the boy thanks him politely.

"That's all right." It's a gift, Little Brother, to feed a small, struggling country.

. 43 .

Black threads sew themselves along the cracks in the walls, on the ground at the edges of buildings. Twilight. To visit the nat tree before it gets too late, the boy has to hurry. He walks quickly, skirting the wall of the kitchen before slipping in to drop off the Songbird's tray. He says hello to the dishwashers and tries to catch a glimpse of the cook. Not for more fish—he receives his payment in the morning only. He just wants to make sure the cook doesn't see him go out to the stream. He's not scared of the crocodiles between the high prison walls, or the ghosts, but it's dark enough for Eggplant to be a worry.

With the cook nowhere in sight, the boy leaves the building through the back kitchen, anxious to visit the tree. He'll be able to think there, about the Songbird and school and reading. He'll say his prayers to the nat.

He takes off his slippers and tucks them in his sling bag, then steps into the stream. With a low clack and loud buzz of electricity, the rampart floodlights turn on, making the boy jump. He scoffs at himself—how silly, to be scared of the light. He starts walking again. Gravel gives way under his feet and his toes sink into the soft mud.

The big lizard is sleeping now. The rats rustle here and there through the shadowy grass, near the big wall. Weeks have passed since he's gone hunting with his stick, but the food from the singer's parcel is finished now. He doesn't like to think about it, but he'll have to start killing rats again.

The water shushes and murmurs around his legs, pulling him on. The ghosts will come out soon enough, maybe even his father. His father was mean sometimes, not friendly like Chit Naing or the Songbird. But the boy is sure he would be kinder as a ghost than he was as a man. Sometimes he suspects Hpay Hpay can see him. That's another reason that he likes to come to the stream and visit the nat tree. His father might be floating around here, drinking tea with the other dead men of the cage.

The branches of the tree are bigger in the floodlights. The tree's shadow spreads across the prison wall like a black-limbed painting of it-self. The boy steps out of the stream and shakes his wet feet.

The morning glories are tightly furled, so he can't leave a flower tucked in the ribbons around the tree trunk. And he didn't bring any rice to make an offering. But he kneels down.

No one can be upset with him if he puts his hands to his forehead like a Muslim, like a Buddhist too—even the Karen Christians do the same sort of thing. If everybody else can do it, why can't he? He whispers to the tree, who has no ears but hears him through its green leaves. To the nat, who must be similar to the Buddha at the shrine, but smaller, small enough to live in the branches of the tree like an invisible monkey. The boy closes his eyes and asks for the word, the beginning word that will open up the books he wants to read. He makes a prayer for bathazaga, the spirit in lan-guage like the nat in the tree. He prays to learn the round alphabet of his mother tongue, of his mother.

And a ghost leaps, furious, onto his shoulder.

His scream is small, one piercing note. He yanks himself away from the claws at his neck. When the creature lets go, the boy flies through the air and falls heavily onto his side at the water's edge. His fingers close on a missile of small rocks and silt as he looks up to take aim at his attacker.

But his hand drops back into the stream. It's not a ghost. In the cross-angles of the floodlights, half of Jailer Handsome's face is sharply lit, the other half is shadowed. The eye in the dark catches light like a broken window.

"You like swimming, do you?" He gives the boy a light kick in the upper thigh, not too hard, just enough to hurt him a little and push him into the water. "It's still rainy season, you know—be careful not to catch a cold." Handsome kicks again, harder this time, at the boy's waist, so his body curls into itself. The jailer's knee immediately begins to burn, but he kicks again, harder, just above the child's belly but below his chest. The kick elicits the telltale snag of breath, the solar plexus in spasm. Funny, but logical: the coughing is quieter than the same sound in an adult man. The little shit is in the stream now, heaving.

The boy feels the cool water soak his shirt, stretch its fingers into his longyi, drenching the turquoise fabric. "Here, let me help you up." Handsome extends a hand, but the boy scrambles to his feet, wheezing and shaking, trying to speak but unable; there's not enough air to make the words.

Handsome takes a step toward him. The boy stumbles backward in the water. He glances over his shoulder, at the tree and its shadow on the prison wall. Then he looks to the big halls. The warders on guard duty must be watching. The nat of the tree must be watching. Why don't they help him? "Leave me alone," he manages in a weak voice.

"Oh, my, the rat-killer is frightened, is he?" Handsome laughs. Then hisses, "I don't have to leave you alone. Got that? I can do whatever I want."

The boy turns his head away from the jailer and spits a gob of phlegm over the narrow stream. Handsome leans forward and strikes, grunting with effort; the thunk of knuckles against the child's cheekbone is surprisingly loud. The boy lands on his back again, this time in the heart of the stream, where the water is deep enough to cover him. He feels the pebbles pushing into his skin as his elbows sink into the soft silt. He lifts his head and chest out of the stream and cries out, trying to stand, but a pawlike hand thrusts him backward again. Opening his mouth to protest, he gulps water, then begins to cough.

Handsome feels a violent craving to *just get it over with,* to step into the stream and grab the child by the neck, hold his head underwater. The Chief Warden's warning—*You have to learn to control yourself, Officer Nyunt Wai Oo*—doesn't matter here; the stream is separate from the compound, and the guards won't stop him. It's the boy's fault. The little rat-killer has been taunting him all this time. When Handsome steps like a giant into the water, the physical relief is as palpable as orgasm. He plants his boots firmly in the mud on either side of the boy's hips and bends forward, his arms reaching out, unstoppable. The ligament in his knee strains away from the bone, sears like a brand; the pain is excruciating but right, stoking his fury. He grabs *FREE EL SALVADOR*, cramming his fists with the threadbare cotton. He hoists the child up sharply, to get a better grip on him, then shoves him in the only direction possible, down, down, the inescapable trajectory of his life, the only choice.

Even the boy sees the inevitability in Handsome's contorted face, a man drowning in his fury as he drowns a child in water, water in the ears, the eyes, the nose, the mouth. The man's strength crashes against the boy's thin, flailing legs, boxing arms all elbows. The breathless choking roars in his ears, fills his eyes with the pressure of his own blood. The roaring heaves and heaves out of him until there is no breath left for sound.

I n the midst of frantic movement, stillness comes quickly, unexpected. The boy stops fighting. His terror is no longer explosion but numbness, an ending, the end of the world. His body was never his own body. There were too many hungers and losses, too many times when it was easier to do this, to slide out of the fearful territory bounded by his skin.

It is magic. He is drowning in the stream, Handsome's clenched hands press him down, but he is also hovering outside, invisible, like the nat. He sees everything that happens to him, but none of it matters. The thin body has gone limp, hardly different from a dead rat, its skin sliding like a velvet sac over viscera and small bones. Underwater, his eyes open to see a blurred shape outlined in light. He thinks, *Handsome is already a ghost!* Then he's gone.

A s quickly as the stillness came, it twists over on itself like a landed fish. Handsome hauls the boy up alive. When his narrow back arches out of the stream, his head snaps into the air, mouth spilling water. He rolls over on his side and begins to heave the food in his stomach onto the gravel. Somewhere close by and very far away he hears Handsome swearing in what sounds like normal human pain. Mid-vomit, he looks up to see the man clutching his knee, stumbling through the nearby grass. The boy wipes his mouth and rolls over, trying to push himself to his feet. If there's something wrong with Handsome's leg, he will be able to outrun him. But the jailer has lifted himself upright too. He glares at the boy, who stands there dripping, bare feet ready to sprint. He's still hacking, but he could run now, if he had to.

The jailer speaks very slowly, through clenched teeth. "Kala-lay, if you stop being so disrespectful, I won't have to hurt you, will I? It has to be *Yes, sir* and *No, sir,* you know that. Now come here."

Water seeps out of the boy's sling bag. His longyi and shirt stick to him. As his coughing begins to subside, he becomes aware of the point on his cheek where Handsome punched him, a sharp ache cutting his face.

"Kala-lay, I just want to ask you some questions."

The boy looks from the kitchen to the lit hospital windows to the first of the big halls, the place where the compound curves, following the octagonal enclosure of the walls. No one will help him. Even Tan-see Tiger's amulets can't help him now. He sees the floodlit figure of a warder on guard duty, the coal of a cheroot burning like a useless beacon.

The jailer is getting angry again. "Get the fuck over here. If I have to cross the stream to talk to you, you'll regret it, I promise you that. I won't save your sorry ass a second time, you little fucker. Just get over here."

The boy would like to curl up, disappear. His voice quavers like his body. "Sir, please don't drown me."

"Just come here. Fuck! Are you deaf as well as stupid?"

Wind moves the leaves of the tree all at once, a susurrus. The boy plods back into the water. He's shivering as he steps out onto the gravel and stands, head down, in front of the jailer, his shoulders tensed. He waits for a slap on the head, or a punch. Nyi Lay wants to put his fingers up to his cheek, to touch the swelling. But he doesn't move.

"I only want to ask you some questions. I think you can help me, kala-lay."

The boy cannot stop shivering. He glances up at Handsome and very quickly drops his eyes to the steady dark shimmer of the stream.

"Remember the big storm last month, when Hall Two flooded?" The man puts his hand on the child's shoulder and kneads the narrow muscles with his fingers. It hurts, but the boy doesn't pull away. He knows he has to forget his fear or Handsome will smell it.

"Do you remember? It was also the day a bunch of politicals were sent to the dog cells."

"Yes."

"Where were you that day?"

Somebody must have seen him near the teak coffin. "In the morning I helped in the gardens, and in the afternoon I was hunting rats."

"Where?"

"Here, by the stream. Then at the back of Hall Two. The rats all came out because of the flood." Weeks ago, the boy made a careful plan about how to tell this lie.

"What about the solitary section at the other end of the big halls?"

"I passed by there on my way to Hall Two, and then again on my way home." Slowly, he loosens his longyi and squeezes out some of the water. He is a fine actor: his forehead furrows with remembering. "My slipper broke. I stopped by one of the solitary houses to fix it. Under the eaves. Because of the rain." Now it doesn't matter that someone saw him by the teak coffin, he has an excuse. He was just on his way home. He reknots his longyi.

Handsome lets go of the boy's shoulder and takes hold of his chin. He bends slightly and hisses in the small, water-streaked face, "You know Sammy, the big Indian? You know how he lost his tongue? Do you?"

The boy's answer is distorted by Handsome's grip on his jaw. "Nah."

"He lied to me, and I cut the tongue right out of his head."

Handsome is a liar too. The boy knows the giant didn't have a tongue when he arrived here. He lost his tongue somewhere else, not to the jailer's knife.

The boy slowly pulls his head back. Handsome releases his jaw. "Sir, I'm not lying. I just stopped there for a second because my slipper broke. Look, I show you—it's tied together with string." He starts to open the bag on his shoulder, where his flip-flops are safely stowed, but the jailer swears in disgust and pushes the boy backward.

"I don't want to see your dirty shoes. I'm looking for something that got lost that day, during the storm. I want to find it."

The boy has stumbled but not fallen. He stands again, head down, his eyes on the jailer's boots. "Sir, I would be happy to help you in your search, if you like. I am very good at finding things."

"Hey, kala-lay. Dirty little Indian, look at me."

The child lifts up his large dark eyes.

Handsome whispers, "I won't cut out your tongue." He leans down and takes hold of the child's jaw again, gently, then moves the small skull back and forth, as though testing the flexibility of the vertebrae. "If you are lying to me, I will kill you."

The boy does not blink.

"Did you find anything in the mud that day, when you stopped by the singer's cell? Hmm? Did you?"

"I didn't find anything, sir."

Handsome shoves him away again. "Go on, then. Get out of here. I'm sick of your smell."

The boy turns and wades noisily through the stream. When he feels far away enough to be defiant, he takes his slippers out of his sling bag and shoves his feet into them, one at a time. There is no string, no broken strap. He strides on, away from the water. He doesn't need to look back. He knows Handsome is still there, watching him.

When the boy disappears between the hospital and the kitchen, the jailer leans down and touches his knee. He would like nothing more than to sit down on the ground. Instead he turns and spits at the little tree. Someone's going to have to cut it down. There aren't supposed to be any trees on the prison grounds. They axed the big ones years ago to stop prisoners and warders alike from thinking that nats would help them escape punishment or get promotions. Superstitious crap.

Handsome puts his back to the tree. If he could, he'd be right on the boy's heels, but he has to rest for a few minutes. When he was showing that little bugger who's boss, something ripped open around the kneecap—it could have been a damn bullet hitting him, that's how much it hurt. He nearly fell on top of the kid. He's still trembling, but he can't tell whether it's from the pain or the excitement.

He looks up. The boy is long gone. *But don't think you're getting away, you little rat-killing Indian shit.*

A couple of warders confirmed it. They saw the boy close to the teak coffin that evening. The only place in the whole prison where they haven't searched for the white pen is the rat-killer's shack. Handsome can't believe he didn't think of it himself; the kid's always put him on edge.

After he caught the boy stealing food, he complained to the Chief Warden, but the Chief didn't care. "What are you on about now? Don't you have enough to deal with, Officer Nyunt Wai Oo? He's an orphan and a good worker. He was eating leftovers off dirty plates? That's hardly stealing. Leave the kid alone." *Leave the kid alone.* Well, he won't leave the little thief alone now. If he steals food right out from under their noses, there's no telling what else he would steal, what else he has secreted away in that doghouse of his. Handsome takes a half-smoked cheroot out of his breast pocket and lights it. For a minute or two he needs this, just this, sweet heavy smoke to calm him. He will take a break and rest his fucked-up knee and then go do what needs to be done.

. 44 .

The singer goes back, before he met Thazin, years before he fought with Aung Min about the right way to win a revolution. He returns to an afternoon without cages, when he was still a boy and his father stood with a bag of oranges at the wooden threshold of the pongyi-kyaung, the monastery school. He bows to the abbot, the smiling Hsayadaw, raising his hands together to show his respect. Then he follows his father into the compound and watches him as he sets up a doctor's office on the table of an open-air schoolroom. Stethoscope in hand, Dr. Kyaw Win Thu checks the boy with fever, the one with an eye infection, another with a lung ailment, the thin child who cannot gain weight. After his rounds, the doctor and the abbot sit under a scrawny tree and share a cheroot, laughing over things Teza cannot understand.

He wanders off. In the room where the orphans eat together on the wooden floor, he begins chatting idly with a novice who's doing schoolwork, his dark orange robe half unbound. The boy complains that he isn't very good at math. Teza finishes the novice's page of sums while the boy rewraps his robe, then they go outside to play.

Unable to remember the boy clearly, he puts Free El Salvador in his place. Perhaps it's all vanity and nostalgia, emotions he believes he's relinquished. Questions replace his memories. Why shouldn't it be possible? The Hsayadaw takes care of so many children. If they bring thousands of men into the prison, why can't they send out a single child? Free El Salvador hasn't committed a crime.

Chit Naing has to help. He will help. He must. If for no other reason, then simply because he feels guilty. The jailer will have to go to the pongyi-kyaung and speak with the Hsayadaw, remind him that Dr. Kyaw Win Thu used to treat the children and the monks at the monastery school. And every year Daw Sanda used to give ahlu—a noble offering of new robes to the novices. At least in 1988 she was still doing this. Teza went with her that year. They also took food to the children. If the Hsayadaw knew where Free El Salvador was from, he would take him in, Teza is sure of it, no matter how crowded the old monastery school might be. Out of love and respect for Teza's parents, he would extend his love to the boy.

But what if the abbot has died? The last time Teza saw him, he must have been in his late sixties, nimble enough but also fragile, parchment-skinned. Teza remembers walking up some stairs behind him. The Hsayadaw hitched up his saffron robes, careful not to trip on the worm-eaten steps. Teza watched the muscles contract in the abbot's long, skinny calves. The parallel tendons at the back of his ankles and knees were like tension cables that held the whole delicate mechanism together. What if the mechanism has slowed to a stop?

Teza taps his fingers on the cement floor. Then he closes his eyes and tries to still his rattling mind. He sees the abbot's face, his eyes almost disappeared in the deep creases of a smile.

Weariness settles into him. Too much thinking. And talking. Speaking with the boy has fatigued him. His jaw is throbbing, pushing pain into the rest of his head. Things get worse in the evening, when the labor of getting through the day leaves him completely wrung out. He will meditate, then sleep. He sits down in the center of the cell and genuflects three times, facing the bars and the world beyond the bars.

Metta.

Karuna.

Mudita.

Upekkha.

These are the Four Divine Abidings. Love. Compassion. Joy in the good fortune of others. Equanimity.

Upekkha. He begins and ends with this word. Equanimity in the face of what must be. The breath travels easily through his body, expanding the muscles of his back over his rib cage, beneath his shoulder blades. It used to be so hard to calm his mind and sit quietly in his body, but there's no battle anymore. He breathes until the word *upekkha* is nothing but an empty form, a skeleton of letters with air moving through it. Then the word itself blows away with the slight wind of the heart. The lungs expand and contract until he feels as if he has no body. The pain joins this lightness, despite its great weight. He carries the burden, though the burden is not himself. He is nothing but a thread of air.

Yet he desires. Precisely this silence, this peace. He wants to stretch it, stay inside it, where he is unbound. Blood pumps bright new shards of glass into his jaw. He feels tendons, muscles in the bottom of his mouth, his tongue, all thumping with his slow pulse. To still the raging mind, to calm the body in great pain: he has found these treasures in his breath.

If desire is the root of suffering, as the Buddha said, is it wrong to crave this peace? The Buddha must have desired enlightenment. Otherwise he would have remained a spoiled prince in a grand palace.

Can it be so easy, to enter the stream? Sotapatti magga. He's impressed with himself for remembering the Pali term. It's been years since he studied such things. Stream-entry is the first step to becoming an enlightened one. To enter the stream is to receive the first glimpse of Nibbana, nirvana, fire unbound from its fuel, gone cold and passionless. That is the nature of the mind released.

His own name means fire. Fire and glory, Teza. How this word strengthened him, tied him to Burma's history. He remembers the beginning, in the interrogation center, clinging so fiercely to the only thing he had: *teza*. Can he desire the end of his own name?

And do what? Take another one, the name of a monk? Becoming enlightened has to be more difficult than acquiring a new name, or sitting through a challenging meditation. Otherwise, wouldn't everyone attain it? The cage would be full of Bodhisattvas, their eyes all shining light as they shat in their buckets and scribbled secret messages to the world. In the Buddha's day, it happened, the texts tell the stories: after the crowds heard the great teacher speak, they attained enlightenment while milking their cows or squatting in the fields. But that was a long time ago. The world must have been simpler when the Buddha was alive.

If his mother caught him thinking of himself as a Hpaya-Laung, an enlightened being, she would scold him and tell him to stop being so immodest.

Perhaps it's not enlightenment he's glimpsed, but his end.

There. Death.

Does it terrify, such a small word? The last one before the next birth. Can dying to the present body be this, passing through all the forms and their skeletons until there is nothing left but empty flesh, its spirit un-housed for a while, waiting?

From far away, he hears human voices. They come nearer now, draw-ing him up from the depths of his breath.

He doesn't want to return. The voices pull and pull. The singer opens his eyes, slowly. To be borne, it must happen slowly. Moving his hands from his lap will be like shifting stones. In less than a minute Chit Naing and the chattering doctor will come around the corner of the outer wall. The singer would like to tell them to visit another time. He is busy now.

He remembers the world, that growing tree of thought and possibility. Images shift through his mind, touch one another, leaves turning to light. Free El Salvador. His mother watering her orchids. Daw Aung San Suu Kyi in her compound, at a small gathering of students, turning to him with an open smile and asking, *Where is your guitar, Ko Teza, will you play some-thing for us?* The Hsayadaw, on reaching the second floor of the monastery school, speaking in a quiet voice, *Teza, you are like a son to me. As your fa-ther was also. So many fine children make me a very fortunate old man.* He stretched his thin arms wide, as though to embrace the whole of the old monastery. In the same instant, two small novices sweeping the compound looked up at the landing and saw their beloved teacher. They bowed to him, and waved, then started to laugh.

Keys clank and ring at the iron bars. Teza grimaces at the sound, magnified in the raw state after meditation. If an ant were on his arm now, it would feel as heavy as a small brown cat. He lets a last breath go and looks up to see Chit Naing peering at him. His glasses flicker as he speaks.

"Ko Teza, are you all right?"

Teza nods.

Chit Naing pulls open the iron grille. Both jailer and doctor walk into the cell. The round-faced doctor in his grubby white coat is all hustle and bustle, unfastening his black bag, pulling things out of it. "First I check your heartbeat, see if you're still alive." He unbuttons the bottom of his white coat and squats down with the snaky stethoscope in his hands. "How is the Songbird doing this evening? Still not singing much, eh? But Jailer Chit Naing tells me you're talking more."

Feeling the warm breath on the side of his face like a wet tongue, Teza leans away and closes his eyes again, repressing a shudder. He does not want to be touched. As the *no* takes form in his mind, the doctor's hand is on his wrist, feeling for the pulse, pressing. Teza pulls his hand away and holds it against his chest. He crosses his other arm on top of it and whispers, "My heart's still beating."

"Your pulse is a little slow."

"I just finished meditation."

Chit Naing says, "See, Doctor? That explains why he's so quiet." The doctor frowns at the jailer, then at his reluctant patient. Chit Naing clears his throat. "Why don't you just give him his injection, Doctor, so we can go?"

"Not possible. For precisely the reasons I mentioned earlier, I want to check his heartbeat."

"You were just saying how late it is. The sooner we finish up here, the better."

The doctor stares rudely at the jailer, clearly miffed by these directives. Crouching puts him at a disadvantage, so he stands, drawing himself up to his full height, still a head shorter than Chit Naing. "Listening to a man's heartbeat does not take half an hour."

"I appreciate that, Doctor, but we are disturbing the inmate."

"Disturbing him?" The doctor ejects a scornful little laugh. "Jailer Chit Naing, I'm sure I don't have to remind you, of all people, that we're not in a hotel. And I am doing this as a favor. Better to say the inmate is disturbing me, keeping me from my family."

The words shoot back and forth over Teza's head. He would like to cover his shaven scalp with his hands.

"That's why I suggest you just give him his injection and we leave."

"I refuse to give him any morphine unless he cooperates. Look at him, skin and bones. He's not eating. Even a man with a broken jaw shouldn't be so thin." He barks at Teza, "You're getting the equivalent of three meals a day. Why have you lost so much weight?" Then he turns back to Chit Naing. "I'm going to check his heartbeat while he still has one, and I'm going to talk to the Chief Warden about this again. Then we can decide how we'll proceed."

Chit Naing has no choice but to acquiesce. He takes a step back and bends down. "Ko Teza, you heard the doctor. I'm afraid he's right. Let him check your heartbeat and he'll give you your shot."

Teza looks into his friend's eyes. "I don't need the injection."

Chit Naing cocks his head, unsure if he's heard correctly. "It's the morphine, Teza, not an antibiotic."

Teza glances at the doctor. "Yes, I know. I don't want it. I don't want any more favors."

"No more favors, eh?" The doctor grunts. "That's fine with me." Chit Naing hears anger in the words. The man's thinking about the money he'll lose. The doctor has wrapped the stethoscope around his hand in such a stranglehold that he has trouble untangling it and stuffing it back into his bag. "I can understand your martyrdom up to a point, but tell me why you aren't eating. If you're talking this much, back on your soapbox, then you are well enough to drink rice soup. What should I tell the Chief Warden?"

"I keep the Eight Precepts."

The doctor looks back at Chit Naing. "You see? I told you." Then he addresses Teza. "Idiot. No food after noon is slow suicide for a man in your condition. You must know that."

Teza drops his head, as if he needs to look at his hands in order to rearrange them on his lap, one on top of the other. He wonders if he is ready to begin. He could announce his decision now, to the doctor. But that would be too fast, a hasty reaction to the man's badgering. First he needs to talk to Jailer Chit Naing about the boy. He will make things happen, but at his own pace.

Angry now, the doctor announces, "This inmate is being uncooperative, Jailer Chit Naing. Injured or not, I hope he isn't beyond punishment."

"Thank you for your suggestion, Doctor."

The man snaps his bag shut and bends down, eyeing Teza. "It makes no difference to me if you starve yourself, but the Chief will have you beaten until you start eating properly. If he wants you to eat, you will eat."

Teza replies, "Doctor, the threat of more torture is enough to ruin anyone's appetite."

"Not mine. I'm very hungry and I'm going home for dinner. Jailer Chit Naing, I will see you tomorrow." The doctor opens the grille and struts officiously out of the cell.

The jailer takes off his glasses, pulls a handkerchief from his pocket, and polishes away, as though clean lenses will enable him to see through his confusion. He can't understand why Teza didn't tell him about the Eight Precepts. He could have arranged for food to be brought to the cell at dawn, so the singer could keep the precepts and still get enough to eat.

He looks carefully at Teza's face. The area around his left eye is still dark and puffy with old bruising. The mouth, of course, will always be askew. It still looks rather gruesome, the sort of deformity people either stare at or turn away from, but Chit Naing is used to it.

He focuses elsewhere, the everywhere of the singer's skin, stretched tight over cheekbones and temples and knuckles and nose and starving knobs of elbows. Surely, the jailer thinks, I've noticed this. How could he have missed those thin muscles tightening in a neck that looks longer, ropier, every few days? The ribbed cartilage of the esophagus has become visible, rung after rung going down.

Yet the singer has never complained. Chit Naing didn't see because Teza didn't force him to the truth. Since they transferred the singer to the white house, he has stopped complaining altogether, stopped even physical gestures of complaint. Chit Naing doesn't understand it, nor does he understand why Teza's passivity frightens him. For weeks Chit Naing's utmost concern has been getting morphine through to the singer and paying for it in the most discreet way possible.

And now he's refusing the damn morphine!

"This doesn't make any sense, Teza. What do you mean, you don't want any more favors?"

The singer exhales a labored breath. The pulsing he felt in his jaw during meditation is a ripping now, red sheets of muscle and fascia torn, one strip after the other. He opens his mouth as little as possible to speak, but each word yanks at the tissue around the original wound. Five weeks ago that stupid doctor said the fracture was clean, but Teza is sure something in him is shattered. Not his spirit, not his heart, but bone.

He would like Chit Naing to come back tomorrow morning, after he has slept and slurped down his morning rice. Then he will have more strength. Now he wants only to close his eyes and lie down.

The jailer squats beside him. "Ko Teza, are you all right?"

These words seem to come from a distance, as if Chit Naing were standing on the other side of the wall. It's very strange. Teza wonders if his ear is acting up again. He lifts his head and exhales the words painfully. "U Chit Naing, soon I will begin a hunger strike." He inhales again, lets the breath go. "But first I need your help."

. 45 .

Jumping over one puddle, two puddles, he pretends there are puddles all the way to his shack. He's careful not to sprint full-out. If he moves too fast, the warders on guard duty will know something's happening. When he gets to his shack, he opens the door and slips inside, pulling the rat stick in behind him. Shivering, he jams the stick diagonally across the door. Stream water drips off his elbows as his hands stretch out in the dark, touch the corner post, and slide down to the brick where he usually keeps his lighter.

But it's not there. It's not beside or behind the brick. Where did he put his lighter? He feels along the bottom of the shack, slides his finger through the little gutter he makes for the rain, but he can't find it. Why didn't he put the lighter back in its place? "Fucking stupid boy!" Only when he swears does he realize that he's crying.

His hands go in the other direction, under the rag bed of damp longyis and old blanket, past the big matchbox with the beetle inside, under the plastic bag that protects his postcards of the Shwedagon Pagoda and the Buddha from Pagan. His fingers close around the other plastic bag, which contains matches. Scratch, scratch, rustle in the dark box, not the beetle but the boy, moving a blind, knowing hand. He wipes his wet fingers on his bed, takes a clutch of matches from the bag, strikes a match once, twice, three times.

The interior of the tiny room flares. Squinting, he lights the yellow candle stub and pushes his rag bed to one side and begins to dig with his tin-can shovel. He digs and digs, he buried it deeper last time. Where is the pen? Why did he put it down so deep? In frustration he stops digging with the tool and starts scraping the earth away with his fingers, where is the pen? Why isn't the nat helping him? Where is the pen? It belonged to the Songbird, and the boy knows his prayers were not enough, his offerings were not enough, is that why he's crying? Yes, the gifts he gave to the Songbird didn't work, not even the precious egg it wasn't enough the nat of the tree didn't help him and the Buddha didn't help him and he lied a big lie and Handsome said *I will kill you* and prayers fail so it's true the junior jailer will kill him.

Chit Naing abruptly stands up, unwilling to believe what he's just heard. He wants to think that this is Teza's idea of a joke, but the singer—sitting like a monk on the floor, bald and gaunt in dirty white prison garb—is clearly serious. Chit Naing hears the treble of anger in his own voice. "A hunger strike? What on earth are you going to strike for? You heard what the doctor just said. Even keeping the Eight Precepts is too much for you." Another emotion unsettles him far more than anger—an intolerable sense that Teza is betraying him.

The singer listens as Chit Naing describes the danger of hunger strikes, how they have almost never worked. The prison authorities do not capitulate to the demands of the prisoners, even when they starve themselves. Teza nods patiently. "Yes, I know. I understand that." He pauses to rest. Chit Naing crouches again beside him. "It will be my own thabeik hmauk."

"Like a monk," Chit Naing says in a defeated whisper.

"Yes. And like a student too." Thabeik hmauk is also the word for a student protest, though its origin is much older than a modern university.

Each man silently remembers the same history, that of hunger strikers from hundreds of years ago, members of the holy sangha. When the monks wanted to protest the corruption and violence of the king and his minions, they paraded through the streets with their alms bowls turned upside down. By refusing to accept offerings from the king, they cut him off from his own wealth—his riches were nothing if he could not make a merit-gift of them for his future lives.

In 1988 many brave monks protested this way. The famous student leader Moe Thi Zon led a group of young monks in thabeik hmauk. As the monks marched along, holding their lacquered bowls upside down, more and more people joined them, until the crowd was thousands strong.

Chit Naing speaks too loudly, clearly impatient, "Thabeik hmauk makes for very moving stories, Ko Teza, but you're not a monk and the cage is not a monastery. Nor are you well enough to begin a hunger strike. It's—" He wants to use the word *crazy* but says, "Dangerous. Why would you do that? Why now? What are you going to protest?"

The question strikes the singer as horribly funny. "Give me paper and a pen. I will make a list."

The joke is lost on Chit Naing. Agitated, he walks out of the cell, strides down the short corridor, then pivots around in military fashion and returns, his face wearing its official mask. He's about to speak, to say how ridiculous this is, but Teza quietly repeats himself, "My friend, before the strike begins, I need your help."

"You need *my* help?"

"The boy needs to learn how to read."

"Ko Teza, what does that boy have to do with you?"

Teza responds by scratching his left underarm: bedbugs or lice? Usually he can tell the difference, but right now he's too tired. Nor does he have the energy to answer the jailer's question. No matter what he says, he fears Chit Naing will misunderstand. It's true: the boy has nothing to do with Teza. Yet it is also true that the boy is inseparable from him. "I want to help him leave. He has to leave the cage if he's going to go to school."

At first, Chit Naing laughs. Another glance at the singer's face tells him that Teza really thinks the jailer can do something. The beating obviously has affected the poor man's mind; he's delusional. "Ko Teza, the boy lives here. He doesn't want to go anywhere."

"He might be afraid to leave, but he wants to learn to read and write. He will never do that if he stays in the prison. Will you help him?"

An irrational bolt of fury hits the jailer. How dare the singer ask this of him! Not only is it a ridiculous request, but he asks it without anadeh, the proper decorum. "Haven't I already tried to help you as much as I can? Now you want me to do more." He stares indignantly into Teza's face. The crooked mouth is parted slightly, the lower lip hanging open, his teeth and blackened gums visible. Saliva drools unnoticed from his mouth, down his numb chin. But Teza returns the jailer's gaze with deep calm and self-possession, apparently unmoved by—and not at all afraid of—his angry words. At the same time, the deepened wrinkles around the dark eyes suggest that the singer is about to smile.

Teza speaks first. "You *have* helped me, and others. You know I'm grateful. If I ask you to do more, it's only because there's so much to be done. We are all tired, U Chit Naing. Daw Suu must be very tired. I know my mother is tired. I imagine the generals are very tired too. And the ones who are fighting on the border, both sides, they must be exhausted." He expels a little laugh. "All this fighting. It's so tiresome.

"I ask for your help because I have no one else to ask. You are one of the few brave enough to make choices. That's what freedom is. We are fortunate, you and I. Even here, I have made my choices. But the boy doesn't have that power. His life is this cage. He barely understands that he wants to leave." Teza hesitates. "Before I begin my hunger strike, I would like him to go away from here."

Chit Naing breaks his gaze and looks nervously to the wall that blocks the white house from the rest of the compound. Soe Thein should be here any minute now for his shift as guard.

Teza doesn't care. Calm he may be, but his voice has a feverish intensity. "There is an old monastery school in Rangoon, in Kyee Myin Daing, on a short lane called Aung Ban Street. My mother knows the Hsayadaw who runs it. You could go to the abbot himself or to Daw Sanda—they would make it possible for the boy to live there. You can tell them he is my little brother from the cage. The Hsayadaw will take him, I know it. Tell him the boy wants to read. That will be recommendation enough. If the boy is called by the Hsayadaw for initiation, the Chief Warden has to let him go. He would lose face if he deprived the boy of the chance to become a novice."

Chit Naing heaves a great sigh. "Ko Teza, it's not so straightforward." The jailer backs away and steps out of the cell, pushes the grille door shut, locks down. Safe on the other side of the bars, he notices Teza watching him with that strange almost-smile on his face. "I'm not sure if you understand that the boy is afraid to leave the prison."

Teza glances down at the aluminum tray, scraped clean. "I understand that very well. But I see something else too. Every time he stands there, right where you are standing, I see how brave he is. His courage is stronger than his fear. He wants to go out and live in the world, but he has to fight to make that choice." Teza looks up at the jailer, who can't avoid his eyes. "The monastery school is called Pyinna Wadi. U Chit Naing, how could you not help him?"

. 46 .

Sometimes Chit Naing wishes he smoked. He has tried many times to start, but both cheroots and cigarettes irritate his throat. One drag of a cheroot can send him into paroxysms of sneezing. It's too bad. If he were a smoker, he would be able to look occupied while doing absolutely nothing. As it is, he pauses some distance away from the white house and pretends to wind his watch. His mind careens forward and back as he tries to fathom all the singer has told him. The sound of Sammy the iron-beater thumps in his ears.

He has never been so relieved to get away from Teza. He would be happy to keep walking at a brisk pace, past the records office and the Chief Warden's building and the warders' quarters, right out the gates and onto the road. Soon enough he will do exactly that, but Soe Thein hasn't shown up yet. Chit Naing looks at his watch; twenty minutes late. He surveys the compound. The regular guards are stationed at their points, but Soe Thein is nowhere to be seen.

The pounding hasn't stopped. It can't be Sammy the iron-beater. Chit Naing juts his head like a blind man toward the sound. Is someone finally fixing the hospital roof? That's what it sounds like, a hammer banging nails into corrugated metal. Where is Soe Thein? The jailer doesn't want to leave the cell unattended. He reminds himself to tell the warder to check in on Teza through the night—he's unwell.

This elaborate scheme to send the child out of the prison is impossible. Nyi Lay may be brave, but he doesn't like going farther than the noodle stand outside the gates. He's never been to a temple, so how could he go and live in a monastery school? Not just any pongyi-kyaung, mind you, but the place where Teza's father used to treat the orphans—how many years ago? Twenty? Teza told him the name of the monastery, he named the street, but that doesn't mean the place is still there. Since 1988, whole neighborhoods of poor people have been sent out to satellite towns. The SLORC has been very busy sanitizing the city's neighborhoods, building up and tearing down, making room for business and tourist hotels. The place Teza remembers probably doesn't even exist anymore.

And—if Chit Naing understood correctly—once the boy is ensconced in this nonexistent school, obediently learning the alphabet and doing sums, the singer intends to announce his hunger strike. Maybe he *is* losing his mind.

Who the hell is making all that noise? What are they doing? No one is fixing a roof at seven-thirty at night.

He removes his glasses and rubs his eyes.

Seven eight nine warders are clustered together outside. Soe Thein is at the front of the group, standing a little apart from the others. Just as he was leaving the warders' quarters for his guard duty, Handsome sent him to fetch a shovel. Now, as the oldest man among them and well respected, Soe Thein is the only one who could say something. But guilt keeps him frozen there; he put that shovel into Handsome's hands. The jailer wields it like a sledgehammer, raising it up over his head to strike, the sweat darkening the shirt on his back.

At the rear of the audience, Tint Lwin shifts his weight from foot to foot, looking around, hoping Senior Jailer Chit Naing or the Chief Warden himself will appear and ask what's going on, why is Handsome doing this—*Stop! Stop it now!* These words are stuck and silent in his own mouth, but he hears them, just as he heard them in the singer's cell during the beating.

Tint Lwin kneads his knuckles to keep himself from speaking. He doesn't want to say anything stupid. But no one has asked if the boy's still in there, too petrified to come out. The young warder is secretly fond of him; he's a polite kid, and curious. Kaung-lay, Tint Lwin calls him affectionately, little creature. Tint Lwin stands on his tiptoes to watch another blow land on the corrugated metal.

Surely the boy can't be in there. Under those blows, he'd already be screaming, then he'd escape. He would run to the young warder, who would protect him fearlessly. Tint Lwin swears this to himself. His imagined bravery calms him. He takes a step closer.

Still pounding away, Handsome is livid with rage. The emotion is contagious. Every man is itching to know if the pen's really in there, wrapped up in a rag or buried. Could this be true, or has Handsome fucked up again?

The men lean forward, half smiling or grimacing. After another solid blow, the buried corner post, its base nibbled by termites, falls over with a hollow *dhoomp*. Roped to the posts, the front wall—three separate slabs of corrugated metal—gives way. Handsome hits the top of the shack once more and stumbles forward in slow motion as the wood squeaks and the metal roof falls in, rattling and scraping.

To keep himself from falling, the jailer drops the shovel blade to the ground and leans on the wooden handle as if it were a crutch. He wipes the sweat from his face and looks at the warders. "What are you waiting for? Take apart this pile of crap and find that fucking pen. It's here somewhere." He spits onto the rubble of the shack because his knee is too sore to kick it.

Chit Naing puts his glasses back on. As he balances the wire-rim frames on his nose and secures them around his ears, the awful pounding stops. He turns his head toward the cessation of the pounding, and there, materializing out of the records office wall, is the boy. He leaps over two puddles, rushing toward Chit Naing.

Out of breath, Nyi Lay pulls up directly in front of him and pokes his rat stick at the ground. He's drenched. The turquoise longyi has turned dark blue with water, though it hasn't been raining. The jailer greets him in the polite way: "Hello, Nyi Lay, have you eaten rice yet?"

"Yes, thank you."

Chit Naing peers down at the small face. A bruise swells around a cut on his cheek.

"I'm doing some night hunting. For rats." The boy's voice is shaking.

"But Little Brother, you're soaked to the skin. What happened?"

As if the boy hasn't heard him, he steps closer to Chit Naing and whispers, "Can I go and say a prayer with the Songbird? I do sometimes, you know. He bows and whispers his prayers and I follow along. Can I visit him? Sir?"

The jailer glances at the bruise. "You can go and see him for a few minutes, no more. He was very tired when I left him. If he's sleeping, you must not wake him." When he sees the relief that washes over the boy's apprehensive face, he realizes the child has come here, to Teza, to seek comfort.

He's already stepping toward the corridor entrance when Chit Naing says, "Stop."

The boy freezes in his tracks and slowly turns back toward the jailer. Chit Naing has never seen such naked fear in him, on him. "It's all right, Nyi Lay, I just want to ask you a question."

"A question?" The words come out flat and high.

Clearly, someone's hurt him. "What happened, Nyi Lay? Where did you get that bruise on your cheek?"

The boy touches two fingers to the blooming cut and represses a shiver, suddenly aware of his cold clothes. "I . . . I fell down by the stream."

"The stream?"

"Behind the kitchen and the hospital."

"You fell down. That's why there's dirt under your fingernails."

"Yes, sir." He immediately wipes his hands on his longyi and starts cleaning the clay out from under his nails.

"How did you fall down?"

"I . . . I don't remember." He stops picking at his nails and holds his right hand toward Chit Naing like a supplicant. "Please sir, I would like to see the Songbird before he falls asleep." *Let me go.*

"Go on, then, be quick. I'll wait here for you." Chit Naing, lacking a cheroot, looks down at his watch.

Nyi Lay has already darted behind the wall.

The long black hand of his watch makes a full round. One minute, then half again, then two. The jailer can't help himself. He approaches the outer wall that surrounds the white house cell and stands motionless, listening hard. He can't hear a thing. He steps quietly along the wall, curious but reluctant to disturb two worshippers. The jailer had no idea that the boy *prayed*—surely Teza's doing. Is it true, though? Are they really praying? Chit Naing stands close to the wall and leans his head around the corner.

The boy is kneeling in front of Teza's cell. He genuflects, bowing once, twice, three times, hands raised in the aspect of prayer. Chit Naing steps into the corridor, presuming he'll see Teza in front of the boy, bowing to an invisible Buddha image. But the jailer is wrong; Teza is curled up, eyes closed, with his head near the bars for fresh air.

As the boy rises, he senses Chit Naing in the corridor and gives the jailer a muted, embarrassed smile. He puts a finger to his lips. *The Songbird's sleeping.* Then he bends forward, grips the cement with his toes, and stands up. Chit Naing, ashamed of his spying, retreats to the compound.

Within seconds the boy leaves the white house and comes toward Chit Naing, whispering, "I did not wake him up. He was already snoring." Nyi Lay closes his eyes, distorts the natural line of his jaw, and mimics the singer's labored snores. Then he returns to his earlier task of quickly and nervously cleaning his nails.

The two of them walk a short distance away from the cell building before the jailer stops. "Nyi Lay, I want you to tell me something."

The boy is a step ahead, but he obediently turns to face him. "Yes?"

"I don't think you just fell down. What happened to your cheek?"

The boy clasps his hands together very tightly and stares at the ground.

The events of the evening crash back into his conscious mind, the stream and Handsome, the drowning and after, water and food wrenching out of him. And then? Skip and leap and try-not-to-run to his shack, and *dig cry dig*. Between his own intent and the calm of Teza sleeping, it's as though the boy really did forget; all the bad things went away for a while. Why does Chit Naing make him remember?

"Nyi Lay. You don't have to tell me. You can lie if you really want to—I won't hold it against you. But it's better if you tell the truth. All right?"

The boy has fixed his eye upon a dark spot of betel juice on the ground.

The jailer asks, "Do you know why the truth would be a good idea right now?"

"Why?"

"Because if someone has hurt you, I can protect you in the future, but only if I know what's happened."

As the boy mulls over this dubious claim, his eyes travel to the jailer's boots and trouser cuffs. The drowning rushes into him. He wants to cry. Staring down at Chit Naing's trouser cuff, he freezes. It has worked in the past, when he's in bed. If he doesn't move, the tears don't come—he just falls asleep.

"Nyi Lay?"

A tremulous feeling, the sensation of cracking, sweeps across his back. He is being broken open like the long thin shell of a tamarind pod. "I . . . I didn't fall down."

"I know that. What happened?"

"Jailer Handsome pushed me." Now something pulls through his chest, like the length of the tamarind fruit yanked right out.

"And you hit your face?"

"No, *he* hit my face *and* he pushed me in the water." Nyi Lay's voice is high and shaky, but he's angry too. "He was going to drown me because he thinks I have the pen that's what he said he's going to kill me and I was in the water and none of the warders stopped him and he hit my face and . . ." The last words are lost in a sob. Chit Naing puts his hands on the narrow shoulders.

"But he didn't drown you, Nyi Lay. Did he? You're with me now. And I'm going to help you."

The boy lets out a low howl. "The warders could see but they didn't care and now he'll get me anytime he wants he'll hurt me like he did the Songbird he'll kill me that's what he said." He tries hard not to let the sounds get out of him, but he can't help it, they're bursting his throat.

In the floodlit night of the cage, two shadows are thrown dark upon the ground. The jailer bends awkwardly. He embraces the thin child and lifts him up, calling him by his real name. Nyi Lay puts his arms around Chit Naing's neck. There is only one shadow now, man and boy joined, crossing over the brick-chip gravel of the compound.

. 47 .

He's all muscle, bone, and heat, crying hard but not making much noise. Holding in his sobs, the boy shakes and idles like an engine. Chit Naing wants to take him back to his little shack, give him a place to rest, but only when he has calmed down. There's no need for the warders to see him like this.

After a few minutes he has tired himself out. Chit Naing hears him catching his breath and swallowing. He wipes his runny nose on the back of his hand. By degrees, the small, frightened child disappears. Wriggling out of the jailer's arms, he drops to the ground and lands back in the body of the wiry boy. Chit Naing reaches down and picks up his rat stick. Nyi Lay takes it, hesitantly.

"We'll go over to the warders' quarters and make sure Handsome has left for the night." Beyond that, the jailer isn't sure what to do. The Chief Warden will have to talk some sense into Nyunt Wai Oo, but that's not going to happen until tomorrow, and it may not be enough to keep the boy safe.

Fighting off the urge to grab the waist of Chit Naing's trousers, the boy grips his rat stick tighter. The two of them begin to walk toward the records office, then along its long western wall.

The moment they round the corner of the building, they stop. Chit

Naing recalls the banging from half an hour ago and immediately understands. He looks down at Nyi Lay, who stares dry-eyed across the compound.

The boy knew it. He knew something awful would happen. He heard Handsome go into the warders' quarters and start yelling at the men. Heart beating in his throat, Nyi Lay knew he had to get away. After digging up the pen, he crept out of his shack, then ran across the open tract of compound to the records office.

The jailer touches his shoulder. He speaks in a quiet, even tone. "Come on. You can gather up your things. I won't let him hurt you." Chit Naing takes a step forward.

The boy doesn't move. He didn't know that it was going to be this bad. He thought Handsome would tear down the door and search everything. But the little house is gone.

Chit Naing looks over his shoulder and waves him forward, murmuring something the boy doesn't hear.

Nothing will be left of the butterfly's wing. It was so crumbly and ant-eaten he rarely took it out of its hiding place anymore. He thinks of his mother's thanakha tin and the beetle in its box. Where is the small lizard now? Two warders are still picking through the debris, making occasional comments to each other in mocking tones.

The boy's eyes rove over bits and pieces he can and cannot recognize from this distance. Cloth from his rag bed; white and colored squares of paper on the gravel, which must be his little collection of postcards and pictures, flung out of their plastic bag. He fearfully recalls his photo-copied picture of the Bogyoke's daughter, Daw Aung San Suu Kyi. He knows it's illegal. The books too: they're illegal. And the piece of broken transistor radio. He sees very plainly, trampled on the ground, the big pair of underpants. That's all right—he would never be fat enough to wear them. He was just waiting for the right moment to trade them for something more useful.

He wonders, practically, if his green school longyi and white T-shirt are still whole and dry. If Handsome doesn't kill him first, he would like to change out of his wet clothes. There's a piece of material on the ground that might be the longyi, but everything's drained of color under the floodlights—maybe it's just one of his bed scraps. It would be such a relief to be warm and dry and sleeping under his blanket and old longyis. But Handsome has thrown his rag bed all over the ground. He sees the torn blanket of Chinese felt. He will pick up all the scraps and wash them and make his bed again. But where will he sleep?

He's ashamed to see his treasures thrown about like this, his very own good things. His eyes are drowning again. Stupid! He will not cry. He must not cry in front of the warders. Unshed tears thicken his voice. "Saya Chit Naing, why did he do it? He could have looked inside without tearing it all apart." Staring straight ahead, he picks and pulls at a thread of dry skin from his lower lip, until the soft skin bleeds and he stops pulling and bites the thread away and sucks at the blood. One pain reminds him of another. He carefully puts his fingers up to his cheek and touches the cut in the center of the bruise.

Chit Naing leans sideways and whispers, "Dwa-may. Ma-jow-ba-neh." Let's go. Don't be afraid. Nyi Lay sighs as the jailer steps forward, but he falls in beside him so willingly, so trustingly, that Chit Naing feels a pang of regret.

A warder has seen them. As he straightens up, one of the child's belongings falls from his hand. He vacillates, looks to the warders' quarters and back over to Chit Naing. He mumbles something to his workmate, who lifts his head and sees the boy. Without a moment's hesitation, this man calls Handsome in a loud voice. "Jailer Nyunt Wai Oo, you better come out here right now."

Many months later, after his court-martial and interrogation, after the beatings, the kneeling in glass, after the vat of excrement where they leave him for an entire day and night, with maggots crawling into his nose and ears, burrowing at his closed mouth, into the corners of his eyes, he will be transferred to a prison in the north, where he will have plenty of time to think. In his cell, pondering, remembering all that went before, he will recognize this as the defining moment in which he could have chosen between yes and no.

But right now Chit Naing acts with such clarity of purpose that no one, including himself, could imagine a choice exists. Handsome comes out of the warders' quarters with the wooden baton already in his hand. The smile on his face is indistinguishable from a grimace of pain. The warders file slowly out of the building behind him. Chit Naing is surprised to see how many men there are. Most of them should be at home by now, except for Soe Thein, who ought to be standing guard duty. Chit Naing inclines his head to the boy and quietly makes a promise: "You will be all right." They begin to walk forward. The boy's small fingers tighten around the senior jailer's belt.

When they are ten paces away, Handsome bellows, "Give him to me."

Chit Naing calmly replies, "There's no need to yell."

"Give him to me!"

"Officer Nyunt Wai Oo, I will not give him to you. What do you think he is, a dog?"

"A dog who can talk, and I intend to interrogate him."

"You will do no such thing. The boy is not an inmate, and you have no right to interrogate him. I think it's time you went home."

"Don't talk to me about that little fucker's rights. He has the pen. I know he has the pen—he's hidden it somewhere. Under interrogation, he's going to tell me exactly where it is."

Chit Naing raises his voice and speaks slowly, enunciating each word, making sure the other men can hear. "Junior Jailer Nyunt Wai Oo, you are not going to interrogate a twelve-year-old child. Destroying his hut and attacking him earlier this evening were quite enough." He runs his eyes over the group of warders, noting the range of expressions on their faces. Curious. Embarrassed. Ashamed. That flat, uninterested look he reads as secret glee. It's not often they get a chance to observe their superiors engaged in open combat.

He addresses the men, none of whom will meet his eye, not even Soe Thein. "Your duties do not include destroying the shelter of an orphan." The boy, horrified to be the object of so many eyes, shuffles behind Chit Naing. "Did anyone check with the Chief about doing this?"

Handsome answers, "The Chief's not here tonight. He's in the city."

"So you thought you could have some fun. Is that what this is all about?" He glares at the men again and then steps to the left, so the boy is in clear view. "I suppose *this* is the enemy, if you could do that to his house." He looks from the face of one warder to another and another. "Why didn't anyone come to find me? Look at this kid! He's armed with a stick against the whole troop of you. He came to find me with the news that Handsome tried to drown him, because he supposedly has the pen. Well, here is your terrible thief! But you didn't find anything, did you?" He turns his head to Handsome. "Did you?"

"We found books and a picture of that bitch Suu Kyi."

"He probably doesn't even know who she is."

"Oh, fuck off, Chit Naing! Why would he have a picture of her, then?"

Chit Naing sucks in his breath at the risk of it and turns to the boy. "Nyi Lay, why do you have a picture of Suu Kyi?"

"Who is Suu Kyi?"

Chit Naing smiles at Handsome. "I rest my case."

Handsome roars, "What an answer! That's exactly why he needs to be interrogated." He rushes forward, spitting out the words, "Why did you have that picture, you little bastard?"

Chit Naing puts his hand up. "Don't come any closer." Still holding his hand between the two of them, Chit Naing addresses the boy again. "Suu Kyi is the woman in the picture that was in your shack. Why was it there?"

The boy is staring at his bare feet.

Chit Naing nudges him. "Go ahead. You can tell us."

He begins to talk very quietly, and Handsome shouts, "Louder!"

Without looking up, the boy says in a clear voice, "Tan-see Tiger has a nice picture in his cell, and I wanted one too."

Chit Naing says, "You wanted a picture of a woman."

The boy wrings his hands and whispers, "A smiling picture."

Chit Naing puts his hand on the boy's shoulder again and calls out, "Did you hear that, men? The kid wanted a picture of a smiling woman! Who can blame him? Which one of you dangerous elements put up the picture of that pretty lady singer in the warders' quarters? Officer Nyunt Wai Oo wants to interrogate you too!" When several warders start to laugh, Chit Naing knows he has stepped on firmer ground.

Handsome yells, "This is bullshit. Everyone knows that only politicals have pictures of her."

Chit Naing smiles and gestures at Nyi Lay. "Now he's a political pris-oner? It must be some kind of record. The first illiterate twelve-year-old political prisoner in the history of incarceration in Burma. Officer Nyunt Wai Oo, look at him! He's lived in here since he was seven years old—he has no conception of politics. I suggest you write up your extraordinary findings in a report, then you and the Chief Warden can have a long meeting about it. But now it's time for you to leave. Your shift is over. If you hurry, you'll make the nine o'clock bus."

Handsome speaks through clenched teeth, "Just give me five minutes with that little fucker and I'll find out everything. Come here, dirty kala-lay!" He reaches out to grab the boy's T-shirt, but Chit Naing steps between them and pushes Handsome hard in the chest, sending the heavier man into a backward stumble.

If not for the shovel lying on the ground, Handsome might have recovered his footing, but his heel catches it and his opposite leg with its bad knee can't take the full weight of his body. He falls on his backside, arms akimbo, and screams, "Don't think you can get away with this, prick! You'll pay for it, both you and that stinking little bastard." Still cursing, Handsome twists over and tries to jump up, but the ripping sensation in his knee is so fierce that he's stuck there, off balance, still touching the ground with his hands and trying to rise up on one leg. He bites his lip and raises his upper body slowly but surely, furious at looking so ridiculous in front of the men. The fall has turned him around, so he's facing the pack of them now. "What the fuck are you staring at, you assholes? It's my knee— he's fucked up my knee."

Tint Lwin takes a small step forward, his arm extended, but the gesture is more than Handsome can bear. "Don't you fucking touch me. Stay away! You useless shits, what are you looking at!"

Soe Thein is the first to move. Without a word to anyone, he walks past Handsome, past Chit Naing and the boy, and disappears around the corner of the records office, ready to begin his guard duty at the white house. The other warders disperse more slowly, some back into the quarters to fetch their things and to whisper to each other as they glance out the window. Three men, including Tint Lwin, go off toward the gates and home.

While they're leaving, Handsome tries to turn around to face Chit Naing again, but he can't place any weight on his bad knee. The torn joint is loose and burning. Once he's steady on one leg, he bends down and grabs the shovel. Using it as a cane, he hops around to face Chit Naing and the boy.

"Where is it, kala-lay? Where'd you put the pen?"

The boy stares into Handsome's eyes like a fox about to disappear into the forest. He has never spoken back. Until recently, he has rarely thought about retaliating against insults, slaps, cuffs on the head, stabs of laughter. His fear and obedience were absolute, and life-preserving. So he is surprised at the feel of the words in his mouth, like a taste of something new. *Fuck off,* he wants to say. But he just tells the truth. "I don't have it."

Handsome lifts the shovel and strikes the ground. Grit flies into the air as he strains to keep his footing.

Chit Naing steps forward. "Officer Nyunt Wai Oo, you should have that leg looked at."

"Fuck you," Handsome says. "This isn't the end of it, I promise you that."

Chit Naing smiles. "I know. Who can tell when we will come to the end of it, Officer Nyunt Wai Oo? It might take years."

"You and I will be done sooner than that." Handsome hobbles over to the warders' quarters, where he yells to one of the warders for his jacket.

After the junior jailer is gone, Chit Naing watches the boy search through the various bits of cloth on the ground. He's looking for dry clothes. Eventually he finds them and changes into his green longyi and white T-shirt. He shakes out his muddy felt blanket and wraps it around his shoulders. Then he starts to pick methodically through his possessions. In what used to be the center of the shack there is a knee-deep hole, like the beginning of a grave. When Handsome saw the disturbed earth under the rag bed, he made the men dig deeper.

The boy sits cross-legged at the edge of the hole, examining various things, turning them over and over in his hands before throwing them into the little pit. The iron-beater strikes out nine o'clock. Chit Naing looks reflexively at his watch, thinking that it's probably too late for a trip into the city. If he goes tonight, he'll have to call his wife, give her some explanation. And he will have to leave soon. He looks at Nyi Lay, wondering what to do with him.

The boy is relieved to find his father's tooth, but the thanakha tin he kept it in is crushed. He keeps the tooth but drops the tin into the hole. Boot treads have defaced the postcard of the Buddha from Pagan, but he's keeping it, along with the torn postcard of the Shwedagon Pagoda. And he finds his nail. The idiots trampled it under the brick chips. He carefully scrutinizes the torn matchbox, but there are no signs of beetle blood. And the lizard must have run away.

Gone, all the beloved paperbacks. The picture of Daw Aung San Suu Kyi is gone too. The photo of her father, stuck on the corrugated metal with rice paste, tore in half when the walls fell down. There's not enough left of the great Bogyoke to bury him. Dry-eyed and thoughtful, the boy carefully examines the wrecked beetle box. Only one side is torn. He will fold the cardboard out and use rice paste to glue it back together. It's a good matchbox, extra-large. He doesn't want to lose it.

Chit Naing crouches behind him. "What did you used to keep in there?"

"A beetle."

"A live beetle?"

The boy sighs. "Yeah. I used to feed him and everything."

"Maybe they took him away to interrogate him."

Nyi Lay quickly twists his head around. "Saya, they could not interrogate a beetle."

Chit Naing smiles. "I'm sure Handsome would like to try."

Nyi Lay allows himself a faint, bitter grin. "Yeah, he's such a fucking idiot." Shocked by his own audacity, he glances up to see if Chit Naing will scold him. But the jailer only laughs, which encourages the boy, who goes on in a low voice, "I bet he could interrogate a rat."

"He certainly speaks the language."

Nyi Lay grins. Clearly he has permission. "Handsome could interrogate flies. And maggots. He speaks *maggot*-language." He pauses to search for the end of the insult. "And he wants to interrogate the maggots about *shit*." Chit Naing and the boy both start to laugh.

When the laughter peters out, the boy throws a mangled candle stub into the hole and returns, in his practical way, to the problem at hand. "Maybe I should go and stay with Tan-see Tiger. He'll let me sleep there."

"In his cell." It's not exactly the ideal solution.

In a stern voice, the boy reminds Chit Naing, "But I'm not a prisoner, Saya."

"No, Nyi Lay. I know you are not a prisoner." The senior jailer scratches the back of his neck. All right, then. He will call his wife with a good excuse and travel tonight into the city. If he goes on a bus most of the way, then takes a cab, it can't take more than an hour to get there.

The boy is staring into the hole. Suddenly he cocks his head to the side and leans back, frowning at the pile of boards and corrugated metal that used to be his shack. "Listen, Saya. Do you hear that?"

Chit Naing raises his eyebrows. "Hear what?"

"He's scratching!"

The jailer stands at the edge of the hole. He can't see anything but raw clay and the bits and pieces the boy has discarded.

"He's scratching, Saya! That means he's hungry!"

"Who's hungry, Nyi Lay? What do you hear?"

The boy jumps up and starts throwing things in the air, like a dog searching for a bone long buried. "Not in the hole, Saya—he's somewhere over here!" He tosses a board out of his way, and a tangle of rope from the corner posts. He pushes aside a long narrow scrap of corrugated metal. "He's here, look! They didn't steal him!" He whirls around to face Chit Naing. In his fingers, he delicately holds a carrion beetle by the carapace. Six sturdy black legs march purposefully through the air. The boy places the creature in his palm and lets it crawl from one hand to the other. He walks over to the eastern wall of the warders' quarters and carefully sets the beetle down in a jungle of weeds. Noticing the boy's reverent expression, the jailer stops himself from laughing. He turns in the opposite direction, toward the watchtower, but he can still hear Nyi Lay whispering to the beetle as it disappears into the green tangle.

. 48 .

Thankfully, the bus is almost empty, and the tired people already on the line don't raise their heads to look at him. Staring down at cheroot butts and betel stains and ticket stubs, he falls to examining his own tired feet, separated from the dirty floorboards by the thin soles of his flip-flops. Chit Naing's feet are like the rest of his body, long and angular, a collection of finely sculpted bones. The second toes are longer than the first. His feet are much paler brown than his face and hands, because he's worn boots six days a week for more than twenty years. When he leaves the cage in his street clothes, there is often this moment of unrecognition, sheer surprise, as he looks down and sees his toes clinging to their simple slippers, just like everybody else, like a regular man.

He gets out when the bus stops near Hledan Junction. Though he rarely takes cabs—they're much too expensive—tonight he has no choice. He goes from one street corner to the next, asking one cabbie after another if he's ever heard of Aung Ban Street in Kyee Myin Daing. He doesn't want to mention the name of the monastery school. Taxi drivers are in an ideal position to work as paid informers, especially in this township, so close to the university and not so far from the prison. Their job combines a handy mobility with plenty of spare time for observation: who's going into which building, for how long, who stays the night—spending the night in a house not your own is illegal—and, naturally, who's going where.

Chit Naing glances at his watch. It's getting too late to go knocking on any doors, especially those of a monastery. He approaches the last cabbie in the row, a slick young fellow sitting on the hood of his car, showily engaged in pulling a cigarette out of a packet of Lucky Strikes. Upon hearing the name of the street, he asks, "What's it close to?" Chit Naing replies that he doesn't know. "Listen, Uncle, if you don't have a landmark, how can I help you? There are many monasteries and pongyi-kyaung in Kyee Myin Daing, but I've never heard of Aung Ban Street." He lights the cigarette and exhales a smoky suggestion. "If you go over there—see?—up that little road to the second noodle stand, there's a short, chubby driver named Than Thaik. He just ordered his dinner. The guy's a walking map—he'll probably be able to help you. He's finished for the night, though, so he might not want to take you there." As Chit Naing begins to walk away, the young man adds, "But if he does, tell him he owes me one!"

The jailer heads up the noodle stand street, which is very dark save for battery-powered light bulbs hanging over the great sizzling pans of fried noodles. The heady smell of garlic snapping in oil makes his mouth water, but he won't even think of dinner until he's either fulfilled or failed at the task before him. He trips on a chunk of cement and swears under his breath. Either there's a blackout in this particular part of the grid or the entire street has no proper lamps. He curls and uncurls his stubbed toe while scanning the dark tables. A dozen of them are occupied. He approaches the only corpulent body he sees. "Ko Than Thaik?"

"Yes, sir?"

The *sir* throws him for a moment, but perhaps the man is very polite, or impolitely ironic. Chit Naing steps nearer the table and quietly explains himself, naming the township and the street.

"I do know where it is, yes, indeed I do. There's a little fabric and odds-and-ends market at one end and a football field at the other. A couple of apartment blocks with shops under 'em. That's about all there is, sir. It's a short street. You know what house you're looking for?"

Chit Naing smiles tightly. "I do, thank you."

"Well, I'd really like to help you, but unfortunately I'm finished working for the day. Been up since four in the morning with some very nice English people. We went to Inle Lake to see the jumping cats. Very interesting what those monks can get a cat to do. Amazing, really. Those cats kind of reminded me of a lot of people I know, jumping on command. Have you seen 'em?"

"Ah, no. No, I haven't." Chit Naing frowns. "I . . . I would be willing to make it worth your while. I need to get there tonight."

"To Inle Lake to check out the jumping cats?" The chubby driver guffaws at his own joke.

It's the laugh that makes Chit Naing remember. Everything else about Than Thaik, including his name, has changed. "No, Ko Than Thaik. I need to get to Aung Ban Street. And you will help me, won't you? In the name of an old friendship?"

Than Thaik shifts away from the rickety little table, slaps his hands together, and laughs again, deeply, from the belly. "Took you a while to recognize me, didn't it? No fucking wonder—I've gained thirty-five pounds since those vile days. Thirty-five! Just let me finish eating, okay, Jailer Chit Naing? I'm bloody hungry. I'm always bloody hungry. Since the cage, I've never worried about being fat, only about starving. Have you eaten yet?" Before Chit Naing can reply, Than Thaik shouts, "Another plate of khauk-swe, Daw Thida, we're still hungry!" And to Chit Naing, "You didn't know me at first, eh, but I pegged *you* right away, as soon as you turned up the street. You're still thin as a rail and you got the same professor glasses. I recognized you even without your outfit."

Chit Naing is caught between feeling great relief at finding the right cabdriver and great consternation at finding the wrong one, a man who knows him well. But he sits down at the table. Two minutes later a plate of fragrant fried noodles is placed before him. Despite his worries, the scent of the steaming food overcomes him and he quickly begins to eat.

During the drive into Kyee Myin Daing, Than Thaik talks nonstop. Normally this would irritate the tired jailer, but tonight it calms him. He's relieved that the man isn't nosy.

"A couple years after I got out, I stayed on the straight and narrow and my brother got me this job, which isn't bad. There are perks, you know, especially with the tourists. And I'm married now, to a good woman, and we have two little ones. I thought I was going to be a bachelor forever, but that woman just knocked me off my feet and that was that. I'm a family man, and if I get in trouble now, I'll have to answer to my wife, which is a frightening thought." He grins broadly and glances at Chit Naing. "I'm a very lucky man and I know it.

"After that big fight on the grounds, the Chief Warden wanted to turn the whole lot of us over to the military. We would've been sent up as weapons porters to the front line. And everybody knows what happens to those poor fuckers. By now I'd just be a skeleton in the jungle if you hadn't stepped up for me and talked to him."

"I believed you were innocent. Besides, if I remember correctly, you couldn't have been involved in that fight because you had a bad case of dysentery."

"That's true. I had nothing to do with that business. I really didn't. But in the cage it doesn't matter whether you're innocent or guilty. All that matters is who you know." He vigorously shakes his head, as if tossing away unhappy memories.

They've pulled onto a quieter street. "We'll be making a turn at the bottom of this long boulevard," he says, then points out a few perfectly mundane sights, a habit he's picked up from driving foreigners around. "And now we just go down here." Bald tires screech as he brakes for a sharp turn. They cross a larger thoroughfare of shops and restaurants as well as houses and apartment buildings. A few corner tea shops and noodle stands are still serving, but it's past ten o'clock now and very quiet. He turns onto another little road. It's a residential district, poor and very old, with banyans and palms and neems shading the roadways. Than Thaik goes left, then right—Chit Naing is trying to keep track—down streets of confused architecture, one-story concrete bungalows mixed in with two- and three-story apartment buildings with shops underneath. Ten minutes away from the main road, Chit Naing has no idea where he is.

But he suspects they're very close to their destination, because Than Thaik has slowed down for the first time since they began their journey. Past a boarded-up market empty of wares, the cabbie turns to him and asks, "You do know the number, don't you, sir, the number of the building?"

Chit Naing responds, "It's best if you just let me know where to go from here, Ko Than Thaik."

"Oh, but this is it, sir. This is the street." He smiles. "Don't you trust me? Not to worry, my friend. I'm just a taxi driver now. I have no nasty work on the side." He smacks the steering wheel with the heel of his hand. "Those military creeps—I wouldn't give them the fucking time of day."

Chit Naing thinks to himself that the time of day is the last thing MI agents would be interested in. "I do trust you, Ko Than Thaik. But it's best if I just get out here. How much do I owe you?"

"Suit yourself, sir, but keep in mind that if I leave you here now, it's going to take you half an hour to get back to the boulevard, if you can find your way at all, and then maybe, just maybe, if you're lucky, another cab will pass by at this time of night. But maybe not." Than Thaik rubs his nose and turns to look directly at Chit Naing, though he can't see much of him but streaks of light sliding over his glasses.

"U Chit Naing, you can trust me. Let me do you a favor, okay? If I'd been sent out as a porter with the other men, I would have died. You saved my life." He laughs again, to take the edge off his seriousness. "It's not much of an exchange, my life for a cab ride! But it is something. Let me help you. That's why you turned up at that noodle stand. So Than Thaik could repay you, even if it's just a fraction of what he owes."

"Ko Than Thaik, I am not a moneylender. You don't owe me any-thing." To trust or not to trust? The question is pointless. He has already trusted the man too much. "Let me off here and please wait for me around the first corner."

"Excellent, sir. I'll catch a nap while you're doing your business. Un-less . . ." He lowers his voice. "Unless this really is about a woman. I can't wait around all night, sir. If you know what I mean."

Chit Naing lightly punches his shoulder. "I'll be finished quickly enough. She won't want anything more than a little chat and a kiss."

"Ah-ha! So it *is* about a woman! I knew it."

Shutting the door as quietly as possible, Chit Naing waits for the cab to drive off, then begins to walk along the unlit street. There's no sidewalk, and twice he detours around small, stinky hills of garbage. Because the electricity has been cut in this area, he sees candles in the interiors of some houses. In others, flashlights beam and flare against the walls. For once he's relieved that the SLORC is useless when it comes to public utilities. The darkness makes him feel safe. He startles, though, when he unexpect-edly crosses paths with a large rat.

Near the end of the dirty little street, a crumbling brick wall surrounds a two-story building that reminds Chit Naing of an old colonial school. The high gate is closed, but when he pushes on it, the hinges creak loudly under his hand. A dog barks inside. The jailer squints into the courtyard, trying to see where the animal is. Beside a small temple stands a much larger building, which he realizes must be a residence for the orphans. Wooden huts, monks' cells, flank the temple.

When the dog barks again, he turns his head to the sound. On his right, almost invisible in the darkness, a makeshift shack three times the size of a sentry box is built against the monastery wall. Seconds after his eyes distinguish the lines of this little building, a creature like a large white rabbit comes hopping toward him at an alarming speed, yipping and growling ferociously. The suddenness of the attack sends the jailer tripping back into the street. An old man's voice bawls a series of very unreligious expletives. Poised and growling at the threshold of the gate, the small dog drops to its belly for a moment, stands again, barks once in Chit Naing's direction, then walk-hops slowly back to the shed, anticipating punishment.

The jailer is embarrassed; his mouth has gone dry with fear. He laughs nervously. *I was attacked by a three-legged dog but survived to tell the tale!* He looks up the narrow lane, where other mutts, hidden from view, have joined in the barking, aware that it's their duty to alert the entire neighborhood to a stranger's late-night visit. Chit Naing hears the voice again: "What's this all about, now?" Then he makes out a small man, growling like the dog. "Who's in the street? What's going on out there?"

"I am looking for the Hsayadaw U Sobana. Are you the custodian of the monastery school?" The old man mishears him and announces vigorously, "No, I am not the venerable Hsayadaw, I am not his venerable self." His voice trails off into a forgiving chuckle. "I am the cook. And, on occasions such as these, the night watchman."

"I apologize for coming so very late, but I need to speak to him."

"Yes, it is very late." The old man wags his head slowly from side to side, cogitating, as far as Chit Naing can tell, on the lateness of the hour. The jailer sees that he has no front teeth.

"I am very sorry for appearing like this, but I need to speak to the Hsayadaw on urgent business."

"Yes, well, it's rather late for urgent business. Don't you think, young man?" Chit Naing is amused to hear the slight swagger of power in the old fellow's voice. "Everyone is sleeping, you see. The boys and the novices too. Even their teachers, the monks, they are sleeping. This is a monastery school—we all get up at four in the morning. Some of us get up even earlier. Myself, for example, despite my great age, and I go to bed the latest too, because I have so much work to do. It's hard for me, especially with the rains, as I've got terrible rheumatism. What a blessing that the monsoon is almost over!"

Chit Naing clasps his hands together. "I'm very sorry for your rheumatism, Grandfather, and for coming so late, but I must speak to someone tonight. Could you please wake the Hsayadaw for me? It's very important. I need to talk to him about a boy."

"One of our boys?" The cook wrinkles his nose and takes a step forward.

"No, Grandfather, another boy. An orphaned child who wants very much to come and live here."

"Oh, we're full up with boys. There's not a mat in the place for another body, no matter how skinny. They're almost sleeping on top of each other already. As for me, I sleep in that little shed there, and the roof leaks, which is terrible for my rheumatism. Look at that box—they don't even have a proper room for an old gardener."

"I thought you said you were the cook."

"I'm also the gardener, sir." His voice sharpens with pride. "I have many titles."

"Could you please wake the Hsayadaw? I need to speak to him."

"The Hsayadaw? Oh, he's not here. He's in Sagaing for three more days, and we miss his venerable self a great deal." The old man sucks his upper lip into his toothless mouth. "I'm afraid you'll have to come back later if you want to talk to the venerable Hsayadaw."

Chit Naing rubs the middle of his forehead, where a small invisible drill is making an invisible hole. "I see," he says very politely. "Is there anyone else here in a position of authority—the Hsayadaw's assistant perhaps, one of the other monks? Someone I can speak to about this child?" He hears the frustration in his own voice.

"There's not a spare mat in the place." The old man clears his throat. "And the kid can't sleep with me. There's no room in that shed, as you can see. It's very small, too small for an old man who's lived a life of dedicated service. It's like a box, as you can see, that's how they treat old men these days; even venerable monks treat me poorly. It's pitiful, don't you agree?"

"I agree completely." Chit Naing doesn't want to do it. He shouldn't do it. He knows it's the wrong thing. But it's like being locked out of a house with a glass door. It's not the safest thing to do, it lacks wisdom and patience, but he draws himself up, pushes back his shoulders to assume a military bearing, and, with a strikingly officious voice, smashes the glass. "Grandfather, I am the senior jailer at the prison and I'm here on the business of the prison authorities. I cannot and will not come back later, Grandfather. I must speak to someone in a position of responsibility right *now*." He utters the last sentence in a low barking tone. The dog lying near the shed yips back, noticeably braver than the poor old man, who has shrunk visibly under the weight of the jailer's announcement. He opens his mouth, closes it, opens it again.

Chit Naing is ashamed of himself, but pleased when the old man finally manages to find his tongue. "I . . . I . . . I will go and wake up U Rewata, sir, he'll be able to help you directly. Yes, one moment, please, I will be back, he'll be down in a moment, he sleeps upstairs, I need to go get my flashlight, one moment, sir." Despite his terrible rheumatism, the old man nimbly backs away, glancing over his shoulder with a gaping mouth as he disappears into his shed. Chit Naing hears him whispering to himself or to the dog. He quickly reappears with a flashlight and bows as he moves past Chit Naing, then speedily mounts the outdoor staircase to the second floor.

As the wood creaks under the old man's feet, Chit Naing relaxes his military stance and sticks his fingers under his glasses to rub his eyes. The brave dog growls again. Will it race out of the shed and attack him? That would be too much.

He watches the old custodian rush along the outside corridor, one hand on the sagging wooden railing, the other holding the flashlight in front of him, its beam cast in a steady yellow line through the air to the floor. He raps hard on the door at the end of the hall and quickly disappears inside.

Chit Naing's eyes linger there for a moment, then rise to the gracefully peaked roof of the building. For a moment he thinks *fire*, but then he realizes the bright glow comes from the rising moon. Daw Sanda. Her name is the Pali word for moon. Suddenly self-conscious, he is aware that he stands in a place where she has stood also. She's visited the monastery to give alms and new robes to the boys.

He looks nervously into the dark courtyard, as though someone might be there, reading his mind. But it's just him, alone, realizing that he's come to the monastery school not only for the boy and not only for Teza. He is here for her too, Sanda, the intelligent, elegant woman he loves, a widow (though the term seems so wrong for her, at odds with the long black hair, the beautifully tailored clothes, her smile). She appears at that tea shop, this biryani shop. Sometimes they meet "accidentally" at a crowded pagoda. She walks slowly, searching through the crowd with an open face until she finds him. Then, very naturally, as though greeting her cousin or her brother or her husband, she smiles and begins to speak, fearless and discreet in equal proportion. The last time they were together—she gave him more money for Teza's morphine—he asked her, "Aren't you afraid of what will happen if they find us out?" She smiled. "I have nothing to be afraid of. My conscience is clear. I act out of compassion for my son. Any mother would do the same. It is you, Chit Naing, who risks everything by helping us. That's what I worry about."

When Teza makes his hunger strike public, there will be an uproar, not only in the prison but in the government too. Chit Naing will have to stop meeting her then. The thought of not seeing Sanda, of never again being close enough to touch her, upsets him as much as the prospect of getting in trouble.

He thinks of her remarkable son, leaning toward him and whispering the name of the street and the Hsayadaw's name, as if the urgency of his voice would ensure their existence, make the place and its querulous old keeper be here still. And here they are.

A door opens and closes. The flashlight beam flashes into the second-story corridor, lighting the faded burgundy robes of a monk who walks on the other side of the gardening cook. As they descend the stairs, Chit Naing goes forward to greet the senior monk, bowing low. Now that he's before the robed man, he's mortified by his earlier behavior—bossing around the old custodian, forcing him to wake the monk at this late hour. Head down, he quietly offers his respects and his apologies.

"Yes, yes, I accept both. This is a very unusual visit. Come with me, please. There is a little office next to the schoolroom where we can talk."

. 49 .

This is a different vision.

He dreams of himself from the outside, and high above. Has he become the cell, his body a wall of bricks, his eyes inside that wall? At the rim of his dreaming mind is the conscious one, asking questions, wandering around, trying to understand what's happened. Has he returned to the teak coffin and become the spider who watches the man in the cage? No. He knows he is still Teza. He sees himself stretched out on the floor, naked, quiet in the dark. Not shivering. Sleeping perhaps—his eyes are closed.

Then how can I see myself?

Am I dead?

No, wait. It's not the teak coffin, not the white house. Look at the floor. Instead of cement, it's stone, old and hewn stone. His eye travels around the outline of the sleeper, following the surface and the lines of separation between enormous flagstones. Excitement flushes through him, almost happiness.

Neither cell nor cage, this place, but temple.

One temple on a plain of two thousand temples and pagodas. His mind struggles to wrest itself from dreaming, to wake up and remember the ancient city of Pagan, where he visited the holy sites with his family. His mother fed them rice in the shade of the walls of Lemyethna, Temple of the Four Faces, under the trees dwarfed by Thatbyinnyu, Omniscience of the Buddha. Could he have come at last to the long ordination hall of the beloved monk Upali Thein? Or found a resting place half hidden in the face of a cliff, the rock-tunnel temple of Kyaukgu Umin? A weary man might find refuge in any of these places, in all of them. Kandawgyi. Apeyadana. Dhammayangyi, rising like the Dhamma itself, the great mountain of the Lord's teachings.

He might be dreaming of the Temple Nagayon, Protected by the Naga, where nine centuries ago a young serpent-dragon took care of the future king Kyansittha, who was so exhausted by his flight from an enemy that he fell into deep slumber right there, on the spot where the temple now stands.

Teza could be in any of these places. He could have fallen asleep in the cavernous halls of the great Ananda, white-tiered, four terraces gleaming like polished ivory. Anantapanna, Infinite Wisdom of the Buddha. It's true, the four porticoes of the hall are as intricate as wisdom, honeycombed with alcoves of treasure, green-glazed plaques of clay, devas painted with marks of auspiciousness on their palms. In terra-cotta, the Jatakas tell the stories of the Virtuous One's past lives, and the high windows rain light on the Buddha's head.

Then why such darkness, Teza?

Because we've come to the end of night. But dawn has not yet broken. The dream pulls him back into itself.

He sees through the high arched door. He feels stone-cool air on his skin and smells stone dust, akin to the scent of cold water. The vaulted room opens into archways, one in each of the world's directions, east, west, south, north.

How small he is! (Who am I?) The mind laughs, delighted by the discovery: he is clinging to the shoulder of the statue that faces the northern archway. He is the smallest man, his tiny hands scaled and clawed and four. (Who is that other one below, sleeping on the temple floor, he who loved his name?)

There is (*I am*) a lizard on the shoulder of the Buddha, the Buddha made of plaster and brick, the brick made with riverbed clay eight hundred years ago and fired here, in Tattadesa, The Parched Land, Pagan, City of

Temples. Gautama the Buddha's left hand rests in his lap, palm up, and his right hand reaches down to touch the earth, to call upon the earth as a witness to the worthiness of his enlightenment. The Buddha stares toward a river still invisible in darkness.

The lizard's skull swivels toward another open stone archway. At the eastern edge, there is the beginning of light, the slow paling of the sky, as the earth, his witness, rolls to face the burning star of the sun. The light comes in a slow flood, washes of pale pink, dark rose, mauve, deep red. In that light he sees the silhouettes of two people. They come up the steps, a man and a child. He sees the khaki uniform, the green T-shirt and turquoise longyi. Both of them are barefoot; they've come to pray.

The boy, Free El Salvador, and the man, Jailer Nyunt Wai Oo. Handsome. And he is handsome, beautiful, his face unlined, without the cutting mouth and angry eyes. How can this be, the two of them, coming into the vestibule, walking toward the sleeping man, the Buddha rising high above him? The boy is smiling shyly, as if he has something to say but is embarrassed. Handsome looks down at him and opens his mouth to speak. No sound comes but the harsh sigh of the vaulted ceiling. The first line of bricks buckles and begins to fall.

It happens slowly and quickly both. The stone pediments give way; the bricks crash down like the mud they once were, flowing, sliding (there is no sound but the susurrus of water), the Buddha himself tumbles over, burying man and child and sleeper, not out of anger *there is no place for anger here* but out of love. *How can this be?* Am I the temple, embracing them, falling to keep them inside me, like the relics of the Holy One buried deep in the heart of a pagoda?

The temple has fallen. (What am I now, my face against the stone?) He is outside as well as inside, watching. Before him lies rubble, a huge, uneven pile of bricks, out of which rise broken clay limbs, the dusty hands and rounded knees and elbows of the Buddha. His chipped face stares straight and blind into the bluing sky. Where is the lizard? Where is the boy, the jailer? (Where am I?) What have we become?

The same hearts and bones, swallowed by ancient clay. *We are the same life and death, the same fear, one flesh, our blood indistinguishable among these ruins.* Suddenly a bird is startled out of a crevice among the shattered bricks. His body jerks into the air, then lifts, lifts lightly, quickly. I am the sparrow also, whose feathers once were scales, whose wings were feet, whose feet are still the lizard's claws. I wake to fly and below I see the plains, dark gold and brown, the color of human skin, my skin when I was human. I see the river too, silver and twisting like a naga in the morning light, the immense Irrawaddy, one of the great rivers of his people, of my peoples, of the earth.

There is water on the singer's face, water on his fingers like a blessing as he touches his eyelids. But when he opens his eyes, the bare light hanging from the ceiling makes him shut them again. He knows the hardness under his head is cement, not stone. He stretches out his arms; it's not the temple or the plain. *Why did I have to wake?* He strikes the floor and brushes his arm in a long arc over the cement, pulling his head back under the edge of his blanket. He wants to curl up, to fold into himself, but his elbow knocks the strange thing close. Hardness butts against his ribs. Teza has no idea what it is; the shape has become foreign to him. Panicked, he tosses off the corner of the blanket and picks up a tattered, damp ledger. With one stunned hand, he lifts the thing over him—*a book!*—upside down, askew. The stained cover swings open like a door. And a pen, the white pen, falls onto his chest.

Teza begins to laugh. It hurts his mouth, but he cannot help himself. The laughter throbs right into the back of his skull, but he keeps laughing as he clicks the nib of the pen in and out, in and out. He props himself up on an elbow and inspects the ledger with his free hand. He moves slowly into a sitting position and shushes himself, trying to hold the weird mirth in. The laughter travels down into his shoulders and he finds himself shaking with silent giggles, which hurts more, so he lets the sound out again, and wipes the tears from his face, and wonders if this is still his dream.

To express his gratitude for being allowed to sleep on a mat beside Tan-see Tiger's bunk, Nyi Lay has been tidying the cell, washing longyis, and killing cockroaches since lights-on at six. For reasons no one can explain, the roach population of the hall has reached plaguelike proportions. The other inmates have left for workshop or cleaning duties, but Tiger is exempt from such menial labor. He sits cross-legged on his bunk while the boy brushes the small straw broom across the floor. Haltingly, by a route as meandering as the one he follows to sweep out the crushed roaches, the boy has told the tattooed convict what happened to his little house.

"That guy's the asshole among assholes. You gotta get the fuck outta here, kid."

The boy looks up with wide eyes.

"Not outta my cell, boy—you can stay here as long as you want. I mean the cage, you know? It'd be better to work outside than get smacked around by these pricks. You know, my cousin's husband has a tea shop. Maybe we could make an arrangement. You could go stay there and work. They're straight folks too, not like me. You'd get a day off and some money every week, and they let their boys sleep on the tables at night. It's not a bad life. You'd have a bit of cash, and there'd be boys your age all over the place, and pretty little girls selling cigarettes and betel. You know, Nyi Lay, girls! Pretty girls! We gotta get you the fuck outta here before you turn into a faggot. Really. I've seen it happen to a lotta guys. It's time for you to fly the coop, kid."

The boy holds the broom off the floor and theatrically cocks his ear toward the sound of the iron-beater. One strike. "It's ten-thirty, isn't it?"

The tan-see ostentatiously swivels the loose gold watch to the top of his wrist. "On the dot."

"I better go do my work. Can you call the warder to let me out?"

Tiger raises an eyebrow. "Why don't you just stay here until Jailer Chit Naing comes back to fetch you? He didn't want you to be on the grounds, Nyi Lay."

But the boy is already lifting the long strap of his sling bag over his head, onto his right shoulder. He pushes its bulk from his opposite hip to his back, so it doesn't swing against his legs when he walks.

Tiger laughs. "You're loaded up like a pony, kid. You can leave that stuff here, you know."

Nyi Lay doesn't reply. He just adjusts the cloth strap protectively across his chest. Inside the sling bag are the only treasures he has left. He's willing to leave his spare clothes and his blankets with Tiger, but he doesn't trust the other men who live in the cell.

"Why don't you just hang around until old Chit Naing turns up? You know, it's probably safer for you in here. No telling where Handsome is right now."

For a moment the boy thoughtfully chews his lip. "But we have to do our work, Saya Gyi, and who will feed the singer if I don't? I know the warder won't do it." He lowers his voice. "Saya Gyi, the Songbird's already so skinny, it's very bad. I need to take him his food. It's my job."

Tiger is impressed with this long speech; obviously the boy is keen to see his singer. He grins broadly, amused as always, and flattered to be called saya gyi, great teacher. Dressed only in a frayed ochre longyi, the tan-see stands and hails the warder. Then he whispers, "You just watch out now, Little Brother. If Handsome wrecked your house, he'll be happy to wreck your head too, the prick. Go to Sammy if you need to—he's beating time at the watchtower all through this week, double shift. Or run your ass straight to the Chief Warden. Even if you just get halfway to the office, they'll hear you screaming." The tan-see pauses, eyebrows knitted. "That's what you do, Little Brother, if there's trouble. Scream your fucking head off. After last night, the warders know Handsome's in some kind of shit, so they'll be more likely to help you now."

"Yes, Saya Gyi, tzey-zu-tin-ba-deh." The boy looks at the roaring blue cat on the man's chest. There's another one, with bigger teeth, on his leg. He glances surreptitiously at the rows of numbers and letters tattooed into Tiger's torso and upper arms. He knows they're for luck, for warding off bullets and knife wounds, but he's always been too shy to ask the tan-see what they say. If he ever grows big like Tiger, he will find some lucky words to write forever on his skin.

Usually when the boy goes to pick up Teza's food tray, Eggplant is busy cooking the Chief Warden's lunch in the back kitchen. But today Eggplant is sitting outside the kitchen on a tea-shop stool, his feet planted wide apart to make room for his belly. The boy wonders why the stool hasn't splintered into pieces under the man's bulk. Eggplant's red-checked longyi rides up high on his legs as he leans over and tamps his cheroot against a windowsill. Someone else sits on a stool across from him, his narrow back to the boy, but Nyi Lay recognizes the rusty scalp gleaming through the gray hair.

A few steps away now, he averts his eyes from the cowled fat around Eggplant's bare knees.

"Look who's coming—our little friend the rat-killer."

Sein Yun glances over his shoulder, then turns back to Eggplant and announces, "That's not his name anymore, my friend. They call him Tiger Sucker now." He turns to the boy again and leers, all pointy gold caps and betel teeth. "They call him Lover Boy. We hear you spent the night with your good uncle the tan-see. How nice!"

The boy pulls his sling bag around to his front. He smells the dirt in the palm-reader's words but can't understand it.

Sein Yun throws his head back and guffaws. "Come on, little Tiger Sucker, stop pretending. You know exactly what I'm talking about." He reaches out and snatches the cheroot from Eggplant's fat hand. Making a circle with his left thumb and index finger, he pokes the cheroot through quickly, half a dozen times. The cook slaps his bare knee, and the men erupt into unrestrained laughter. Sein Yun tosses the cheroot high in the air, back to the cook, who catches it with ease.

The boy looks from one man to the other, still confused. The palm-reader knows Tiger isn't like that. He doesn't fuck boys, or men, or any-one in the cage—he pines for faraway girlfriends. But Nyi Lay isn't sure how to refute the palm-reader's insinuation. He opens his mouth, simply to say *no*, but Eggplant cuts in, "Lucky, lucky boy. Did you like it? Hmm?"

In a menacing flash of comprehension, the boy realizes that Eggplant and Sein Yun have been waiting for him. That's why they're sitting out here, in the late morning, when there's still so much work to do. Goose-flesh rises on his neck and arms.

Eggplant leans forward on his opened knees, holding the cheroot in the curl of his fingers. "I bet you really liked it, little boy. Why don't you come with me to the back kitchen and I'll give you some nice oil to drink? Hmm? You'd like that too, wouldn't you?"

The boy has stopped at the threshold of the kitchen. He could go in and fetch the tray. It's not that the two men block his passage; they're sit-ting off to one side. But their voices hold him still. Ten seconds pass, twenty, half a minute. He knows that the cook doesn't like to be stared in the face, so he stares him hard in the face. Eggplant ignores him by light-ing his cheroot. His huge body is more unfathomable than usual, because the boy is standing so close to the thick flesh slabs of the upper arms, the breasts full and jiggling under the threadbare undershirt, the wrists packed tight with fat like a folded-over Chinese sausage. Sweat and cooking oil and charcoal smoke come like a vapor off Eggplant's skin. The boy glances once more at the palm-reader, who grins so hard he resembles a half-decayed human head.

Step by slow step, the boy backs up. When he's over the threshold of the kitchen, he turns and marches across the big serving room to the inmate who prepares the food for solitaries. After the man loads up Teza's tray, the boy walks back out into the fresh morning air.

Without so much as glancing at the two men, he carries the tray with his head held high, his skinny shoulders thrown back. He doesn't know the word to describe his steady stride, this new willingness to be visible, unhidden. Eggplant and Sein Yun see it. They know what it is. Dignity. And they laugh.

. 50 .

No, sir. I questioned the boy myself, and as far as I could tell, the charges against him were unfounded. Officer Nyunt Wai Oo was very angry, and he wasn't thinking straight. I wondered if he was drunk." It's a talent, keeping the voice flat, disconnected from the words themselves and where they might lead. Chit Naing is managing quite well. From his calm face, no one would be able to guess the shredded state of his nerves, nor the acid twisting his guts. "The child had no idea what Jailer Nyunt Wai Oo was talking about. As you can imagine, sir, he was very frightened, and the loss of his house—"

The Chief Warden snaps, "Yes, I know, you've already told me about that." He thrums his fingers on the desk and stares down at the notes in front of him. One is a two-line memo from Senior Jailer Chit Naing, requesting this interview. The other is a long letter from Nyunt Wai Oo, delivered at dawn by a timid, stuttering young man who lives close to the jailer's house.

That little scene took place before the Chief had finished drinking his tea. What a way to start the day. The petrified, acne-bitten messenger, who on further investigation turned out to be the junior jailer's nephew, explained that Junior Jailer Nyunt Wai Oo would not be able to come to work for several days, having been laid up with a seriously injured knee. The fellow, almost unable to talk for nervousness, then unable to stop his jabbering, went on to testify that he had s-s-seen it h-h-himself, the j-j-j-j-joint swollen to twice its normal size. Bowing deeply, he gave over Nyunt Wai Oo's letter as though passing on a plague-laden envelope. He bowed repeatedly as he backed out of the office.

Written on two sheets of paper, the letter is a document of convoluted fury. The Chief wonders if it's possible that Junior Jailer Nyunt Wai Oo is going insane. The letter makes no mention of how he injured his knee, though the sentences are full of accusations, oaths against the boy and Chit Naing, and constant references to that ridiculous pen. It occurs to the Chief that if the bloody thing is ever found, he would like nothing better than to stick it down Nyunt Wai Oo's throat.

He glances up at Chit Naing, who is polishing his glasses. Without the wire rims, the jailer looks younger, almost vulnerable. Chit Naing meets his boss's eye calmly. Then, longing for the thin protective veil between himself and the world, he quickly puts his glasses back on. The two men are in the downstairs office, with a long wooden desk and files lining the back wall. Chit Naing's eyes flit from the Chief's jowled face to the faded portrait of Bogyoke Aung San that hangs above the file cabinets. He takes it as a good sign, somehow; the Chief Warden still respects the general. In some government offices they've taken away the Bogyoke's famous picture because it reminds people too much of his daughter.

Just as quickly, Chit Naing redirects his gaze to the open window, which gives onto the compound and the first of the big halls. A group of inmates shackled in leg irons walks across his field of vision. *Clank clank clank*. For perhaps the thousandth time, Chit Naing thinks of rattling elephant chains and how the scrawniest mahouts control such powerful animals.

What if the Chief won't let the boy leave? Chit Naing looks down at the palm of his open hand, trying to affect disinterest.

"Did he hurt the kid?"

"Earlier in the evening he found the boy by the drainage stream and tried to drown him. You know what he does to the inmates in the shower rooms sometimes? He did that to the boy. He could have killed him. The boy didn't want to tell me anything about it. I had to coax it out of him. Jailer Nyunt Wai Oo also hit him. There's a big cut on his face. He came to find me and I accompanied him back to his hut, which the junior jailer and some warders had already destroyed. When we showed up, Jailer Nyunt Wai Oo wanted to get his hands on the boy, but I wouldn't let him. He was acting like . . . well, like a lunatic, sir. All of us could see that. He wanted to interrogate the child." He allows a weighted pause. "As he would a political prisoner."

The Chief Warden expels a short, sharp breath. "Seiq-nyit-deh! Bloody irritating. He wants to be an interrogator so badly that he'll work on errand boys to prove it. I will need to speak with the boy myself, just to make sure there's nothing to Nyunt Wai Oo's claims, but before that happens, tell me about the *helpful possibility* you mentioned in your note." Chit Naing can hear a twinge of irony in the Chief's tone. Fortunately, he hadn't dared to write *solution*.

Lightly, lightly; it can't seem too important to him. He leans back in the wooden chair. "Well, sir, I'm not really sure if this would work, but it's something to consider. Until yesterday, when Officer Nyunt Wai Oo attacked him, the boy never wanted to leave the prison. Quite the opposite, in fact. But now he realizes that there are all kinds of dangers for him here. I can only imagine what he's already experienced. The prison isn't . . . it's not . . . the right place for an orphan. Sometimes I think I should have gone ages ago to find him a placement in a monastery school. That's my idea, you see, sir. I know a very good pongyi-kyaung in Rangoon, in Kyee Myin Daing. I think the Hsayadaw might agree to take the boy as a novice. With your permission, of course, sir." Another pause, to give the Chief the space to speak if he wants to. But he doesn't say a word. Chit Naing continues. "Shall I ask him?"

The Chief Warden stands up, pushing his chair out behind him so it grates against the floor. Chit Naing, who has started to lean forward, sits up straight and gazes at the portrait of Bogyoke Aung San. The Chief paces to one side of the small room, turns, returns to his desk, and takes a package of cigarettes from his breast pocket. He rarely offers his pack to the senior jailer because he knows Chit Naing has never smoked, but there is something distinctly proprietorial about the way he flicks open the little box and turns away slightly, as if to say, *These are mine.*

Ignoring Chit Naing's question, he asks one of his own. "How do you know the monastery?"

The jailer is disheartened, though the passive expression on his face doesn't change. He feared this might happen—a little interrogation. The story he has prepared is the only possible story to tell, the only plausible lie, but taken together with other evidence, in the months to come, it will lead to his undoing.

"My wife gives alms there sometimes. At the beginning of the rainy season, we try to donate a few new robes to the novices." The Chief Warden would not believe for a second that Chit Naing, on his own, might give alms to a monastery school. Only his wife, with money from her family, would buy robes or food to give to hungry orphans. A senior jailer doesn't make very much money, especially if he doesn't take bribes.

With the mention of Chit Naing's wife, the Chief seems slightly mollified. He even smiles a little. *Ah, the generosity of the weaker sex*. Or perhaps he is thinking, *How easy it will be to catch you out, liar*. He takes an ashtray from a little side table and places it carefully on his desk but still does not sit down. He paces the length of the room again. Chit Naing is keenly aware of his bulk, the solid mass of him. The Chief is not a tall man, but he wears the power of his position like he wears his military rank. The silence is his to control. He lets Chit Naing sit in it like a cat in water.

"Does this Hsayadaw have a history?"

"A history, sir? Of political activity, you mean?"

"Yes, Officer Chit Naing, of course that's what I mean."

"Well, sir, I really don't know. I haven't checked. He runs a school. Most of his pupils are under fifteen, so they're not . . . they're not like the university students. It's a rather poor orphanage, crumbling to the ground, really. I suspect they worry more about food than politics."

"That's as it bloody well should be. But you know that some of the older monks get big ideas. They can be dangerous. Remember the one who hid the student rebels in his monastery?"

"Yes, sir, of course I remember him." Chit Naing couldn't possibly forget that fearless old monk, his skin like holy parchment. *My son, this body is a dirty shell. Do whatever you want with it*. He died in his cell, still sitting in his meditation pose, his back against the brick wall.

"We treated him with kid gloves and he went and croaked on us anyway, the old bugger."

The way the Chief speaks about the monk is repugnant, but Chit

Naing nods his head. He's ashamed to take part in this theater, but there's nothing else he can do. Is the Chief trying to bait him? Belying his composed expression, Chit Naing feels a shiver across his shoulders.

"You know what those people are like, don't you, Officer Chit Naing? Always up to something, making demands they have no right to be making. It's just like that colonialist collaborator Suu Kyi. You know they're letting her speak to the people on the weekend? From behind her gate, if you can believe it. You heard about that, didn't you?" His voice amplifies.

"Yes, sir, I think I did hear something about it."

"She stands up there and says whatever she wants to say, talks to the people, answers their questions with lies, smiling and showing off for the foreigners who come to take her picture. What does she know? What could she possibly know about this country when she spent most of her life in England fucking white men? I don't understand why the First Secretary allows it, I just don't understand. Or why General Ne Win would allow it. They should have just killed her, you know. I've said that for years—they should have shot her and all her traitor friends a long time ago."

According to the part Chit Naing plays, he must say something, anything, to assure the Chief Warden of his position, his rightness in all things; that is how the balance of power holds. But Chit Naing sits in mute astonishment. He cannot do it. Right now, this moment, he has to say something. Though the instant is passing, it's not too late.

It's gone. His eyes are fixed on the portrait of Daw Suu Kyi's father. The Bogyoke loved Burma so well; he worked tirelessly for his people. Some forty years later, with history still bearing witness to the magnitude of that love and work, it's almost impossible to believe that anyone wanted to kill him. Yet a jealous rival did want him to die and did murder him, spilled his blood like that of a mere animal, less than an animal, whose dying might have served a purpose. If Chit Naing agrees with the idea of assassinating his daughter, if he nods his head and eats that lie with a smile, how would it be different from celebrating her father's death? He cannot do it.

While the jailer stares at the portrait of the dead hero, the Chief Warden frowns at the jailer. The ash on his cigarette has grown so long that it falls off; he jumps and brushes the live cinders from his shirt. Then he carefully sets the cigarette in the ashtray. His voice is very quiet. "Officer Chit Naing, she is not what he was."

"Excuse me, sir?"

"The Bogyoke and his daughter. They are not the same people."

This is not so hard to manage. "No, sir, they certainly are not." *She is still alive.*

"You agree with me there?"

"Absolutely."

The Chief stands up straight again, suddenly brusque and businesslike. "This Hsayadaw, then, he's not full of big political ideas, is he? Hmm?"

"The Hsayadaw has never spoken to me, sir, about politics." *Actually, he has never spoken to me at all, but he'll be back from Sagaing in two days.* "I don't think he's interested in politics, sir. If you would like, I'm sure we could arrange an interview."

"Oh, I'm sure we could. It's not that I don't trust you, Ko Chit Naing." Though he has used *Ko,* the less formal manner of address, the words he has spoken hang testily among the blue nooses of cigarette smoke. "You know I'm fond of the boy. I just don't want to hand him over to a bunch of troublemakers."

Chit Naing clenches his jaw. Only a devotee of the military government could have spawned such absurdity. A school run by monks is cause for concern while the prison is safe haven for a child. Chit Naing clears his throat. "I know exactly what you mean, sir. I feel the same way."

. 51 .

They stare at each other through the bars without talking. Free El Salvador has pushed the rice gruel through the trap. His eyes move from the tray to Teza's face to his blanket and sleeping mat. The singer says, "Little Brother, you brought me gifts last night."

But he sounds strange. And there is no smile around his eyes. Unsure of what to say, the boy looks down and rubs at a patch of rust low on the bars.

"Why did you bring those things to me?"

Free El Salvador's voice is defensive. "But the pen is yours. You lost it. I brought it back." He adds in the quietest whisper, "Now you can write."

"But where did you *get* the pen? *How* did you get it?"

The boy sniffs. "Outside the coffin. The day of the beating."

As Teza stares at him, the distended jaw and open mouth become part of an expression of pure disbelief. His mind jumps and weaves, trying to grasp the many implications of what the boy has said.

Free El Salvador abruptly stands, runs down the short corridor, and checks the compound. He waves at Teza and mouths the word *warder*. But the warder passes by. A few seconds later the boy returns to the cell. He whispers, "The pen is still good, Ko Teza. Really, there's lots of ink inside. I only used it a few times, hardly at all. It's yours. I brought it back to you." The singer hears what he's really saying: *This is my gift to you. Aren't you pleased?* He's longing for what comes after a gift is given: words of praise and gratitude. Teza forgets sometimes. He forgets that Free El Salvador is a child.

"Nyi Lay, thank you. I thank you for the pen and the ledger. I'm just very surprised. This morning, when I woke up, I couldn't believe they were here. It was like magic. But I still don't understand. Chit Naing told me about the search. Handsome turned the cage upside down, looking for the pen. He said warders and inmates were hunting for it, poking around, bribing people. How did you do it?"

The boy slyly narrows his eyes. "Handsome didn't think of me. He knows I can't write. He didn't search my place." Then his face changes. "Until yesterday."

"He figured it out?"

"He broke apart my house and threw my things out into the compound. The warders dug a big hole, trying to find the pen. But they didn't find it, Ko Teza. They tore up my shack and took all my stuff, but it was too late." The full, boyish lips curve into a cautious smile. He whispers, "He didn't get the pen!"

Teza finds it hard to keep his jaw immobile and his voice still, not to whoop with the admiration he feels for the boy crouching in front of him.

"He didn't get the pen because you brought it to me. Along with that ledger."

"*Ledger* is the book of lines and numbers?"

"That's right. The clerks keep track of accounts, money spent, by writing down all the numbers, the dates. Where did you get that?"

"I found it in the garbage outside one of the offices."

"The garbage?"

"Ko Teza, you can find many good things in the garbage," the boy explains earnestly. "Sometimes food, sometimes wires and plastic bags. Once I found a pencil and traded with an Indian for three chapatis. Sometimes I just get mango pits and bags of la-phet with a few peanuts or tea leaves still stuck inside. No one's supposed to throw away papers or books or anything important in the garbage baskets, but sometimes they're too lazy to take their garbage to the big office."

"But how did you leave the ledger here last night? Didn't the warder on guard duty see you?"

"Only Saya Chit Naing was here."

"U Chit Naing *knows* about this?"

"Oh, no! He didn't see anything. I said I wanted to pray with you. He stayed on the other side of the wall when I came in. You were sleeping. So I stuck the book under your blanket."

Free El Salvador and the singer stare at each other. Then, at precisely the same moment, they begin to laugh. Teza breathes out his ragged, syncopated *Heh heh heh* and the boy covers his mouth with his hands. After a few seconds he suddenly becomes serious and whispers, "I thought Handsome was going to kill me. But Chit Naing would not let him."

Teza is silent. What can he say? "Oh, Nyi Lay, please be careful."

"I'm always careful. But if somebody really wants to kill you, it doesn't matter what you do. He'll get you in the end." The words are so brutal and true that Teza cannot respond.

Nyi Lay briskly rises and reknots his longyi with sharp movements, then sinks again into a squat. "But you know what? On my way over here, I heard the news from a warder that Handsome didn't come to work this morning. Everybody's talking about it. So for today I'm safe."

Yet the boy is very nervous, Teza notices, constantly fidgeting and straining to hear what's happening in the compound.

"Maybe Handsome's quit his job."

"Oh, no," the boy replies. "He loves his job. Tint Lwin told me something's wrong with his leg, so he can't walk. But when he comes back, he'll come after me again."

Teza watches the boy carefully. "Sabado, this is your invitation."

"My invitation?"

"To go away from here. If you leave the cage altogether, Handsome won't be able to hurt you."

The boy rubs the back of his hand across his nose. "I have other work to do now."

Without thinking or planning his words, Teza begins. "Sabado, you can rush off now, but take this idea with you. Think about it. Why did you bring me the pen, the ledger? Because you understand how important words are." The boy turns his face away, stubbornly, but can't pull himself out of the man's orbit. "Nyi Lay, when I was really small and didn't know how to read and write, I used to cry because I wanted so badly to learn. Then I went to school, and I learned. You want to learn too, don't you? Don't you? Then you have to leave the prison. You're already so brave, living on your own here. I admire you. But to get out of this place, you'll have to be braver."

"I don't want to talk anymore. I have to go now." The boy clenches his fists.

The singer cannot stop himself. "U Chit Naing will help you, Nyi Lay. Other people will help you. But you have to let them. You have to trust us. You have to trust *me*."

Teza has stretched out his hand in a pleading gesture, and the boy wants to knock it against the iron bars. Instead he scrambles backward, not losing his balance but springing to his feet, so angry he can't breathe. *Trust!* Yon-kyi hmu, at the heart of love and betrayal both, a word he understands but has never lived. How would he live it here, who would have taught him to believe in its power? Yes, he might trust Chit Naing and Tan-see Tiger and Sammy the giant Indian. He might trust Teza, but one question keeps him separate, caged within the cage: *Why? Why should I trust any of them?*

He chokes, not on water like last night but on tears. Drowning again, he stifles his cries, but the force of them makes him shudder. His arms lift away from his sides. It almost hurts to touch his own body. Abandoned, he stands in front of the white house and sobs.

"Nyi Lay!" The voice comes across a chasm three feet wide and a universe distant, but it's the same place, the same cage, because the boy can hear Teza. "Nyi Lay, come here." Teza stretches his hands and voice through the bars. "Come here," he whispers again. In the midst of the wave that carries him forward to take Teza's hands, the boy might be safe, even beloved. But the wave rolls back. He draws his hands from Teza's and twists away. Swallowing his tears, he spits out the furious words, "Why should I trust you?"

Teza meets the question with silence. He is thinking, *Why? Why?*
"Because *I* trust *you*. That's the only reason. And I love you as much as I
love my own little brother."

This declaration has an unexpected effect on Free El Salvador. It
shakes him out of his hurt. "You have a *brother?*"

"A younger brother. But not little like you."

"I'm not little."

"No. I guess you're not."

"What's your brother's name?"

"Aung Min."

"Does he live in Rangoon?"

"Not anymore. He's somewhere on the border."

"The border?"

"Between Burma and Thailand."

"Sometimes the Thai prisoners give me food."

"That's kind of them. Their country is right beside Burma. And the
place called the border separates our two countries, and joins them."

"At the same time?"

"Yes. Like the walls around the prison keep us from the outside but remind us that the world's right there, just a few steps away."

"Is Aung Min in prison too?"

"No. He's a revolutionary."

"Like Bogyoke Aung San!" Awe deepens the boy's voice.

Teza immediately thinks of how pleased Aung Min would be with this
comparison. "You know about Bogyoke Aung San?"

"Tan-see Tiger talks about him. He has a framed photograph of the
Bogyoke in his cell. Bogyoke Aung San was the great revolutionary general who chased away all the Japanese and English." The boy isn't sure exactly what Japanese and English are. When Tiger talks about them, they
occasionally seem human. Other times, the boy is convinced they're wild
animals. But he knows for certain that Bogyoke Aung San made them leave
Burma. "Does your brother chase away Japanese and English?"

Teza gives Free El Salvador a sad look. "No, he fights against Burmese
soldiers." Teza has no idea, really, what his brother does, and how. He's
not even sure that Aung Min is still alive.

"*Our* soldiers?"

"Yes. The Burmese army. And their leaders." How to explain civil war to a child? "Many of the soldiers are cruel, because the men who lead them are cruel. You know about the other political prisoners, right?"

"They can read."

"Yes, they can. And they can write. And they talk to people about changing the government. The army doesn't like that, so they put the politicals in the cage. But thousands of other politicals don't live in the prison. When the generals started to kill them, they went to the border, to work against the army from outside Burma. There are many different groups of people working against the government."

"What's the government again?"

"The government's made up of the men who run the army and their friends. The SLORC."

"Oh." The boy nods.

"If you disagree with them or ask them to stop hurting the people, sometimes they become very cruel."

"Like Handsome."

"Yes. A lot like Handsome."

"Why are they like that?"

Teza looks at Nyi Lay's hungry-to-know face. "Because they're afraid. They're afraid to give up their power, or all the good things they've stolen from people. And they're afraid of how angry the people are."

"What people?"

"All the people who've been hurt or whose families have been hurt by the government. All the people who aren't allowed to be free and do what they want. But do you know what terrifies them the very most?"

"What?"

"Change." Teza doesn't let go of the boy's eyes. "They don't want to change. They want all the old ways to keep going. They're not very good Buddhists."

"Why not?"

"Because the Buddha taught us that things change all the time. It's like the weather. The monsoon's almost over, isn't it, even though it still rains at night. And now it's warm enough, but soon the cold season will begin, and then a while later it will get hot again and more rains will come. It's the same for everything—people, animals, plants, all the things we make and build. Even if people or things look the same, they're always shifting or growing or dying. Nothing stays the same for any of us. So we try to have upekkha, to live with upekkha. That means to accept the change that comes and to be calm in it."

Free El Salvador glances toward the corridor and quickly puts a finger to his lips. The old warder is coming to take Teza out for a shower. The boy recognizes his footsteps. And sensing the hidden message Teza is trying to pass to him, he is glad to end the conversation. "The warder's coming. I'll take your pail off to the latrine hole."

He walks toward the outer wall. If the stooped old fellow's in a good mood, he might give the boy a candy.

Teza quickly whispers, "Nyi Lay!"

He turns his head.

"Be very careful."

Just as the old man appears, rattling a handful of keys, the boy gives Teza a smile like a small jewel.

. 52 .

Once more he's found a tribe of ants. They lived in the white house before his arrival, but those first weeks after the beating, all his energies turned inward. In the past few days, with a sense of purpose returned to him, he has started to observe the ants with his old keen eye, wondering about the minutiae of their lives. It's easier to see them too, because their trails, once close to the ceiling, now switch back and twist farther down the wall. Teza has tempted them down with grains of rice on the floor. He saves any gristle or vegetable in his morning meal for the boy, but part of the rice gruel goes to the birds, to the ants, to the twitchily enthusiastic cockroaches.

The rest of the morning gruel he eats himself, though eating is still his most dreaded activity. He can't apply any pressure to grind his teeth. Even swallowing uses muscles that have not healed. It's excruciating, but it concerns him less and less. Soon it won't concern him at all. Most days he meditates, four, five, six hours. When he is done, his exhaustion is complete. He can only do sitting meditation now. In the teak coffin he often meditated by walking, observing each footfall, the heel, middle foot, ball of the foot, toes bending. Though his broken toes are much better now, they're very stiff. He hobble-walks without grace. Ya-ba-deh. Never mind. His toes are so far from his heart, he's already given them up.

His body is often tired, the long muscles squeezed empty and thin. His distillation continues apace, as the pulp gets sucked out. The leftover shell is not dry husk but essence, pure oil or alcohol, sharp and eye-brightening despite his weariness. When he doesn't meditate, he sleeps, and when he doesn't sleep, he thinks about the pen, so remarkably returned to him, and the ledger with its stained but mostly empty pages, and his little brother, and words. Of all the words there are in his mind, in his life, of all the words in the world, which ones must be spoken to paper? What will he write? Sometimes he lies on his back, face turned to the ceiling, where lizards pivot and run in their hunt for insects.

It's just as it was in the teak coffin, yet everything has changed. He composes long letters in his head while watching the creatures do their jerky dance, small jaws snapping. They eat and eat: moths, mosquitoes, small and larger flies. It's almost unbelievable that the singer ever ate *them*, the small reptiles. He shakes his head when he thinks of it.

He looks from the ceiling to his slice of blue sky beyond the cell. Last night he saw the moon, half waxing or half waning, like a sad face turning toward him. Lying close to the bars, he intended to watch it drop across the short chasm between roof and wall, but he was so tired he fell asleep after two minutes. He woke to watch the gray dawn become mauve become rose-blue become blue sky, and he knew it was a whole blue sky, without clouds, wide open over the prison, over Rangoon. The colors made him think of his mother, her flowers and plants growing in their compound. He remembered the little wooden gate. Surely it's covered in lime-green moss again, after the monsoon. Scrub brush in hand, Daw Sanda has already complained about it to the neighbor, as she does every year, and she has promised to get an ugly iron one, which she never does and never will do. A gate made of iron bars looks too much like a prison door.

With this thought, Teza's eyes shift. Because he's still lying down, the first thing beyond the grille of bars that hits his eyes is a pair of boots. The sight of them so close to his face frightens him. An uneven cry rises three octaves "Waa-aa-aah!" as it flies from his mouth. He's already rolling away as a glimpse of the face registers in his mind. It's not Handsome but Chit Naing, his friend.

"I'm sorry, Ko Teza. I thought you heard me."

With the rush of adrenaline, Teza has become both nervous and dazed. Very slowly he rolls onto his side and sits up. "No, I . . . I was thinking about something." He wonders if he has gone completely deaf in the damaged ear. He moves his head back and forth, as though rattling a faulty gadget.

Chit Naing bends down. "The doctor wants to come by to see you again."

"Today?"

"Oh, he's not that dedicated. But soon. He mentioned it to me this morning when he signed in."

"Has he spoken to the Chief Warden?"

"I don't think so. But he will, Ko Teza. And if you are serious about a hunger strike, you must know that the Chief Warden won't let you go through with it. They will beat you again. You have to know that. They'll make you eat."

"What are they going to do, break my jaw again to stuff food down my throat?"

"Possibly. If the Chief's feeling generous, he might strap you down in here and hook you up to an IV."

Teza looks at him suspiciously. He doesn't believe the prison authorities would handle any problem with such finesse. "No one will do that immediately."

"So you *are* serious about the hunger strike."

"You thought I was pulling your leg?" Genuine bemusement lightens Teza's voice.

The jailer closes his eyes for a long moment. When he opens them, he asks, "What are your demands?"

Teza slowly crosses his legs, so that the ankle of his bottom foot presses against the dirty weave of his mat. He lifts the other foot and nestles it in the cradle of slack thigh and calf. Then he says, "I have no demands."

"But if it's a hunger strike, the prisoner always has demands."

The senior jailer sounds like a petulant child, Teza thinks, scratching the rash of scabies along his shin. He shrugs. "If I must have a demand, then I demand to be released so that I can go eat curry and rice with my mother."

"Ko Teza, please don't make stupid jokes."

"That's my demand. Surely it's no more stupid than my being here in the first place."

"I cannot tell that to the Chief."

"I could tell him. I'll explain why now is the perfect time to release me."

Chit Naing smiles nervously. "Even if you ask politely, I don't think they'll let you go."

The two men look at each other. Teza's voice is clear and resonant. "No, they won't let me go. I know that, U Chit Naing. But I intend to release myself. I'm ready to leave the cage."

Chit Naing gets out his handkerchief, takes off his glasses, and squints at his friend's blurred, softened face. "You have to serve out your sentence . . ." He is aware how ridiculous these words sound, but he can't help saying them, holding on to this reality, this version of how things must be. Teza will serve out his sentence, thirteen more years, less if there's an amnesty. There might be amnesty next year, or the year after; sometimes it does happen. It's happened before, when those human rights groups in the West have campaigns for certain political prisoners. It makes the generals fret about the bad publicity, and they let the person go. It's happened before. Look at Daw Aung San Suu Kyi. They've released her from house arrest.

Teza stares at Chit Naing with a sympathetic, almost fatherly expression. "I know all about serving my sentence. That's not what I mean."

"What do you mean, then?"

Teza stares past his friend's shoulder, up to the left, at the slice of blue sky. Then his eyes return to Chit Naing, who hasn't been able to resist cleaning his glasses. The singer waits until the polishing is over and the jailer has put them back on. He's about to speak when Chit Naing starts to fiddle with the wires behind his ears, making the lenses flash once, twice, again, like signal mirrors. His left eyebrow and cheek have tightened up, as though he has a bad toothache.

When his eyes are visible again, and steady, Teza answers his question. "I mean that I am ready to leave this body behind."

Chit Naing stares at him for such a long, stunned moment that Teza starts to wonder if the jailer has understood. Will he have to be more explicit? But then the torrent of words begins. "Ko Teza, stop. It's the beating. The beating took something out of you. Obviously it was awful physically"—he lifts his hand in the general direction of Teza's face— "but psychologically, your mind, you haven't been the same since. And you've been fasting already—you've lost so much weight, no wonder you haven't gotten better. You need to drop the Sixth Precept. Start eating your evening meal. I will get the boy more rice. I will, I promise you. I know he eats your food. The guys in the kitchen take some too—it's a double portion. If you just started to eat more, you would feel better. And the morphine. You need to take it, Ko Teza. The pain is too much, you see—it's affecting your mind."

The jailer is gesticulating now, as if talking to himself. "It doesn't make any sense. You have to think of . . ." The word comes out in a barely audible whisper, "The movement. All you've worked for. And Daw Aung San Suu Kyi. She's free now. And your . . ." Teza knows what he's going to say. "Your mother. Think of her. She's already lost so much. If you just give yourself time to get better, you will change your mind. I am sure of it. You are depressed because of your injuries." Like a flare in empty ocean, the jailer throws his final argument out into the cell: "To live through so much, and then to give up!"

Teza lightly responds, "U Chit Naing, don't say that. I'm not giving up. I am ending the war."

"What? What are you talking about?"

"I can't hate them anymore. I don't hate them."

"Who?"

"The men who put me here, who keep me here. The generals, the MI agents. The Chief Warden. All of them. Even Handsome. I must not hate him for what he did to me." His voice is warm but eerily toneless.

Chit Naing's eyes have grown amazed, even incredulous, behind his glasses, but he sounds impatient. "Ko Teza, what do you mean?"

"I mean that I have ended the war. My own war. It's done."

"I don't know what you're talking about."

"I do not want to die hating them, the terrible *them*. Who are they? They are my own people. You were once *them*."

"Fine, Ko Teza, I will agree with you if that's what you want, but can't you end your war without a hunger strike? You have to fight against them, Ko Teza. Don't you remember what you told me once? I remember exactly. You said, 'In the cage, the only weapon I have is my own life.' How can you give that up now?"

"What I said was true. But look at my body. Look at my face. I don't need to defend myself now."

"Why not?"

Chit Naing sounds offended. "You forget that people still listen to your songs. You are the singer. Don't you remember why you're here? Because of the struggle. How can you abandon it? Think of your brother on the border—he's still working."

"If he's still alive, yes, I imagine he's still working."

"He's mentioned regularly in the newspaper as an enemy of the people, so he must be alive. If he'd been killed, the government would have made a big celebratory announcement."

Teza laughs quietly.

"What's so funny?"

"I'm just thinking of how pissed off they'll be when I . . . go."

"Ko Teza, you are not going anywhere!"

Teza ignores him. "Their power takes such unexpected forms. Sometimes killing is the power. Sometimes keeping someone miserably alive is the power. Those two things look so different, but they are the same— they come from the same will to control, to violate. It's true that my life has been my weapon. But death can be a weapon also."

Chit Naing has started to feel nauseous. He stares at the singer, who calmly, almost blandly, returns his gaze.

"U Chit Naing, do you know about the hunger strikers of Coco Island?"

The jailer has never told Teza that his father was a chief warden of Thayawaddy Prison and, years before that, an overseer for the work camps on Coco. "Yes," he mumbles, deflated, his sense of indignation gone. "Yes, of course I know."

"The prisoners who staged those hunger strikes knew that choosing their own death was a better choice than enduring degradation day after day. They *chose*. They died in their friends' arms. Did you know that? Their friends helped them to die with dignity."

"Yes, Ko Teza, but they died and their friends got off the island alive."

"We have to respect the choice they made. Their deaths forced the authorities to pay more attention to the camps. Their friends were released sooner because of the strikes."

"But who will be released sooner if you die, Ko Teza?"

"Me. I will be released. You see? My decision is a selfish one, finally. I am very tired. I am ready. The only one I worry about is the boy. I want him to leave before I begin the strike."

"Listen, we'll talk more about this strike business later. I have to go. But about the boy—I went to the monastery school last night."

"It was still there, wasn't it?"

"Yes."

"And the Hsayadaw is still alive."

"He is, but he's away in Sagaing for a couple of days. The pongyi-kyaung is very full, but I think they'll find a place for him. I've spoken to the Chief Warden. He's willing to let the boy go. Last night I talked with the Hsayadaw's assistant, a monk who grew up there. He knows you, he said, you played together as children. And he knows the songs."

Teza puts a hand to his chest in a gesture of thanks. "This is the best gift, U Chit Naing."

"But we can't be sure if the boy will want to go."

"Oh, don't worry. I'll talk to him again. He's close to making the decision for himself. He's just getting ready. It takes time. Doesn't it?"

The two men look at each other without speaking. Teza sits cross-legged in his cell and Chit Naing crouches in front of him, one hand gripping an iron bar for balance. He knows he must quell his rising emotion. It's disconcerting to realize how much he draws his own strength from the presence of this wasted prisoner, Teza of the beloved songs, the man in solitary who endures with dignity, grace, and humor. Where to put the unfathomable idea of his absence? He staunchly refuses the word *death*. The hunger strike won't work. They'll force him to eat. Chit Naing is ashamed to hear the thought forming in his mind, *I will force him*.

Teza no-longer-here shakes the very center of his mind. He grips the iron bar, the muscles in his hand and wrist and lower arm contracted and aching, until Teza whispers, "U Chit Naing, are you all right?"

The jailer blinks at him. He releases the bar and pulls his hand across his mouth. Before rising, he whispers, "If I can, I'll come again tomorrow." The visit will be for himself, he knows, as much as for Teza.

Sein Yun stares at the Buddha's face. He's trying for a holier-than-thou expression and thinking about water buffalo. About that proverb actually, so dear to his heart: When the buffalo fight, the tender grass gets trampled. Oh, well, that's tough for the grass, isn't it? Everyone has their karma in this shitty life.

Straightening the hair that kinks from his chin, he tries to throw a religious glance back across the compound. He's waiting for Soe Thein to come by with a little package of quinine for a prisoner in Hall Three. The guy's sick with an attack of malaria. Soe Thein is okay, he's useful enough—he got Sein Yun some pills for his hepatitis—though he still refuses to bring in the hard stuff; he's a warder with principles. Chuckling under his breath, Sein Yun shuffles away from the praying ground of the shrine and spits his betel juice, then returns to wait for the warder. Bloody principles! Their inevitable erosion is always pleasant to observe. Quinine and new syringes today, amphetamines and smack tomorrow. Or next week, or next year.

There will be a next year, and a year after that. Maybe more. Handsome is a fucking idiot. Why didn't the palm-reader see that from the beginning? He's done so much work in the past two and a half months. That whole laborious setup with the politicals, all the pen-and-paper-ferrying and rah-rah-rah-ing for the revolution, the bloody mess with the Songbird. Not to mention weeks of looking for that stupid pen. And what has all his magnificent bullshitting accomplished?

Handsome sent him a note last night. He was in a fit, an absolute *fit*, after another fuckup with that kid. Just what did the note say? Was it a thank-you note, commending Sein Yun for his psychic detective work? Was it perhaps a little poem, praising his great dedication to the retarded junior jailer?

No, it was two scrawled lines of poison cursing Sein Yun's name and mother. Not only has the palm-reader lost his sentence reduction, but for the next two years he'll have to put up with that asshole who couldn't even manage to shake down a twelve-year-old. He didn't find the pen. Sein Yun pulls and pulls on his unruly hair.

He *knows* the kid has the pen. He can feel it. He would bet every palm he's ever read on it: Cut their hands off! The boy has that precious piece of contraband. Or he *had* the damn thing and somehow got rid of it in the nick of time. Unbelievable. Not once but twice—*twice!*—the palm-reader serves up exactly what Handsome orders and the idiot wastes it.

The more he thinks about it, the more pissed off he gets. The prison kings got what *they* wanted. Better said, they'll give away what they want to give away when all the contraband cases go to trial next month. Right now the politicals are still in the dog cells, edging away from the tide of their own shit and enjoying the last of the monsoon on their bare heads. But at the end of October's hearing, the Chief Warden will hand out about eighty years' worth of extended sentences to the letter-writers from Hall Three.

So something went wrong with Teza. Is that the palm-reader's fault?

Handsome was the one who screwed up, all because of a brat with a rat stick and a smart-aleck stare. How could they have been outsmarted by an illiterate, garbage-eating *child*? It's disgusting. All those free palm readings, what does he get for them? Dick all.

Buggered.

The word makes him think of their own resident water buffalo. Forget the nickname Eggplant, the cook has more in common with an ox. His fleshy lower lip droops, as though the tendon that holds it up has been cut away. His big bottom teeth are almost always visible, the horizontal grain of them stained brown, just like a water buffalo's.

The palm-reader's scowl slowly turns into a smirk, which spreads into a smile. He thinks again about the little creature—kaung-lay, kala-lay, nyi lay, they call him by so many names—and remembers the school longyi the boy was wearing this morning, wrapped tight around his skinny hips, bright and deep green both, and he renames the child so easily, so *aptly*, it makes him laugh: little jungle snatch, little tender-assed patch of grass.

. 54 .

Teza sits and breathes. He unfolds his legs and opens his eyes to look at them, so thin and long on the cement floor that a vision of a praying mantis clambers into his mind. He thinks, Exoskeleton. His bones are so close to the surface of his skin that he might wake one morning only skeleton and rise up to do a clackety little dance.

That has been the meditation theme of his morning, not macabre but practical. The meditation of unmaking the body, letting it decompose and pass away, as it will, as it must. It's fascinating to him that he feels so light, so lit from within, when he has spent the last two hours envisioning himself without life, the whole of him and the parts, inside and outside, rotting away and putrid. The stench of a rotting body is a disgusting one, but foremost in the meditation is detachment: that horrid reek, like the pain, is not him. It will not be him.

Ironically, he is most attached to what he cannot see, the most broken piece, his own face. After that, he mourns his hands. They are made for grasping, picking up, holding; it is not easy for the mind to let them go. To think of losing his hands is to remember the disappearance of his father, who had the same long, double-jointed fingers, like a dancer's. The hands are his memory of music, fingers spidering over frets, stretching and bunching up for the unfamiliar chords that he used to impress his classmates, guitar-strummers all. Oh, the hands, which keep and give, which touch or stay folded with shyness. He looks around the cell, gazes at the bricks in the wall, the bars, the blocking wall beyond them. Human hands built this cage, just as they built the temples and painted a myriad of faces of the Buddha.

Teza refolds his legs. He closes his eyes again and breathes, inhaling and exhaling the passage of an hour, two hours, until he has died and bloated and rotted clean away. His rib cage sits open like an empty basket. Inside, his invisible heart beats, jumps like a bird or a frog. Or a lizard. Like any small animal waiting to get out of its cage.

Here is something new, and strange, and fine: he does not worry himself about the pen, or the ledger. The book is barely a quarter used; the spillage occurred on the last page bearing figures—there the writing is completely illegible, drowned in some mystery substance. He sniffs the paper. Ink, and mildew, or sour milk, and . . . tea? Can he smell tea? Tea! It would be nice to have tea, wouldn't it, but in a tea shop, on the open street one evening, surrounded by friends.

The whole book is ruined, at least for the purposes of proper bookkeeping. Someone must have copied what figures he could before throwing the ledger away. Teza holds it in his hand, very happily. He turns it over and opens it and brings the wrinkled paper to his nose again. *Tea*, it whispers to him again, la-phet-yeh. Despite the damage, it's still a sturdy book, paper-and-cardboard-bound with a dark purple cover. Pieces of black binding tape are folded over each corner.

The pen, of course, is familiar to him. After fishing it out of his clothing stash, he holds the plastic vein of ink on his palm and stares at it, marveling at how it helped to cause so much agony.

Tsshik-tsheek. The nib is thick with a glob of coagulated ink. He wipes it away with his thumb, then walks to the other side of the cell. "So you have come to me again, little troublemaker. This time I shall put you to better use." He sits down against the brick wall that faces away from the white house entrance. If a warder appears unexpectedly, Teza will have a few seconds to hide his new book and his old pen. Sitting here is as much precaution as he will take. He is neither nervous nor afraid. On the contrary, a lightheartedness holds him, moves him slowly like sunlight moves a plant. The long meditations tire his body, but they almost always leave his mind spacious, as open as a plain. He can see all around himself, forward and back, his whole life and his one death in his hands. The simplicity of it brings tears to his eyes, not from sadness, or grief, but from clarity, and love.

Let the warder find him. One of the old songs warms in his throat; as much as he can, he smiles. Let Handsome himself come in and see the pen in his hand, scribbling verses, or a list of food he will never eat again, or the day from his childhood that he remembers so often, when Daw Sanda caught him and Aung Min breaking the First Precept and sent them alone to the pagoda. Laughter sighs out of him, mixes with the remnants of song. He mouths a few words. Oh, to sing at the top of his lungs again, to get his hands on a guitar and feel the thin wood warm as he plays it. Let the prison kings read his memories, or whatever else he might write— nursery rhymes or poems for his lovely Thazin or a letter to the world he loves and will leave, is leaving now. He balances the open ledger on his knees and takes up his pen and begins, whispering the words to himself as he goes. Finally the singer writes his first prison song.

Dear Nyi Lay, you are so far away
I can see you only with my eyes closed
while I hum the songs that separated us
my ardent phrases for the revolution
Now those boys love one another
by map and moon and lizard
clinging to brick wall

If you examine the map with care
you will see men with Hpay Hpay's hands
lighting their cheroots at the tea shop
behind the jute factory
The twin boys born without fingertips
still crawl among the low tables
They have a big business now

digging bottle caps
out of the dirt with a pointed stick
Remember? We once bought them mohinga
They laughed to the bottom
of the bowl then danced for more

My Brother my dreams
have changed but sometimes
I walk down the same street to an old house
where a woman summons moonlight
to help her orchids flourish
under tattered nets
If there is a wind
white sheets snap
on the lines nearby
the starched arms
of shirts twist and flail
like ours did when the soldiers
came out with Bren guns
with bayonets

Nyi Lay
I wish I could touch your eyes
and wipe away what they have seen
visions that ravage the iris
and drop shards of broken skull
down the pupil's black hole.
The dish of the ear still fills
with cries from a road
where the blood
stayed for many days.

Remember their cautious gasps,
the people who came slowly out
of their hiding places to collect
the slippers, the hand-painted signs.

Still they are gathering the words
from frozen-open mouths.
We must remember the voices
of dead women the voices
of dead men the voices
of children
our own voices.

My Dear Nyi Lay,
I am happy
because you will understand
every message in this little parcel.
Do you still have the slingshot?
If there is a telephone in your jungle
do you dare call the woman of orchids
our mother May May?
Sometimes I lean over my own map
here in the cage   pattern of grit
on the floor   wet trailings
of roaches after they drink my soup
the lines on my hands make this map
and I see a night when the guerrillas
come drunk and singing up the hillside
young men thin as corpses but laughing
Hunger you say
keeps them alive

I stand behind you
in the shadows you stand
before me near the fire
not a gun
but a warped guitar in your arms
One of the men roasts
a small bird on a stick
You strum one of my songs
but they are too tired

too hungry to sing it
I lean over my map
and see your face lit by flames
You refuse to eat the flesh

I venture a prediction: in peace
you will become a passionate vegetarian
like our mother.

Now we are men! Finally we know
what she was doing down there at night
among the flowers in their clay pots
surrounded by her orchestra of crickets and frogs
She was cleaning the salt from her eyes
crying pure water into the orchid pouches
Dear Brother, I've never told you this before
because you would have laughed
Still you will laugh but now I am glad
Nyi Lay I heard her voice
before my birth
I remember May May
singing to me inside her
That's why I grew into music
like one of her orchids purple open mouth
crying out the truth of its own color

Dear Brother, here where all the doors are closed
I have learned to walk through brick walls
A copper-pot spider was my good friend
and many lizards fed my heart
Now every dream I see assumes
the shape of a skeleton key.

Once I heard Grandfather's voice
calling me back through the trees

but I can't go home that way
I will return by an older path
over the plain on the river
My offerings as I travel
through the city of temples
will be bones and tears

Burma, the generals say Myanmar
to make us forget our country and
their crimes but we will not forget
they built a cage around our lives
Only the ants know the strength
the weakness of its walls
and perhaps the child knows
who knows too much   the white ghosts
of maggots on the edges of my pail
the dark ghosts of men who haunt him
He knows the living tree of language
but cannot climb it yet
my broken face he knows
he knows my hunger feeds him
as yours feeds the men on the border
as May May became a vegetarian
when Hpay Hpay died so her sons
might devour the meat in every dish

Everything shattered is sharp
and often shines
A sliver of glass in the hand
can make the history
that alters history
here in the cage and there
in your cramped room in that house
without nation the new country
is no distance away at all.

Sometimes I almost see it
growing like a web
now invisible now
suddenly shining

Nyi Lay, here where the flesh
becomes spirit
the borders dissolve
with the flayed skin
Here there is no separation

Brother, sometimes I fear for you
Will you enter a new era
only to make up another word
for murder?
I cannot see the weapons you carry
only that warped guitar

As for me I have forsaken
every weapon but the voice
singing its last song
And the hand Dear Brother
my own hand
writing it down

with metta
Teza

. 55 .

The iron-beater strikes five o'clock. Dinner hour. Teza looks up and sees four sparrows bathing in the puddle near the outer wall, shimmying water over head and wing. In response to a chirp from him, two of them pause expectantly, then flutter out of the puddle. Hop-hop, a little closer. Hop-hop to the left, then more quickly again, to the right, undecided. Teza chirps again—the tongue sucking, clicking lightly away from his palate. It hurts, but not so much. One small skull tilts sideways at the sound. Hop-hop on spindly legs, straight toward the cell. Teza sits a couple of feet behind the bars.

"Soon, little one, soon enough, a bit of rice." The sparrow eyes him.

Another bird comes hopping up and gives its companion a peck on the shoulder. The first bird rises into the air, wheels away, then returns and pecks back. The well of space between the outer wall and the cell quickly fills with small raucous argument, four sparrows taking sides. The other two bathers, still puffed up like miniature feather dusters, fly up and drop closer to the cell, shivering water off their backs as they scold each other.

Teza laughs behind his bars. Still watching, he slowly lies down. The birds abruptly take wing, lifted into the air by an invisible communal net and pulled over the wall.

Teza looks toward the entrance. He didn't hear Free El Salvador's footsteps at all, but here is the boy, carrying a loaded tray with both hands. The singer motions his head toward the bathing puddle. "You frightened them away."

"They'll come back. They know I'm bringing their dinner." The boy hesitates before the bars. "Do you want your rice?" He's asked this question several times in the past few days, just before squatting down to eat the singer's meal.

"No. You go ahead."

But the boy still hesitates. "Ko Teza?"

"Hmm?"

"Why won't you eat?"

"I am no longer hungry."

"But you are so thin." The boy places the tray on the ground without looking at it.

"I've told you before, Sabado. I'm doing what the monks do, fasting after my morning meal."

The boy picks his nose and thinks, *You are full of shit*.

Teza says, "You will leave some rice for the birds?"

But the boy has no desire to change the subject. "You are not a monk."

"No, I'm not. But I am keeping the Eight Precepts, like a monk."

Making a dissatisfied clatter with the aluminum tray, Free El Salvador spoons up rice soup and stands very quickly. Near the edge of the puddle, he upturns the spoon: food for the damn birds. Then he returns to the tray and scrapes out another spoonful of gruel, draining away as much liquid as he can before returning to the birdbath and dumping out the sopping rice. That's it; he will eat the rest himself.

Teza's voice is almost timid. "You are kind to them."

The boy watches the rice settle against the cement, a waste. He walks back and squats down beside the tray again, fixing the singer with his unwavering gaze. "Ko Teza?"

Teza looks up from his hands.

"When will *you* get out of the cage?"

Teza thinks, I have underestimated this child from the start. He shifts himself slightly to see Free El Salvador's whole face without the obstruction of the iron bars. "Soon, Sabado. I'm going to leave soon. That's why I want you to leave too."

"So we can see each other outside, in Rangoon?" When the brittle tone cracks open, a child's voice is inside, raw with longing.

"No. We won't see each other. But that doesn't matter. My mother used to say that it doesn't matter how far away you are from someone you love. The person might even disappear, but the love always stays."

The boy skeptically explores his lower lip with his upper teeth until he finds a chapped shred to tear away. Then he replies, "That's not the same as having them close to you."

"That's true, it's not the same. But love is very strong. It's the most powerful thing in the world." He pauses. "Nyi Lay. Sabado. And by your birth name, whatever it is. You know I am like your brother. You know I love you as I love my own little brother, who's very far away."

The boy stares at him. He's still squatting, arms wrapped around his knobby knees. He's so thin that his opposite hands are able to reach and hang on to his elbows; he grips them hard. Teza knows the boy is waiting for something else, something more, and he feels a pang of sorrow shoot from his throat right into the mess of his cracked mouth. What more can he give?

He whispers, "Nyi Lay, we can love the people we don't see." The boy says nothing, but stares at him so relentlessly that Teza loses the contest and drops his eyes. He looks at the boy's bare feet, toes splayed on the concrete. The moment the words are out of his mouth, he regrets them: "We can love the dead."

The boy cries, "Ko Teza, you can't die."

The singer reaches through the bars and takes hold of Nyi Lay's hand. But this time the boy resists the gesture and makes a fist. Teza holds on to the knot of bones and smiles at the boy, sadly but without apology. He whispers, "Just remember what I told you. And I will tell you something else. If you love the dead, they will teach you many things about being alive."

The boy eyes him contemptuously, unable to speak. Words are useless. His chest feels hollow, empty, like the hole that has taken the place of his little house. Is loss the only thing he is allowed? If there are words for his unhappiness, he doesn't know them. Nor does he care to learn. Stupid paper, stupid words, the stupid pen. He's glad he gave them back. He pulls his fist out of Teza's grasp and barks, "Give me your tray."

The command hits Teza like a blow. He moves away from the bars. "It's there, at your feet, Nyi Lay. Please eat the soup."

"I mean, give me your dirty tray, from the morning. I need to return it to the kitchen."

Teza slowly reaches behind him and picks up the empty tray. Just as slowly he turns back, lifts the little metal trap with one hand, and begins to feed the tray through. Free El Salvador grabs it; iron bars screech against aluminum like fingernails. Cursing under his breath, the boy half rises from his squat and pulls harder. Trying to steady himself, he shifts a foot into the wrong place and suddenly the dinner tray in front of him flips over, spraying his knees and outstretched arm with sopping rice.

He looks down at the wasted food. It spreads amoeba-like over the concrete, nudging his toes, sliding into Teza's cell. As the liquid soaks into the porous cement, bubbles form and burst. For a long appalled moment, the singer and the boy stare at the mess.

Teza says, "It's all right, Nyi Lay. It was an accident."

But it's not all right to the child. Nothing feels like an accident; everything is preordained disaster. Dangerous words flare up in him again, curses he would like to yell at Handsome, that asshole Sein Yun, and anyone else who would hurt him. Before he knows it, he swears, "Fuck off! Fuck off and leave me alone." All the warders in this end of the compound probably hear him, but he doesn't care; why would he care about all those stupid bastards? For good measure, he throws "Stupid bastard!" into Teza's shocked face. When he finally manages to dislodge the tray from the trap, he stands up, breathing hard. Furious, he also feels instantaneous regret, and fear. What has he done?

He stands frozen between the cell and the outer wall, wanting to run away but unable. He avoids Teza's eyes, staring instead at his head, his hair, black bristles among bald patches.

What has he done? Why did he swear at Teza? He grips one tray in his hand but is too ashamed to pick up the other one, flipped over on the ground—that would mean stepping close to the singer again, bending down to help him clean up the mess. His face burning, he breaks out of his stillness and runs down the short corridor, takes a sharp corner, hanging on to the white house wall with one hand. Teza calls out, "Little Brother!" but the boy doesn't stop running until he's past the records office and a warder coming onto his shift shouts, "Slow down, kala-lay! Now!"

The boy stops short, panting, his eyes big and glassy as he lifts his head and looks across the narrow end of the compound. The wreckage is still there, outside the warders' quarters. In his agitation, he completely forgot. He was running home, but his shack has been replaced by a pile of old boards and sheets of rusted metal. As he walks toward them, he hears the men inside the warders' quarters, drinking tea, talking. A woman's voice, high and plaintive, rises out of the dusty tape recorder.

He drops the aluminum tray on the ground and lifts up the biggest slab of corrugated metal, balancing it on his knees to get a better grip before heaving it off the top of the pile. He tosses a lighter piece of siding into the hole where the shack used to stand. Wood and iron and wads of dirty cloth and broken bricks: he throws them aside methodically, a digging animal, searching for something he can't name until he reaches the earth and sees it, covered in ants.

He has no doubt that it's Nyi Lay, his lizard, crushed among the boards when Handsome tore them down. The boy flicks the ants away until gray-green skin shows, flayed here and there but still attached by sinew to bird-thin bones. Dozens of small scavengers rush around in great indignation. The boy reaches into the bottom corner of his sling bag and finds the big matchbox, where he used to keep his beetle. Though he's already repaired it with a bit of paper and rice paste, it's not sturdy enough for anything alive.

He's turned it into a coffin. He opens the little drawer and shakes his father's old tooth into view. Then he taps away the last of the persistent ants and lifts the finger-long skeleton off the ground. He carefully inserts the lizard into the box, closes the drawer, and buries the coffin in his bag.

Rising voices and a clatter of spoons inside the warders' quarters rouse him. He remembers the aluminum tray on the ground, his last job of the day. Now he regrets spilling Teza's rice for a purely pragmatic reason: his stomach is growling.

56

The boy sees Sammy the iron-beater under the watchtower, smoking a cheroot and waiting for six o'clock. The hulking Indian waves, and Nyi Lay waves back, tentative but grateful. He knows Sammy will not hurt him. Walking along the edge of the shit-stink gardens, he sees the small tea-shop stools sitting outside the kitchen. A third one, knocked upside down, rests there also, wooden legs sticking up in the air. When he's closer, he spits at one of the upright stools, wishing that Eggplant were still sitting there. Pleased with his aim, he hawks another gob at Sein Yun's stool. He grins for a split second, glancing into the kitchen to see if anyone's caught him in the act.

But the kitchen is very quiet. Usually a work detail of dishwashers mills around after dinner, but the place is empty. He stands at the threshold, tapping the dirty tray against his leg as he leans in and listens, looking to the left at the big serving pots, to the right at the washing area. Then he searches deeper into the building, eyes sliding along the big chopping counters, over the pile of rice sacks. Where is Eggplant?

He turns back toward the shrine and the hospital. Hall Five is in the opposite direction. Two warders on guard duty stand there, chatting. He hears the muted voices of the inmates inside the big hall. Farther along the ring of big buildings, Tan-see Tiger's probably sitting on his bunk in Hall Four, all those lucky words inked into his skin, and maybe he's picking his teeth with a nail, because he's the tan-see and he always eats a good dinner, with chicken in his curry, even beef. This thought becomes a small vise that squeezes the boy's stomach.

He lifts his head and double-sniffs, delicately the first time, then harder. Four sniffs tell him that leftover curry is cooling on one of the burners at the back of the kitchen, maybe with shreds of meat in it still, floating in the Chief Warden's deep-bellied frying pan. Close by, perhaps on the neighboring burner, there's a big pot of fresh, high-grade rice, fragrant and sweet, without a chunk of dirt or a bit of gravel in it. A bowl of mandarins sits on the rice sacks where Eggplant likes to nap. One of the mandarins has been peeled, pulled open through the middle, and half eaten. The uneaten half sends its sweet, citrusy scent to the hungry boy.

He takes one step inside, hesitantly, waiting for someone to scream, *Thief, thief!* But no one yells. He glances left, right, behind. There's not a soul to stop him. All right, he thinks, I have to hurry. Wherever they've rushed off to, they'll be rushing back soon enough. As he steps forward, his sling bag knocks against his thigh. What good fortune to have it. He'll put a whole chunk of rice inside.

Soundlessly, he hurries down the length of the chopping counters, then cuts in at the rice sacks that form a half-wall between the rest of the kitchen and the stash of the Chief Warden's food. The boy goes directly to the deep frying pan balanced on the gas burner and lifts off the lid. The smell of curry rises into his face, sweet dust of cumin and coriander and turmeric floating in oil, blended together like a garden for the nose. His eyes, open above the essence of garlic and chili, join his mouth in watering. He glances over his shoulder again. No one is there.

On the other burner is a big pot of fresh rice. He lifts away the aluminum top and carefully sets it on the counter. He bunches rice in his fingers, scoops it through the leftover curry, and stuffs it, dripping, into his mouth. He chews for two bites, swallows, squeezes more rice together, his mouth already open for the next mouthful, it's so delicious that he smiles as he eats, good rice, spiced oil, such happiness. He swallows once more as his hand reaches for the rice pot again, his fingers digging gently through the soft white grains. No, he thinks, no, just put a big scoop of rice into your bag and swallow down the oil quickly, *go*, but he can't resist the combination, the curry and scoops of fine rice together, so once again he squeezes the rice in his fingers and dips.

He's still chewing as he lifts the heavy pan and rests his lower lip against the metal rim. Then he tilts it up and watches the fragrant oil slide toward his mouth. It surges heavy and warm against his upper lip; he opens his mouth wider. One gulp, and a swallow of mushy cauliflower, two gulps, three. He feels oil running down his chin. He knows he needs to leave some; he can't drink it all. Carefully again, with hardly a scrape of noise, he lowers the pan to the burner and raises his eyes.

He didn't think, did he? No, he wasn't thinking, he only wanted food. He didn't check the back kitchen. How could he have made such an awful mistake?

Fifteen paces past the gas burners, Eggplant stands in the doorway, his fleshy lips slightly open. The boy turns his head, looks past the rice sacks and stacks of crated vegetables and shelves of trays, down along the counters. The double doors opening onto the twilit compound seem very far away.

With Eggplant's voice comes the strong smell of his sweat. "Don't even think about running. I've caught you stealing the Chief Warden's food. Now you're in big trouble, little boy. *Big* trouble." Eggplant takes a step toward him, and the boy takes a step away from the burners.

"If you run away, you'll get in more trouble, I promise you that."

The boy is not convinced, but he's lost his voice and can't respond. He remembers what Tiger said—*Scream your fucking head off*—but how would he know how to scream? He can't remember screaming, ever, not once in his entire life. And why would he, now? The cook is right about the stolen food. The boy's eaten the Chief's good curry and rice, not just leftovers off plates in the warders' quarters. Of course he must be punished.

Eggplant walks toward him, holding the knot of his longyi against his great belly. "Get down," he says, so quietly that the boy wonders if he's heard right. His mind jumps to a forced task, punishment, *Get down, wash the floor*. He senses the violation but imagines the clearer forms of violence—getting thumped on the head as he's scrubbing away, having water thrown on him . . .

The next whisper is louder but still quiet enough to confuse. "Come on, kala-lay. Get down on your knees." Eggplant sounds almost gentle, ca-joling. When the boy doesn't move, though, he gets agitated. "Hurry up!" Nyi Lay takes another step backward, comprehension dropping around and through him like a dark blanket. Eggplant doesn't yell because he doesn't want anyone else to hear the command, which he repeats: "Get down, cocksucker!" One sausage hand waves *down down* while the other hand gathers bunches of his red-checked longyi, which he pulls up over his big legs. He tucks the loose material over the waist knot. The boy, still standing, turns his head to the side, stunned. Understanding, not under-standing, he thinks, Eggplant is going to *piss* on me!

The thought fills him with revulsion, but the reality is worse, and arranges itself quickly, relentless as a nightmare. Eggplant puts his hands on the boy's shoulders and pushes; a weight like a load of bricks bears down on his thin skeleton. His knees buckle very easily. He's bending, falling forward; now he has knelt and his face presses against the soft flesh of Eggplant's inner thigh, close enough to inhale the heavy sexual scent there, sweat in the tight hair, the musk of testicles. Eggplant bends his knees, lowers himself, all the while gripping the boy's skull tight. With his other hand, he rubs his penis over the small nose, the fine high cheekbones. The boy's eyes follow the dark brown-purple cock, realizing what's hap-pening. Words crash through a wall, old words newly understood *cock-sucker, eggplant.* The man's nickname is his cock—his cock, purple and curved like an eggplant. It's supposed to be funny but the boy gags, be-cause of the smell, more intense now. That stink wakes him to his fear and he throws his body back, away from the cook. His torso and arms and hips jerk violently in the direction of the rice sacks behind him, but his skull does not move, only feels half torn away from his vertebrae. Eggplant's thick fingers dig into the soft pads of the boy's temples. One of those fleshy arms is stronger than the boy's entire body.

"You're not going anywhere, my little friend. You're going to play with me now. I've left you alone all this time, and now I hear you've gone to live as Tiger's boy. Tricky little fucker! I want to get my share right now, be-fore he loosens you up too much." Eggplant bends down while pulling the boy's head up. They look each other in the face, but the boy can't keep his eyes still. He keeps glancing down, looking for the swollen cock still gripped in the cook's hand.

Eggplant's voice is low and guttural. "You do this for me and I'll do you a favor. I'll keep your thieving a secret. You tell anyone about our little meeting, I tell the Chief Warden about you stealing his food. You know what will happen to you then, kala-lay? They'll lock you up forever, you stinking thief." Concentrating, sucking in his big bottom lip, the cook maneuvers his hips to line up his cock with the boy's mouth.

The boy knows something about the things men do, the things that can be done to men, but it's happening to him so quickly, and he hates it. He can't move his head. He can't get away.

He opens his mouth, but there's not a single word in there; no scream comes out. Eggplant whispers, "That's right, open up wide. Get me good and wet and then I'll turn you around and you can be my nice little girl." He abruptly pushes the boy's head back and thrusts his hips forward. There is no stream, no water, but the boy is drowning again. Eggplant's penis fills his mouth, pushes against the back of his throat. His eyes slide rapidly back and forth, trying to see beyond, above, around the cook's body, but flesh envelopes him, pushes into him, pushes in, pushes in. Even when the cook slides his cock out slightly to thrust again, it's not enough to let the boy inhale. The man swallows the boy even as the boy gags on him, his eyes bulging out with violently suppressed choking, the reflex trapped, backfiring. He chokes without choking because no air enters him, only this man, plunging his cock into the passageway that cannot scream. Eggplant groans, grips the boy's head harder. Hot skin and wiry hair bang against the small nose and forehead and chin.

Why is this happening? The boy does not think the question. His body becomes it, demanding an answer as his muscles twist and writhe a mute, fierce protest against the fat cook. He's big as a battalion, a whole army bearing down on a small country. A moment later there is no question, no answer, only a rare child, dwarf-king of many names, whose flesh decides *this is the end*, not knowing what is ending, his life or this violation, he's so old though still too young and terrified to know and he cannot scream but he can bite, *he can bite*, as he has seen a rat turn at the last possible instant and leap toward the stick, mouth open, teeth closing upon the wood that lifts him up like lightning and shakes him loose and strikes him until he's dead.

• • •

Time stops. Only because Sammy the iron-beater, timekeeper, does not care about striking the next hour, six o'clock. If he could talk, he would tell the story later and it would become a prison myth. Unfortunately, his tongue has not grown back yet. His ears have grown keen, though, and his eyes. With his giant's slow but fast amble, he's already heading for the kitchen, wondering about the boy. Because Sammy's a timekeeper, friendly with the right warders, he has compound privileges and is allowed to move at will in certain areas of the prison. When he's more than halfway to the kitchen, a high-pitched scream careens like a flock of bats out the open doors. The giant Indian walks only slightly faster. Compound privileges or not, he would never run in the cage.

A bellow follows the scream. The timekeeper recognizes this as the unrestrained cry of great pain, extremely loud and unself-conscious. This cry joins the human to the animal world like no other sound but birdsong. In the briefest flash, Sammy recalls a scene from the village where he grew up: the buffalo that turned craftily against the knife, outwitting the slaughterer but then suffering much more as a result.

Bloody warders, lazy bastards, he's beat them to it, though he sees Soe Thein jogging over from Hall Five; he'll be here in less than a minute. Sammy walks into the kitchen just as the keening begins, repeated howls in a low register. That's shock, he knows, sinking into the body by way of the throat. Safe inside the building, the tall man moves faster, one wide step, two, three. He's half loping alongside the chopping counters when the boy, eyes huge with fear, mouth and chin slathered in blood, bursts out from behind a pile of rice sacks and crashes right into his long legs. Sammy grunts his sound for *Stop* and reaches out to grab him, but the boy screams and twists away from his hand, slipping on the wet floor with a slap of bone. A split second later he's up again, scrambling into a full-out sprint. Sammy grunts as articulately as he can, knowing exactly what he's saying: *Nyi Lay, don't run! The warders are coming. Don't run!* But the boy does not stop. The big man makes a wolfish sound for the word *Fuck* and stands there, long, muscular arms spread in hesitation—should he go after him or not? He stays put, watching the boy's dirty bare feet wink back at him. The kid's so fast, already clearing the doors now, turning to the right, at least—away from the open compound. The iron-beater snorts toward the sound of wailing behind the rice sacks. *Shut up already!* He looks back toward the open double doors, hoping the warders won't do anything stupid when they see the poor kid making a dash for it. You can never tell with those assholes.

A few steps closer to the keening, he finds the fat cook fallen against the rice sacks, clutching the length of his cock in one bloody hand and what must be the bitten head of it in the other. The red gush is unstoppable, dripping rapidly into a pool between his massive legs. His legs are spread, knees up, oddly like those of a woman in labor. The timekeeper stares at the small crimson handprint splayed on one of the white sacks. He knows this is where the boy, choking on semen or blood or both, wiped his mouth before pushing himself back and up, vaulting away.

When Eggplant sees Sammy looming over him, he cries out, "Help me, help me!"

The timekeeper shakes his head in disgust. He glances over the cook's head to the famous little shelf high above the gas burners. The glint of the well-guarded cleaver catches his eye. If the boy had been tall enough to see that shining blade, he would have known the cook was around, because Eggplant never leaves it out unless he's nearby. Soe Thein, entering the kitchen, shouts, "What's going on in here?" as if Sammy might call back an intelligible answer. He looks down at Eggplant again and spits on him, then glances back at the cleaver. There is still plenty of time to kill him. That would be the best way to shut down the whining siren of his voice. It would be nothing, absolutely nothing, to cut his throat. If the cleaver were really sharp, Sammy could lop off his head with a few solid hacks. He knows how to do this, from his time on the boats.

But then he would never get out of this shithole, and the warders might think he had something to do with the mess of Eggplant's dick too. Now there's a *really* stomach-turning thought. Besides, if they don't hurry and sew him up, the cook just might bless the world and die from blood loss. Sammy grits the teeth in his spacious mouth and puts his hands on his hips. It's a feat of discipline to keep his hands off that cleaver. Never mind cutting the cook—the blade would be worth a great deal of money.

But time is short, and there's something he wants even more than the cleaver. He steps forward, bending slightly at the waist, as if to take a concerned look at the carnage of the cook's dick. Soe Thein is walking toward them now, and another warder is close behind. Leaning in quickly, Sammy slaps the cook's face, open-handed but very hard. Then he straightens up, following the motion through with thigh, bent leg, raised heel, which delivers a deep jab to Eggplant's stomach. The keening abruptly becomes wheezing as the cook doubles over with new pain.

Sammy takes two steps into the aisle that leads to the back door, one hand pointing at the mess. Soe Thein strides past him, turns in at the rice-sack wall, and swears when he sees the blood pouring through the cook's fingers.

Eggplant cries as he gasps for breath. He looks up at Soe Thein and whispers, "Help me. The little fucker bit me."

The warder leans down, just as Sammy did, and asks, "The kid bit you, did he?"

The cook nods his head tearfully.

"It's about time somebody did." Soe Thein turns to the timekeeper with the order, "Go find the doctor." Sammy gives him a look of friendly insolence, eyelids drooping, mouth a mixture of pout and smile. "What the fuck are you looking at me like that for? You heard me! Get the doctor. Hurry up!" Sammy shrugs his shoulders. For a man with such long, strong legs, he walks away very slowly.

57

They've cut down the monsoon grass that grew on the banks of the stream. His feet notice immediately. It's like walking on the bristles of a shorn head.

No matter how many times he works his tongue around his mouth and spits, and spits again, the taste remains, soaked through like oil in a rag. He smells it all over his face, a stink with a rhythm to it, the same pulse as his inhalations. Semenblood, semen-blood. Breathing through his mouth doesn't help; it's up his nose. Dried around his lips, on his chin, the blood smell's stronger, but that juice of metal and stone from the male body sticks at the back of his throat.

The warders will kill him now. First they will make him stay in one of the dog cells because he ate the Chief Warden's food. They won't give him back to Eggplant—the warders hate the cook, because he's fat and rich—but maybe the Chief Warden will give him to Handsome and Handsome will take him to a trough in one of the shower rooms and drown him. The junior jailer won't do it in the stream—it's too shallow today.

The boy leaps over the water to the side where the tree grows, and he spits again, in a manly way, just like Tan-see Tiger, making a big noise. Then he bursts into tears. If the men leave flowers and ribbons and water and food, where is the good nat of the tree? Believing in that spirit, he brought morning glories and whispers like prayers. But his faith and his gifts were no protection, not from Handsome or the cook or Sein Yun. That jaundiced face with its slashed red grin flashes into the boy's mind. In their different ways, all three of them want to drown him.

And so they will. That's how it is with big people. They can do whatever they want. He will die, like his father and his mother and Nyi Lay his lizard. He hits his sling bag, the heavy pouch hanging at his thigh; he pounds it once as hard as he can, feels the blow against his leg. The possessions hidden in there are useless. No one would call them treasure but him. During the past two days, the crimes against him have wrought another crime: they've made him old enough to recognize his poverty.

Who among the men of the cage hears the sound that rises now, that old ever-new cadence from a child's throat, the crying that comes before language and carries beyond it? Warders stationed around the hospital hear it. Men doing guard duty at the watchtower hear it and come across the compound, curious about all the commotion. As they get closer to the kitchen, the boy's cries are drowned out by Eggplant, who moans and begs for his penis to be saved. The medic adds his droning voice to the cacophony. Judging from his glazed eyes, he's probably stoned; he is definitely unfazed by the growing red lake, one shore soaking the bottom rice sacks, the other shore coagulating on and into the concrete. Tossing the black mop of hair out of his eyes, he explains to the Chief Warden that the doctor left over an hour ago and there are no empty beds in the hospital. If Eggplant is to receive care, one of the inmates who has paid for a bed will have to be dragged out of it, but the medic certainly can't do that on his own. A high-ranking warder or the senior jailer will have to be sent. Someone goes to find Chit Naing, and ten minutes later, four men and a stretcher carry the bloody cook to the hospital. Chit Naing watches the men carry the moaning cook away and then takes stock of the mess behind the rice sacks. Standing still, looking at the blood on the floor, the jailer hears it too, the rising wails that break and stutter as they fall. He knows the boy is crying, but he can't leave the kitchen until he receives orders from the Chief, who approaches him now.

Rather than looking down at the mess, the chief very pointedly looks up at the shelf above the burners. "Make sure to take that cleaver out of here tonight, would you?" More quietly, he asks, "What about the mona- stery? Will the Hsayadaw take the boy or not?"

Lying with admirable self-possession, Chit Naing assures him, "Yes, there's a place for him. The abbot would be happy to take another child." In fact the jailer still hasn't met the Hsayadaw, who returned to Rangoon only this afternoon. Chit Naing has an appointment tonight, to meet him for the first time.

"I'm glad the monastery will take him. It's either that or a state-run house for delinquents. Get him out of here as soon as you can. This is ridiculous." The bald man waves his hand over the rice sacks, still not looking down. "We can't have him running around here if he's getting vi- olent. Who knows what he'll do next? I'm just glad that the cook didn't say anything about pressing assault charges."

Chit Naing opens his mouth and closes it. Then opens it again. "Sir, you don't mean to say that . . . The boy was . . . He was protecting him- self, sir. Against the cook. We all know——"

The Chief cuts in. "We all know that what the cook does is his busi- ness. You can't tell me that the boy doesn't have his own business too, if you know what I mean. Usually he's a good boy, I grant you that, but he's hardly an innocent child. What the hell was he doing in here so late, on his own? This looks like a very ugly, and very messy, lover-boys' quarrel. Dis- gusting pigs, all of them." With the sneer still twisting his face, the Chief turns to go, then abruptly stops. "Oh, I forgot to tell you. I expect the jun- ior jailer to report for work quite soon. In the next couple days. Perhaps even tomorrow. You won't have to work so hard anymore. His knee seems to be much better."

Two warders follow the Chief Warden out of the kitchen at a safe dis- tance. Unlike him, they take a quick turn behind the building, know- ing the kid's gone back there. In the falling light, they see a little human crouched down under the tree. The high-pitched cries catch in their ears, but they know it's not the crows come back to roost on the prison walls. A minute later the crying changes rhythm. Comforting themselves with the thought that he must be calming down now, they return to their duties.

They are wrong. The boy isn't calming down. He's hyperventilating.

There are words in every tongue for *grief fear terror broken* but none so eloquent, so precise as this, the sound of a child who cannot breathe for weeping. And there is no cowardice so profound as the adult's who cannot bear to hear it.

The boy knows he has to stop this breathless sobbing. He crab-walks to the edge of the stream and feels himself sinking slightly, his toes involuntarily clutching mud. He touches the water. His fingers stretch down into it and squeeze up a handful of gravel. He wills himself to take a breath, then another. And another. He doesn't dare rinse his mouth out with the dirty stream water, but he washes the blood and semen from his hands and face.

He puts his skinny arms around himself and rocks back and forth. Then he turns from the stream and crawls up the bare mound of earth where the tree grows. When he looks at the small canopy of leaves still glowing in the last light of dusk, he wants to cry again. The tree could be cut down any day, by the same men who scythed the grass.

In its solitariness, the tree also seems to know this, and stands there astonished, astonishing, like an early memory of the human, limbs stretching toward the sky. There are no clouds now, only dark blue opening into mauve above the first brick wall and the second brick wall, those borders between two worlds that are the same world.

The crows are coming home to roost in the ramparts. Half a dozen of them turn, wheel against the sky like dark fan blades before they flap back to the outer wall. *Caw-caw caw-caw* come their raspy voices; they are as short-tempered as old prisoners, the fathers who lived here before and lost some shining thing in the prison. That's why the crows always come back; they're looking for whatever it is they lost. The boy watches them carefully, as he often did in the evenings, when he lived in his little shack. He hears the throaty warbles and clicks the birds make, talking to each other as they settle in for the night.

The floodlights crack on, changing all the colors to chalk, making him squint in the harsh light. He blows his nose like a cannon, finger to nostril. Then he looks up at the shadow of the tree immense against the brick wall, big enough to climb. He cannot remember ever climbing a tree, though he would like to. Not this one, of course. Even if the nat doesn't protect him, he must live here still, invisible among the branches, admiring the colored ribbons of cloth and the flowers. The nat must be waiting for the boy to leave. Then he will swing down and collect the offerings left for him.

The boy stands up, steps closer to the sand-colored bark. Wedged in the crook of the lower branches rests the upright box, the simple altar. Inside it are two strings of jasmine, a small plate of rice, and a glass of water. The boy swallows, coughs. He smells and tastes the cook in his throat.

And he hears boots. Not Handsome's gait, and thinner than Soe Thein's. It's a measured walk, slowing down now. It has to be Chit Naing. The boy lets go of his held breath.

"Nyi Lay?"

"Yes?" He doesn't turn around but keeps staring at the altar box, the glass of water.

"Are you all right?"

That's a funny question. Nyi Lay blinks hard, several times—no more crying—then focuses his eyes on the glass. "Sir, I am very thirsty."

The senior jailer, standing in the mud on the other side of the stream, doesn't know how to respond. When he jumps across the water, the boy startles away from him. He takes two slow steps toward Nyi Lay, who still faces the little tree. Chit Naing would like to touch the child, lay a hand on his shoulder, comfort him, but something keeps him from making the gesture. He follows the boy's thirsty gaze. "There's water in that glass, isn't there?"

"That water is for the nat of the tree."

Nyi Lay, Chit Naing thinks, nats do not exist. He pulls an open hand down over his mouth and chin. Who knows how the boy has come by his nat worship? His mother probably believed in spirits. After all that's happened, Chit Naing doesn't want to take anything else from him, even a superstition. He says gently, "I think the nat would not mind, this once, if you drank his water. The nat of this tree is very generous."

The boy gives him a peculiar look, as though appraising Chit Naing's qualifications for making such claims. Then fear crosses his face. "Will I get in trouble?"

"No, you won't. It's all right, Nyi Lay. You can drink the water."

The boy extends his arm, puts his fingers around the glass, which is not glass at all, but clear plastic, cooler than his palm. He pulls it out of the box without disturbing the jasmine or the small plate of rice.

Sweet without sweetness, the clear liquid slides into him, its own element, and he swallows it down without choking, which seems a feat unto itself. He drinks slowly at first, then gulps, his head angling back until the glass is empty. He puts it back into the box. Then he turns around.

"Saya Chit Naing?"

"Yes?"

"What's going to happen to me?" He is full of weariness, and acceptance, like an old man who's made a hard journey to the wrong village. It is night. There is nowhere else to go.

Chit Naing takes a step closer, lowers his voice. "That's what I want to talk to you about. I've already spoken to the Chief Warden. He came down to the kitchen when he heard what happened." The boy's shoulders curve inward as he pulls his sling bag close to him.

"No, Nyi Lay, it's all right. Don't be scared." Chit Naing decides very quickly to lie again, in an effort to reassure the child. "The Chief's not angry at you about . . . being in the kitchen. The cook's in trouble, not you. You didn't do anything wrong. Do you understand that?"

Later, much later, the boy will remember Chit Naing's voice and his face, drawn and thin, the brow wrinkled against the top of his wire-rimmed glasses. The words will become a mantra, an acrid blessing: *You didn't do anything wrong.* But right now he believes himself to be the sole author of various disasters. It's his fault that he went into the kitchen, that he stole the pen and made Handsome angry.

It's his own fault that he lived. The roaring truck struck his father, who died, and his mother died too. The shame of surviving sticks in his throat like a fishbone. He reaches out to steady himself and touches the smooth bark of the tree.

Chit Naing steps closer. He would like to pick the child up as he did the other night, but Nyi Lay moves away from him.

"The Chief Warden isn't angry at you. He's angry at the cook, who did a very bad thing. We talked about you, Nyi Lay. There's something we want you to do."

Always there is something, the boy thinks, some deal or trade-off. "What?"

The jailer hears the challenge in the small word, the hardness. He doubts Nyi Lay will take up the offer. "There is a pongyi-kyaung in Rangoon."

The boy quickly replies, "I know about that place. The singer told me." They're all in it together, the singer and the jailer, even the Chief Warden.

"The Hsayadaw takes in children, and teenagers too, boys who don't have a family."

"I don't need anyone to take care of me."

"I know that. We were thinking about something else. Something very important."

"What?" The word snaps out and hits Chit Naing like an elastic band.

"If you went to live at the monastery, you would learn to read. And write. The Hsayadaw would be kind to you. He's a good man."

The boy's fingers spread wide over the light brown skin of the tree. A slight breeze makes the leaves tap against each other, a thousand tiny doors. Still gazing hard at Chit Naing, the boy asks, "When do I leave?"

Chit Naing accompanies the child back to Hall Four for the night, walking him all the way to Tan-see Tiger's cell. The men, in the throes of gossiping about the events in the kitchen, quiet down when they see the senior jailer and the warder with his fistful of keys. The boy walks between them, staring at the ground. He knows that he's become a topic of conversation. News travels fast in the cage, but Nyi Lay has never been at the center of it before. He wants to disappear. All five of the tan-see's cellmates are here, smoking cheroots and picking their teeth after dinner. The old man who's blind in one eye is working on a basket, weaving threads of stretched plastic. Tan-see Tiger is sitting on his bunk, a ragged book in his hands; he's *reading*. When the warder opens up the grille, the other prisoners make way for the boy to pass. Tiger looks up at him, sadness plain on his face.

Scrawny Hla Myat runs his long-nailed fingers through his greasy hair and greets the boy, then pokes the convict beside him in the ribs. This man, a diminutive car and truck thief with a nose splayed wide beneath restless eyes, is called Kyaw Kyaw. A big joker, Kyaw Kyaw can't help muttering something under his breath to the two other inmates of the cell, who burst out laughing. Tiger warned them not to make jokes, but they're already failing miserably. The temptation to pervert the usual greeting—Tamin sa bibi la? Have you eaten rice yet?—is simply too great.

The tan-see and the old weaver are the only men in the little group not involved in the muffled but increasingly raucous laughter. After the boy drops into his nest beside the tan-see's bunk, Tiger growls at his men, "Would you guys shut the fuck up? Can't you see the kid's worn out?" Discreetly avoiding the pervertible question, Tiger asks, "Do you want something to eat, Nyi Lay? Can I get you something?"

What the boy really wants is a shower, with real soap and a lot of water, but that's not an easy thing to arrange. At night the shower rooms are off-limits to the inmates, and he wouldn't want to go to shower alone with a warder. He whispers, "Water. I'm thirsty." When Tiger waves his hand, the basket-weaver puts his work on the floor and dips an aluminum cup into the clay water pot, then gives it to the boy. Nyi Lay drinks deeply, but his throat is sore and his stomach is churning. He sets the cup of unfinished water in front of him on the floor and nestles into his felt blanket, pulling a corner of it over his head like a shroud. He wants to wait a few minutes, gather his wits, then change into his other pair of clothes—the lime-green *FREE EL SALVADOR* T-shirt, the turquoise longyi—but he falls sound asleep.

Hours later he wakes with a low moan, belly clenched in a painful cramp. Still shrouded, he doesn't know where he is. He tears the cloth away from his head and sits bolt upright, a yelp escaping him. *Tiger's cell.* The pounding in his chest is so loud that he's sure the men would be able to hear it if they were awake. He pulls his sticky legs apart, sniffs. *Oh, shit.* He's already lost some of it, shit and piss mixed together, on his longyi, soaking into his felt blanket. Ugh! His belly tightens and twists again. He looks around, taking in the four bunks of snoring convicts and Hla Myat and Kyaw Kyaw asleep on the floor. The events of the evening tumble in slow motion through the boy's mind, gathering speed until the memory with its blood taste crashes down like a falling wall and he has to go, he can't wait, *quickly, quickly, the latrine pail.*

He clutches his belly and hunches over, not wanting to shit in front of the men—he's not used to it, he tries to do his business in private—but at least they're sleeping. He stands up quickly, unsteadily, knocking over the aluminum cup, which clanks and rolls toward Hla Myat, who turns over on his mat and groans. *Quiet! Don't wake him, or he'll never stop teasing you.* The boy steps gingerly around the sleeping bodies, his face sweating now, twisted by the spasms in his gut. He's afraid he's going to lose it while walking, *no no no,* the mess would be horrible, *hurry.* He bunches his longyi up around his waist—it's wet with stink—and with great relief squats over the latrine pail.

A few minutes later, when he's finished, he feels lucky to be in Tiger's cell. There's real toilet paper here, a whole roll of it rigged on the wall beside the pail. The boy unravels an extravagant handful and cleans himself, then pats his green longyi. The smell doesn't go away. He'll have to scrub it later, with soap and water.

He walks to the front of the cell. Two water pots are there, one for drinking, one for handwashing; the extra bucket, with soap, is further evidence of Tiger's status. Trying hard to be quiet, he lathers up his hands and splashes them clean.

A ragged breath catches in someone's throat, becomes a cough; the boy goes still. Drops of water *dap-dap-dap* fall from his fingers. He holds his breath until the cougher falls silent again. In the corridor, moths and lizards move in their old dance around the light. He hears the small flutter and thump of wings. And the syncopated snores of the men. He hears his own breathing. It makes him remember: *I will leave this place soon. Tomorrow.*

He reaches over to the clay water pot. Standing there, the cup in his hand already dipping down into the cool water, the boy truly wakes up. He senses the small weight of his own life, its particular shape. That shape is bounded only by time, the time he himself is filled with, like the water that fills the clay pot. His hand is still poised, the cup completely submerged, completely full. He raises it, dripping, out of the water, and takes a long, slow draft.

Back at his sleeping place, he changes into his clean turquoise longyi, then takes the dirty one off the floor and rolls it into a small, discreet ball. The problem is his felt blanket, wet and reeking and big, too bulky to be tidily folded. He bunches it up and puts it in the corner, where it sits accusingly, stinking at him. He takes off his T-shirt—it's dirty anyway, streaked and blotted with brown roses of blood—and stretches the stained cotton over the blanket. There, that's better, now it's just a pile of dirty clothes.

He settles down on his rags again and pats the bulky blue pouch of his sling bag. Everything's all right. His treasures are safe.

Ssst. Hey, Little Brother. Come 'ere."
The boy whips his head around. It's Tiger. He crawls over to the tan-see's bunk.

Tiger has raised himself up on one elbow. He sniffs a couple times and looks over at the boy's blanket. But he just says, "You okay, kid?"

"Yeah."

"Crazy place, isn't it? You did the right thing. In the kitchen, I mean. Though the guys were making fun, they're proud that you took care of yourself." He whispers more softly, "But I have to tell you a few things, kid. It's not gonna get any easier in here. I'm gonna do what I said, get in touch with those folks of mine in the city." He puts his big, heavy paw on the boy's arm. "It's hard to believe, but that fuckin' cook has friends. You can't stay in the cage. You know, 'once blood is spilled' and all that. Believe it or not, kid, we've tried to watch out for you. We warned the cook years ago, when your dad first died—Eggplant knew he wasn't supposed to lay a hand on you, the dirty pig. That's why Sammy went into the kitchen, Little Brother. He's always kept an eye on you. And you know what?"

The boy's voice is a tiny sliver. "What?"

"Sammy wanted to cut off Eggplant's head. But you . . . well, let's just say you'd already done the job." The tan-see ruins his whispering by laughing too loudly at his joke. "Get it?" The boy stares at him; he does not get it. Tiger clears his throat.

"Sammy feels real bad that he was too late to help you. We let you down, Nyi Lay. First that bullshit with Handsome, then the cook, who's more of a creep than the jailer, believe it or not. He'll get somebody to hurt you. If he lives, that is. They can't do more than sew a few crooked stitches around here, so they took him to Rangoon General. But the word is they never have enough blood for transfusions. And when they do it's full of malaria! Or HIV!" More laughter rumbles from Tiger's throat. The boy has no idea what a blood transfusion is, but he keeps quiet and the tan-see keeps talking. "So maybe that creep will die. But if he lives, he'll come back to work. And then you'll really have to watch out, Nyi Lay. You know what I mean?"

The boy nods gravely. "I know, Saya Gyi. Saya Chit Naing wants me to go too. To a pongyi-kyaung."

"Aha! That's what he was up to! Sneaky jailer. He said he was trying to arrange something, but he wouldn't tell me what. Hey, this is good news. A monastery school is much better than a tea shop." Tiger puts his free hand on the boy's shoulder. "You'll go to the treehouses in the People's Park. You'll eat biryani and fried noodles instead of the shit they give us in here. And you'll go to all the temples and pagodas! When you first walk up the stairs to the Shwedagon, your head will spin like a top, it's so beautiful, like nothing you've ever seen in your life." Tiger knows that orphans in monastery schools have little chance of eating biryani or going on tours of the city—from what he remembers from his own childhood, the monasteries are desperately poor—but what the hell, the kid has to have something to dream on. Even a lie. The smallest and the grandest of lies, he muses, can keep you going your whole life.

"Saya Gyi?"

"What's up?"

"Will the monks really teach me how to read?"

"That's what they do in those monastic schools—they teach boys their letters and then they teach 'em the scriptures. I learned to read in a monastery school in a little village near Mandalay. Then I ran off to Rangoon and got all mixed up with some rough fellows. Don't you go and hang out with pickpockets and black-market boys. They'll just lead you into trouble. Then you'll end up right back in here." He peers into the boy's eyes, wanting to believe that there's still time for the child; his life might be different. Better. That's probably bullshit, of course, but he tries to be encouraging. "You're meant for something else, Little Brother. Just stay put with the monks and do as you're told. They'll take care of you."

The boy drops his head, chin to chest, and glances timidly at Tan-see Tiger's extravagant white grin. Then both of them look up and listen. The iron-beater is striking *one two three*.

"Do you know when you're leaving?"

"Tomorrow."

"Hmm. It's three in the morning, Little Brother. That means it's already tomorrow."

Nyi Lay's stomach lurches and cramps. *Oh no, not again.* But the lurch rises out of his belly and wraps around his chest like a rope. How can he be leaving, and so soon? He won't give Tiger his massages anymore, or watch the purple cats roaring on his skin. He won't see Jailer Chit Naing anymore, or the Songbird. It's unfair that tomorrow is already today. Soon someone will come from the monastery to pick him up. In a taxi. The boy will have to ride in the taxi, which Chit Naing says is the same as a car. The boy has never been inside a car before. All motorized vehicles remind him of the truck that killed his father. A great sigh empties him out.

Tan-see Tiger whispers, "Oh, I know. It's hard to be out there at first. I've been through it a couple times. Just like it sucks to be in here when you first arrive. But you get used to it. So don't worry about being scared shitless. It happens to all of us."

Incredulous, Nyi Lay asks, "Even to you, Saya Gyi?"

The feared criminal laughs again, more loudly this time. The man in the bunk above him mutters in his sleep. Tiger reaches out and punches the boy lightly on the shoulder. "Yeah, Nyi Lay, me *especially*. I'm the biggest chickenshit around here. Why do you think I have to be so tough?"

The boy laughs too, not believing him. "Saya Gyi, you're joking!"

"No, I'm not."

Tiger smiles with his strong white teeth. *Saya Gyi,* he thinks to himself. Not very many people would use this respectful title for a smuggler convicted of murder. Funny kid, he thinks, a good kid, so damn sharp. He regrets not feeding the boy better. Not getting him out of here sooner. He regrets . . . Oh, fuck it, the list is too long, and involves a lot more than the orphaned rat-killer. Tiger's smile falters, then closes into a tight line.

"Now go back to sleep," he whispers. "You have lots to dream about, Nyi Lay."

. 59 .

Senior Jailer Chit Naing's businesslike walk is slower than usual. He's not used to carrying a tray loaded with a double portion of boiled rice. To do so is a glaring breach of protocol, but he doesn't care. He slipped some money to the new cook—brought in on emergency from a military barracks—to throw in a boiled egg. An egg! As if a fucking egg is going to put flesh on a skeleton. As he passes the shrine and the hospital, Chit Naing repeatedly checks the congealing mush of rice, wondering how much of it the singer will eat. He has the distinct impression that Teza has started his hunger strike without making a formal announcement.

When he comes around the outer wall, he finds the gaunt man sitting in half-lotus position, right leg folded on top of the left. His eyes are closed. The jailer stands perhaps eight paces away, watching him through the bars. Chit Naing hasn't seen him for two days. In that short time, Teza's face has changed. The skin is slightly loose and wrinkled under his sharp right cheekbone, but tight where his left jaw juts out in its brokenness. Because he's thinner, the deformity of his face is more pronounced. His neck is all ropy tendon and muscles around the rungs of esophagus. If his blanket were not wrapped around his shoulders and chest, Chit Naing would see collarbones pushing like tent pegs against his white prison shirt.

It's peculiar to see how calm he is, his face serene in its unmaking. As his physical body becomes more worn down, worn away, something else becomes evident, glimmering, like the sheen in old silk just before it tears.

What a life, Chit Naing thinks. What a life this is. Not far from the meditating, starving prisoner, the inmates and warders of the cage discuss the latest gossip insatiably, like feral dogs around a dead goat. Just how badly did the boy bite Eggplant? Will the cook survive the blood loss? Most inmates know that Eggplant was in critical condition because it took a long time to find enough blood of his type. Most of them don't yet know that the Chief Warden requested blood from the military hospital, which is always better supplied than Rangoon General. Alas, the cook is not going to croak after all. But will he survive not being able to screw boys for however long it takes his dick to heal? Here is the question that elicits the most raucous laughter and the most extravagant betting: What if they've had to *amputate*? And has the cook already paid someone to kill the sneaky little kala-lay who bit him? The rumors are flying.

Undoubtedly the palm-reader has set up a betting racket regarding the exact number of stitches. Chit Naing exhales his disgust. Weary of holding the tray, he slouches against the dirty white wall and sighs again, louder, hoping to rouse the singer from his meditation.

Eyes still closed, Teza asks in his warped but resonant voice, "What happened last night? A man was screaming bloody murder, but not because of a beating."

Chit Naing pushes himself off the wall, spilling some of the rice gruel on his trouser leg. He swears under his breath, then says out loud, "I thought you were going deaf in one ear."

"In one ear only." Teza opens his eyes. He looks up at his slice of sky: blue, blue, blue. It's such a relief to see it, almost every day now, this sea bath for the eyes. Only after tasting the blue does he look at Chit Naing. He sees the tray in the jailer's hands and immediately asks, "Where's the boy?"

Chit Naing kneels down. The aluminum scrapes through the metal trap.

"Where is Nyi Lay?"

The jailer stares at the wet slop of rice as he tells the singer about the screams he heard last night. Teza listens in silence, eyes cast down to the hands in his lap, right upturned palm resting on the left one. When Chit Naing finishes speaking, Teza asks, "But is he all right?"

"I don't know. He seemed to be fine. Who knows what's going on up here?" The jailer taps his forehead with three fingers. "Or in his heart. I did what I could. I'm not sure . . . exactly what happened to him."

"Maybe a doctor . . ."

"No doctors. I asked him if he was hurt physically. He said no. I think he was telling the truth. It would be more frightening for him to see a doctor than just to do what he's always done."

"Which is?"

"Look after himself."

"But he's a child. I don't even know how old he is. Ten, eleven?"

"Twelve, maybe close to thirteen. He's small because of malnourishment. I hope the food will be better at the monastery." Until now the jailer has been talking to the tray, pushed through into Teza's cell. Now his eyes meet the singer's. "That's the only good thing to come from this mess. After last night, the Chief Warden *wants* to send the boy out." He pauses, knowing he shouldn't tell Teza more than he needs to know. But Chit Naing wants to tell him. He wets his lips and whispers, "I finally met him last night. Your Hsayadaw. He was just back from Sagaing, very tired from traveling, but he listened to what I had to say. He's agreed to take the boy. The monastery is badly overcrowded, but he said there has to be a way to fit in one more sleeping mat. He really is a generous man."

"My father loved him very much. My mother loves him still."

"I can understand why. It was after midnight when I left. He's the sort of person you can talk with for hours."

Daw Sanda's face flashes into the jailer's mind and leaves him speechless. Teza is quiet too. Both men listen to the sounds of the cage beyond the white house, past the outer wall: the shuffle of feet and the clank of manacles as new prisoners are escorted to their assigned hall, the jeers of their warder, the low murmured talk of three guards hurrying across the compound. And from somewhere nearby comes the argumentative chatter of sparrows. Soon, when Chit Naing is gone, they will swoop over the wall and wait to receive their daily portion of rice.

Teza asks, "When will the boy leave?"

"The Hsayadaw will come for him early this evening."

Teza has been waiting for this. He wants it. But he turns away from the news and stares dumbly at the back wall of his cell. He has longed for the child's departure, imagined and helped to engineer this feat of escape while sitting right here. Yet his voice sounds shaky in his own ears. "Will I see the boy before he goes?"

"For a quick visit. I'll let him bring over your dinner tray."

"Yes," whispers the singer.

"I know it's sudden, Ko Teza, but with all that's happened, it's the best way. And Handsome is supposed to be coming back to work. He hasn't shown up yet, but when he does, he'll make trouble for Nyi Lay. It's better to get the boy out of here as quickly as possible."

"Yes, I know. I agree."

Chit Naing knocks the metal frame around the food trap. "Have you already started your strike without telling me?"

"It's always hard to eat. Very painful."

Chit Naing gives him a level look. "You can't live on talking." He gives Teza a grim smile. "I brought you an egg."

"Thank you. I will eat it." He returns Chit Naing's look. "Yes, sir, I *am* eating. A little every morning. I'll begin the strike when the boy is gone. Tomorrow, I guess. Tomorrow."

Chit Naing still cannot understand. His voice is foolishly loud. "Ko Teza, what about everyone else? The ones you're choosing to leave behind?" It's not possible for him to say, *What about me?* In the silence after his questions, he realizes that a warder passing in the compound could have heard every word he's said. Called back to himself, he quickly pulls away from the bars and straightens up. "I'm sorry," he whispers.

"Ya-ba-deh. It's all right." Teza has been watching him intently. "You're exhausted, aren't you?"

"Yes, I barely slept last night." He rubs his forehead for a few seconds, surprised by how his skin aches, not just the muscles beneath it. He looks down at Teza and sees him clearly: a man he loves but cannot comprehend. That must be why I'm so angry, he thinks. Like a child worrying a scab, he continues, "Ko Teza, wouldn't it be the ultimate failure, to protest with your death? Isn't that what the generals want of you?"

"U Chit Naing, there is really no point in talking anymore about failure or protest. Every day I've lived here, I've succeeded, because I've continued to love. Even a spider, even a big Indian with no tongue." He exhales laughter. "Even my good jailer. That is no failure. But something in me is finished. I am empty. The only way I could keep going now is to return to those old sources of inspiration. Anger. Passionate hatred. And I won't do that."

"Do you think they care about that, whether you hate them or not? Do you think they care about you at all?"

"Oh, the Chief Warden cares a great deal. As do the generals. If they didn't care, I wouldn't be here, would I?"

"Ko Teza, seriously, do you think they care?"

"I am serious. In this time, in this life, the way their lives are, of course they don't care—not in the way you mean. The torturer cannot allow himself to care about the person he hurts: his job is to destroy the body and the spirit. And the soldier's job is to kill. That's his duty. But they *know* they are destroying, killing. If they admitted their guilt to themselves, it would be the end of their lives as they know them."

"As it will be the end of mine?"

"Probably," Teza responds lightly. Again he breathes out his laugh. "But you already accept that the life you had before is over. Usually that makes you happy. If such a transformation happened to you, it could happen to any number of them too. I believe this. We all sleep. You, I, the generals. The ones who run the cage. Everyone sleeps, some more deeply than others. And everyone can wake. That is what the Buddha taught."

"Ko Teza, think of Handsome. Or the MI agents who tortured you. You think these men will wake up and suddenly care about what they did, to you or to anyone else?"

"I don't know if they *will*. But I know that they *could*. It's possible. You might think this is pure foolishness, but I often wonder what would happen if the generals went away for one month—just a single month—of meditation retreat. To simple monasteries, just to sit and meditate during the day, and listen to a few lectures by good teachers. When the chiefs—the big ones, Ne Win himself and Khin Nyunt and Than Shwe and the rest of them—came away from retreat, I bet they would begin a dialogue with Daw Aung San Suu Kyi and the NLD. I bet they would disband the dictatorship of their own free will."

"You would bet on it, would you? I'll be sure to mention that to the palm-reader as a possible racket. Maybe he could get the whole cage bidding on the results. Except that such a thing will never happen, Ko Teza. Dictators don't like sitting on the floor."

"I know. It's very un-Burmese of them, isn't it? They should try sleeping on concrete through the cold season. My rheumatism was bad enough with the rains, but it's getting worse as the weather cools. My hips are so stiff that it takes me half an hour to rise in the morning. Worse than my grandfather! The cage makes us old. Even Nyi Lay is a little old man." He shifts his legs again. He needs to lie down; the talking has worn him out. He closes his eyes and murmurs, "I hope he'll get to be a child when he leaves here."

"The boy's not so keen on games."

"He might learn." His eyes open to Chit Naing's face. His voice pulls in on itself, tightens. "He'll take his belongings with him, won't he?"

"Yes, of course."

Teza's words are like simple loops in rope. "It's not like he has very much to carry."

"No. His little sling bag. His collection of useless knickknacks. He's a bit of a pack rat. He won't be able to leave that stuff behind." Chit Naing squints, trying to see where the singer wants to lead him.

The loops close, complicate into a knot. "They probably won't even search him. Or maybe they will?"

Understanding what he's being asked, the jailer quietly answers, "No, I doubt anyone will search the boy. We know he has nothing to hide." The young warder Tint Lwin will be in the releases room, and Soe Thein will be on the gates tonight. The boy's not an inmate for release, anyway, and there are no instructions for him to be searched. Chit Naing takes a deep breath, as though preparing himself to voice the question in his mind: *What are you going to do?* But he stands up and bids his friend good-bye.

. 60 .

In Tan-see Tiger's cell, the men are finishing breakfast and getting ready for their work details. Hla Myat stands at the bars, clearing his throat like a consumptive. When he lustily hawks a gob of phlegm into the corridor, the attending warder spins around and yells at him. Hooting like a schoolboy, the young convict leaps away from the grille and swaggers deeper into the cell, until he's standing at the end of the tan-see's bunk.

Nyi Lay is there, kneeling on the floor, arranging and rearranging his belongings, wondering how to take everything with him. The important treasures are in his sling bag, but he doesn't want to leave the extra longyi and the blanket behind. The bloody shirt doesn't matter, he'll throw that away, but his Chinese felt blanket and his green school longyi are coming with him. Could he just carry them, as a bundle, under his arm? He's mulling over this question when Hla Myat leans down and pokes him, very hard, in the ribs. Still on his knees, Nyi Lay jumps sideways and up onto his feet like a cat beside an exploding firecracker. A high-pitched, uneven yowl escapes him, and his face contorts with fear.

But stupid Hla Myat is only making a joke. "Scared ya, didn't I? Ha-ha, I hope ya didn't shit yerself again, kiddo." The gangly young man snorts at the air and quips, "Is that stink the latrine pail or you? Where's it coming from?"

Nyi Lay gives the man a black look and pushes the bundle of dirty cloth under the end of Tiger's bunk. "Leave me alone," he snaps.

"That's a nice way of washing clothes, you stinker. Hey, Tiger, how do you like that—he just put his shitty blanket under your bed!"

Tiger has been watching everything from his preferred position, half sitting, half lying at the head of his bunk. He blows the dust off one fingernail and starts filing the next. His morning voice is deep but croaky. "Hla Myat, you're left-handed, aren't you?"

Hla Myat replies in a guarded voice, "Yes, Tan-see, I am."

"That's what I thought. Because that's the hand you poked the kid with. But I wanted to be sure. Now leave him alone, asshole, or I'll break your thumb and index finger. On the left hand, of course."

This sturdy promise makes the whispering men go quiet. "Hey, kid, come 'ere. Sit over with me while the men get ready to go." Tiger pats the mattress.

Rubbing the spot where Hla Myat poked him, the boy pads over to the tan-see's bunk and leans tentatively against it.

Tiger smiles. "Come on, kid, hop up here." The boy pushes himself onto the bunk and sits cross-legged. "There ya go. That's more comfortable, isn't it? Pretty soon these devils will be out of here and we'll have room to dance around, okay? Or play a game of football!" Nyi Lay leans his back against the brick wall and gives the tan-see a very small smile.

A few minutes later a warder comes to take the convicts away to their work details in the workshops and gardens. Only the weaver remains with Tiger and Nyi Lay. Though he's a taciturn old codger with tobacco-stained hands and lips, Nyi Lay is comfortable with him, and fascinated by his blind eye. Far from being dead, the white-scarred pupil slides around with deftness and purpose, while the other eye seems to follow it, squinting in the same direction, trying to catch a glimpse of what the blind eye sees. Nyi Lay finds himself doing the same thing, though more surreptitiously. When the old man breaks from weaving to stretch his neck, the ruined eye gazes upward. The boy follows it, hoping to discover something more than bricks and water-stained ceiling.

Not long after the convicts leave for work, Soe Thein appears and opens the grille like a man unlocking his own house. He seems to be on very good terms with Tiger, greeting him politely and nodding amicably to the old weaver. "You shouldn't be working so hard, Uncle. You're supposed to be on vacation in here." The men laugh. Tan-see Tiger pulls a cheroot from under his pillow and takes it as a gift to the warder. Then he turns around and announces, "Come on, kid! It's time you had a good shower."

The tan-see crosses the cell and pulls a big striped carrying bag out from under his bunk. He grins at the boy, who's sitting wide-eyed on the mattress. "Hey, look what I've got for you. Here's a nice clean towel." He plunks it down in front of Nyi Lay. "And a new bar of soap with *perfume* in it. Oh, and look at this, a pot of thanakha too. One of my ladies sent it to me, but you take it, so you leave the cage smelling fresh and clean." Tiger piles these valuable items on top of the towel. "We might even be able to find a new toothbrush for you. Shit, have you ever brushed your teeth?" He looks up inquiringly, but Nyi Lay's chin has dropped against his chest. "Hey, Nyi Lay, what's up? Hey! What's going on? Kid! Your face has sprung a leak!" Smiling, Tiger puts his face close to the boy's, examining him. The boy blinks; tears slide down. "Two leaks! The plumbing in this place, I tell ya. I'm going to complain to the Chief Warden. Where's this water coming from? It's the monsoon all over again." Pretending amazement, Tiger spreads his muscular arms—the tiger on his chest stretches out—and stares up at the roof of the cell, looking for rain. Nyi Lay starts to laugh, crying at the same time. The tan-see says in a louder voice, "You think it's funny, do you? It's not funny, it's a disaster, but I'm glad you're laughing. Now come on, cheer up, the warder's going to take us to the shower room. Grab that stuff. You'll feel better when you're all cleaned up."

Soe Thein escorts them out of the cell and to the end of the row. They walk through another long corridor, turn right, and arrive at the shower room of Hall Four. The warder unlocks the double doors and Tiger says, "Go ahead. I'll wait right out here. The warder and I are going to have a smoke and solve the country's problems." Soe Thein laughs very loudly at this comment, but the boy doesn't think it's funny at all. Tiger hands him a plastic pot for scooping water. "Go crazy, kid—use as much water as you want."

The warder has heard this exchange. He reassures the boy, "On the last day, we don't count scoops."

It's a big room, cavernous and gray, with hooks on the walls and two long troughs, one for washing clothes and one for bathing. As he walks beside the concrete trough, he checks over his shoulder several times. But no one else is here, no one is following him. The room smells of water and dust. He holds the tin of thanakha up to his nose and inhales the fragrance of small ivory flowers, skin of the thanakha tree. And his mother. The orange oval of soap is like fruit candy mixed with slightly rancid lime juice. To a boy thrilled by the luxury of soap, this is a wonderful smell.

The concrete floor is cool and wet in some places but not in others. He looks around again. Seeing his wet footprints on the dry stretches of concrete, he whispers, "I am following me." The sound of his own voice reassures him.

After hanging up his towel, he takes the soap and scooping pot to the trough, which comes up to his rib cage. He stands in front of the water as straight-backed and concentrated as a diver. When he unknots and steps out of his longyi, the leftover stink of his nighttime accident hits him in the nose. He begins his bath with great enthusiasm, plunging the pot into the trough and pouring water over his head more times than the prisoners are allowed when they come here every morning, more water than the Songbird was ever allowed.

He washes his backside first of all, lathering up and sluicing away the soap with cool water. He rubs down his chest, as if he's giving Tiger a massage. Everything needs to be washed, scarred knees and skinny shinbones and dirty ankles and leathery feet, bisqued with brick-chip dust. Greedy to get as clean as possible, he stretches his hands over his shoulders, around his waist and up, to scrub his back, all the small muscles braiding and unbraiding under dark brown skin. Then, remembering two places he usually doesn't bother with, he returns to the top and washes right inside his ears.

Shivering, the boy douses himself with water once more, fervent as a duck. He sees with great satisfaction that the waterline of the trough has fallen significantly. Toweling off—with a real towel, not an old piece of cloth—he also notes with pride that there is not a dry spot on the concrete floor for ten feet. Before dressing, he makes a paste of the thanakha and smears it on his legs and arms, his neck and face. When he emerges from the shower room, he fastidiously dries off the orange soap with a corner of the towel, then politely holds soap, towel, and thanakha out to the tan-see, who smiles down at him. "No, they're *yours*, Nyi Lay," he says, laughing. "To keep. You know, as a going-away present." The boy does not know. He's never had a going-away present before. But he draws the bundle of items to his chest, cradling them, and walks back down the corridor with Tiger and Soe Thein.

Tiger and the weaver do not seem to be worried about lunch. Usually the rich prisoners have a midday meal, but the iron-beater pounds out twelve strikes, then one strike an hour later, and the two men don't discuss food at all. Neither does the boy. He is already very grateful for the tan-see's generosity, so he doesn't dare say that he is hungry.

Sometime past three o'clock, Tan-see Tiger's men begin returning. Knowing the cage routines, Nyi Lay can't understand why the prisoners have come back so early; most of the other inmates are still out in the workshops or gardens. But he's more surprised to smell them as they file back in, talking and teasing each other as always. They smell like *food*, and food is what they carry: la-phet in small bags and three kinds of curry in stacked bamboo bowls, fragrant rice in a dented aluminum dish, fresh tomatoes and shredded cabbage and new-fried garlic slices for the tea-leaf salad.

The boy catches the scent of each man as he walks in. He looks from one criminal to another in contained confusion, his mouth flooding with saliva. Roused by the spices and the pungent scent of pickled tea and a salty whiff of dried fish, his guts immediately start churning and groaning again. He looks from the criminals—Kyaw Kyaw the truck thief is busy spreading a big cloth on the cell floor—to Tiger, who is rubbing his hands together like a giant about to devour an ox. The tan-see speaks in a booming voice, "Well done! I was starting to get unbearably hungry. I bet you're hungry too, eh, Nyi Lay? I know you've had a good shower, but I want you to wash your hands again, with soap. That's why we have the extra bucket, so we can eat with our hands instead of those damn metal spoons." The boy jumps up and speedily scrubs his hands. The convicts follow suit.

"Now you sit close beside me, otherwise these guys will elbow you right out, the pigs." When Kyaw Kyaw and Hla Myat protest like scolded children, Tiger responds, "It's true, you eat like animals. Remember, this is a meal for the boy, a feast of shin-byu. He's going to be ordained as a novice!" He looks down at Nyi Lay, who is already sitting cross-legged beside him. "When a son enters the monastery for the first time, his family gives him a big ordination feast. Usually the shin-byu takes place at the monastery, so maybe when you get your robes, the monks will give you a big feed too. But who knows? There are lots of boys at the monastery schools, and lots of boys eat piles of food. It's probably too expensive to have a party for every one of them, so we're having one for you here. What do you think?"

It's hard for the boy to take his eyes off the food—all the dishes have been placed on the eating cloth—but he looks up at Tiger and answers solemnly, "Saya Gyi, I think it is a very good idea."

The tan-see laughs and squeezes Nyi Lay's shoulder. Hla Myat hands the boy a bowl of rice, and Tiger says, "Go ahead, new novice, you begin."

The moment the boy picks up a deep-fried chicken foot, the men set to in a graceful frenzy, hands and tattooed forearms crossing over and under each other to scoop up chicken or bean-curd curry, another handful of rice. Fingers tear open a dried fish and more fingers rush in to pry the oily flesh away from the sharp skeleton. The scents of cumin and turmeric and crushed chili swim into the boy's nose. The freshly steamed rice is still warm, a rare treat for him, and for once he doesn't listen to the men, who talk as they eat, exchanging gossip about warders and each other and new arrivals.

The boy picks up another chicken foot. They are one of his favorite things to eat, even though there's hardly any meat on them. Something about all the gnawing satisfies his jaws. He cleans three toes, then returns to the curry, has more rice, eats another crunchy mouthful of tea-leaf salad. There's not a single pebble or bit of chaff in the rice, which makes the boy wonder where Tiger got it.

The tan-see is the first to sit back, away from the feast. He burps loudly and says to the boy, "Well, eat as much as you want, but there's no need to stuff yourself. We'll put some food in a plastic bag and you can take it with you on your big journey. Hey, now that's a good smile!" Tiger looks at his fancy watch. "You're a lucky fellow—you'll be outside soon enough."

In a wistful voice, the little truck thief Kyaw Kyaw observes, "And there'll be so many pretty girls to see."

Tiger grins at Kyaw Kyaw and sighs. "Ah, beautiful women are all over Rangoon." He smacks his lips so appreciatively that the boy wonders if he's put more food in his mouth.

The basket-weaver shakes his head and turns to the boy, admonishing, "But there won't be any girls in the monastery."

"You mean it's like the prison?"

Tiger interrupts the old man, "No! No, it's not like the cage. There are girls all over the place, just not right in the monastery, not in the compound. But you go out a lot, into the streets, the markets, the temples. You'll see lots of girls. The prettiest girls give the tastiest alms. Alms collecting was the beginning of my downfall as a novice. The girls were just too lovely. You know, the head monks will say that you shouldn't have anything to do with them, but you should, Little Brother, oh, you definitely should. Girls are very important." The boy is mystified. What are alms? Why does Tiger care so much about girls? Too embarrassed to ask, he just nods.

Tiger looks at his watch again. "Are you ready, Nyi Lay? Chit Naing is coming soon, at five o'clock." The boy gets up and pulls his flip-flops out of the side pocket of his sling bag. Lately he's been going barefoot as much as he can to save the soles of his slippers, but he wants to wear them for his departure. It's the done thing; even the very poorest convicts wear something on their feet when they leave.

Before putting on his flip-flops, he gets down on his knees and pulls his dirty felt blanket and longyi out from their hiding place under Tiger's bunk. Hla Myat whistles. "What the fuck are those things still doing in here?" He shoots an accusing glance at the tan-see. "Why didn't he throw them away while we were out?" Then he growls, "Kala-lay, could you at least wait until we get the food cleared away?"

The boy stares at Tiger and says matter-of-factly, "I want to take them with me."

"Nyi Lay, I think they'll have nice clean blankets for you at the monastery."

"But this one is *mine*. And the longyi is a school longyi, and I'm going to school at the pongyi-kyaung, so I want to take it with me. I'll wash everything when I get there. With my new soap."

"Come on, Little Brother, don't be stubborn. At the monastery you'll wear robes, orange or burgundy robes, you won't need an old green longyi. Hla Myat is right, though as usual he expresses himself like a talking dog. That stuff doesn't smell very good. And you've had a nice shower and everything, to be clean for your big trip."

The boy repeats, "I want to take them with me." Like the treasures in his sling bag, these are the last vestiges of his little shack. He doesn't care if they have a bad smell. They're his, and the smell is his too, and he's not leaving them behind.

Tiger asks, "How are you going to carry them without getting dirty?"

The boy looks down at his things. If the bundle were smaller, he'd be able to fit it in a plastic bag—he is taking half a dozen plastic bags with him—but the Chinese felt is bulky, and the bags are too small.

"I don't know."

As he gathers up the eating cloth, Hla Myat mutters, "It's just disgusting! He's like a barnyard animal. So much for a civilized shin-byu."

"Hla Myat, shut up before I stuff some of that blanket in your mouth! You're insufferable. It's a good thing you can cook and clean, you skinny prick, otherwise you'd be out of here."

The old weaver coughs politely. His blind eye is examining a secret point on the ceiling, his other eye is squinting after it, but his voice is aimed like an arrow at the boy. "Nyi Lay, you can put your blanket in the big basket I've just finished making. It'll fit in there. It's a tight weave, so the . . ." He pauses delicately.

The boy finishes the old man's sentence, "The smell won't get through."

Hla Myat can't restrain himself. "That was going to be my laundry basket!"

Tiger throws a cheroot butt at him. "Didn't I tell you to shut up?"

The boy looks up at Tiger. "Is it all right?"

"Of course it's all right. Uncle is offering you a gift. That's very kind of him." He gently elbows Nyi Lay toward the old man.

The boy gets up as the weaver retrieves the basket from among his things. The boy accepts the gift with a gesture both servile and courtly; his left hand cradles the elbow that extends the right hand to receive the basket. It's like a carrying bag for the market, wide at the bottom, narrower at the top where the looped handles face each other and close together, two perfect circles. It's made of blue, green, and pink plastic threads, which the color-hungry boy likes very much. He thanks the weaver with a slightly bowed head.

"Ya-deh," comes the old fellow's gruff response. He's examining the basket with his sighted, critical eye. "It's not much of a suitcase, but it's the best I could do on such short notice." The boy glances from the weaver's seeing eye to the white-scarred one, which is already looking somewhere else. Nyi Lay follows the direction of his gaze across the room. There, on the other side of the bars, stands Chit Naing.

. 61 .

They make an odd pair, the tall, bespectacled jailer carrying a dinner tray and the small boy with a large market basket knocking against his leg. For balance, he wears his sling bag over his opposite shoulder. They walk to the white house the long way, around the other side of the compound, so that the boy doesn't have to pass the kitchen. He understands this. That's why Chit Naing picked up the tray on his way over.

"Saya Chit Naing?"

"Hmm?"

"Does the Songbird know I'm going away?"

"Yes, he does. I told him that we've found a pongyi-kyaung for you. He'll miss you, but he's glad that you're going." The tray in Chit Naing's hands wobbles slightly.

"Saya Chit Naing?"

"Yes?"

"Why are you taking the Songbird his food?"

Chit Naing dodges the question. "*You* are going to take it to him."

The boy is nervous about seeing the singer, and ashamed. Only yesterday he spilled the rice gruel on the cement and cursed Teza, though it feels like a long time ago. "Maybe I shouldn't see the Songbird, Saya Chit Naing. Maybe he doesn't want to see me."

"Nyi Lay, that's not true. He wants very much to see you. He told me so himself."

"Did he?"

Chit Naing hears the rawness in the child's voice. "Yes, he did, this morning. You know how much he cares about you. Don't you?"

"Yes, I know." He confesses, "Saya Chit Naing, Teza gives his food to me. Or to the birds."

The jailer doesn't get upset. He just sighs. "Yes, I know. Ko Teza is not very hungry anymore." The two walk past the sentencing halls.

"Saya Chit Naing?"

"Yes, Nyi Lay?" The jailer doesn't let impatience sharpen his tone.

"Teza doesn't want to be in the cage anymore, does he?"

"No, he does not."

The boy bites his lower lip and walks more quickly. He waits a whole minute before making his announcement. "After I leave the cage, Teza will also leave."

Chit Naing frowns and glances down at Nyi Lay's head, wondering what's going on in there. Soon that small skull will be bald, shaven clean, and the scrawny body will be wrapped in the robes of a novice. The jailer watches the narrow neck swivel; the boy is gazing toward the watchtower.

Over two hundred feet away, Sammy leans against the iron timekeeping pole. He's just finished beating out five o'clock. The boy doesn't stop walking, but he slows his pace and tentatively raises his hand. Sammy smiles and waves back enthusiastically. The boy wants to run to him and say good-bye, but he does not; he's carrying too many things, and he's shy, with a thumping heart because they are getting closer to the white house. But he already regrets it, with the confused anxiety of a child, and he will regret it later too, with a deeper knowing, that he didn't go to the man who came to help him, who was so much like him—silent, Indian brother, separate from the others, the timekeeper.

When they are steps away from the white house and the wall that surrounds it, the boy thinks, *After this, I am leaving!* The thought tires him out. He yawns, infecting the jailer, who also yawns. The two of them smile at each other, but they are sad because Teza is there, on the other side of the wall. After the boy says good-bye to the singer, their lives will change. They themselves will change, like one animal turning into another or stone becoming flesh or a cascade of blue water bursting into flame.

Look who's come to see you," says Chit Naing, but Teza, sitting close to the bars, already knows. The boy's eyes dart from Teza's broken jaw to the inner walls of the cell to his own clean feet, wearing his two differently colored slippers. Not far from his toes, a dark stain of moisture has settled into the concrete. The spilled rice gruel from yesterday.

Chit Naing kneels awkwardly and starts to push the food tray through the metal trap. Nyi Lay reflexively squats and holds the trap fully open, lifting the tray so it slides through with ease.

And there he is, in the same position he was in yesterday when he got so angry. But now Teza is sitting close to the bars. The boy lowers his head to speak. "Ko Teza, I am sorry. For yesterday."

"Ya-ba-deh, Nyi Lay." It's all right. "Geiq-sha ma shee ba boo." No problem. "I had my servants come in and clean up the mess."

The boy takes up the joke, just to keep talking. "That's not true."

"Yes, it is. The pigeons came first, but they make as much mess as they tidy, so I sent them away, and the sparrows came. Then the cockroaches, and after them the ants. Later the cockroaches returned to make sure the ants had done a proper job, because they're real sticklers when it comes to a messy cell. See how clean the floor is?"

The boy steals a glance at Teza's face. There are many things he would like to tell the singer, but something as hard as iron is stuck in his throat. Words. Words are as hard as iron.

Teza puts his fingers around one of the bars. "And you're clean too. I can smell the soap."

The boy looks up, abashed. He is also grateful that Teza has spoken again, about something so easy. He responds with boyish enthusiasm, "I had a shower in Hall Four. In a proper shower room with as much water as I wanted. Tan-see Tiger gave me soap and then I put on some thanakha and he let me keep the whole tin of it too, and a real towel, and . . ." The boy, in his nervousness and longing, begins to talk.

Teza closes his eyes to see what the boy speaks, *water soap thanakha towel*. The mention of these simple things sends a thin, sharp blade into his chest. Now that blade flicks out, further, right to his edges, flaying him from inside. He gasps and leans forward, his face almost touching the bars. There is no physical ailment, no real blade. Yet how this skinlessness hurts him, this loss of everything: bathing, clean water, the boy, shy and lively at once, talking about food now, *tamin ne hin la-phet ayun gaund-ba-deh*. The blade is the sound of the boy's voice. It make a deep wound because Teza knows he'll never hear it again.

So the singer, who thought he knew all the reasons, learns another one for beginning the hunger strike that will end in his death. Without the boy, he doesn't want to live here anymore. The hungry child has fed him too well.

He opens his eyes. *FREE EL SALVADOR*—there is the faded slogan on his favorite shirt—is staring at the singer's face. They look at each other intently.

Teza makes a request. "U Chit Naing? Can you leave us for a few minutes?"

The jailer has stood above and apart from them, awkwardly, trying not to watch their exchange but watching anyway, compelled and unsettled by what he sees. He's almost relieved to leave them alone. "For five minutes. Maybe a bit more. The Hsayadaw will be here at five-thirty. We have to be as quick as we can."

"Yes, I know."

When Chit Naing is gone, Teza rises and walks over to his mat and blanket. He returns to the bars with the purple ledger in his hand. "I want you to have it," he whispers. Then he reaches to the back of his longyi and pulls out the pen. "And this too. Take them with you. U Chit Naing will get in trouble if anyone finds them in here."

The boy is staring at the water-stained ledger. "But Ko Teza, I . . . What can I do with the book?"

"You'll read it."

"But I don't know how to . . ."

"You *will* read. Some of the words are about you. Some are for my other little brother, the one on the border, but I don't have his address, so I can't send it to him, can I?" He smiles with his eyes. A pool of saliva forms in the corner of his mouth and begins to slide down his crooked chin. "Some of the writing is for my mother. And I wrote down some of our stories, yours and mine." Teza taps the hard cover. "All these words are your words too, because you brought me the paper and the pen. Understand? You don't know your letters yet, but you helped me to write this."

The boy swallows. "What if they search me and find it? What if they find the pen? Then we'll both be in a lot of trouble."

"Jailer Chit Naing said no one's going to search you."

The boy sucks in a sharp breath. He'll take the ledger with him because he wants it. He used to have so many books in his shack, until Handsome stole them. He would like to have Teza's book in his hands, to sit somewhere quiet and turn the pages slowly and follow the lines with his eyes. He can't read, but when the old paperbacks were in his possession, he *did* read, all the time; he held the text right side up and sent his eyes through page after page of lines made of letters, letters that made words, and inside those words—he knew this—were human voices.

If he gets caught with the ledger and the pen, he'll have to stay in the cage. The Chief Warden will sentence and imprison him and he'll go back and live with Tiger! The thought doesn't disturb him in the least. On the contrary, it makes him feel calm and slyly hopeful. If he could live with Tiger in his cell, the tan-see would protect him and feed him, and he wouldn't be alone. He stretches a thin arm toward the bars, and Teza meets him halfway with the ledger. The weight passing into his hand sends a shiver into his arm, over his shoulders.

In the middle of the corridor he sits on his knees, takes his old possessions and his new presents out of his market basket, and sets to rearranging everything, to hide the book and the pen. Teza watches anxiously, especially when the boy starts unrolling his bulky felt blanket. "Hurry, Nyi Lay. U Chit Naing will come back soon."

Wanting to reassure Teza, the boy quickly twists around, sweeping his hand lightly across the blanket, the floor, where his fingers hit the white pen. With a quiet whir, it shoots over the cement toward the cell.

Teza and Nyi Lay watch it come to a stop. It points at the singer, who is close enough to reach down through the bars and pick it up. But at the same moment an awful, familiar sound distracts them both, and they look up, toward the crunch of boot on brick gravel. The boy blinks. Chit Naing is standing at the entrance to the corridor, not fifteen paces away, his expression neutral but for his mouth, which is open. He closes it and takes two steps into the corridor, not wanting anyone in the compound to see him hesitating there, between one cage and another. He isn't looking at the boy. He isn't looking at Teza. His eyes are riveted on the mute, insignificant, made-in-Thailand pen. He knows without examining it that the plastic casing is carefully marked, at the bottom and the top, little cuts with a razor blade. Identifiable.

Teza stares at the jailer. He is worried for the boy. For himself, he is simply defiant. Very slowly, Nyi Lay sits back on his heels. His face is drained pale; his eyes are round black questions. The jailer watches him lean forward, his shadow covering the ledger.

The pen seems to glow on the gray floor. Chit Naing blinks. How did it come to be here? There is no time to find out, to ask, to make the right decision. There is no time, yet how the moment lengthens, turns into a minute, a minute and a half, and swerves in Chit Naing's mind, twists in on itself, the way the whole cage now twists into this one corridor, this cell, this man and child at the center of the labyrinth. Here. The pen. He shakes his head, then whispers, "You have to give it to me."

The boy remains motionless but Teza begins to protest. "But the writing is for—"

"I don't mean the notebook. He can take it out—no one will search him. But if I keep the pen, I can use it against Handsome. I don't know how, I don't know what I'll do yet, but if *I* find the pen . . ." He silently corrects himself: *I* have *found it*.

He steps forward very quickly and bends at the waist in a smooth, graceful movement, no one will know; the pen is already sliding with his hand into his trouser pocket as he straightens up. Then he feels awkward, to be standing above them, his boots close to the boy, who is still kneeling. The pen burns through the lining of his khaki trousers. He didn't know until he saw it just now how much he cared about the mystery of its disappearance.

The jailer looks from Teza to the boy. "Nyi Lay, look at me." The boy solemnly raises his head. "This didn't happen. Do you understand? I didn't see anything. I am still standing on the other side of the wall." He smiles hesitantly, trying to reassure the child, who just stares at him.

Chit Naing takes an unsteady step backward, then turns with a pounding heart and leaves the corridor. Standing on the other side of the wall, he glances back and forth, wondering if anyone has passed by the entrance to the corridor. No, he would have heard feet on gravel. He takes a deep breath and tries to calm himself. What has he done? The slender piece of contraband against his leg is unexpectedly heavy. He tries to push it deeper into his pocket, hoping no one will see the top poking out.

All right, calm down, he thinks to himself. It's just a pen. I can throw it away if I want to. He watches a work detail pass by on its way back to one of the halls and waves at the warder at the end of the row. Then wipes his forehead. He's sweating. Did the warder notice anything? He makes a silent wish: let no one pass by and talk to him. He slowly removes his glasses but doesn't clean them. He simply stands there, motionless, unsure of what he's done. If only he hadn't stepped into the corridor at that moment. Of course he suspected something—most probably a message scratched onto a plastic bag. But a notebook—a prison accounting ledger, no less. And that bloody pen.

Such a small weight. It rests against his thigh and slowly burns. There's nothing I can do, he thinks. I picked the damn thing up. *It belongs to me now.*

Something akin to fear cuts through him quickly, unexpectedly, faster than fear, like a blade so sharp and quick that the cut turning crimson shocks you. How did this happen?

He wipes his forehead with his hand again and puts his glasses back on, telling himself once more to calm down. But regret is settling into him like sickness. He wishes he hadn't seen it.

He thinks, That's the story of my life. There is so much he wishes he'd never seen. The beatings, the poke-bar stabbings, so many men violated and violating in turn, every year, tens, hundreds, thousands of them, angry, frustrated with the lives allotted to them, with the injustices they survive only to perpetrate upon others, returning to the cage the next year, two, five years later. Over and over again he has watched despair attach itself like an immense leech to the human heart. He wishes he knew nothing about all that.

But now his knowledge of the other side doesn't make him feel any better, and endangers him far more. He has seen the goodness that thrives in the human, the love that grows right here in the cage, among the most battered, the most insignificant. And what he has seen, what he knows to be the truth, can so easily become evidence against him.

Why did he pick up the pen?

If it's not the pen that undoes him, won't it be something else? The terror lies in this inevitability. The unraveling may be unexpected, accidental, the mechanism set in motion at a party, where the Chief Warden will mention a certain wife, niece of a senior MI officer, who donates to a certain monastery school; and a woman, daughter of the same officer, will raise her bejeweled head and ask in an arch voice, *Oh, really? Where did you hear that?* Or one of the underground agents from over the border will be arrested, and he also will know what he should not, that a jailer supplied trial documents and information about certain politicals. Or in the next ten minutes, if the boy is too nervous and makes the warders suspicious—so suspicious they become fearful—the net could close on all of them very quickly.

He brushes his wrist against his trouser pocket. Yes, there it is, his own piece of contraband, his own crime.

I'm done!" the boy whispers breathlessly. He looks down at his handiwork; the thick felt blanket bulges from the mouth of the basket. He stuffs the blanket in deeper and turns to the singer. "But Saya Chit Naing took—"

Teza waves his hand back and forth, brushing the words away. "No. He didn't. If anyone asks you, he knows nothing about this. Do you understand?"

The boy echoes, "Saya Chit Naing doesn't know a thing."

"Well done." Teza takes a deep breath. "Nyi Lay, before you go, I would like you to give *me* something."

"What? What can I give you?" He looks up, considering. "I know! My new thanakha! You can put it on your sores." He nods at the singer's shins and forearms, scratched red and raw. "Also some soap, I have some soap for you."

"Nyi Lay, thank you, but I don't need those things. I want something else. It's small, but very important. And it's invisible. When you give it to me, I'll be able to see it."

"And *I* have this thing?"

"You do."

This is a riddle; he's heard the men tell riddles before. "Ko Teza, I don't know! What do I have that's invisible?"

Teza waves his hand toward his own chest. *Come closer.* The boy turns his head against the bars to let the singer deposit the secret of the riddle into his ear, which he does with a warm whisper, "Your name."

The boy rears back in surprise. "My name?"

"Not Nyi Lay or kala-lay. None of the names I've heard the jailer or the warders call you. Not Sabado, Free El Salvador, those words on your shirt. Your *own* name."

The boy's mouth has opened into an *O*, the letter of sheer surprise. He puts his face close to the bars again and whispers back. "Zaw Gyi is my name."

"Zaw Gyi, my friend. Thank you."

"No, not Zaw Gyi. Zaw Gy*ee*, the long sound."

"Really? Are you sure?"

Is he sure? The answer rises unbidden into his mouth. "My mother said Zaw Gy*ee*. Always. With the long sound. I remember her voice."

Teza speaks through laughter. "Do you know what your name means?"

"It doesn't mean anything. It's just my name."

"But all names have a meaning. Zaw Gy*ee* especially. He's the al-chemist. From the old stories. When you're settled in at the monastery school, ask the Hsayadaw about him."

The boy shakes his head. "What is the alchemist?"

"He's a very wise man who lives in the forest. He knows all kinds of extraordinary secrets. The Hsayadaw will tell you. Our monks used to know a lot about alchemy. How lucky you are, Zaw Gyi. You have a very special name."

"I do?"

"Yes. I'm glad you told me what it is. I won't worry so much now, be-cause I know you have a strong name to help you."

Chit Naing walks, rather noisily, around the outer wall. The singer slips his arms through the bars and takes the small, hard hands in his own. He whispers, "It's time for you to go."

A small cry escapes the boy. He can't leave Teza, he can't leave Tiger. He turns his head and casts a grim look at the jailer, who arranged all this; Chit Naing is making him leave the cage. *I will not go.*

But even as he silently makes this pronouncement, he grasps Teza's hands tighter and presses his forehead against the bars. "Ako, I will miss you."

"I will miss you, too, Nyi Lay. Ma jow-ba-neh. Don't be afraid."

Chit Naing politely coughs and glances at his watch. "We've got to go. The Hsayadaw has already arrived."

His eyes and Teza's meet above the boy's black head. Chit Naing sees that the singer doesn't care that he took the pen. It really doesn't belong to him anymore. Despite his ruined face, Teza seems to be smiling. But maybe it's the angle of his head, which turns away now and drops closer to the boy. The two of them lean together. Chit Naing can't tell if their foreheads touch through the bars, but their fingers are still intertwined. Teza whispers to the boy, who murmurs back, and the singer whispers again, and everything they say—Chit Naing can't make out a single word—is sung in the faint music of shifting tones and breath. Teza pulls back first, to look at the boy. Then he takes his hands from Zaw Gyi and places them on his own knees, in the attitude of a meditator.

The boy stands, puts his sling bag back over his shoulder, and picks up his basket. He wants to cry and scream. He wants to pass through the bars of Teza's cell and stay with him in there, talking. But he just says, "Ako, now-muh dwee-may." See you later, Older Brother.

"Yes, I'll see you later, Zaw Gyi." The boy turns, and Chit Naing turns, and they walk. Turquoise longyi. Lime-green, ragged T-shirt *FREE EL SALVADOR*. Two mismatched flip-flops, slapping away.

For a few seconds Teza does not breathe. He listens to the thwack of slippers on brick-chip gravel. The steady beats are already fading. He turns his head to catch the last of the footsteps. Then he can't hear them at all. Exhaling, he presses his forehead against the bars, where moments ago he felt the child's skin against his own.

Upekkha. Upekkha.

The fourth of the Four Divine Abidings. Equanimity. To let be what one must let be.

Teza remains sitting cross-legged. When he reaches for his blanket and pulls it around his shoulders, his position shifts only slightly. Just as he doesn't permit himself to think about food, he takes his mind away from the friend who has left him. The child. His own child.

Upekkha. Upekkha.

The sky between roof and wall is a deeper blue now. He's had many evenings watching that small bridge where birds and clouds cross over. He once saw the moon passing there. Sometimes he found a faint trailing of stars. And always this: the gradation of light through hours, one blue like fresh-dyed silk, another like worn turquoise cotton. Now dusk-mauve darkens the sky, and just before the big lights crack on and erase everything, a flood of indigo ink writes up the night.

Teza closes his eyes. He follows his breath through his body, down night-black lanes into streets of light and bone. It's hard to sit in the evening, he's so worn out by the day.

He finds himself leaning, falling over in slow motion, which strikes him as comical, and sad, because he doesn't have the strength to halt the slow toppling. He ends up sitting sideways on the floor, stuck. Awkwardly, patiently, he scissors his legs apart and slowly stretches them out. He thinks, Ya-ba-deh, I will meditate this way, lying down.

After the necessary shifting, he finds his breath again, he comes back to his meditation word. Upekkha. But it's not long before the word escapes him, and he sleeps.

Already the dream has come to him several times, and here it is again. Companionable now, it no longer confuses or pains him. Whether he wakes or sleeps on, the vision is the same. In old Pagan, Tattadesa, the great temple falls, with the Buddha and the boy and the man inside. The lizard, caught beneath the bricks, becomes a bird and flies. He dreams himself, flying, the earth spread out below him like a living body, his own and all that he loves.

. 63 .

The moment Senior Jailer Chit Naing steps into the releases room, he puts a prophylactic smile on his face and thinks, What a bloody nightmare.

Then, as he ushers the boy into the room, he thinks again, If only this *were* a nightmare, I might have the great relief of waking up and drinking a glass of water.

His mouth has gone bone-dry. Reflexively, he tries to lick his lips, but his tongue sticks between them like fine-grade sandpaper. At the same time—oh, such irony!—he feels the sweat begin under his arms. Within a minute, slick, narrow streams will be running down his sides. Turned away from the long table where possession searches take place, he quickly draws his hand across his upper lip. Smiling, murmuring to the boy, he pivots back, almost sick with the movement, because he can feel the pen shift in his pocket, sliding upward. He tries not to press his shirt against his body with his arms. He doesn't want the Chief Warden to see the coming deluge of perspiration.

Because there he is, the Chief, leaning on the edge of the table, his arms crossed over his big chest, his bald head like wet bronze under the light. His pack of Marlboros is on the search table; his gold lighter glimmers beside it. The bastard. He is not supposed to be here.

Yesterday afternoon he told Chit Naing that he had no interest in seeing the boy before his departure. He actually said, "The sooner the kid goes, the better, with as little noise as possible." Stupidly, inadvertently, in some small gesture or flicker of eye, Chit Naing must have been visibly relieved, and that unconscious signal made the Chief suspicious. It's Chit Naing's own fault. He has conjured the man like a demon, and the Chief wears a demon's grin to mock the senior jailer's terse smile.

But it's worse. Young Tint Lwin stands on the far side of the table, his hands obviously clenched together behind his back. The stricken expression on his handsome face whispers, *I'm frightened.* What is immediately clear is that Tint Lwin is frightened for him, for Chit Naing. Can he see the pen? It's everything Chit Naing can do not to look down at his own hip, and he doesn't want to put his hand in his pocket either. He gives Tint Lwin a sharp glance, wishing the young warder would pull himself together. There's no telling how quickly the Chief might turn around and see that desperate look.

Soe Thein is here too, standing a few steps away from the door. How predictable. These two men—one low-ranking, one senior—both have reputations as decent, nonviolent warders. Soe Thein is careful not to be overtly sympathetic to political prisoners, but a few people know how much he respects Daw Aung San Suu Kyi and her party. Through his network of eavesdroppers and whisperers, the Chief Warden must also know. As for Tint Lwin, he's just green, a good boy who isn't cut out for the prison. Yet here he is, working in the cage, his wages feeding who knows how many people. Such men are always viewed by their superiors with suspicion. Just a sympathizer waiting to happen.

Chit Naing believed their duties here were a gratuitous blessing, a good and lucky chance. What a fool! He realizes that both of them are here to receive a warning. And if there is a more serious lesson to learn, they will learn it right now.

Being older and smarter than the young warder, Soe Thein doesn't allow his deeply lined face to show any emotion. But when Chit Naing meets his eye, he hears the warder's crusty voice quite clearly: *I hope the kid's not carrying anything out or you're both fucked.*

Trying to calm his breathing, Chit Naing stands one step behind the child, whose head is bowed in deference. The Chief pushes himself lightly from the edge of the table and stands up to his full height. His voice is very loud, and reverberates in the bare room. "So today's your big day, eh, kala-lay?"

"Yes, sir," the boy replies in a respectful voice. Chit Naing swallows. No saliva goes down.

"Your life sentence is finished! Congratulations!" The Chief Warden chuckles at his own joke. "You must be very happy."

The boy whispers, "No, sir."

"What? What's that?"

"No, sir. I am not happy. I want to stay here."

A stillness descends upon the four men. Taken aback, they stare down at the boy, who keeps his eyes on the cement floor.

Chit Naing knows he has to speak first. He clears his throat. "But Nyi Lay, the Hsayadaw is waiting for you. He's come to take you to the monastery school."

"Yes, Saya Chit Naing, I know."

"And you're all ready to go. You've said good-bye to everyone here, you've packed all your things."

"Yes, sir."

The Chief Warden opens his Marlboros, picks up his gold ingot, and lights a cigarette. Exhaling a bluish cloud, he begins. "But you *are* leaving, kala-lay. Good Jailer Chit Naing and his wife have gone to all this trouble to find a place for you at the pongyi-kyaung, so you mustn't be ungrateful now. Right, my boy?"

"Yes, sir."

While the Chief is talking to the boy, his eyes bore into Chit Naing's cheekbone. The jailer is careful not to look at him. He stares at the boy's head, the words *his wife* reverberating like distant artillery fire. Sweat shows through his shirt now, long bars of it under his arms. He doesn't want to turn around lest the Chief see the round, damp target in the center of his back. He puts his hands in front of his body and clasps them together, but it's too much, too close. His fingers let go of each other and he thrusts his right hand deep into his pocket. There it is, the pen. His hand closes around the plastic casing, pushing it down again, the nib against his thumb.

"You see," the warden continues, his voice smooth and deep, "that's why I've come down to bid you farewell, kala-lay. I just want to take a look through your things before you go. Could you put your bags up here on the table? There we go. That's a good boy." The Chief slides to the left as the boy shuffles forward, pulling the handle of his sling bag over his head. He places the bag carefully on the gray metal table. Then he hoists the woven market basket into the air. "This one too?"

"That one too."

Smelling the blanket, the boy wrinkles his nose as he swings his colorful suitcase up on the table. The Chief won't mind a little shit-stink, especially if he finds the ledger. That would make the big man happy, and Nyi Lay would get to stay in the cage.

"My boy, no need to keep staring at the floor. Lift up your chin." As the Chief talks, he watches the boy's face. He opens the blue sling bag by touch, without looking down at his hands. "I just want to make sure that our friend Junior Jailer Nyunt Wai Oo is as crazy as everybody seems to think. When he heard you were leaving, he called me. I know he's not too friendly, but he's a hard worker, even when he's away from the prison. This little search was his idea."

The Chief sees that the mention of Handsome doesn't intimidate the child; his knees certainly aren't knocking together in fear. On the contrary, having received permission to lift his head, Nyi Lay stares into the Chief's eyes. The bald man sniffs the air, looks left and right, and sniffs again. He seems about to say something, but instead just tosses his cigarette on the floor. Nyi Lay doesn't jump away from the arc of the red coal. He doesn't even look down, nor does he cower when the Chief Warden takes a quick step toward him and squashes the burning cigarette with the toe of his boot.

The man slides his cigarettes and lighter out of the way and upends the sling bag, shaking its contents out onto the table. In the space of fourteen seconds, he undoes the boy's careful packing.

The only thing that immediately interests him is the nail, which clatters on the metal table. Prisoners use them as weapons against each other. He picks it up by the pointed end and asks in an almost sexual voice, "You're not an enemy of the regime, are you, kala-lay?" He isn't looking at the boy now but at Chit Naing, the grin on his face like the nail in his hand.

The boy answers, "No, sir, I'm not an enemy of the regime, sir. I want to be a prison warden when I grow up." All the warders love it when he tells them this.

The Chief Warden laughs loudly, predictably flattered. "You do, do you? My, my, that's quite a grand hope for such a little boy. It's not an easy job, you know. This nail"—he wags the point of it at the boy—"you can't keep this nail. It's prison property."

"Yes, sir," replies the boy. The Chief keeps pawing through his things. He touches the new bar of soap, opens up the thanakha tin. *His going-away presents.* The Chief unrolls the new, still-damp towel and shakes it out with a snap. Nothing hidden there. Two bent, tattered postcards are splayed on the table—the Shwedagon Pagoda and a Buddha from Pagan—but they don't interest the Chief. One by one he examines several bags of food: pickled tea leaf and deep-fried beans, a big clump of rice, green spirals of cabbage and lettuce. He pushes them away with the nail, puncturing each bag in turn.

"What's this?" He picks up the matchbox and shakes it.

The boy hesitates. "Hpay Hpay . . ." His eyes are on the matchbox. "Hpay Hpay . . ." he begins again. The word for father. The other words are stuck.

"What's in here, kala-lay? Hmm?" The Chief Warden glances at the tongue-tied boy, then brings the box closer to his face and slides open the little drawer. At first he doesn't understand what he sees. There is a pointy cylinder of pale wood, brown and bonelike at one end. He tilts the box toward himself and something else slides into view just as the boy finally spits the words out, proudly, "My father's tooth."

But the Chief isn't listening. He sees the lizard now, half skeleton, half flesh, the flesh part moving slowly, sensuously, many small white mouths, chewing. "It's full of fucking maggots!" he shouts, thrusting the box away in disgust. It falls open on the table, dislodging perhaps a dozen maggots from their meal. The tooth has also jumped out and dropped with a musical *tink* on the Chief's gold lighter, from which it bounces to the floor.

Repulsed, waving his hands, the Chief steps back. "Bloody filthy! Filthy. Get them off the table!"

Zaw Gyi drops to his haunches. His hand darts out and grabs the tooth off the cement. He quickly stands again, and not knowing what else to do with the maggots, he tweezers them up in his fingers with the deftness of a gem dealer. One pinch at a time, he deposits the wiggling creatures back in the box and closes the drawer. "Sir, I am sorry. Sir, I am very sorry," he whispers, hunching his shoulders up around his ears.

But the Chief is too upset to hit him. Those maggots were a mere foot away from his mouth. "Ugh! Ugh!" he says, grimacing and wiping his hands on his trousers. He walks behind the table and circles past Tint Lwin, then paces to the other side of the room, where Soe Thein stands, his face still unreadable.

The Chief addresses him for support. "Wasn't that revolting? What a weird little bugger he is."

Soe Thein agrees in a low voice, "Yes, sir. But the cage is a weird place for a boy. That's the problem."

The Chief nods briefly, impressed by his employee's logic. "You're right, Warder Soe Thein. You're quite right." He strides back to the table and scrutinizes the surface to make sure that the maggots are all gone. "All right, let's get on with this, shall we? Warder Tint Lwin, check the boy."

Tint Lwin rounds the table and searches the boy gingerly, running his hands down the boy's back and front, relieved to find nothing tucked in his longyi, nothing under his arms or tied to his legs. "He's clean, sir. Just taking out his own skin and bones."

"And a box of fucking maggots. Great. Now, what do we have here?" The Chief pulls the market bag toward him and opens the twin handles. His hands are already tugging on the rolled blanket when the dank smell rises into his face, but this time he doesn't push the bag away; he just yanks his hands off it and steps back. "And what the fuck is in there? No, don't tell me, I can guess. He's smuggling out a latrine pail!"

Fallen from grace because of the maggots, the boy has lowered his head again. He bites his lip. The Chief looks at Chit Naing in bewilderment. "What the fuck is in that basket?"

Preparing to remove his hand from his pocket, Chit Naing presses the pen down hard, ready to leave it there, safely stowed. Instead he hears a sound as loud as a human voice: *Tsshik-tsheek.*

The boy's head jerks toward that inky word. He raises his eyes to the Chief and begins, very loudly, in a tone of adolescent righteousness, "Sir, that is *my* blanket and I want to take it with me to the monastery. I'll wash it there, sir. I will. Please let me take my blanket with me."

Chit Naing's mouth is so dry only a croak emerges. His explanation begins with a ragged cough. "Sir, the tan-see told me that the kid had a little accident during the night but there was no time to clean it up." He attempts to clarify. "He had the runs, sir."

"Yes, I have a nose, Officer Chit Naing, but why the hell is he taking that filthy blanket to the monastery school?"

"He's very attached to it, sir. It's from his shack. He insisted on taking it with him. I gave him permission. He has so few possessions." When Chit Naing pulls his hand into the air, he feels the sweat streaming down his side. He gestures stiffly to the boy's belongings. "As you can see, sir. He has nothing."

"Novice monks are supposed to have nothing. A shitty blanket! I'm sure the abbot will be very impressed." He waves his hand in front of his face. "Bloody hell, what a reek! I've been wondering what that smell was from the moment you two walked in here. I wish Officer Nyunt Wai Oo could have done this search himself. What a dirty job it's turned out to be." He reaches over to pick up his cigarettes and lighter, then takes another big step away from the table.

Chit Naing doesn't let his face change. He doesn't move. Nor does the boy, except for his nostrils, which dilate as he takes a conscious whiff of his accident. It really doesn't smell that bad. The Chief Warden should try emptying out latrine pails.

The chief lights another Marlboro and takes a deep drag. He looks from Chit Naing to the boy and back to Chit Naing. Then he taps the ash off his cigarette and gestures to the things on the table. "You can pack up your stuff, kala-lay." He glances back at the senior jailer, whose eyes are hidden by a streak of light across his glasses. "This has been great fun, Officer Chit Naing. I look forward to next time."

The jailer manages a strained smile. "Yes, lots of fun, sir. Thank you." He watches the boy stuff his belongings back into the sling bag. Then he carefully asks, "May we go, sir? There's a taxi outside the prison gates. I'm sure the Hsayadaw has been waiting a long time."

The Chief Warden replies, "And I'm sure such a wise man knows that state security is more important than anything else."

For an instant the two look into each other's eyes, with nothing between them, no screen of reflective light, no words. Chit Naing has the distinct impression of being offered a reprieve, which he warily accepts. "Yes, sir, you're absolutely right."

The Chief addresses Zaw Gyi. "Well, off with you, then. I'm sure the abbot will be happy to meet his new student, despite what you've got in that basket. May you become a good novice."

"Yes, sir." The boy settles the strap of his sling bag across his shoulder and picks up his woven plastic suitcase. Chit Naing's warm hand grasps his shoulder, nudging him toward the closed door.

The boy is the first to step out of the releases room. As one flip-flop settles into the gravel, the Chief's voice stops him. "Officer Chit Naing." The senior jailer turns back. The boy waits, facing the compound. It's late twilight and the floodlights are already on.

The man's voice booms out of the bare concrete hollow. "When you're finished seeing the boy out, could you come back in here for a moment? I want to talk to you about something. Something quite important."

"Yes, sir. Of course. I'll be back directly."

Saya Chit Naing's voice has become very small, which frightens the boy. But the tall, thin man touches him again on the shoulder. "Let's go, Nyi Lay." Once they've taken a few steps, he speaks again, more quietly, "Hurry."

The only sounds between them are their feet crunching gravel and the boy's slippers slapping his soles. In another minute Soe Thein follows them, the Chief Warden's keys rattling in his hand. The three of them stare at the iron-banded door built into the high gates—it seems to grow taller and heavier as they approach it. Soe Thein waves to the guard in the sentry box and bends down slightly, to see the locks and bolts better. After a few seconds, he pushes the heavy door open.

A light wind gusts in, carrying the scent of green stuff, weeds and ripe fields beyond the prison. Now comes a heady draft of car exhaust. The chubby driver is already behind the wheel, revving his engine, but the old monk in burgundy robes remains standing beside the taxi, watching the prison gates.

The boy looks up gravely at Chit Naing, who whispers, "Nyi Lay, don't worry. We'll be fine in here and you'll be better out there. Look, the Hsayadaw is waving at you."

The boy gives the jailer a grin like a spark of fire and glances at the road. He lifts his hand and shyly waves to the old abbot. Chit Naing nods toward the open door.

And Zaw Gyi walks out of the cage.

A NOTE ON BURMESE
PRONUNCIATION
AND TERMS

In traditional Burmese, surnames do not exist. People are identified by their birth names only, which are chosen carefully by parents and advisers, usually according to the day of birth and astrological influences.

> *ky* is pronounced *ch*
> *kyi*, as in Aung San Suu Kyi, is pronounced *chee*
> *gy* is pronounced *j*
> *gyi*, as in *longyi*, is pronounced *gee*

In daily conversation, honorifics are very important. The speaker chooses an honorific according to his own and the other person's age, status, and sex. The most common honorifics in the novel are

> Ko—for older brothers, for young men equal in status, or for men
> slightly older than oneself
> U—for uncles and older, respected men
> Nyi—for younger brothers (as spoken to by other men)
> Daw—for aunts and older women

Ma—for older sisters, for young women of equal status, or for
women slightly older than oneself

Saya—for a respected man who is a teacher or who acts in a
teacherly fashion

In this book I have used various terms that are "Burmese English," the
elegant, colonial, British-influenced English spoken by Burmese friends in
Burma.

ACKNOWLEDGMENTS

Despite the solitary nature of writing, this novel has been a community project. It could not have been written without the help of many Burmese people of various ethnicities, who spoke to me about life under the dictatorship that rules their country. These conversations spanned several years and continents, but in the beginning people entered into them with little regard for their own safety or privacy, recounting painful and sometimes harrowing experiences for the sake of a stranger who said she was writing a book.

I am thankful to many people, from former political prisoners to unemployed prison guards, from young tea-shop workers to old betel-nut sellers. Those who still live in Burma must remain anonymous, with the exception of Daw Aung San Suu Kyi. Her books were important during the writing of this one, as were the interviews I conducted with her and her colleagues in the National League for Democracy in the mid-1990s. Many Burmese writers, journalists, and artists helped me understand the suffocating power of the censorship under which they live and work. Someday the government of Burma will change, and I will publicly thank each of you by name.

The prison in this novel is a composite of several different prisons and work camps in Burma. Insein Prison, near Rangoon, is its architectural model, but the real Insein now stands in the midst of a bustling township. Needless to say, though based partly on historical events, this is a work of fiction.

For associations and friendships that began in 1996, my gratitude goes to many men and women on the Thai-Burma border who are or were members of the following political parties, armies, and dissident groups: the All Burma Students Democratic Front (ABSDF, both sections), the Democratic Party for a New Society (DPNS), the National League for Democracy Liberated Area (NLDLA), the Karen National Liberated Army (KNLA), the Assistance Association for Political Prisoners (AAPP), and the Burmese Women's Union. Some of these groups have morphed into other organizations, but the names of generous individuals remain the same. My sincere thanks to:

Win Naing Oo, with whom I did my first extensive interviews about prison life, and whose writings, especially in the ABSDF publication *Cries from Insein*, helped me to build a fictional prison. Many of ABSDF's publications were indispensable to my understanding of prison life in Burma. The punishments in the novel, created around seemingly innocuous contraband—pen and paper and words—came directly out of the shocking book called *Pleading Not Guilty in Insein*, a translation of an official court document that was smuggled out of Insein Prison. It records the trials of twenty-two political prisoners whose cells were raided and whose sentences were increased substantially on the basis of the contraband found therein: pens, paper, political poems, old copies of English magazines, congratulatory letters, and notes to Daw Aung San Suu Kyi.

Min Min Oo, Zaw Zaw Htun, and the others from the days in Mae Sarieng.

Soe Aung, Zaw Min, and Dr. Naing Aung, for border trips, military camps, malaria, dysentery, and many late-night conversations.

Political activist Moe Thi Zon, whose love for his country and for his imprisoned comrades helped me to imagine my two Burmese brothers into existence.

U Aye Saung, U Soe Pyne, Tennyson, and the journalist U Aung Phay, for telling me about his time on Coco Island; Win Min, Bo Saw Tun, Kyaw

Thura, Thet Hmu, Yeni, Pet Thet Nee, Lwanni, and Mun Awng. The story of my young musician is not entirely fictional: Mun Awng's famous songs of defiance were the soundtrack to my writing.

My gratitude especially to Aye Aye Khaing, Aye Aye Lwin, Ma Ae Ae Muh, and Ma Su Pwint.

The irrepressible poet and great teacher Sayagyi U Tin Moe.

Bo Kyi, Aung Din, Min Mon, and the others at AAPP, for long discussions and for tireless work on behalf of those who are still imprisoned. Thanks especially to Bo Kyi for his miraculous sense of humor.

Dr. Cynthia Maung and numerous members of the staff from the Mae Tao Clinic.

Aung Naing Oo, for his political insights, and Shona Kirkwood, for her sustaining friendship and for her comments on an early version of the book.

The self-effacing but nevertheless remarkable Pippa Curwen, and the staff of the Burma Relief Centre, for many different kinds of help and support. Everyone at Images Asia, in particular Lyndal Barry. Heather Kelly and Marc Laban, for bringing me back to Southeast Asia in 1996 and encouraging me to visit Burma.

I have been fortunate to find a friend as well as a writing colleague in Aung Zaw, the journalist and editor of *The Irrawaddy*. He and his brother, Kyaw Zwa Moe, have spoken with me at length over the years, not only about their experiences in Burmese prisons but about many different facets of Burmese politics, Buddhism, and culture. Thanks too to Moe Kyaw, Win Thu, and the other staff members at *The Irrawaddy*.

The works of Burmese writers were important to me in my research, especially those by Ludu U Hla, Mya Than Tint, Journalgyaw Ma Ma Lei, Moe Aye, Pascal Khoo Thwe, and numerous short story writers still in Burma. My thanks also to several dedicated translators of Burmese, in particular Anna Allot and Ohnmar Khin. Anna Allot and Colleen Beresford read early versions of the novel and provided much-needed encouragement when I was poor and doubtful in Greece. Thanks also to Daw Nita in London, for her courage and grace.

I am grateful to Bertil Lintner and other Western writers for their excellent books about Burma: Edith Mirante, Christina Fink, Minke Nijhuis,

Martin Smith, and Alan Clements. Alan's interviews with Daw Aung San Suu Kyi and senior members of the National League for Democracy were integral to my understanding of a vital and politically engaged Buddhism.

While based in Vancouver, I had the great pleasure of yelling through a bullhorn at Canadian companies (such as Ivanhoe Mines) that continue to do business with the Burmese junta. For that experience and others like it, I thank the members of the Vancouver-Burma Roundtable. They and other activists continue to remind the Canadian government that Canada has another deep, very expensive connection to the narcodictatorship of Burma: Vancouver is the major Western port for Burmese heroin.

The Karen, Shan, and Burman communities of Vancouver, Ottawa, and Toronto have kept me connected to Burma even when what I love about that country has felt far away. I am grateful for their wonderful hospitality, enthusiasm, and support of my work. I can say the same for several other Burmaphiles: Christine Harmston, Katrina Andersen, Corinne Baumgarten, other Canadian Friends of Burma, and the documentary filmmaker Holly Fisher.

Dr. Simon Bryant, Dr. Duncan Nickerson, and Dr. Win Myint Than offered excellent medical expertise on the subjects of dysentery, malnutrition, and distended jaws. The therapist Audrey Cook shared with me her wisdom and her extensive knowledge of child sexual abuse and the cyclical nature of trauma; she taught me a great deal about "the child in prison," and how many imprisoned children live all around us. The trauma research of Bessel A. Van de Kolk, Judith L. Herman, and Sandra Bloom provided me with a crucial education. The line quoted on page 64 is from Pema Chödrön's book *When Things Fall Apart*.

Soe Win Than from the BBC read the manuscript and offered invaluable criticisms—he has been a great friend to this novel, and to me. Other excellent readers were Soe Kyaw Thu, Dr. Win Myint Than and her family, Libby Oughton, and my heroine, Nancy Holmes. Thank you all for making me a better writer. And *tʒey-ʒu-bay* to my wonderful teachers of Burmese at SEASSI, in Madison, Wisconsin. For crucial financial assistance, I am grateful to the Canada Council and the Alberta Foundation for the Arts.

Writing about prison life and its many kinds of violence was often painful and difficult, but the work was made easier by supportive communities in Canada, Greece, and Thailand. I have been blessed throughout the writing and beyond it by the friendship and love of Libby, Nancy, Maria Coffey, Dag Goering, Beth Kope, Sandra Shields, David Campion, Linda Griffiths, Mireille and Panagos Katirzoglou, Andreas Amerikanos, Vangelis Ikonomidis, my Thai brother Goong Samakeemavin, Ajahn Champa, and the late Timothy Findley.

I owe debts of gratitude both to my wise and persevering agent, Jackie Kaiser, and to Anne Collins of Random House Canada. In the final stages of writing, I had the unexpected pleasure of working with Lorna Owen of Nan A. Talese/Doubleday New York. Beyond the brilliant editing, both her and Nan Talese's enthusiasm and willingness to take the risk has brought this story of Burma to a much wider audience; I know I'm not the only one who is thankful for that.

While I was working on this novel, my brother and I engaged in a correspondence that spanned the length of his prison sentence in Alberta. Though Canadian and Burmese prisons are very different places, his letters gave me a unique perspective on the day-to-day psychology of imprisonment. His prison stories also convinced me that, contrary to popular belief, we *do* have political prisoners in North America. But we prefer to call them mentally ill, drug-addicted, Native, and black.

I am grateful to my family, especially to my mother, Jackie Henry, who has taught me much about the saving graces of generosity and humor and the elasticity of love. Hers has stretched with me all over the planet, making me a most fortunate daughter. Last but not least, I thank my dear friend and husband, Robert Chang, whose presence in my life is a daily blessing.

In the mid-1990's, Karen Connelly visited Burma numerous times, until she was denied a visa by the military regime. She then lived for two years on the Thai-Burma border, among Burmese exiles and dissidents. Years earlier, she had emerged on the Canadian publishing scene with the publication of *Touch The Dragon*, which won the Governor General's Award and remained on bestseller lists for two years. The same book was published in the U.S. as *Dream of a Thousand Lives*, and was a *New York Times* Notable Travel Book of the Year in 2002. Her first book of poetry, *The Small Words in My Body*, won the Pat Lowther Award for best book of poetry by a Canadian woman. She is also the winner of the Air Canada Award. She is currently working on a book of explorations and encounters set in the refugee camps, border towns, and rebel army camps of the Thai-Burma border. She has two homes, one in Toronto and the other in a Greek island village. *The Lizard Cage* is her first novel. In 2005, it was nominated for the Kiriyama Prize and in 2006 was longlisted for the Impac Dublin Award.

For more information about this author, please visit www.karenconnelly.ca.

A NOTE ABOUT THE TYPE

THE LIZARD CAGE is set in Fournier, a digitized version of the original font cut that was part of the Monotype Corporation historical typeface revivals in the 1920s.

Fournier was created by the typographer and printing historian Stanley Morison (1889–1967) and grew out of his admiration for the type cuts of Pierre Simon Fournier (1712–1768).